UNDERGROUND

KIT SERGEANT

THOMPSON BELLE PRESS

OTHER BOOKS BY

Kit Sergeant

Thrown for a Curve

What It Is

355: The Women of Washington's Spy Ring-Women Spies Book 1

L'Agent Double: Spies and Martyrs of the Great War (Coming Spring of 2019!)

Sign up for my mailing list at kitsergeant.com to find out how to get a FREE copy!

Copyright © 2018 Kit Sergeant
Published by Thompson Belle Press
All rights reserved.
ISBN: 1726237575
ISBN-13: 978-1726237574

Although this book is based on real events and features historical figures, it is a work of fiction. Most of the dialogue and incidents in the story are products of the author's imagination and should not be construed as historical fact. For more information on fact versus fiction in the Civil War, see the Epilogue at the end of this book

This book is dedicated to all of the women who lived during the Civil War and whose talents and sacrifices are known or unknown, but especially to the real-life women these characters are based on

CHAPTER 1

HATTIE

FEBRUARY 1861

*B*altimore's men were up in arms. Even at the unseemly early hour of three in the morning, shouts from angry secessionists echoed through the slats of the depot, drowned only by the train whistles announcing each new arrival.

"It will be coming soon, boys," a man in a straw hat and full beard announced. "Remember," he told the men who gathered around him, "no damned abolitionist shall pass through this town alive."

Hattie Lewis's eyes shifted to her friend and supervisor, Kate Warne, who stood just to the right of the mob. Kate's face held her usual inscrutable expression, but Hattie could tell from the way she gripped her handbag that she was as uncomfortable as Hattie. Most of the employees of the Pinkerton Detective Agency had arrived in Baltimore only a few days prior, but the depth of the anti-Union sentiment had greeted them almost as immediately as the concierge

1

at the Barnum Hotel. Maryland was a swing state, and its Rebel proclivities had boiled over with the election of the anti-slavery Lincoln to the Presidency.

Hattie turned at the sound of horses approaching. A plain coach stopped near the tracks, the horses whinnying as the driver pulled them to a halt. She hurried toward them. As she entered the coach, snatches of Dixie followed behind her, ceasing mercifully when she shut the door.

"No doubt there *will* be a good time in Dixie, by and by," a deep voice offered.

Hattie gave the man a tentative smile. The President Elect was dressed in a simple traveling suit, the shawl draped over his head taking the place of his stovepipe hat, which was placed beside him. She'd read multiple descriptions of Abraham Lincoln in the papers —most focused on the newly grown beard in response to the young lady Grace Bedell's request for him to cover his sunken jaw—but none of them had properly described his dignified manner, nor the fact that the beard still grew sparse over his gaunt cheeks. His eyes held an amiable crinkle as they focused on Hattie. She regretted that the tight quarters of the coach offered no room to show Mr. Lincoln the proper obsequies. She introduced herself to Mr. Lincoln and then told him, "Miss Warne has arranged an empty sleeping car for our purpose."

He nodded. "I am to be your brother, then," he stated, addressing Hattie.

She cast a sidelong glance at the man sitting beside her, her employer, Mr. Allan Pinkerton. He leaned forward. "It is for your safety." Even though he'd been in America for nearly two decades, his accent still resonated Scottish when he was anxious.

"I still think it is all nonsense." Ward Hill Lamon, Lincoln's personal bodyguard, sat back into the ripped velvet of the coach. "And ridiculous for our new President to be skulking about a city, unknown, in the middle of the night."

"It would be even more ridiculous to have our new President not arrive to his inauguration alive," Pinkerton replied evenly. He opened the door to the coach. With a swish of her satin skirts, Hattie scooted past him to retrieve the wheelchair the driver had unloaded. Lincoln looked down and sighed before climbing out of the coach and arranging himself into the chair. He made to replace his hat, but Hattie pulled the shawl up to obscure his face instead, knowing his customary hat would only serve to give him away.

"Brother, I believe our train has arrived." Hattie's hands tightened on the chair as she pushed forward toward the station. Lincoln was so tall he nearly reached Hattie's height sitting down. She did not look up, even as she passed by Kate, who stood in line waiting to board a car near the front of the train.

"May I be of assistance?" Hattie was about to refuse the train operative who loomed in front of her until she recognized him as another Pinkerton employee, Timothy Webster.

Hattie affected a Southern accent. "We have reserved the back car. My brother here needs to be isolated."

Timothy, with his usual capableness, bent down to hoist the front of the wheelchair up the steps to the car. Hattie, pushing forward, peeked at the man in the straw hat. He and his companions stood with their arms crossed, searching the crowd. According to the posted schedule, Lincoln's train was not due to arrive for another several hours. After uncovering a potential assassination plot, Pinkerton had insisted on rescheduling and sending the President-elect in on an earlier train from Philadelphia. Hopefully the man in the straw hat would not realize he'd been outwitted until long after Mr. Lincoln arrived at the Capitol Building for his inauguration speech.

At last Mr. Lincoln was safely ensconced in the sleeping compartment. Webster locked the door behind him as he left, and Hattie allowed herself one sigh of relief before retrieving the small pistol hidden underneath the seat of the wheelchair. Lincoln had boarded the train, but that did not mean his life was no longer in danger.

Mr. Lincoln had to double up his legs to fit in the sleeping berth, a position that, when Hattie dared to cast her eyes at him, seemed too lowly for a man of his status.

She stretched her cold hands to the warmth of the stove as she heard the cargo door bang shut. She immediately cursed herself for leaving her gun out of reach. *Newbie.* But the intruder was only

3

Allan Pinkerton, come to check on the precious cargo. As usual, the heavy smell of Cuban cigars clung to his clothing and beard. Hattie assumed he'd been chain smoking them on the bridge.

"How does he sleep like that?" Pinkerton wondered aloud as the train whistle blew.

"How does he sleep at all, knowing what he knows?" Hattie asked in reply. It was not just that his life was in danger, but he was about to take on a nearly impossible role. Seven states had already seceded from the Union in protest after his election. It was up to him to try to repair the conflict that was building between the North and the South and to solve the moral question of slavery as a whole. Hattie knew she and Pinkerton were of the same mind as Lincoln, but that the rest of the country would not come to an agreement so easily. "I am fairly sure I will not be able to get a wink in myself."

Her boss smiled wryly. "The nature of the job. We Pinkertons never sleep." He went to the window. A flash of light broke through the darkness. He tapped the window. "All's well," he said, turning back to Hattie. She knew Pinkerton had placed several operatives at train stations along the way. They were instructed to flash lanterns stating that no known evil forces were at work.

Hattie glanced again at Mr. Lincoln, visions of all the ways the plotters could still attack temporarily blinding her. They might be out of Baltimore, but henchmen could still burn bridges or derail the train. "Let's hope it stays that way."

The train arrived in Washington, mercifully without incident. The Pinkerton detectives unloaded from different cars, avoiding each other's eyes, but silently congratulating each other nonetheless. Hattie marveled that no one would ever know of the danger their new President had been in, and that the threat of murder could have been resolved not by apprehending the alleged criminals, but by a mere switching of the train time table.

And yet the guilty parties walk free, Hattie reminded herself as she scanned the people surrounding her. Mr. Lincoln was still wrapped in his shawl and the crowd seemed blissfully unaware that the potential savior of the Union was the man in the wheelchair.

A man dressed in a fitted frock coat walked rapidly toward Mr. Lincoln. Hattie fingered the pistol in her handbag. The man extended his hand and was about to give a salutation when Hattie stepped forward.

"Sir?" she asked quietly.

He looked Hattie up and down before turning back to Mr. Lincoln. "Mr. Presi—"

"My brother here is very tired," Hattie declared, conscious of the lanky figure in the wheelchair attracting multiple pairs of eyes.

"This is Miss Lewis. She is a friend of the railroad company," Mr. Lincoln told the man.

The man, obviously catching on to Mr. Lincoln's double meaning, nodded. "Your carriage is waiting, sir."

Pinkerton appeared next to the man. "Miss Lewis. You can ride in my car."

Hattie relinquished her grip on the wheelchair as her boss and the man exchanged pleasantries.

Mr. Lincoln reached out to grasp Hattie's hands in his. "I am aware that you put your life at risk for me last night. I truly thank you for your service," he said in his quiet tone.

"Thank you for yours," Hattie replied. She wanted to say more, that she knew he had a lot riding on his shoulders, although if anyone could save the Union, he could. But, knowing her place, she kept quiet.

Pinkerton had one final question for Lincoln. "Mr. President, shall we move forward with arresting the would-be assassinators?"

Mr. Lincoln focused his solemn eyes on Pinkerton. "No. I do not wish to make martyrs out of cowards and madmen."

Pinkerton bowed his head. "As you wish."

They followed Lincoln's carriage to the Willard Hotel off 14th Street and watched Lincoln exit, glancing up and down the street as he did. He was still in disguise and seemed curious as to why none of the passersby paid him any note. Lamon, his chief of security, came out of the hotel and hustled him inside. Pinkerton gave Hattie a wry smile before nodding his head at Pennsylvania Avenue just behind them. "Lincoln's only steps away to the White House now," he said with a wink.

Hattie sat back. "Thanks to you."

"And you, Miss Lewis. You have proven yourself."

She nodded, pleased. She'd been with the agency for nearly a year now, but the Lincoln plot had been her first major assignment, and one of national importance at that. Hopefully she had indeed finally shown her fellow agents what she was capable of.

The Pinkertons were off-duty for the inauguration, but Hattie could see many policemen spread far and wide over the city, watching for any sign of trouble. The day had dawned gray and rainy, but it was now bright and sunny. *Just like our country: what began today in darkness as a fractured nation will now come together in light and jubilance under our new President.* There were thousands of people spread on the grounds of the unfinished Capitol building: the vivid parasols of women sprinkled throughout the neutral suits of the men. When Mr. Lincoln appeared on the platform erected on the eastern portico of the building, the crowd greeted him with thunderous cheers. After the marine band played "The Star-Spangled Banner," Senator Baker introduced the new President. Mr. Lincoln walked to the front of the podium and bowed to the enthusiastic approbation. He put on his spectacles and rearranged the papers in front of him before beginning his speech. Lincoln's booming voice had a musical lilt to it, and, despite her distance from his podium and the hordes of people in between them, Hattie could hear him clear as day. As she had predicted, Lincoln urged reconciliation and discouraged secession. He closed by saying:

We are not enemies but friends. We must not be enemies. Though passion may have strained, it must not break our bonds of affection. The mystic chords of memory, stretching from every battlefield and patriot grave, to every living heart and hearthstone, all over this broad land, will yet swell the chorus of the Union, when again touched, as surely they will be, by the better angels of our nature.

As he spoke, Hattie could not keep her eyes from shifting over to that fire-eating Texan, Senator Wigfall. If anyone was Lincoln's enemy and not friend, it was he, who leaned against the Capitol building with his arms crossed over his chest. Hattie felt heat rise in her face. Texas was the most recent state to secede from the Union and, along with the rest of those deserters, had formed the Confederate States of America. Consequently, he should not have even been there. *You have your own slave-holding, supposed president,* Hattie thought. *What do you want with ours?* Wigfall made a sudden movement and Hattie pulled her bag, with the gun concealed within, closer. But Wigfall merely nodded to himself, as if he had made a silent decision.

CHAPTER 2

BELLE

APRIL 1861

"*B*elle! Belle Boyd!"

Belle looked up from the book in her hands. She'd been trying to read it for half an hour, but the delightful Baltimore spring day had proved much more interesting than perusing the treatise on femininity she'd been assigned. Her best friend at school, Virginia, was running toward her. Belle smiled, thinking what the author of the tome would say about a young woman running through the mud, skirts hiked up and showing more than a little ankle.

Virginia reached the tree Belle had been using for shade. She bent at the waist in an effort to catch her breath.

"What is it, Ginny?" Belle demanded.

"Shots have been fired." Virginia gasped, still breathing heavily. "Fort Sumter. War has started."

Belle waved her fist in a most unladylike manner. "Finally! Maybe now we can get that rail-splitter Lincoln out of office."

Virginia straightened. "But what will become of us? We are in Northern territory here." She crumpled a handkerchief in the palm of her hand. "And God hates the Yankees."

"Yes, why don't they just leave the South alone? They can let those darned abolitionists have their way and let us keep the traditions laid down by our forefathers." Belle cast her eyes around the campus of Mount Washington Female College, as if the lush landscaping could belie the official political leanings of the school. Maryland was still a slave state, but its proximity to Washington made its status as Union or Confederate unclear. "I must get home to mother as soon as possible."

Virginia shook her head. "You know Headmistress Staley is a staunch Unionist. She will not allow you to go home as long as your tuition is paid up."

"We shall see about that," Belle said, hiking up her own skirts and heading toward the headmistress's office.

"Absolutely not." As predicted, Headmistress Staley refused to let Belle leave the school grounds. "There is a war brewing in our fair Union. It would not be safe to let you leave."

"But Headmistress—"

"Your parents have entrusted me as your guardian. You are under my care, hence you will obey my command." Never once in Belle's tenure at the school did Headmistress Staley ever waver in her principles. Miss Staley ruled the girls under her like a temperate overseer, molding them into submission with threatening words instead of fists while teaching them both the classics as well as how to be a proper lady. As the attendees were from both the North and South, Belle often felt that the mannerisms she was taught contradicted greatly with the feminine ideal of a Southern woman, but that was no matter, since Belle herself was in contradiction to those same ideals.

Realizing she was as likely to change Staley's mind as she was to take up arms and join the war effort, Belle gave a half-hearted curtsy before exiting the headmistress's chambers.

Virginia was waiting for her outside. She need not ask for the outcome of Belle's plea since the disappointment was written on her face. Virginia joined Belle's quick pace and walked beside her. "What shall we do now?"

Belle stopped and stared helplessly at the sky. She could see the entrance to the grounds, the starred-and-striped flag that graced the hill, flapping in the breeze just beyond the driveway. Belle felt a sudden rush of hatred for that once beloved symbol of a country that no longer felt like hers. A plan began to form in her mind. "Ginny, do you still have that pearl-handled pistol your father gave you?"

Virginia nodded. Her father manufactured such items back home in North Carolina.

"Go and fetch it for me."

Virginia, used to Belle's odd demands, did as requested.

"You aren't going to shoot anyone, are you?" Virginia asked when she returned with the gun.

"No." Belle walked quickly across the sprawling green lawns of the college. "I won't be shooting a person." She paused near the flagpole and peered up at the flag. Squinting against the bright sunlight, she grasped the pistol with both hands and took aim. Belle shot the gun with the expertise of someone well accustomed to a firearm, not even startling at the kickback. Virginia glanced up, noting the bullet hole that was located where one of the Union's stars should be. Belle repeated the gesture and managed to take out another star. The lawn soon filled with young women chattering at a safe distance from the line of fire. Belle used up the entire round, managing to take out four stars in total.

"Miss Boyd." The headmistress, who had waited until there were no more bullets left to shoot, appeared next to Belle.

Belle opened the chamber and held the gun handle toward Staley. "I suppose now you will choose to expel me?"

Even after three years of Belle's antics, Staley was clearly surprised by this newest one. She merely nodded. "I will make the arrangements immediately.

Belle nodded and headed to the dormitory to begin packing.

CHAPTER 3

MARY JANE

APRIL 1861

"Give me liberty or give me death!" Patrick Henry's famous words echoed in Mary Jane's head as she glanced up at the towering spire of the church. The day was gray, but somehow the white paint of the wooden structure was still blinding and Mary Jane had to shield her eyes with her hand, the lace on the sleeve of her finest red dress billowing in the wind.

"It is for your own protection," Miss Lizzie had appeared beside her, in her usual sly manner. Stealth was as natural to Miss Lizzie as her notions of abolition, borne by her education in Philadelphia.

Mary Jane dropped her arm. "I don't love him."

"I am aware. But marriage and love don't always equate. Look at me… I was in love too, a lifetime ago." Miss Lizzie had once been beautiful and, according to her, had been a much sought-after Virginian belle. But her fiancé had died of yellow fever in the epidemic of 1841, and now, at forty-three, with her blond hair graying and her face becoming thinner and more pinched by the day, she was an established spinster. "Perhaps love will develop out of affection. Besides, Wilson Bowser will make a perfectly adequate husband."

"He is a slave." Mary Jane's anger was swift and sudden. For most of her young life she had been ruled by Miss Lizzie's desires—she'd gotten an education up North and then spent some time in Liberia, all at Miss Lizzie's expense. But her choosing Mary Jane's life partner was too much to bear.

"A slave who is working to pay for his freedom." Miss Lizzie turned her hawkish face to look Mary Jane squarely in the eyes. "After what happened last year..." Miss Lizzie's voice faded out. She disliked talking about Mary Jane's arrest even more than Mary Jane herself. Miss Lizzie switched to a different tactic. "Let's not forget you too were born a slave." Miss Lizzie broke eye contact, as she always did when she mentioned Mary Jane's status.

They both turned as a carriage pulled up a safe distance away from the women so as not to muddy their dresses.

"Miss Richards!" A black man several years older than Mary Jane climbed down from his post next to the driver.

"Mr. Bowser," Mary Jane acknowledged. "Seeing as we are about to get married, you might as well call me by my Christian name." She had not a little pride that she had been baptized at the very same church they were about to enter. Mary Jane knew that was another source of gossip for the Richmond society: St. John's Church was a white people's church and it was highly unusual for black marriages to take place there. But Miss Lizzie was not one to heed anyone else's desires but her own, and so it came to be that she'd scheduled Mary Jane's wedding to be held there, in the same spot where Patrick Henry had given his instrumental speech 86 years prior. A strange coincidence, considering that just a few days ago, Virginia had voted to secede from the United States.

"Mary Jane, then." Bowser—Wilson—replied. He led the way into the church, which was sparsely adorned. Unlike her fellow Richmonders, including her sister-in-law, Miss Lizzie had no desire to be ostentatious, either in dress or decoration. She had invited many of her most influential neighbors, but most refused to attend a

Negro wedding. A few servants filled the family pew along with Miss Lizzie and her brother John. Their mother, Mrs. Van Lew had sent her best wishes that morning, but she was suffering from another one of her headaches and could not leave her bedroom.

Mary Jane replayed the Patrick Henry speech in her head during the ceremony. She'd memorized it in its entirety long ago, much to Miss Lizzie's delight since he had stood in what had eventually become the Van Lew family pew as he called such prominent Virginia colonials as Thomas Jefferson and George Washington to arms. Mary Jane wanted to concentrate on anything besides the commitment she was making, another mistake possibly, just like going to Liberia had been. Miss Lizzie had convinced her that Liberia would have been Mary Jane's ticket to freedom, once and for all. But Mary Jane's roots had always been in Virginia; it was where her mother had lived and died, and, if Mary Jane couldn't be with her, at least she could be near her burial site. In her letters, Miss Lizzie had included accounts of the unrest the nation was feeling, especially in regard to the question of that peculiar institution of slavery. Mary Jane realized they were on the brink of another revolution: this time for the rights of blacks instead of American men and begged for Miss Lizzie to pay for her return. She had finally relented, and after Mary Jane had been arrested, arranged for her to marry Wilson Bowser.

The white minister united them in matrimony within the Episcopalian tradition: there would be no jumping over broomsticks in St. John's. He asked that the couple turn as he presented the rings. Wilson stared at the ground as the minister spoke and Mary Jane used that time to study him. He was a good twenty years older than herself, with a sturdy figure. His skin was blacker than hers, darkened by many days spent toiling on the Van Lew farm outside of Richmond. But his eyes, which were walnut, like the cabinet work in Miss Lizzie's parlor, were kind. He was dressed in the livery uniform of the Van Lew household: dark blue with yellow accents, complete with a white cravat. He had been a relatively new addition to the family's slaves—or, "servants" as Miss Lizzie preferred them to be called. Her father, Old Man Van Lew, though a Northerner by birth, had accumulated a healthy supply of fifteen slaves, including

Mary Jane and her mother, and put a stipulation in his will that they remain his property upon his death. Senile as he was at the end of his life, he must have had some inclination of his wife and daughter's abolitionist proclivities. But Miss Lizzie defied her father in death as she never would have done in life and began freeing his slaves by way of hiring them out to employers and letting them keep a small portion of their earnings in order to ultimately buy their own freedom. She then used some of her father's estate to purchase more slaves in order to set them free. Wilson Bowser was part of the latter group of purchases; even with the prospect of war, their mistress wanted to give them what she could.

An admirable act, as was most of Miss Lizzie's work, especially given the Southern ways that dictated normal Richmond life. But, as always, Mary Jane suspected that Miss Lizzie's actions included an alternative clause and there was something she wasn't telling her.

After the ceremony, and the resulting congratulations by the few attendees, Wilson gently took Mary Jane's hand and led her out of the church to the awaiting carriage. He nodded to the driver, a man whom Mary Jane recognized as an occasional attendant of Miss Lizzie. "I thought we could take a ride to view the sights of Richmond before we arrive back at the Van Lew Mansion," Wilson stated.

Mary Jane hesitated. She knew that most of the white population of Richmond would view her marriage as a farce—so much of a farce that many refused to honor the commitment and would sell a slave wife away from a husband faster than a whip's crack, at the right price. At any rate, she didn't feel like parading around now. Normally spring in Richmond was glorious with magnolia blooms and luscious greenery but there was a pall over the city for any abolitionist or Union sympathizer. There had been large parades of people carrying Southern flags after both the news of the surrender at Fort Sumter had reached the city and then again after the Ordinance of Secession had been passed by the Virginia Convention. The massive Union flag that had waved from the corner of Franklin and Governor Streets had been recently taken down to great fanfare, and been replaced by Virginia's state flag with its emblem: Death to Tyranny. And there was much of Richmond that Mary Jane purposely avoided at all costs: namely the auction blocks at Lumpkin's Alley and the Negro jail at Shockoe Bottom where she had recently spent time.

"Or we could just head straight for the farm," Wilson added. He must have sensed that Mary Jane was uncomfortable.

"No, Miss Lizzie would be mad if we didn't return to the mansion. She's had the cook in the kitchen all day, brewing up a mighty feast."

"Miss Lizzie is awfully kind in that way," Wilson offered. He seemed disappointed when Mary Jane's only reply was a slight nod.

A crowd had gathered at the Church Hill mansion when the newly-weds arrived. Mary Jane's heart began to thud upon spying some of the Van Lew's more secesh neighbors. She steeled her spine as she exited the carriage, the large hoop skirt that she had borrowed for her wedding making the process all the more difficult. She prepared herself to accept the insults about her marriage that were sure to ensue, but the Southerners had their sights set on the Union flag that flew in front of the main house. That flag—much larger than the standard—had always been Miss Lizzie's pride and joy. The last time she'd taken it down was when Kansas had become a state. Then she'd sewn another star on it, rejoicing in the fact that another free state had joined the Union. Mary Jane led Wilson into the big house through the back door. Miss Lizzie had never insisted upon her servants using a different door, but Mary Jane thought it would be better than walking through the angry crowd.

Miss Lizzie's voice was equally angry as she shouted, "I won't do it, John."

John Van Lew, Miss Lizzie's younger brother stood with his hand on the knob of the ornate front door. "We both know which side we support, but to continue to back the Union outright will be a danger for us all."

"I won't—" Miss Lizzie started to argue, but John was already out the door. The three of them—Wilson, Mary Jane, and Miss

Lizzie—stood in silence until John returned, the flag reverently folded. He handed it to Margaret, another servant, who had come in from the parlor. Without a word she took it and brought it upstairs.

Miss Lizzie stood with her arms crossed, muttering to herself. "I may not be able to display my Union loyalty in this Confederate town, but there must be other ways to help the Cause."

Mary Jane heard John reply in a whisper as he passed by, "Your mouth may need to remain shut, but you can keep your eyes and ears open." All three pairs of eyes then focused on Wilson Bowser, who had taken a sudden interest in a hallway vase.

The next day, Wilson brought Mary Jane to his cabin on the family farm. But Mary Jane panicked. All she could think about were her mother's stories of her grandfather's time as a cotton picker—a field hand—on a New Orleans plantation. Her mother had always revered her status as a "house slave." As such, it had always been a threat that a misbehaving house slave would be sent to work in the fields, where the workload was heavier, the food was worse, and there was less freedom to come and go as one pleased. It seemed that the Southerners weren't the only ones whose prejudices endured.

Wilson dismounted and pointed toward the horizon. "Massa John says that this little patch of earth will be mine one day. We can work our own land."

Mary Jane, remaining on her horse, held up both palms. "These hands were not meant for farming." She said nothing of her mind, which had always been her greatest asset. Miss Lizzie had taught her to read at a very young age. She saw this instruction as part of her Christian duty, never fearing that it was illegal in Richmond, but she never came across anyone who learned as fast as Mary Jane.

On Sundays, her mother, Mrs. Van Lew, would read the Bible to her slaves and teach them how to pray the white-people way. Many fellow Richmonders opposed this education of slaves, fearing that they would then demand equality and endanger a practice that had defined the South, and without which cotton could never have been

King. Old Man Van Lew was one such advocate of the practice, and Mrs. Van Lew would change her sermons according to her husband's presence. "Slaves, obey your masters according to the flesh, with fear and trembling in the sincerity of your heart, as you would Christ." Old Man Van Lew would nod his head in agreement as Mary Jane's juvenile sense of defiance would rise up. She hated the old man as she hated anyone who was pro-slavery. Her mother had established from an early age that blacks were just as good as whites, though whenever Old Man Van Lew was around, Mama was sure to curb her tongue. But alone, she would tell Mary Jane that the drudgery of slavery on Earth would be more than made up for in Heaven.

After Mary Jane's mother had died, Miss Lizzie sent her North to be educated. Her teachers had declared her intelligence as "on par or better" with a white person. Mary Jane could not explain to her peers how she had come to memorize anything she read, including the Declaration of Independence or Thomas Paine's pamphlets on the American identity. And she definitely could not explain the same to her new husband.

Wilson took her soft hands into his rough ones. "Mary Jane, I'm working for us. For our family, as it is now, and as it will be in the future."

Mary Jane's eyes filled with frustrated tears. She knew the meanings of thousands of words, but sometimes could not use them to express what she felt. She did not love Wilson Bowser, but she did not hate him. She'd long ago become numb to the strong feelings that most people experienced—it was easier to endure life that way. After what had happened last year, Miss Lizzie thought that marriage would be a safeguard, an extra layer of protection. So far Wilson had only treated her with kindness, but Mary Jane knew that she needed to be in Richmond, the now declared Capital of the Confederacy, if she were to accomplish any of her goals. She cleared her throat and thought about how best to appeal to her new husband. "I may be free, and you might be soon, but what of our brothers and sisters of color? They might never be free unless the Union wins this war."

Wilson's glance darted around him, as if seeing who might have heard, but there was not a soul around. He stepped in closer anyway. "Wife, you speak of treason."

"I do." Mary Jane's voice rang loud and clear. "Treason might be the only way to win this war."

Wilson shook his head. "You are putting the both of us in danger."

Mary Jane took a deep breath. "And that is why I must return to the Van Lew Mansion. I wouldn't want to put you in any more perils than you are in for being a slave in a Southern city. You are subject to any white man's will. Regardless of whether your current master is kind, you could be sold to a cruel man at his will. I would not want my children brought up in that atmosphere." With that, she kicked her heels and steered her horse in the direction of the Van Lew Mansion.

CHAPTER 4

BELLE

JULY 1861

*M*uch had changed in the months since Belle had left her boarding school. There was no place in the world more scenic than where she had grown up, but she had been dismayed to find out that her hometown of Martinsburg, Virginia, was the only region in the Shenandoah Valley that had voted against secession. She knew the issue currently dividing the nation was that of slavery, and Belle recognized that the practice, while necessary, was imperfect and would someday come to an end, but the Federal government had no right to demand the immediate abolishment of it. Her family had always had slaves, including Mauma Eliza, who had run away from an intolerable master when she was little and who became Belle's personal maid. The other five slaves in her family mostly helped out on her father's tobacco farm.

The majority of the Martinsburg males had enlisted with Company D, the 4th company of the 2nd Virginia Infantry, including both Belle's father and her many beaux. Mr. Boyd had been offered an officer's position but declined in favor of joining the ranks with his fellow townsmen, under the command of Colonel T. J. Jackson.

"You must look after your mother while I'm gone," Ben Boyd told his oldest daughter as he packed his bag. "In war, boys become men as soon as the first shot is fired. But for now, it's time for my little girl to become a woman." He smiled. "I know how you've always been eager to be older than you are." Her father loved to tell the story of how an eleven-year-old Belle, dismayed to hear that she was too young to attend a dinner her parents gave for prominent Virginia politicians, led her horse, Fleeter, into the dining room and demanded that, since Fleeter was old enough to attend, he should be set a place at the table. Although Mauma Eliza was fit to be tied, the guests insisted that Belle join them for dessert. A house servant led Fleeter back to his stall in the barn as Belle enjoyed a custard to the delight of the Boyds' important visitors.

"I will, Papa," she replied.

He went to his top drawer and pulled out his Colt revolver. "I'm going to leave this with you." He put a hand on Belle's head. "I know you know how to use it."

"Of course." Despite the fact that she desperately feared for her father, and all the boys going off to war, she refused to cry in front of him. There was something so unfair about men marching off to war while their women stayed back at the house and wept, and she knew her father was counting on her, his oldest daughter, to take care of the family in his absence. Belle turned the gun over, checking to see that it was loaded. If only she could join the war and use the gun to shoot Yankees!

Belle watched them march off, old men such as her father with graying mustaches and whiskers, accompanied by boys still in the flush of youth, some barely able to shoulder a musket. Belle had just turned 17—a year older than her mother had been when she got married—and she felt not just a little dismay as she noted Cliff McVay, a once promising beau, march off toward the gaps in the Blue Ridge Mountains to the destination of Harper's Ferry.

22

Belle knew that she was no great beauty: her nose was a little too hawkish and her eyes a bit too beady to be considered the conventional kind of pretty so valued in the South. However, she had never wanted for male attention. She'd made an effort to dress in the latest fashions; her figure was fine and the Virginia sun lent a reddish tint to her brown hair. She knew how to flirt and use her long lashes, framing dark blue eyes, to command men to do her bidding. Her wit was quick, her cunning daring, and she possessed the most graceful curtsy in all of western Virginia. As much as she hated watching her future prospects leave for the front, Belle was eager to do her own part for the war effort. Belle joined the sewing circles composed of cousins, friends, and other debutantes to make clothing for the troops.

Her mother, having never spent any significant amount of time away from her husband, grew unbearably needy. Belle tried reassuring her—explaining that it was destined to be a quick skirmish, one sure to end in the South's favor, and it would be only a matter of time before the men of Martinsburg returned home to resume their customary duties of shopkeepers, millers, and farmers—to no avail. Consequently, Belle escaped to go visiting among her friends as much as possible.

One day, as she walked back from such a visit, Belle came upon an old schoolmate, Benjamin Hearst. "Why Ben, have you already been granted a furlough?" she asked.

"No." Ben shuffled his feet. "You know that mother is very ill."

Belle placed a hand over her mouth in shock before removing it to say, "Do you mean to tell me that you have not enlisted?"

Ben met her eyes. His contained more than a hint of defiance. "Yes, that is right, Miss Boyd. As I have said, Mother is sick and needs someone to look after her."

"Is that not what your slaves are for—to take care of domestic duties? Yours is to fight for your country."

Ben tapped his hat. "Good day, Miss Boyd."

Belle watched him shuffle down the street with narrowed eyes. How dare he linger about his daily life when the other boys and men of the town were risking theirs for the South! Upon arriving at home, she went to the attic to dig through boxes until she found a petticoat that no longer fit. She wrapped it in parcel paper and attached a note addressed to Mr. Benjamin Hearst, declaring that he should enlist immediately rather than join the ranks of the petticoat warriors. Belle did not receive a reply, but the next time her mother paid a visit to Mrs. Hearst, the old lady was in mourning over the fact that Benjamin had joined the Union army

In early July, Belle was dismayed to see men clad in Union blue march down Queen Street. Belle's Negro maid, Mauma Eliza, joined her at her bedroom window, mirroring an equally disdainful expression.

"Look at them, Mauma. Why does their flag still contain thirty-four stars? It should only be twenty-three now."

Mauma Eliza's eyes narrowed as she watched one soldier spit on the street. "Them Yankees have no respect. No respect at all."

Belle silently agreed as her eye caught a familiar figure. "Why that's Ben Hearst. How dare he come marching through his town wearing that despicable uniform? He would have been better off in the petticoat I gave him."

"No respect at all," Mauma Eliza muttered again as she turned away from the window and began pulling the bedclothes off Belle's bed. "Indeed," she harrumphed to herself as she left Belle's room, her arms full of dirty sheets.

Two days later, on the 4th of July, Belle was disappointed to hear of the Confederacy's defeat at Falling Waters, a beautiful spot just eight miles away. Only three Yankees had met their maker as a result of that battle and now Martinsburg was under Union control. That, combined with the date, was enough to make Belle's blood boil. Only one year ago her family had picnicked at Falling Waters in celebration of the holiday. Now Belle had come to hate the holiday and the archaic Yankee traditions it brought with it. *What would the Founding Fathers have thought if they knew their precious Union had willingly let 11 of their states secede?*

Belle grimaced and backed away from the window as the men

below began singing "Yankee Doodle." She reached for the blinds and yanked on the cord. The thin wood did little to drown out the drums, bugles, and fifes, however.

The men were celebrating both America's eighty-fifth birthday and their recent victory, and soon became belligerent with drink, terrorizing the Confederate citizens of their new dominion. Belle could hear the shouting and screaming before she caught sight of the blue-coated men stomping the grounds just outside her bedroom window.

She ignored her racing heart and picked up her father's Colt pistol, opening the barrel to check that the bullets hadn't mysteriously disappeared. She descended the stairs and then began counting to ten in an effort to slow the canter of her heartbeat. On five, a pounding on the front door commenced. At eight, the Yankees burst into her parents' home, the broken door practically falling at the feet of Mauma Eliza.

Mother jumped up from her nervous perch on the settee. There were four of them, and Belle could smell the whiskey on their breath from across the room. Instead of fearing the soldiers, she felt only hatred—what right did they have to invade her home? She had heard of the barbarism the Union soldiers had inflicted upon their Southern neighbors, plundering homes and violating women. It had gotten so bad that Confederate husbands and fathers were demanding that Jefferson Davis appoint contingencies to protect their helpless women. But never once in Belle's seventeen years had she felt helpless, and she was not about to start now. She tightened her grip on the gun.

The biggest one cast his eyes around the parlor and then settled on Belle. "Are you with the Union or are you one of those damned rebels?" he asked in a heavy German accent.

Belle folded both hands, including the one with the pistol, behind her back, and matched his disdainful tone. "I happen to be a secessionist."

The sneer on his face grew larger. "So you are. And do you have any reb flags hidden in your dwelling?"

Belle didn't answer, not wanting him to know that a Confederate emblem spanned the wall in her room directly across from the window. Out of the corner of her eye, Belle watched Mother sink back into the couch before giving the most imperceptible nod at Mauma Eliza. The slave crept back upstairs, unnoticed.

The tallest of the other three soldiers stepped forward. "With the Confederate loss at Falling Waters, this town is now under federal command. We intend to hoist a Union flag above your house as soon as possible."

This was too much for Mother to bear. She rose to her feet, her voice void of its customary lilt as she stated, "Every person in my household will die before you dare raise that flag over our heads."

Belle gasped as the German man marched over to her mother. Time seemed to slow as Belle watched him stare her mother down before grabbing her waist and pulling her close to him. Mother's struggles to get free were no match for her captor's brawny arms. The man paused as he took in her brown eyes and well-rounded figure. His big, ugly lip curled outward as he bent toward her. Her head flinched in time and the soldier's lips met empty air. This threw the soldier off balance, and he dispatched a slew of obsceni-ties directed at both Belle's mother, whom he had been forced to let go of, and the Confederacy in general.

The blood coursing through Belle's veins was as hot as a boiling kettle as she saw the German's hands again seize her mother's waist before everything in her sight disappeared into a haze of crimson. It took her nearly a full second before she realized that the voice shrieking, "Let go!" over and over was hers. She lifted her arms and squinted her eyes to block out the redness, aiming the gun square at the German. Her intent was to frighten him into releasing her mother; she wasn't aware that her finger had coiled around the trigger until she heard the gunshot and sensed the recoil in her arms.

At first Belle felt only numbness, no anguish for the blue devil lying prone on the parquet floor, no remorse over what she had done. The still smoking pistol was warm in her hands and, as she carefully set it on the armchair beside her, she felt bile rise in her throat. Surely there would be repercussions from the fallen man's comrades.

Mauma Eliza had reappeared and both her and Mother's mouths were open, but Belle barely heard their screams. Her concentration was gathered on the other three soldiers who were approaching her, guns raised. She let her gaze fall to the Yankee's motionless body before holding up her arms. She had never seen so much blood before but she refused to let the Yanks see her fear. Steadying her voice as best she could, she declared, "Shooting a woman is an act of a cowardly man." She met the eyes of the tallest man. "Are you a coward?"

He returned her stare as the other men rushed to their fellow soldier hemorrhaging on the floor and hoisted him in their arms. Mauma Eliza's screams had turned into earsplitting shrieks as the tall man finally broke Belle's gaze. He holstered his own pistol before snatching the one Belle had used. Without a word, he left the house to follow his men with the dead Yankee in their makeshift stretcher, leaving the women alone to clean up the mess.

CHAPTER 5

LORETA

JULY 1861

*L*ieutenant Harry T. Buford was fixin' for a fight. He had traveled to Virginia with his slave, Bob, determined to prove that he was as honorable as the scores of men who had taken up arms for the Southern cause. He was not afraid to die in battle—the only true fear that Harry had to contend with was missing the action, as people were saying that the war would be over in no time. The last thing Harry wanted was to return to New Orleans without ever having shot a Yankee.

Harry hadn't joined a regiment, knowing he'd have more freedom to follow the action as an independent soldier. He'd arrived at the station near Manassas Junction on a train from Richmond. He'd left that city to a cheering crowd, a Confederate cockade—a gift from an admiring female—pinned to his uniform.

For the past three days, Harry had been participating in skirmishes with the enemy outside Blackburn's Ford, near the muddy

Bull Run Creek. One of the Yankee generals must have thought that the road to Centreville was clear through and began to advance. General Longstreet's men, with whom Harry had currently taken up arms, commenced firing. To Harry, it was more like a series of duels between enemy soldiers and not a true battle. He'd exchanged gunshots with a few Yanks, but did not wound anyone seriously, despite having picked up and fired a dead man's musket at a fleeing Federal.

"Hah!" a fellow soldier commented as the Yanks started to retreat. "Those blue devils thought they'd march right into the South to take our property, set the niggers free, and drag us back into the Union by our kickin' feet. How wrong were they!"

"Serves them right for thinking they could force us back under their will!" Harry agreed. He joined in the gleeful shouting of insults at the Federal soldiers before the men were compelled to participate in another institution of war—the burial of the dead. There seemed to be only a few boys lost, yet they toiled under the July sun for hours, digging three-foot holes in the ground and then depositing the next poor fellow in, clothing, shoes, and all, accompanied by a short prayer, until both Harry and his darkey Bob were exhausted. Harry was sorry for the loss of his comrades; some of those boys who lost their lives at the dawn of the war were very young, never having a chance to prove themselves. He wondered if they had a family at home, or, like him, had no family to speak of anymore.

Despite the afternoon's drastic circumstances, Harry slept well. In the short time that had elapsed since he became a soldier, he'd learned to sleep as soundly on the cold hard ground as he once did on the expensive couch in his ma's living room. When he rose at four the next morning, he felt sore from the previous day's exertions.

Harry marched with the brigade through Ashby's Gap, reaching the small town of Piedmont, located on the Manassas Railroad. They were ordered to halt there. Over the next few days, more Southerners came with various regiments. The talk of the army was of the impending Federal attack on the 21st. According to one of Brigadier General Barnard Bee's men, the Confederates had ample knowledge of the Union army's movements.

"How did they get that information?" Harry asked him.

The soldier shrugged. "They say that there is a Confederate woman in Washington City who uses her..." he cleared his throat, "powers of persuasion on high-ranking Union men. She sends messages to our leaders through an underground network."

Harry smiled to himself, picturing a courageous seductress in the Federal Capital, ferreting out reports on troop movements from unsuspecting Yankee scamps.

The soldier continued. "We'll be able to defeat them Yanks with one blow and then this war will be over just as fast as it started. Everyone knows that one Confederate is worth five Yankee men."

Harry nodded, hoping that it would not be finished before he had a chance to show his worth. The previous day's skirmishes had only served to provoke his desire for a real battle. He'd dreamed about such an adventure his whole life. He'd read every book about soldiers, kings, or adventurers he could get his hands on, and, as a child, begged his father to tell him about his exploits as an officer in the Mexican-American War. Like Harry, his father had fought against the United States, but he had been a much more reluctant soldier.

On the night of the 20th, Harry assumed he might be too excited to get a good night's rest, but he fell asleep right away, the bare ground being a welcome coolant for his sunburned face.

July 21, 1861 dawned bright and clear. Harry arose with the sun and shrugged on his uniform, smoothing down his mustache and combing back his hair. In his excitement, he found it almost impossible to keep still.

"Look at the little dandy independent, ready to do battle!" one man at his camp called.

Harry steeled himself but did not reply. If he allowed himself to be bothered by every enlisted man who thought themselves better than he, he would have gone back to Richmond several days ago. He'd come this far, experiencing ordeals and circumstances that these mocking officers would never have to go through. He had no thought of turning back for any cause, especially not because of officers who were too big for their britches.

As the sun rose higher in the sky, it cast its light upon thousands of Southerners ready for battle. Harry decided to post himself with General Bee's men, leaving Bob to clean up the camp.

The brilliant sunshine of the morning gave way to sweltering heat at the same pace as some of the men gave way to their inner fears. As Harry scrambled up the hill for an ideal position, he passed by many men with white faces and trembling hands holding their muskets, ascending very slowly, looking for any excuse to slip back down the hill. *Cowards.* He almost wished he felt even just a hint of fear, if only to sympathize with the chicken-hearts behind him.

The mist from the morning dew disappeared, only to be replaced by the faint clouds of dust from thousands of enemy feet marching toward the hill on the opposite side. As Harry bent forward to get a better look, he caught an occasional glimmer of a bayonet through the trees. Adrenaline surged through him as the tiny figures in blue uniforms grew closer. *Every man marching on that side is my personal enemy,* Harry told himself. He raised his musket as a gunshot sounded.

The sounds of many rifles firing soon filled the air, along with the roar of military shells exploding. To Harry's delight, the moment he'd dreamt about all his life was upon him. The first major battle of the war had finally begun. The air became clogged with acrid smoke which burned Harry's eyes and caused incessant coughing from the men around him. As more and more Federal soldiers entered into view, it became evident that the Confederates under General Bee were vastly outnumbered, although Harry noted with satisfaction that the men in grey still managed to hold their own. When he heard someone shout, "Fall back!" Harry assumed that the command had come from a Yankee general. But the men beside him began hightailing down the hill—it was General Bee who was ordering his men to retreat. Harry bit back a rage of indignation. He briefly considered disobeying Bee and continuing to shoot at the Yanks. His rage, however, turned to shame. He might have not had an official commission, but he was a soldier, and a Confederate at that, and the gallant men who fought for their independence always listened to their commanding officer. So, with all the mortification of someone admitting defeat, Harry turned and fled.

Bee had an alternate plan, however, which Harry quickly surmised as the general led his men to the rear of a nearby house and ordered them to halt. Soon, Harry was elated to see more and more Confederate reinforcements arrive.

After they'd had a chance to catch their breath, Bee turned to his men, and with a voice as loud as thunder, said, "My boys, at them again! Victory or death." He gestured toward the newly promoted Brigadier General T.J. Jackson, who stood in front of his brigade of fearless Virginians. "See how our Jackson stands there like a stone wall."

A thousand men echoed Bee's roar as they made another go at the enemy, cheering for "Stonewall" Jackson as they did so. They rallied behind the Confederate flag, "The Stars and Bars," which, in Harry's opinion, was a little too similar to the detested Yankee flag.

When Harry glanced up at the hill that the Confederate's bravest generals had occupied that morning, he saw it covered with men desperately fighting. Their shouting, combined with the deafening sounds of the guns, made for a roar that became a constant buzzing in Harry's ear. The more intense the conflict became, the more determined he became to avenge the Southern cause as well as vindicate his comrades lying slain on the ground beneath them.

Jackson pressed forward, ordering his men to reserve fire until the enemy was within 50 yards. "Then charge, boys, and yell like furies!" The Confederates did as they were told, pushing through the lines with their bayonets pointed and emitting a guttural howl, an unearthly sound that would come to be known as the "Rebel yell." The last of the men in blue were pushed off the hill by late afternoon.

Although the Confederates were eventually victorious, their losses that day were great, including General Bernard Bee himself, who was mortally wounded only a few moments after giving General Jackson his nickname.

At the end of the day, Harry's exhaustion from the day's trials was mixed with exhilaration from both the victory and the fact that he had accomplished something he had dreamt of doing all of his life.

Something that everyone, including poor William, God rest his soul, had told him was impossible.

As Harry headed back to his tent, he reflected that if anyone were to ask his fellow soldiers how he had fared, they would reply that Lieutenant Buford had fought just as valiantly as any man on the field, perhaps even more so.

After double-checking that the tent flaps were closed, he removed his shirt. He unwrapped the soiled wrappings on his chest, taking one free deep breath before replacing them. He then used a hand mirror to take off his fake mustache in order to reapply the glue that held it in place. For a brief second, the face that stared back at him was not that of Harry Buford, but that of his real identity: Loreta Janeta Velazquez Williams, a recent widow who had a sympathy for the South that was as strong as anyone's: male or female.

CHAPTER 6

MARY JANE

JULY 1861

*W*hen Richmond became the capital of the Confederacy, the once quiet city was overrun with government officials—the Confederate Congress was installed in the State Capitol Building and the Post Office was established in the basement of the beautiful Spotswood Hotel. Jefferson Davis, the newly elected President, had arrived to the salute of 15 guns—one for each Confederate state.

After the Battle of Manassas—or Bull Run to the Federals—train after train arrived bearing the pine boxes of the dead and wounded soldiers. Many of the "brave boys" were welcomed into private homes to convalesce when the hospitals grew too full, but others were not so lucky and the streets were thronged with bruised and bloody men from both sides of the war.

"Come with me," Miss Lizzie commanded Mary Jane as she returned to the mansion after an errand. Mary Jane helped her down the steps. She trailed after her mistress down Grace Street, puzzling over her fine attire: a blue silk dress trimmed with yellow ribbon and a matching parasol. She contrasted greatly with the soldiers who wandered the streets as though they were the walking dead, which, Mary Jane mused, with their faces black with gunpowder and blood-soaked bandages over every appendage, they nearly were.

"Miss?" the man's throat was surely so parched he could barely croak the words out.

Miss Lizzie paused and took in the man's appearance. His head was wrapped with a yellowing bandage and another was wrapped around his right knee, the leg below it gone. He used his musket as a makeshift crutch.

"If I had to give a quarter for every wounded soldier, my father's fortune would disappear in no time," Miss Lizzie muttered, more to herself than to anyone else. But she dug change out of her reticule, anyway. She placed it square in the man's open palm and then folded his fingers over it, as if to say, "Don't tell anyone I gave it to you."

She motioned for Mary Jane to continue on, checking to make sure there were no carriages in the vicinity as she crossed Franklin Street. "Damned wounded rebels," Miss Lizzie murmured. "If I could guarantee that for every quarter I pay to them, the impaired Federals would receive the same, I would indeed spend every penny of the money Daddy left me." She gave Mary Jane a searching look before adding, "For the cause."

Miss Lizzie stopped abruptly at the corner of Main and 25th Street as Mary Jane peered up at their apparent destination: the former tobacco warehouse belonging to Mr. John Ligon. The tobacco factories of Richmond had been infamous for their tales of cruelty to the slaves who labored in the warehouse, pressing and preparing the tobacco leaves and stuffing them into the massive hogshead barrels.

A crowd had already formed outside the three-story brick building.

One woman pointed her parasol toward the building and

shouted, "Nothing but cowards in there, not even daring to show their face at the window!"

"Of whom do you speak?" Miss Lizzie asked the woman.

"The blueback malingerers in there." Again she waved her parasol. "They've been taken prisoner and we are here to stir up the Northern lunatics."

Mary Jane caught sight of a young man in a blue uniform, staring out the barred window as though he were a wild animal in a cage. Another woman, this one younger than the one beside Miss Lizzie, shouted, "Even if you end up killing all our men, we women will make more soldiers!"

Mary Jane bit back a giggle as the other woman planted the tip of her parasol on the ground. "Why, Sarah, just because the Yankees are rude, that doesn't mean we need to be as well."

The woman named Sarah opened her mouth and then shut it, glancing at the rest of the crowd, who were snickering at her remark. "I didn't mean we'd make more, as in... make more ourselves. I meant we'd take up arms if need be."

"That's even funnier," a young man, clearly not old enough to enlist, commented. "Women taking up arms."

The woman with the parasol found a new target. "You sir, you don't think women could fight the Yankees as well as you?"

"Not me," the young man conceded, shaking his head. "Not until I'm 18."

"See there," the women replied, shouldering her parasol. "There are other ways to go to battle with the Yankees."

Miss Lizzie marched up to the door and held it open for Mary Jane. "Give them officers hell!" an unknown female voice shouted before it faded when the door slammed shut. "I'd like to see the officer in charge," Miss Lizzie stated to a guard.

"Who are you?" he demanded.

"Miss Elizabeth Van Lew," she said, not without a little pride.

The man, a Richmond native, Mary Jane could only assume, nodded with deference at the name and disappeared behind an inner door. In a few minutes, he was back to escort them into the former owner's office.

The man rose upon their entrance. He looked to be in his early thirties. He had a full goatee and mustache, both black as pitch without a hint of gray. His dark eyes seemed to match, and they became darker as they fixed briefly on Mary Jane standing behind Miss Lizzie before flickering back to the seated Miss Lizzie. Mary Jane could detect a hint of alcohol in his breath as he introduced himself as Lieutenant David Humphries Todd. He pronounced his name with half as much pride as Miss Lizzie used earlier. Mary Jane knew him to be the half-brother of Mary Todd Lincoln, a native of Kentucky. It had been rumored that some of her kin had joined the Confederacy, and, judging by the battered gray uniform, this would be one of them.

If Miss Lizzie recognized the family name as belonging to the First Lady, she did not show it. "Lieutenant, this prison must contain wounded soldiers, and, as such, I would like to be appointed nurse to them."

Todd narrowed his eyes and glared at Mary Jane.

"My servant," Miss Lizzie replied to his unasked question. "She will be of assistance to me."

"Miss—"

"Van Lew," Miss Lizzie supplied.

"You are the first and only lady to make any such application," his voice, slightly slurred, was more of a growl than anything else. "You are aware that we house Yankees here, not gentlemen."

"Yessir," Miss Lizzie's voice had affected a Southern drawl. "But if we wish our cause to succeed, we must be charitable to the thankless and unworthy as well."

His black eyebrows, previously knitted together, became two again at the mention of the words, "our cause." He pulled a pen out and scribbled something on a piece of paper. "This is a pass to see General John Winder, the provost marshal of Richmond. You will find him next door at Howard's factory."

"Thank you, sir." Miss Lizzie rose.

His eyes followed them. As soon as the door shut behind them, Mary Jane thought she heard a drawer open. She pictured him uncapping a bottle of Kentucky bourbon and taking another swig before returning to his paperwork.

· · ·

"Miss Lizzie," Mary Jane hissed once they were past the crowd outside the prison. "What was all of that about 'our cause'?"

"You can kill more gnats with honey than you can with poison," Miss Lizzie said cryptically before entering the adjacent building. They entered directly into a cavernous room, with multiple rows of wooden structures that Mary Jane guessed were tobacco presses. A gray-haired man in an officer's uniform stood in the middle of it all, barking orders at two other uniformed men, who seemed to be running around in circles.

Miss Lizzie waited for a lull in the commands before tentatively calling out, "General Winder?"

"Yes'm?" he replied, marching closer to the women.

She stuck out her hand. "I am Miss Elizabeth Van Lew. Lieutenant Todd sent me here to speak to you about the federal prisoners being housed at Ligon's Warehouse."

"Yes. Eating utensils," he shouted at one of the soldiers nearby, who marked something in a notebook. Addressing Miss Lizzie, he said, "We've already reached capacity there and plan on moving some of the officers here as soon as we can ready it."

"Sir, that's exactly why I'm here—I want to help. A man of your authority shouldn't need to worry about such trifles as forks for the Yankees."

Winder sighed. "Indeed, it is a thankless position. I was a major in the US Army." He pointed to a scar running the length of his cheek. Everything about his countenance was gray, from the dull eyes devoid of color, to the unruly tufts of hair that stuck out underneath his hat, to the stony expression on his face. "Got this in the Mexican War, fighting for the Union. But they have no right to use force to keep the Union intact."

"Ah, I would have never noticed your scar. Your hair is what distracts me—it belongs in Rome among the Gods, not here in Richmond."

The taut line of Winder's lips extended, as if he were attempting a smile that did not reach his eyes. "You say you want to help the prisoners."

"I know the good women of Richmond will tend to all of the

needs of the Confederates, but the federal prisoners will need provisions as well."

He nodded. "You there," he called to a passing soldier. "Write Miss Van Lew a pass to visit the prisoners at will."

Even Miss Lizzie seemed taken aback at Winder's easy compliance. He excused himself and returned to his spot in the middle of the warehouse to bellow out more items for his men to procure. The other soldier returned with the requested pass and Miss Lizzie bid him good day. When they left the dank warehouse and the sun was once again warming their shoulders, Miss Lizzie congratulated herself. "I'd heard Winder's vanity was great. Now I know I can flatter anything out of the old man."

Mary Jane thought once again of that gray face, lined with knowing wrinkles. Perhaps Winder wasn't completely blinded by arrogance and those colorless eyes saw past Miss Lizzie's flattery to her true intentions.

Mary Jane assisted Miss Lizzie in gathering fruit, bread, books, boots, and other various items for the prisoners. They loaded her wagon until the wheels threatened to stay buried in the mud. Miss Lizzie's sister-in-law Mary watched the goings-on from her perch on the porch. "Elizabeth," she called as Miss Lizzie made another trip from the kitchen to the wagon.

"Yes, Mary?" Miss Lizzie asked as she carefully balanced a basket of socks on the pile of supplies.

"Why do you insist on aiding those miscreants? If freed, they would rape or murder us in an instant."

Miss Lizzie pasted on a smile. "All Yankees are not criminals, just as all Southerners are not gentlemen. There are evil-doers on both sides of the war, just as there are noble men. Our purpose is not to judge, but to aid."

"You are aiding the wrong side. You could be considered an enemy under Jeff Davis's new proclamation," Mary stated.

Mary Jane knew that the Confederate Congress had recently passed an act declaring that any person "adhering to the Government of the United States and acknowledging authority of the same" would be treated as an alien enemy.

Miss Lizzie motioned for Mary Jane to climb into the front seat of the wagon. "That act only applies to male citizens," she replied, ascending the block to take her place beside Mary Jane. "God knows it's the least we can do," she said, more to herself than anyone else as the driver picked up the reins and the horses began to pull the wagon slowly out of earshot.

CHAPTER 7

HATTIE

JULY 1861

*A*fter helping deliver Lincoln to his inauguration in one piece, Pinkerton and Co. settled back in their Chicago office. Even though Fort Sumter had fallen, resulting in a war between the states, the criminals were still at work, and the Pinkerton operatives resumed their status quo.

Since Hattie was the new girl, her day mostly consisted of completing paperwork and sketching. Hattie knew she had been hired in large part because Pinkerton had spotted her talent for drawing. She would draw a likeness of a suspect based on the hair color, eye color, chin shape and physical abnormalities dictated to her by an informant or victim. The picture was then hung in the "Rogues' Gallery," a hallway which was also filled with daguerreotypes and tintypes of criminals the Pinkertons had arrested through the years. To Hattie's immense pride, a few of her depictions had resulted in arrests—in her own way, Hattie contributed to getting dangerous criminals off the street. But still, she longed for a larger role.

When strangers insisted on inquiring after her occupation, Hattie told them she was a dressmaker. Most people assumed she was a widow, like her supervisor Kate. She did not correct them, for they would think it impossible for "a respectable married woman" to remain virtuous in such work. Pinkerton did not agree with such musings and told Hattie so when he encouraged her to stay in Chicago and work for him, stating that "the position of a lady operative is as useful and honorable of employment as can be found in any walk of life. It is no less respectable or honorable than that of a lady copyist or clerk."

When Hattie was clearly still hesitant, he added, "And actually, your virtue would be even more safeguarded than those aforementioned jobs, since the operatives in my company know that their conduct is under constant surveillance."

Pinkerton knew the value of a beautiful operative, having employed Kate Warne for six years. After being left destitute at a young age upon the death of her husband, Kate sought work from Pinkerton. She managed to convince him that he needed her type of tact and discretion as well as her uncanny ability to read anyone's inner motives, which indeed he did need. After a successful trial run —and her subsequent hire—Pinkerton sent Kate out on various assignments. The Pinkerton Detective Agency's largest clients were the railroad companies, who hired the agency to guard their rails and prevent theft on the trains. But the Pinkerton operatives also solved fraud and counterfeiting claims, and even murder cases. Kate's duties usually involved becoming a mistress to suspected criminals—in that way she could achieve the confidences of difficult subjects and get them to divulge information they would not to a male operative. Once Pinkerton realized the advantages of having a woman on staff, he quickly promoted Kate to head of the female unit and hired more female detectives.

Kate had reopened the murder case she'd been working before she left for Baltimore. She had befriended the murder suspect's girlfriend and, a few days after returning to Chicago, came into the office with a quickened gait and a thoughtful expression. She disappeared into Pinkerton's office and emerged several minutes later. "Hattie! Are you ready for your next undercover role?"

Hattie dropped her pen. "Of course!" Hattie followed Kate into the back "disguise" closet. Kate began tossing women's clothing all around until she found a flowing silk scarf. "Miss Davis just told me that Mr. Pattmore believes in fortune tellers." She draped the yellow scarf over Hattie's head and they both gazed at her reflection in the mirror. With Hattie's dark eyes and hair, she already had an exotic look to her, made even more so with the scarf.

Pinkerton paid for Kate and Hattie to go to a fortune teller that night. Kate pretended to be interested in having her fortune told while Hattie memorized the soothsayer's rhetoric and jerky movements. The woman foretold that Kate would soon be pregnant.

"But my husband is dead," Kate replied.

Undaunted, the woman stated, "You will be married again within the year."

Kate cocked an eyebrow but did not say anything as she rose from the chair. "Your turn, Hattie."

"That's okay. I think we've learned enough tonight."

"Come on, Hattie."

Hattie shrugged. As close as Hattie and Kate were, Kate was, after all, still Hattie's boss. She sat down and placed her hands palm up on the table.

As soon as the fortune teller laid her hands over Hattie's, she pulled them back, as if Hattie's palms were red-hot pokers.

"Is something wrong?" Hattie asked. She looked down at her hands, fearing they had betrayed her past to this strange woman.

"I'm tired," the woman replied. "It's been a long day, and my third eye has closed."

Hattie glanced at Kate, whose eyebrows were furrowed.

"That's fine," Hattie said, grabbing her purse. She threw a few dollars on the table and the two operatives left. They headed to the "office" located across the street from Pinkerton and Co. Pinkerton had purchased it a few years ago to utilize for various cases—its most recent use had been acting as an accountant's office for another undercover operative. Kate and Hattie worked late into the night to cover the windows with dark drapes, creating an atmosphere more akin to a fortune teller's place of business.

"Do you believe in any of that stuff?" Kate asked once they were on the street again.

Out of habit, Hattie checked to make sure her revolver was secure in her handbag. "No."

"Me neither. I don't ever want to marry again, let alone in the middle of the war. The only man worthy of my love would be fighting for the Union, and I don't want to spend my time worrying if he lives or died in battle."

Hattie gave her friend a tiny smile. "Agreed."

As Hattie climbed the steps to her apartment, she reflected on what Kate had said. There had only been one man that Hattie had ever met that she felt would be worthy of her love. And it wasn't her husband.

After Hattie had unlocked the door, she was grateful to note that her landlady was not home. She headed to the room that she leased and pulled a small box from the upper corners of her closet. The box contained papers from her past life: mostly newspaper clippings of her brother's exploits, but it also included her marriage certificate, the train ticket from Iowa City to Chicago, and a small folded paper, which she removed before replacing the lid. The paper was a sketch of one of the men who had accompanied them on the journey from Kansas: Captain Lawton. He was the bravest man Hattie had ever met, refusing to give in to the slaves' fears that they would be caught and whipped, or, worse, sent to the gallows. Hattie traced her finger along the etched lines. She'd completed it by memory after she arrived at the Chicago safe-house. The woman of the house had made up a guest room for Hattie while some of the slaves were herded into a small room off the basement to await the next leg of their expedition. The others went to various other refuges—called "stations" in terms of the Underground Railroad— located throughout the city.

The owner of the safe-house happened to spot the drawing amongst her things while Hattie was packing. "Did you draw this?"

he asked, picking it up to examine it closely. Even that early in their relationship, Hattie could tell that his sharp eyes did not miss much.

Hattie suppressed the urge to snatch the drawing back. "Yes sir."

He set down the picture and turned his penetrating eyes on her. "You intend to go to Canada with the rest of them."

"Indeed, sir." Hattie tucked some clothing into her carpetbag.

"Are they relatives of yours?" His finger pointed downward, referring to the slaves hidden away in the lower reaches of the house.

"No, sir." Hattie refused to meet his eyes.

"Then why? As I'm sure you're aware, the journey is exceedingly dangerous."

Hattie could have laughed aloud. Of course it was dangerous: she'd already spent weeks traveling the frigid prairies, traversing creeks swollen with ice-cold water, and dodging armed bands of men intent on murdering their leader—in their words, "that damned nigger thief" John Brown.

"Why then?" he demanded when Hattie did not reply.

Hattie blew out a breath of air. There was something about this man's demeanor that coaxed the truth from her. "Aaron Dwight Stevens is my brother."

She assumed correctly that he was aware that Aaron was one of the warrior abolitionist Brown's most devoted followers. "That does not answer my question." His voice softened. "While I agree with Brown's viewpoints on slavery—I personally despise it and see it as a curse upon all Americans—I disagree with his vigilante methods. The pro-slavers wouldn't hesitate to kill him and his disciples on sight. Including your brother."

"I know," Hattie said softly.

"And Captain Lawton as well. None of them are long for this world if they keep up their escapades. Which puts you in the same danger as them." He once again picked up the drawing. "I own a detective agency. Your artistic gifts would be of great use in capturing criminals."

Hattie refrained from gasping aloud. She knew the safe-house had been owned by a Pinkerton, but she didn't realize it was *that* Pinkerton. Hattie was an avid newspaper reader; she'd developed the habit at an early age, sneaking the paper into her room and scouring it for any word of Aaron. Later, she'd search through the obituaries, hoping that news of her husband's death would make it into the Chicago papers. She'd come across stories on the exploits of the Pinkerton National Detective Agency many times. "I read about how you solved that post office robbery."

"Yes," Pinkerton scratched at his beard. "I was undercover, working as a clerk, and I saw that rascal Dennison sneak envelopes into his waistcoat. We did a thorough search of his apartment but turned up nothing until I had the idea to look behind the many pictures he had on his walls. There we found thousands of dollars." He met Hattie's eyes again, and this time Hattie didn't turn from his gaze. "It's that kind of quick thinking that helps solve cases. Your brother must be a quick-thinker to have survived this long. Surely you are as well."

"Thank you, sir."

Pinkerton must have realized that Hattie was intent on continuing to Canada because he tried a different tactic. "I managed to scrape together some funds to help get the slaves to freedom. But it's not much money and it could go further if there was one less mouth to feed along the way." He put his hand on the doorknob. "The party plans on leaving tomorrow night. You have some time to think it over."

Indeed she contemplated Pinkerton's words after he'd gone. Now that she'd left her husband once and for all, Hattie knew that she would not have a lot of options for earning an income on her own. Jobs for women were few and far between, mainly consisting of three options: factory worker, which offered little job stability; house servant, which meant that Hattie would have to live in her employer's household and give up her freedom of movement; or prostitute, whose drawbacks needed no further explanation. But it was the mention of the slaves that did her in. She knew of the hazards they had faced in their old life, especially from Hattie's own husband, who treated his slaves even more brutally than he treated his wife. One of the men on the journey had been a free man until captured under the Fugitive Slave Act and brought to Kansas. Although Hattie's husband had never owned him, he said that he did anyway, and beat the man senseless as a lesson for the other slaves never to run. Hattie had been shocked by the scars on the man's back—revealed the day he'd removed his shirt to serve as a makeshift blanket for a baby—and couldn't imagine the wounds he carried on the inside.

And so Hattie stayed in Chicago, reconciling with the fact that she'd never again lay eyes on Captain Lawton, who represented everything a man should be and everything her husband wasn't: an abolitionist who wasn't afraid to stand up for what was right. That fall, John Brown organized the doomed raid on Harper's Ferry in an attempt to trigger a slave uprising. Although Aaron was shot four times, he managed to survive and was arrested along with Brown and his other followers. Aaron wrote Hattie one last letter from his prison cell. In it, he stated:

I do not feel guilty in the least, for I know, if I know anything, that there was no evil intention in my heart. I thought I should be able to do more good for the world in this way than I could do in any other. I may have erred as to the best way, but I think everything will turn out for the best in the end.

I do not expect to be tried until next Spring, when I expect I shall be hanged, as I think all the rest will, as Slavery demands that we should hang for its protection, and we will meet it willingly, knowing that God is Just, and is over all. There seems to be no mercy for those who are willing to help those who have none to help them.

My heart feels like bleeding to think how many thousands are worse off in this land than I am now. Oh, that I could see this country free, I would give a thousand lives if I had them to give.

Hattie wrote to him, vowing to help him see that goal of a free country in both the North and the South, but her letter was returned to her. Aaron, Brown, and the others were sent to the gallows in March of 1860. Hattie pored over every paper she could get her hands on, but she found no mention of Captain Lawton.

. . .

The next day, Kate's suspect, Mr. Pattmore arrived with his mistress, Miss Davis, at the makeshift fortune teller's place of business. Although unduly nervous in her fortune teller disguise—she'd worn a flowing silk dress and the requisite scarf and carried an oddly carved wand donated by one of the other operatives—Hattie was determined to prove once more that she could be a successful operative.

Mr. Pattmore was a well-dressed, rather handsome man, with dark hair and eyes.

"What do you seek to know?" Hattie asked.

"The outcome of the war," Pattmore replied.

Hattie tried to meet the man's gaze in order to ascertain what side he had allegiance for, but his eyes shifted in every direction but hers. Unable to get a fair impression, she rotated her head, mimicking the fortune teller's movements from last night. In this way, she was able to make momentary eye contact with Kate, who stood behind Mr. Pattmore, half-hidden by a black curtain.

"Rebs," Kate mouthed.

Hattie moved the wand back and forth. "The Confederacy fights well. And though they are outnumbered—"

"Yes?" Pattmore leaned forward.

"The outcome is favorable."

He nodded and sat back in his chair.

Hattie refrained from frowning. "Do you wish to know your own future?"

"She is a fortune teller," Miss Davis cut in. "Isn't that what you paid for?"

"Indeed," Pattmore placed his hands on the table.

Hattie pretended to take her time examining the inside of his palms while recalling what Kate had told her about her suspect. "Your parents are dead. You had one brother, who died at an early age. Most of the money your father left you is gone."

Miss Davis gasped. "You can tell all that from the lines on his hand?"

"Shh." Pattmore directed his attention back to Hattie. "What else?"

"There was a man." Hattie shifted her eyes to Miss Davis. "Your husband, I believe?"

The woman, clearly under Hattie's spell, nodded.

Hattie turned Pattmore's palm over. "He is no longer with us as well." Hattie focused once again on Miss Davis. "I am sorry for your loss."

"It was no great loss on anyone's part," Pattmore muttered.

"Indeed not, although she got a great amount of wealth upon his death." Hattie widened her eyes. "But it seems that you had something to do with his death."

"Of course he did not." Miss Davis stood. "What kind of sooth-sayer are you? You know nothing."

"Quiet, Cecile," Pattmore commanded. "I want to hear more."

"These are just lies."

"Oh, but they are not, my dear." Pattmore gestured for her to sit. "I did have something to do with his death."

"What?" Miss Davis fell back into her chair. "How?"

Pattmore seemed more angry than agitated now. From behind the curtain, Kate rapidly circled her hand. *Keep going.*

Hattie traced a line on his palm. "You paid someone to off him."

"No, he didn't." Miss Davis said. She faced her fiancé. "You wouldn't do that, would you Benny?"

He removed his hands from the table and stood up. "How else would you have gotten your inheritance from the old man?" He puffed out his chest and looked down at Miss Davis with cold eyes. "He was onto our relationship. It was just a matter of time before we were discovered and you were disinherited."

Miss Davis gasped as Kate and Sam Bridgman, another Pinkerton operative, appeared from their hiding places. "You're under arrest," Bridgman said as he bound the criminal's wrists in handcuffs. "Nice work, Lewis," he told Hattie as he escorted a protesting Pattmore out.

Kate pulled off one of the window coverings, flooding the room with light, before turning to Pattmore's bewildered mistress. "You are free to go, for now. But Miss Davis, make sure to choose your beaus with a greater amount of prudence from now on. Your future husband's life may depend on it." After Miss Davis promised to be more careful, she left.

Kate hugged Hattie. "Thank you. This is the second time you've proven yourself a worthy operative."

"Hopefully now the Boss will give me other work besides drawing and being his secretary."

"He will," Kate said as she gathered an armful of sheets. "I know it."

Pinkerton had summoned a meeting to begin at 7 am the next morning for all of his employees in the Chicago area.

As Hattie walked down the hall to the offices of Pinkerton's National Detective Agency, she was surprised to see a new logo painted on the frosted glass: a realistic drawing of an eye. Underneath were the hand-painted words, "We Never Sleep."

"Bizarre, isn't it?" Kate asked when Hattie entered the office. She must have caught Hattie staring at it in the hall.

"Yet somehow fitting," Hattie murmured. The unblinking eye seemed to watch Hattie as she yawned. She indeed had been up all night, feeling at once exhilarated about her role in the murder case, and anxious about today's meeting. Hattie hoped it would be a big case, and that she would have an integral part in it.

Pinkerton ran his business with an iron hand: all operatives— despite his agency's official name, he refused to refer to his employees as "detectives" because he thought it carried an overtone of dishonesty—were required to make daily reports and then to wait for his reply either by mail or telegraph. None in his employ were to make their own decisions unless the nature of the circumstances demanded it, and even then, the agent who acted would have to face a lengthy inquiry by Mr. Pinkerton. Pinkerton had written a reference book, or, as Kate referred to it, a tome, of the edicts his employees had to adhere to, which he presented to every new hire. His operatives were never to stoop to immoral means to complete their investigation, nor would the company take on cases involving divorce or other "scandalous affairs." All employees and their subsequent actions must be "pure and above reproach." Hattie often wondered how much Pinkerton knew of the reason she'd fled to Chicago in the first place, but he never asked and Hattie never offered.

"What do you think Pinkerton's got in store for us?" she asked Kate.

Kate's blue eyes were wide. "Have you heard that Colonel Ellsworth was killed in Baltimore? The secessionists are rioting. They've been burning bridges and they even cut the telegraph wires connecting Baltimore to Washington."

Hattie sighed. "I thought Maryland hadn't seceded."

"I've seen firsthand how those rebels can sow the seeds of revolution," Kate had been undercover in Baltimore for weeks prior to the Lincoln incident, pretending to be a Southern belle and cultivating friendships with the wives and daughters of high-ranking Confederates.

"That's about the only thing they don't need slaves to sow." The voice belonged to John Scully, Hattie's least favorite co-worker, a red-bearded Irishmen who was about Hattie's age. "Right, Warne?" The man had spoken Kate's last name, but his eyes were directed at Hattie.

"Lewis," Hattie replied pointedly. Although the two women had become fast friends the moment Hattie had started at the agency, they looked nothing alike. Kate was slightly taller than Hattie, with short blond hair and expressive blue eyes. Kate was graceful with all the confidence in her abilities that Hattie seemed to lack. Her broad, honest face, lightly sprinkled with freckles, caused fellow operatives and criminals to easily divulge confidential information. Scully should have known better, anyway: his frequent partner on missions was Pryce Lewis, an Englishman, of no relation to Hattie despite the shared last name. Had Hattie realized there was another operative named Lewis in the office, she would have chosen a different *nom de guerre*.

Pinkerton cleared his throat. "Gentlemen, and... ladies." The inclusion of Hattie and Kate was, as always, an afterthought, but Hattie could hold no ill will toward her boss, who was the only man in the world as far as she knew who hired female detectives. "We have been asked to perform a task of great importance. Due to the destruction of the telegraph wires leading to the Capital, Mr. Lincoln has asked me to personally oversee communications from Chicago to Washington. A messenger must be dispatched immediately. It will not be an easy task by any means, but one that will be of honorable service to our country."

At these words, Hattie sat up in her seat. She had no sentiment that she would be chosen for the monumental task, but she had a slight inclination it could be Kate.

"Mr. Webster will be traveling to Washington to offer our services to begin what I'm calling a 'secret service.'" Pinkerton held up a sheet of paper. As Webster rose to accept it, there was a murmur of approval from the rest of the department followed by a modest ovation.

Hattie gave her friend the tiniest of smiles. In truth, Webster's operation was going to be quite dangerous and rebels would not look in favor of a woman trying to get through the lines by herself, pass or not. Kate winked at her and then turned her attention to Webster.

Hattie had not spent a significant amount of time with Timothy Webster, but she knew of his spotless reputation. With his graying hair and eyes beginning to crinkle at the sides, Webster looked to be in his late 30s or early 40s. His eyes were the type of blue that appeared gray at a distance. Surely that, combined with his tall frame, would make him stand out in a crowd and render him nearly useless as a spy. Still, Hattie thought, there was something about his good-naturedness that made you instantly trust him.

Pinkerton turned to the detective to ask, "Timothy, knowing what you know of the task that lies before you, will you undertake its performance?"

Webster drew up to his full six feet. "I understand all perfectly." Even from where Hattie sat, she could see his gray-blue eyes flash. "If my country demands my services, I am ready to perform my duty, even if it costs me my life."

Pinkerton nodded, the slight upturning of his mouth indicating he was pleased with Webster's response. "Miss Lewis." His eyes searched the audience before landing on Hattie. "Your presence is requested."

Hattie's heart thumped in her chest and she rose and stepped forward. Would this be her big break—her chance to avenge the Union? "Yes, Mr. Pinkerton?"

Pinkerton gestured to Webster, and the latter shed his jacket and waistcoat, a well-toned chest and arms were visible beneath his shirt. Hattie dropped her gaze to the ground in an attempt to maintain her modesty, looking up just in time to see Pinkerton grab a pile of papers from the table beside him. He handed them to Hattie. "These will need to be sewn into the linings of Mr. Webster's finery, if you do not mind." Without a word, Mr. Webster extended his accouterments toward Hattie. Shoving the sheaf of papers most unladylike under her arm, she accepted them.

CHAPTER 8

BELLE

JULY 1861

A week passed after the soldier was killed. Belle's fear of Union reprisal diminished with each day that went by without incident. But one morning she had just walked downstairs when she espied a group of soldiers making their way up the front path.

"Dear God," Mother said when she also caught sight of the brigade. She folded her hands in front of her and said a quick prayer before opening the door. "May I help you gentlemen?"

"Is this the Boyd residence?" a man in a Yankee officer's uniform asked.

"It is indeed. I am Mrs. Boyd."

He pulled a notebook out of his satchel. "I am General Patterson and these are my men. We have been dispatched to ask you and your daughter a few questions about what happened during the afternoon of July 4th."

Mother stepped aside and gestured for the men to enter. The man in charge caught sight of Belle on the staircase. He touched the tip of his hat. "You must be Miss Boyd. We'd like to query your mother first, if you don't mind."

Belle nodded but did not move from her post as the men and her mother went into the parlor. Mauma Eliza came into the hallway.

"Remember, Mauma, if they question you, make sure you tell them what the German was trying to do to Mother." The three women had prepared what to say if the Union soldiers came back. Southerners would never dare take a slave's word, but Belle made sure Mauma Eliza had her story correct backwards and forward should the Yanks dare to question her.

When it was Belle's turn to meet with the men in the parlor, she made it clear that shooting the man was her only means of protecting both her mother and herself. Luckily the men did not ask her if she felt any sorrow for what she had done, for Belle held not even a shadow of regret for killing the German. His blood had left not a shadow of burden upon her conscience nor any stain on her soul.

At long last, General Patterson sighed before closing his note-book. "I apologize if Private Martin threatened you harm. I never met the man, but as he was a Union soldier, I doubt he was intent on hurting you or your mother."

"But we will never know, will we, sir?" Belle kept her voice light.

"No." General Patterson gazed at the stain on the floor that, try as she had, Mauma Eliza could not get rid of. "We never will know now. Next time, I advise you to trust in the jurisdiction of the Union before you go killing any more of its soldiers."

Belle bit her tongue from insisting she would never trust a Yankee. She pasted on her most saccharine smile. "I wouldn't be able to anyway, sir. Your soldier has confiscated my pistol."

General Patterson stood. "That is for the best." He nodded at one of his men who stood in the corner of the room. "We will establish a watch outside the Boyd home just in case."

. . .

To Belle's both horror and delight, men were stationed at all hours outside her home. Martinsburg was still under Union control and the federal flag flapping in the square was visible from the Boyds' upstairs windows. Every time she set eyes on that flag, her indignation grew, and she became determined to do what she could to rid her town of the Yankee soldiers.

Lucy Buck, an acquaintance of Belle's, visited for lunch a few days later. Lucy's brother had a furlough after Manassas Junction and had shared stories of the Confederate victory. Belle laughed aloud when Lucy spoke of the Yankees who had ventured out to watch the battle brandishing picnic baskets and wine.

"I guess they must now realize that we will not be defeated," Belle said, taking a bite of a sandwich.

"Indeed. And when General Jackson stood his ground, General Bee likened him to a stone wall. Now that's what they are calling him: Stonewall Jackson."

Belle smiled. She had always had a sweet spot for General Jackson.

"And did you hear?" Lucy continued. "The intelligence that helped us win Manassas was provided by a Southern lady living right inside Washington City."

"What was her name?" Belle asked.

"A Mrs. Greenhorn?"

"Rose. Rose Greenhow." Belle was familiar with her reputation, having spent last winter in Washington. Mrs. Greenhow's parties were the most exclusive, the kind every debutante such as Belle aspired to attend.

"A girl just about our age was the one who delivered the missive. Bettie Duvall," Lucy continued.

"Ah." Belle wrinkled her nose, picturing the thin-boned Bettie, fragile as a bird. "I'm surprised she had the nerve."

Lucy picked up her tea. "Many of us find strength to do what we can for the cause."

Belle nodded. She longed to contribute something other than sewing, killing a drunken Yankee notwithstanding. She wanted other Confederate women to discuss her own daring at tea, to applaud her for her bravery and sacrifice.

59

. . .

That evening, Belle and her mother were invited to meet General Jackson himself at Ramer's Hotel. When the general entered the parlor of the hotel, everyone rushed to greet him at once. Belle hung back, watching while small children pulled at his trouser legs and daughters and mothers batted their eyelashes as they curtsied. Stonewall Jackson was a thin man, dressed in a tattered single-breasted coat. An equally shabby cap was flung over his eyes so coldly blue they were nearly gray. He was a somber man who rarely smiled, but he good-naturedly let some of Belle's mother's friends cut off his uniform buttons for souvenirs, joking that this was the first time he'd been attacked at close range. Finally, Belle saw her chance to approach the general. She walked over and held up a bouquet of wildflowers. "General, do you have any more buttons to spare for my own collection?" She did not have a collection yet, per se, but having one of the respected general's buttons would be an auspicious start.

Jackson threw his head back as if to laugh, but no sound came out. He held out the flaps of his coat like a pauper. "No, ma'am. Not a one." Belle could see the vest underneath had also been robbed of buttons.

Belle batted her eyelashes. "Maybe next time we meet then?"

Jackson nodded before turning to yet another demanding admirer.

Belle watched as his heavily lined face smiled at the newcomer. He was not a handsome man, but his kindness made him attractive. Belle made a vow that there would be another meeting between them.

The next morning, Belle was pleased to note that the Union trooper standing below her bedroom was young and, despite his homely and ill-fitting blue uniform, handsome. "You there," she called from the opened window. She waved a lace handkerchief at him as he looked up. "What is your name?"

He saluted her. "Franklin Smith."

"Where are you from?"

"Ohio."

"What's that?" Belle held a hand up to her ear for good measure. "I can hardly hear you."

"Ohio," Smith shouted.

"Oh bother." Belle hurried downstairs to continue the conversation.

If Smith was startled to see her at street level, he did not show it.

"Is it terribly hard to be so far away from your wife?" she asked him with a bat of her eyelashes.

"I'm not married."

"Your girlfriend, then."

"I've not one of those either."

Belle tilted her head. "How could such a fine-looking soldier be unencumbered?"

The man shrugged. "I was just out of military school when the shots at Fort Sumter were fired."

"Oh, indeed?" Belle asked Smith a few more questions about himself in a lilting voice before warming up to the subject of the Union army. She pretended to brush a piece of lint off of Smith's coat before asking his opinion on General McDowell. "Is it true he is trying to reorganize his scouts?"

"He had a great plan for Bull Run, but most of his troops weren't experienced enough to pull it off. The people in Washington are calling for his removal. They are talking about replacing him with McClellan."

Belle nodded sympathetically, repeating the name McClellan in her head so she would not forget it.

That night, as soon as Mauma Eliza bade her goodnight, Belle re-lit the candle and went to her writing desk. She quickly wrote down everything Smith had told her. She resolved to have Mauma Eliza deliver her letter to General Jackson's camp in the morning, thinking that the Yankees wouldn't question a Negro servant on an errand for her mistress. She was not sure whether the information would be of value, but that was no matter. General Jackson could glean what he could. She paused in her furious writing for only a moment, considering what she was doing might be treason in the eyes of the Union. *It is no matter,* she thought, dipping her quill back in the inkwell. *It is not treason in the Confederacy.* And, after all, if they did not hang her for the murder of one of their own, what harm could a note written by a mere woman do? She signed her name and blew out the candle before retreating to her bed.

CHAPTER 9

HATTIE

JULY 1861

*W*ebster successfully reached Washington and returned to Chicago carrying a message from Mr. Lincoln in a hollow walking cane. Although Lincoln had stated that his services would be a great help to the government, Pinkerton's obvious excitement at the prospect diminished each week that went by with no further communication from Washington.

Finally, a letter came from General George McClellan, newly appointed commander of the Army of the Potomac, directing most of the Chicago operatives to report to Washington City for an undisclosed period of time. Hattie's heart soared when Pinkerton read the missive aloud to the office. It was finally going to be her time to serve the Union!

Pinkerton went on to explain that their immediate concern was whether Kentucky's neutrality was to be maintained or whether the state would become hostile to the Union. In addition, McClellan had requested intelligence regarding Confederate troop numbers, equipment, and intended movements.

"He says Washington City is teeming with spies and it is his suspicion that intelligence provided by them resulted in our terrible loss at Bull Run. We are packing up the entire operation and moving to the Capitol." Pinkerton added as he set the sheet of paper down on a nearby desk. "Oh, blessed be McClellan for his fortitude in seeing the necessity of our service." He nodded at Webster. "Tim and I will go as soon as possible to set up operations in Cincinnati. Mr. Bangs will stay here to run our daily operations."

"Of course, Boss," George Bangs confirmed. "War or no war, the criminals will still need to be apprehended."

With those words, Hattie's heart sank like a brick and she shot a worried look at Kate, who returned a hesitant smile before focusing on Pinkerton.

"Miss Lewis," Pinkerton rose and headed to his inner office. "Will you help me sort what to pack?"

Hattie followed him, determination setting in her soul like a red wine stain.

"Are you acquainted with McClellan personally?" Hattie asked, tucking papers into a carpetbag.

"Indeed," Pinkerton rubbed his chin as he cast his eyes about his office, most likely wondering what else to bring to his new place of operation. "Our acquaintance goes back to when he was vice president of the Illinois Central Railroad. I know him to be a fair and intelligent man."

As she picked up his ledger, she caught sight of a newspaper. "Mr. Pinkerton?"

"Hmm?" he returned, obviously distracted with the task of packing.

"You are aware that some of the suspected spies are female?"

"Yes."

"Sir." Pinkerton finally met her eyes. "Don't you think that you would need females in Washington City?"

"Yes. Miss Warne…"

"I would like to come." Even Hattie was surprised at the

64

commanding tone of her voice. "The Secret Service will need the kind of finesse only a woman could bring."

Pinkerton covered his mouth with his hand and stared at a space above Hattie. "Of course," he said finally. He cleared his throat. "I wouldn't have had it any other way." He gave an uncharacteristic chuckle as he shut his carpetbag. "Did you hear that my dear? This would-be barrel maker is going to head the President's Secret Service!"

"Yessir!" Hattie's enthusiasm matched Pinkerton's as she realized she would indeed have a chance to help President Lincoln in saving the Union.

"Do you trust Pinkerton?" Hattie asked Kate when they had settled on the train to Ohio.

Kate looked at her friend, her blue eyes curious. Thus far, Hattie had only told Kate the superficialities of her story: that she was originally from Connecticut and was married at a young age and moved to "Bleeding Kansas" at the desire of her new husband. "I've never had cause to doubt the Boss," Kate replied. "What is your opinion?"

Hattie gazed upward. "I trust no man more than Allan Pinkerton. Except maybe President Lincoln."

Kate nodded before putting a finger to her lips and gesturing at the strangers surrounding them in the train car.

As Kate shifted in her seat and then shut her eyes, Hattie stared at the passing landscape out the window. Trusting a man was a new experience for Hattie. Her father had been a cruel man and even her older brother Aaron ran away from home at sixteen, leaving Hattie to suffer her father's wrath. She had no idea of her brother's whereabouts, however, and as Aaron's exploits eventually made national news, Hattie's parents were determined to keep Hattie misinformed and away from the public eye. Although Hattie was only 18, they arranged for her betrothal to a family friend, Stewart Smith. He'd been born in Tennessee and was a former slave owner. After they'd married, Stewart took Hattie to Kansas, where he purchased a few slaves. He was brutal to both the slaves and Hattie. She knew he kept a mistress, a beautiful mulatto girl, who became pregnant. When Hattie had the gall to suggest that he free both the mother and his soon-to-be child, Stewart beat his wife until she was unconscious.

When Hattie had somewhat recovered from her injuries, she read that John Brown and his followers were in Kansas, stirring up riots with slave owners. She wrote to Aaron and told him that she needed his help in escaping from her husband. She didn't have a plan, exactly, but knew she had to get away from Stewart before he killed her. Aaron's strategy was simple: the night he arrived, Aaron slipped laudanum in Stewart's whiskey, causing him to pass out. Aaron and Hattie took most of the Smith slaves with them, including Stewart's concubine, who gave birth to the baby along the journey. Hattie never heard any information on what happened to the slaves, but she hoped they found emancipation in Canada.

Hattie adjusted her seat, secure in the fact that even if they hadn't, the nation, under President Lincoln's guidance, would soon see that all men were free. She closed her eyes, pleased in the fact that she would play at least a small part in ending the practice of human bondage forever.

CHAPTER 10

MARY JANE

AUGUST 1861

*T*he *Richmond Examiner* caught wind of Miss Lizzie's aid to the Federal prisoners, stating that she was using her "opulent means in aiding and giving comfort to the miscreants who have invaded our sacred soil, bent on raping and murder, the desolation of our homes and sacred places, and the ruin and dishonor of our families."

"Humph," Miss Lizzie tossed the paper aside. "What causes more dishonor than enslaving people?"

"The paper also warns that you could be exposed as an alien enemy and suffer the ensuing punishment," Mary Jane warned.

"It doesn't mention me by name, though. No one would dare imprison a woman as an alien enemy, not even that traitor Jeff Davis." She caught herself and glanced over at Mary Jane. "If you don't want to continue coming with me to the prisons, I understand."

Mary Jane sighed. "I, more than anyone, want a favorable outcome to this war, I'm just not sure giving them food and clothing is enough of a contribution."

"Indeed," Miss Lizzie mused. "Perhaps we could be doing more."

Miss Lizzie's solution to avoid suspicion was to add to the already circulating rumors that she was a bit mad. She began dressing in well-worn dresses, covering them with a moth-eaten shawl and whispering to herself on the street. But all the Richmonders would have had to do was peer into Miss Lizzie's deep blue eyes to see that her cunning was still intact, her intelligence unscathed.

The next day Miss Lizzie and Mary Jane paid yet another visit to Ligon's Warehouse, this time bringing Lieutenant Todd an offering of gingerbread cookies.

"I've heard that the prisoners are in want of books to occupy their time," Miss Lizzie informed Todd when they reached his office.

"Is that so?" he asked, his mouth full of cookies. "I have doubt those Yanks can read, but," he finally swallowed, "I don't take issue with it, so long as you're not passing out abolitionist trash."

Miss Lizzie held up a copy of *Moby Dick*. "No, sir. You won't find me reading *Uncle Tom's Cabin*."

Mary Jane smiled to herself. Her mistress had given a copy of Harriet Beecher Stowe's best-selling "fictional" account to everyone in her household, with the exception of her sister-in-law. Miss Lizzie's own version was dog-eared and underlined in several parts.

Todd gestured toward the door without rising. "By all means."

The prisoners were, as always, grateful to see the women and even more so when they presented the books, passing them out to eager hands until only *Moby Dick* remained.

Miss Lizzie asked a nearby captain if any of the men knew how to operate a telegraph machine.

The captain indicated a young man in civilian clothes.

"I think you'll find this one quite interesting," Miss Lizzie told the telegraph operator. "Particularly right here," she said, opening to a specific page before handing it to him. Mary Jane had carefully stuck a pin through the margins near the front of the book, using Morse code to ask if they had any information regarding the Confederate troops.

The young man ran his fingers over the tiny holes and smiled. "Thank you, ma'am."

"And I also heard that you men are in desperate need of a needle and thread," Miss Lizzie said in a loud tone.

"Now, wait a minute," the guard started forward.

Miss Lizzie focused her stern gaze on him. "My servant and I can't possibly keep darning these Fed's socks. They will have to learn on their own."

The guard smiled. "Just so long as you don't tell that to my wife." He nodded at the telegraph operator. "I expect to see all those holes in your uniform mended."

"Yessir," the man said, accepting the sewing supplies from Mary Jane.

The following day, the operator handed the book back to Miss Lizzie, telling her it was "very interesting, indeed."

Miss Lizzie and Mary Jane distributed their latest supplies, both women eager to get home and see if the men were able to provide them any information.

The day had dawned cloudy, but it was even darker when the women left the warehouse, the clouds heavy with impending rain. Miss Lizzie wrapped her shawl tighter around herself. The novelty of the Yankee prisoners had gradually worn off and Miss Lizzie and Mary Jane no longer had to deal with angry crowds when going to and from the prison. But today Mary Jane could sense someone following them as they started for home. She quickened her pace, sensing as Miss Lizzie did the same without speaking that she too was aware of their pursuer. Unfortunately, they had to pause at Franklin Street for a passing carriage.

"You dare to show sympathy for those Yankee swine?" a gruff

voice spoke behind them. "I would shoot them as I would black-birds. We know what you and your darkey are up to, and there is something on foot against you now."

Neither woman turned around. As soon as the carriage passed, they crossed the street. When they dared to look back, the man was nowhere in sight. The two took the long way home, walking down Franklin Street instead of Grace, Miss Lizzie glancing now and then to make sure no one else was behind them. Although Mary Jane figured they'd lost their pursuer, both women's steps sped up anyway as they neared Shockoe Bottom, the area that Richmond's slaves often referred to as "the Devil's Half Acre."

While it was true that the Yankee prisons were overcrowded and filthy, they were nothing compared to McDaniel's Negro jail, located on the lowest point of the hill. It was part of a complex of several brick buildings known as Lumpkin's Alley which included the slave-trader Robert Lumpkin's apartments—where he lived with his former slave wife and their many children—and boarding houses where potential buyers from all over the South stayed before they ventured to the nearby auction blocks to take stock of their potential property. The jail served as both a holding pen for its human cargo before they were "sold down river" as well as a prison for misbe-having slaves. Mary Jane had been arrested for being the latter soon after she returned from Liberia—it was illegal for a woman who had been educated up North to return to Virginia. Because Mary Jane was a free Negro that was caught without having a certificate of freedom, according to the Fugitive Slave Act, she could be sold back into slavery if her master did not claim her.

Mary Jane had blocked out most of the memories of her month of incarceration, but now the smell of rot and decay brought a million loathsome recollections back to the surface: the cries of the slaves being tortured in the whipping room, a girl younger than herself being stripped down so a potential buyer could examine every inch of her body, the meager diet of rancid meat and trickles of water. She and the other captives had been kept chained and their clothes grew tattered, their hair and skin fetid with sweat and vermin.

As they passed, Mary Jane sighted the gallows where slaves

whose crimes reached beyond whipping, such as Gabriel Prosser, the leader of the slave rebellion, were hanged. He was probably buried somewhere in Lumpkin's Alley, along with the thousands of others who didn't survive the harsh conditions of the prison.

If Miss Lizzie noticed Mary Jane's breathing had grown heavy, she did not comment and kept her eyes on the street in front of them. Miss Lizzie never talked about Mary Jane's arrest—it was Old Mrs. Van Lew who had paid the fine of $10, telling the judge that Mary Jane was one of her most valuable servants, and if she wasn't to be returned, then the courts would owe her money. When Mary Jane had at last returned home, Miss Lizzie pretended the whole thing had never happened. But the experience lived on in Mary Jane's nightmares and served as one of the reasons she was so determined to help end the practice of slavery.

They finally crossed over to Grace Street and Mary Jane once again tried to put her past behind her, reminding herself that the best way to earn emancipation for all blacks would be for the Union to win the war.

"What does it say?" Miss Lizzie demanded when they were safely ensconced in her room, the door locked behind them.

Mary Jane, somewhat recovered from her earlier panic, flipped to the back of the book. "Let me see." She traced her finger along the new holes. "Gen. T.J.S/ Wash. City." She looked up at Miss Lizzie, her eyes wide. "I think he means Stonewall Jackson is planning an attack on Washington City."

"It can't be." Miss Lizzie sat back.

"But it would make sense. The Confederates are still riding high on their victory at Bull Run. And the Capitol is not far from Manassas Junction." Mary Jane set the book down. "The problem now is how to pass on this information to the Union authorities."

Miss Lizzie nodded. "I will reach out to some of my contacts and see what I can do."

The next day, Miss Lizzie called Mary Jane into the kitchen. Miss

Lizzie's brother John had taken his wife and daughters for a carriage ride in the country, and Miss Lizzie sent the rest of the servants out of the house on various errands. The house was empty save for Mary Jane, Miss Lizzie, and her visitor, whom she introduced as Thomas McNiven, the baker. "He specializes in tea cakes, scones, and running secret messages via the Richmond Underground," Miss Lizzie told Mary Jane.

All three pairs of eyes peered around the kitchen, but they were alone. "I make deliveries in my truck," McNiven said in a thick Scottish accent. "People refer to me as Quaker. I'm told you can read and write."

"Yessuh," Mary Jane affected her "slave" accent.

"You are going to want to code any intelligence you can glean. Take down this cipher. The alphabet will be assigned to numbers, but A will start with number 7, and then continue to 14, except 13. F will be 21, then back to 15. The second half of the alphabet will start with 77 and continue on, except 81 and 84, which will be 13 and 2... why aren't you writing, girl?"

Mary Jane shut her eyes and repeated, "Number 7 to 14 except 13; number 21 back to 15, and then 77 except 81 and 84 will be 13 and 2." She opened her eyes. "Ain't no need to write it down for prying Rebel eyes to find, suh."

McNiven raised his eyebrows as he glanced at Miss Lizzie. "I told you she was good," Miss Lizzie stated.

"I can have one of my contacts stationed outside the Van Lew farm, but you are going to need to get the messages there on your own."

Miss Lizzie turned to Mary Jane. "Isn't it about time you visited your husband?"

Mary Jane narrowed her eyes. She had known that Miss Lizzie had an ulterior motive for her marrying Wilson Bowser, but this seemed almost underhanded, even for her. Had she known about McNiven's underground network all along and was just waiting for the right time? *That seemed too deceitful for even Miss Lizzie, but you never knew.*

· · ·

Mary Jane finished copying the information into a cipher on a tiny sheet of paper and then used the same needle she coded *Moby Dick* with to delicately empty an egg of its contents. She then carefully slid the message into the hollow shell via a small slit and then placed the fragile egg into a basket of unaltered eggs.

"Does my husband know about the Underground?" Mary Jane asked Miss Lizzie as she prepared to leave.

"Yes," Miss Lizzie said simply. "But no one else at the farm. The fewer people who are acquainted with our work, the better."

"Do you trust this McNiven? He knows I can read, now, in addition to this situation," Mary Jane held up the basket. "Not to mention that man on the street the other day."

"That man made idle threats. I haven't thought about him again, and I suggest you don't either. But McNiven is worthy of our trust—I've known his mother-in-law for years. Before the war he was a conductor for the Underground Railroad."

Mary Jane nodded. "And Wilson?"

"He will still be your husband when the war's over." Miss Lizzie focused her shrewd eyes on Mary Jane. "A conciliatory gesture would go far in securing your relationship."

Mary Jane wanted to retort that she needn't take marital advice from a spinster, but she bit her tongue. Miss Lizzie carefully placed a bakery box of cookies on top of Mary Jane's basket. "This was going to be a present to Mr. Bowser from me, but you can tell him it's from you."

The conveyance of the message was the easy part—a rider came to the farm just after Mary Jane had arrived. He tipped his hat, told her his ailing wife would appreciate the eggs, and then rode off.

The conciliation part was much harder. Wilson was understandably upset that his wife had chosen to live in other accommodations besides what he could provide.

"We've had this discussion before, Wilson. Old Mrs. Van Lew needs me at the house."

"Why would Miss Lizzie consent to our marriage if she had plans for you to live there?"

"I don't think she thought her mother would become so sickly." Mrs. Van Lew, in fact, was no more sickly than ever, but Wilson did not know that.

"Well, can we at least be together as husband and wife while you are here?"

The last thing Mary Jane needed was a baby. "I'm sorry, Wilson, I can't." She hoped that he would assume she meant she was having her monthly course, which she wasn't, but it sounded like a valid excuse.

Wilson must have understood because Mary Jane slept in Miss Lizzie's vacant bedroom at the farmhouse while Wilson slept in his outbuilding. She still held no ill will toward Wilson—in fact, she almost wished that she could fall in love with him, if she was still capable of having such feelings. But she knew her mission was hard enough without a family. Perhaps when the war was over, they would be united in freedom like the millions of other families, white and black alike, who had been forced to endure separation because of the conflict.

When morning came, she bid her husband farewell and headed back to her duties at the Van Lew mansion.

CHAPTER 11

BELLE

AUGUST 1861

"*M*iss Belle, you'd better come quick. A Yankee be lookin' for you."

Belle had been enjoying the silence of the peach orchard before Mauma Eliza had bustled from the house.

Belle sighed as she rose. She thought briefly of the letter she had asked Mauma Eliza to deliver the previous week. "You managed to get that letter to General Jackson's camp, didn't you, Mauma?"

"Yes'm I did, Miss Belle."

Belle's heart hammered as she went downstairs, hoping the Yankees hadn't somehow gotten word of her underground activity.

The man standing in the doorway introduced himself as Captain James Gwyn, assistant to the provost marshal of the Union army.

"What do you want with me?" Belle asked.

"I was told to escort you to headquarters." He offered her his arm, but Belle strode past him.

"Tell Mother I might be late for dinner," Belle called over her shoulder to Mauma Eliza. Her confident tone belied her nervousness. Not only was Belle's handwriting distinct, she had signed her name at the bottom of the letter in what she now realized was a foolish move.

Her suspicions were confirmed when she arrived at headquarters and met the colonel, who held that very letter in his hand. "Do you realize the punishment for aiding the enemies of the United States Government?"

"No, sir." She refrained from adding that she didn't care: that her goal was to incriminate pompous Yankees like him.

"I could have you jailed, or even hanged."

Belle met his eyes, giving him her most pitiful look.

"But I won't. Consider this a warning—you must not ever do this again. Do you understand?"

Belle curtsied, hiding a triumphant smile with a bowed head. She had gotten away with only a mere admonishment. The colonel either didn't consider her a threat or else one of her neighbors had intervened on her behalf. "Yes, sir." She let herself out of his office, vowing, not to quit, but next time to disguise her handwriting.

Though Belle's mother was unaware of her daughter's underground activities, she thought it would be safest to leave the occupied town of Martinsburg for her brother's house—Belle's uncle—in Front Royal, Virginia.

Belle had often visited there when she was younger, and delighted in the beautiful town, nestled in the Shenandoah mountains like a baby in its mother's arms. As Front Royal was only about forty miles from Manassas, the local hospital was filled with ailing Confederate soldiers. Belle took a break from her espionage—there were no Union officers around to beguile into passing off secrets anyway—to aid the nurses and doctors.

As soon as she stepped into the hospital room, with the long rows of cots filled with wounded or ill men and the smells of rotting wounds and death filling the air, Belle knew that she was not cut out to be a nurse. She looked away as a doctor dressed the stumped elbow of an amputee. A boy covered with small rose-colored spots lying on top of a dining room table beckoned Belle. She started toward him, but the man next to him began going into convulsions and every able-bodied person in the room rushed to his bedside. Belle, feeling like she was in the way, decided to back away. As she started toward the door, she felt something soft under her foot, and glancing down, she saw that she had stepped on the hand of an amputated arm. And then everything went black.

When Belle opened her eyes, she found she was outside. She felt as though a horse had run over her body and something was preventing her from speaking.

"The fresh air did ya good." An older woman kneeled beside Belle to retrieve the rag that had been stuffed into her mouth.

Belle flexed her stiff jaw before saying, "I'm sorry."

"That's all right. We couldn't save the man, anyway. And I don't think whoever's hand you tramped over minded neither."

Belle shuddered, thinking of that room full of death and decay. "How can you do this every day?"

The woman stood up and held out an arm to Belle. "We all do what we can."

As Belle rose, she couldn't help thinking that she would help her country in any way, save for nursing.

The next day, against her mother's and aunt's wishes, Belle went to visit her uncle, who was a lieutenant in the 12th Virginia, under the command of Stonewall Jackson himself. She blithely informed him that she would like to become a spy for the Confederacy.

Her uncle spit out the chicory coffee he'd been drinking. "You? A girl?"

"Cousin William could use me for the missions. I can ride a horse better than most of the boys here," she cast her arm around camp, "and I've been shooting guns since I was a toddler—"

"All right." Her uncle held up both hands. "You do know your way around the Valley. And I suppose the Yanks would be less suspicious of a woman riding among their lines. I will pass your name on to Colonel Ashby."

And so Belle began acting as a Confederate courier. She rode Fleeter throughout the Valley, passing information regarding army movements back and forth between Stonewall Jackson and General Beauregard. Her uncle taught her the countersigns that were needed in order to pass through the Southern, and sometimes, enemy lines. The signals involved hand gestures such as throwing up her arm or taking off her bonnet and placing it over her chest. Unfortunately, at least in Belle's mind, the excitement of being a part of the Confederacy's underground railroad of information soon wore off as the soldiers became accustomed to her and let her pass easily. Her base was her aunt's home in Front Royal, although she sometimes stayed at her parents' home in Martinsburg, telling her mother she was making deliveries for her aunt as an excuse.

She changed outfits frequently, occasionally dressing in her father's overcoat, her face void of make-up to complete the man disguise. Sometimes she would wear a dress tied with a Confederate tassel belt and a headband decorated with seven stars—one for each of the initial Confederate states. She never ceased to do anything required for the Southern Cause: even sneaking into Union camps in the middle of the night to steal sabers and pistols. She hid the contraband in abandoned barns or buried it, waiting until it was safe to inform other members of the Underground of their presence. One bowie knife did not make it to a hiding spot; Belle was particularly fond of its pearl handle and tied it to her own belt.

CHAPTER 12

LORETA

AUGUST 1861

*W*hile it didn't result in immediate independence, The Battle of Manassas confirmed the view of most Southerners that the Confederacy was far superior to the Union army. Consequently, a multitude of rebels received permission to go on leave. Loreta headed to Richmond, where she found that money was plentiful and the food was good. The drinking saloons, gambling houses, and other places of ill-repute were packed. But Manassas had whetted Loreta's appetite for war and she longed to show more prowess as Harry Buford. She soon became restless with the inaction the continual festivities precipitated. She applied for a pass to head west and got as far as Leesburg, Virginia when she met up with a few men from General Bee's regiment. They convinced Harry to accompany them to Front Royal, assuring her that the Federals were making their way to that part of Virginia.

Front Royal was in a state of celebration throughout the

summer of 1861. Loreta was determined to keep up appearances and frequented the saloons with her newfound friends, although she usually stuck to cider and cigarettes while the other soldiers drank whiskey and smoked cigars.

Major Bacon proved to be quite the ladies' man, and Loreta herself would have found his combination of dark hair, red beard, and blue eyes extremely attractive had she not been acting the part of Harry Buford. After all, Loreta was still a woman and was not immune to a handsome man. In fact, Major Bacon reminded Loreta in a small way of her late husband, William, who had been killed when his weapon had fired accidentally during a training demonstration.

One day Major Bacon and Loreta were purchasing new hats when the major introduced her to a friend of his, Miss Belle Boyd, a strangely dressed woman with a knife fixed to her belt.

"Pleased to meet you," Loreta stated as she extended her hand.

"Oh my," Miss Boyd replied. "Your skin is so smooth."

Major Bacon clamped Loreta on the back. "That's Lieutenant Buford for you. The dandiest dandy of them all."

Miss Boyd batted her eyelashes. Loreta recognized the move as something she used to do before she was married and had to admit that Miss Boyd had the art of flirtation down to a science, which made up for the fact that she was not conventionally beautiful. "Will you call on me later?" she asked Loreta.

Loreta cast her eyes at Major Bacon, who gave her an encouraging nod. A few of her comrades had asked her if she had a lady friend, but she had always declined to answer. At camp, she was always one of the only ones not to pull out a tintype and speak longingly of a fiancé or wife back home. *Miss Boyd might do wonderfully for my cover.* Loreta pasted a smile onto her face and agreed to meet Miss Boyd later that day.

"She's a real strumpet, that Miss Boyd," Major Bacon commented once the lady had left the store.

"Strumpet?"

"She'll latch on to anyone she thinks has money." Bacon let out a hearty laugh. "And she seems to have fixed her attentions on you!"

Miss Boyd's servants had set up tea in the garden in the back of the house. A large, handsome black woman poured the tea and then sat heavily in a chair nearby, sewing.

"My chaperone," Miss Boyd told Loreta.

Loreta nodded. Miss Boyd was even more friendly than she had been at the store. She asked numerous questions: where Harry hailed from, who his parents were, where he'd attended school. Loreta told half-truths, creating the rest of Harry's story as she went along: that her father had been an envoy to the Spanish embassy when he met Loreta's mother, the daughter of a French naval officer and an American heiress. "The blood of Spanish Castilian nobles flows through my veins," Loreta informed Miss Boyd. "One of my ancestors was the Spanish Conquistador Diego Velázquez de Cuéllar who conquered Cuba under the Spanish flag and was governor of the island for many years."

"You must have inherited his sense of adventure," Belle stated.

"Indeed." Loreta had always thought that it should not go to waste just because she was born female. "My father fought in the Mexican War, although on the wrong side. When he lost, our plantation became part of the United States."

"And now you are fighting against them."

"Yes. Fighting for the rights of the Southern sovereignty."

"But you didn't join the army per se."

"No. I'm paying my own way. I don't like to have people tell me what to do." That part was definitely true. Even though Loreta had loved her husband, she had chafed when he told her she could not accompany him when he went off to war. "If I remain independent, I can go where I need to. That's how I was able to fight at Manassas."

Miss Boyd stirred her tea and sat back. "My, you've led an exciting life thus far."

"Indeed." Loreta was careful not to disturb Harry's glued on mustache as she took a sip.

Miss Boyd leaned forward and put her hand over Loreta's. "Pa says the war should be over before the year's end. Do you think you'll stay on in Front Royal on a permanent basis?"

Loreta was taken aback at the woman's forwardness. Evidently her servant was too, as she snorted loudly, causing Miss Boyd to draw her hand back.

Loreta straightened her pant leg before asking, "Why do you take such a fancy to me when we have just met? There must be many elegant, accomplished, and equally wealthy young men in Front Royal with whom you have been acquainted."

"It won't be hard for us to become better acquainted," Miss Boyd stated with another flutter of eyelashes.

Loreta was quite sure that none of the other debutantes back in New Orleans had ever been so bold as this one. "I'm sorry, Miss Boyd. I don't want to deceive you, but you should know that I'm as good as married already."

Miss Boyd's restless lashes were now blinking back tears, and Loreta immediately regretted hurting her. An uncomfortable silence descended upon the couple and Loreta felt the need to fill the lull in conversation. "I am betrothed to a woman of my parents' choosing."

Miss Boyd looked up from her hankie. "You do not wish to marry the girl?"

Loreta shrugged. Miss Boyd's face held the same expression that Loreta's roommate at boarding school, Nellie, had years ago when Loreta had stated that her parents had arranged for her betrothal to Raphael, a handsome Spaniard who lived in New Orleans, and that she would be married when she graduated in two years.

"You cannot be serious," Nellie had replied. "Are your parents from a hundred years ago?"

Loreta shook her head. "It's customary in the part of Europe that my father is from. They say that young people often fancy themselves in love when they do not know what love is."

"Well, no one will tell me who to marry, convenient or not,"

Nellie had declared. "This is, after all, a free country. No one could ever forbid me to marry William."

After that, Loreta had made it her mission to win her rival's dashing soldier beau.

Now Loreta spoke the same words to Miss Boyd that she had told William after they eloped when Loreta was eighteen. "My father said if I don't abide by his wishes, I should consider myself 'repudiated and disinherited.'"

"Oh my," Miss Boyd replied. "I guess you have no choice, then."

"Not if I expect to inherit my father's fortune."

"Don't you think that some things are worth giving up?" Miss Boyd asked with another bat of her eyelashes.

"No," Loreta replied resolutely. "Money can make probable what you think is impossible. The Confederate government knows that—why else do you think we are fighting this war, or any war, for that matter? As much as we fought against sovereignty in the Revolutionary War, King Cotton has been the benefactor that allowed the United States to become the great power that it is."

Miss Boyd gave a clap of her hands. "I wholeheartedly agree. And it will remain so, however fractioned the Union becomes."

"Indeed." Loreta rose and placed a hand briefly on Miss Boyd's shoulder. "I must wish you good evening now, miss."

Miss Boyd buried her head in her hands. When she looked up, she was rather pitiful with her red face and wet eyes. "Will I ever see you again?"

"Perhaps, if I am not killed in battle."

"Oh, do be safe. God willing you will survive."

Loreta nodded and, once again, bid her adieu. She expected that Miss Boyd would soon recover from the heartbreak of Harry T. Buford and set her eyes on another, hopefully more consenting, beau.

As she made her way back to the hotel, she reflected on what she'd told Miss Boyd about Harry's background. Though the estrangement of her family had caused Loreta considerable grief, it was a small price to pay to have won William from Nellie.

Loreta had always had a penchant for battle and occupied the long hours when her husband was training by studying past military tactics. After Lincoln was elected and South Carolina seceded, Loreta figured it would not be long before the fighting started. She'd eagerly scan the papers every day, making a notch in a leather belt as state after state left the Union. When Texas finally seceded, she threatened to forsake William if he dared raise his sword against the South.

The night after William informed her he'd reluctantly resigned his commission as a Union officer, Loreta surprised him by dressing in one of his old army uniforms, adding a drawn-on mustache to convince him she'd make an excellent Confederate soldier. The shocked William had been adamant that no wife of his would be accompanying him to war.

But then William had gone and killed himself accidentally even before he had seen battle and Loreta had no choice but to avenge his death by taking up arms.

CHAPTER 13

BELLE

AUGUST 1861

*B*elle watched Lieutenant Buford as he walked out of the garden. Although she still found him somewhat dashing, there was something definitely odd about him, from his thin figure, to the obviously fake mustache, to that wild tale about his Spanish ancestors. He had said his father was a Spanish envoy and inherited a large estate in Mexico, but the name "Buford" didn't exactly sound Castilian. In fact, *Bouffard* in French translated to "blowing." While his last name didn't match his story, it certainly fit his inflated sense of self-importance, the sort of arrogance not usually found in a Southern gentleman. Belle suddenly sat up in her chair, wondering if perhaps the lieutenant was really a Yankee spy in disguise. She chided herself to be more careful as she went back into the house.

. . .

A few days later, her resolution to undertake more caution forgotten, Belle delivered stolen Union weapons to General Beauregard's camp. The Confederate soldiers there were even more gallant than Lieutenant Buford, and Belle attempted to win their favor by bragging about how she had killed one of the enemy.

"I doubt that's true," one man replied. He was large, with an unruly rust-colored beard. "But I'll be more inclined to believe you if you brought any whiskey along with those guns."

Belle's lip curled. She knew that the soldier could be punished for drinking, but she also knew that Mother could use the money. "Two dollars."

"One," the man responded.

"Forget it," Belle said, standing.

"Not so fast." The man pulled at Belle's belt and then put his hand under her skirt. Belle grabbed her pearl-handled knife as the man, finding a bottle of whiskey hidden underneath her hoops, uncapped it and began to chug.

"Sir!" Belle shouted but the man paid no attention as he wiped his mouth with the back of his hand and then tucked the bottle into his coat pocket.

Belle pointed her blade at the man's chin and tried to hold both the knife and her voice steady. "Give it back."

The man got to his feet, towering over Belle. Her knife was now level with his chest. "What are you going to do, little rebel?" he asked.

As she heard the words, "We're with you, Miss Boyd," Belle glanced backward. Several men stood behind her. She recognized the man who had spoken as Private Winfried; he was from Martinsburg and had known Belle since she was a girl.

Other men gathered behind the soldier who had stolen the whiskey. The two parties of men faced each other, wondering, like Belle, what would happen next. The large man pulled out Belle's pilfered bottle and took another drink.

That was enough for Belle. She charged forward, knife pointed. The man reached his hand out and planted it on Belle's forehead. She shouted and swung her knife, but he kept her at bay and the knife only connected with air. The soldiers behind her fell into action and clashed with their comrades defending the large man. Belle, realizing the danger, headed for the hills, watching the fight she had started from a safe distance.

CHAPTER 14

MARY JANE

AUGUST 1861

*T*he fighting between Mr. John and Miss Mary, which had been almost constant before the war, grew everlasting. She frequently accused Mr. John of being a Union sympathizer, or, in her words, an "enemy of the Great State of Virginia," an accusation she often extended to Miss Lizzie and their mother, the widow Mrs. Van Lew. Miss Mary had been born into the prestigious Carter family, who had long ties to Virginia. She considered the entire Van Lew family to be nouveau riche trash while she was a full-blue blood of the Old Dominion.

When Mrs. Mary called Mary Jane a "nigger" for accidentally spilling wine on the tablecloth in front of her, Mary Jane began referring to her as Witch Mary in her head. Mary Jane had been called a nigger very few times in her life, and she resolved to not stand for such a low blow coming from a guest in Miss Lizzie's house. Not to mention Mary Jane had more intellect in one little finger than Witch Mary had in that tiny brain of hers.

Mary Jane gave Miss Lizzie a heated look.

Miss Lizzie set her fork down. "You will not refer to my servants as 'niggers,'" she spat the word out with obvious distaste, "ever again. The Negroes in this house may have black faces, but their hearts are white."

John focused his soft brown eyes on his wife. "We treat our servants here as though they are family."

"Servants, indeed," Witch Mary returned bitterly. "They should be slaves. This is Virginia. How dare you question an institution that was good enough for George Washington and my own cousin, Thomas Jefferson, true Virginians if there ever were such a thing. Both the niggers' hearts and brains are smaller than ours. They were destined to serve the white men."

Mary Jane again glared at Miss Lizzie, but her mistress discreetly held up one finger. Mary Jane knew that Miss Lizzie gave Mrs. Mary a wider berth than normal because of their prison visitations, but it was getting to be too much for Mary Jane. She was tired of living in a nation full of bigots like Witch Mary—it was time for Southerners to learn to do a true day's work of labor and let her people be free to live their own lives.

When Mary Jane bent to pick up a plate, Witch Mary pinched her. Mary Jane looked to the other diners, but no one else had seen. She was well aware that Witch Mary, with all her connections, could make Mary Jane's life miserable in revenge should she dare to confront the woman. Concluding that it was wisest to disappear, Mary Jane deposited the plates in the kitchen and then retreated upstairs.

"You must forgive her," Miss Lizzie said later, appearing in Mary Jane's doorway. "Slavery is as much a part of her life as the water she drinks or the air that she breathes. She knows no different, and someday people like her will need to be educated."

Mary Jane looked up from her desk, where she had been coding

90

another message to the prisoners. "She would never willingly learn the errors of her ways."

Miss Lizzie reached out and grabbed Mary Jane, her claw-like fingers wrapping around Mary Jane's skinny brown arm. "Mary Jane. I alone know what you are capable of, but we must keep that a secret and not let anyone, or anything, threaten that. We both know that your intelligence can be a great help toward a Union victory. Richmond will rise from its intolerant ashes and once again become a great city of the United States. But none of that can happen if Mary finds out what we've been doing."

Mary Jane rubbed at her arm. There were splotches from where Miss Lizzie's fingers had dug in. "So I must keep my mouth shut while she berates and insults everyone around her?"

"It won't be forever," Miss Lizzie promised.

The next day, Mary ventured into the kitchen while Mary Jane was preparing Mrs. Van Lew's tea. She watched Mary Jane for a moment before stating, "I know who you are."

Mary Jane looked hopelessly around but they were alone. Resolved in her decision that the best way to deal with Witch Mary was to try to speak to her as little as possible, Mary Jane picked up the tea tray. As she started to head out of the kitchen, Witch Mary suddenly stepped in front of her, causing a stream of tea to spill out of the kettle.

Witch Mary folded her arms in front of her chest. "Haven't you ever wondered why your skin is so pale compared to the rest of the Van Lew darkeys? Aren't you curious as to why the Van Lews treat you like family?"

Mary Jane set the tray down and fetched a rag to wipe up the spill. From the parlor, the wavering voice of Mrs. Van Lew called out, "Mary Jane? Is that tea on its way?" As Witch Mary stepped away from the doorway, Mary Jane picked up the tray and headed to the parlor.

"You know you have white blood in you, don't you, girl?" Witch Mary's voice followed Mary Jane out of the kitchen.

Mrs. Van Lew eyed Mary Jane as she arranged the tea tray.

"Was that Mary you were speaking with?" Mary Jane returned the old woman's searching look. Mrs. Van Lew's hearing was bad, but the thought occurred to Mary Jane that she'd indeed overheard and was pretending she didn't.

"Yes'm."

"Well," Mrs. Van Lew sat back on the chaise, tea cup in hand. "Mary likes to fill people's heads with gossip and rumors. Pay her no heed."

"Yes'm," Mary Jane repeated.

Mrs. Van Lew's gaze fixed outside the window to soldiers marching by on the street. "That'll be all for now, Mary Jane."

Mary Jane headed up to her room. It was true that she was lighter than most of the other servants, lighter than many of the Richmond slaves she had interacted with over the years. Of course she had heard the rumors of her parentage—the other slave children had often teased her when she was a little girl that her daddy "musta ben white." It was a fact of a slave woman's life that their masters saw them as property and could have their way with them, in the process creating more slaves for their collection or to sell off. Mary Jane saw the prospect of her paternity as an advantage: she knew that some white folks held mulattos in a higher esteem than pure negroes because of the white blood in their veins. Mary Jane's mother never confirmed nor denied the rumors. They had come from another plantation in Virginia to the Van Lew Mansion when Mary Jane was a baby. Right before she turned ten, her mother had died, taking the secret of who Mary Jane's father was with her to her grave. Mary Jane assumed it was someone on that old plantation, possibly the master, the overseer, or even one of the half-breed children of the master. She suspected both Miss Lizzie and Mrs. Van Lew knew who it was, but they denied so whenever Mary Jane had asked. At this point, Mary Jane figured it didn't matter: she was who she was and knowing her father's identity wouldn't change that. And Witch Mary's conduct in the kitchen only served for Mary Jane to ignore the narratives even more.

· · ·

"I want out," Mary Jane told Miss Lizzie the next day.

"Out? What do you mean, out?" Miss Lizzie's head swiveled around the parlor before she bent in toward Mary Jane. "How shall we continue our aid to the prisoners if you leave?"

"Helping the prisoners is not enough for me."

"Is this about Mary?"

"Somewhat. But it's more about this." She tossed a newspaper onto the parlor table. On the front page was an article about Jefferson Davis and his family's new residence at the former Brockenbrough house.

Miss Lizzie picked up the paper. "It says that Mrs. Davis is hiring qualified servants."

"Indeed. She'll be in need of discreet maids, maids that would need to dust the President of the Confederacy's office, with all of his papers and plans in plain view."

"Mary Jane, although this is a brilliant idea, it is also an exceedingly dangerous one."

"Miss Lizzie, think of how this information could help our cause. Remember what we read about Rose Greenhow and how she got information from those men in Washington City?"

Miss Lizzie's face wrinkled in concentration for a moment before

she spoke again, a twinge of hesitation in her voice, "I think I will pay a social visit to Mrs. Varina Davis, and recommend a wonderful servant for her new house."

CHAPTER 15

HATTIE

AUGUST 1861

*P*inkerton rented a house on I-Street, out of which he established both his Washington City office as well as the living quarters for him, his wife and three children. Pinkerton's first order of business was to assume a new *nom de guerre* as his own had become synonymous with detectives. "I will now be referred to as E.J. Allen," he informed the travel weary operatives as soon as they had arrived.

According to Pinkerton, the main duties of the Secret Service of the Army of the Potomac was to gather military intelligence as well as ferret out any suspected counterespionage activities, hence Timothy Webster was sent to Memphis, beyond enemy lines, in order to retrieve the desired information. The experienced detective needed no instruction regarding the delicacy of his mission. The rest of the Washington staff settled in to contribute to the war effort.

· · ·

One dismal rainy afternoon, none other than the assistant secretary of war, Thomas A. Scott, himself visited the I-Street office. He and Pinkerton were sequestered in the inner office for over an hour. After Scott finally left, Pinkerton asked Pryce Lewis and Sam Bridgman, the former soldier, to conference with him.

"And you, too, Miss Lewis," he said as he passed by her desk.

She grabbed her sketch book and a small notebook before she walked into his office, expecting more secretarial work.

Pinkerton put his hands behind his head. "It seems that the widow Rose Greenhow has fallen under official suspicion."

Hattie nodded, recognizing the name. She'd read several wires in which Webster mentioned her as being a possible spy for the Confederacy.

"Scott has requested that we arrange a surveillance team in order to pass on any information that might be of use." Pinkerton rose heavily from his desk. "Miss Lewis, we will need you along as an intermediary."

Hattie got eagerly to her feet, tucking her books behind her skirts. "Yes, sir."

"Now, boss?" Pryce asked, his eyes focused on the pouring rain outside the window, darkening the already dimming light of late afternoon. Hattie had to stop herself from glaring at him. *Don't you ruin this for me,* she commanded him silently.

"Indeed." Pinkerton grabbed his hat and coat off the rack. "I will accompany you to find a good place to set up watch outside her home."

The three men and Hattie started out from the office and walked toward the White House. The miserable downpour could hardly dampen Hattie's spirits, however. She paid no heed to the lightning that streaked the sky, nor the thunder that boomed overhead. All she could focus on was that she'd finally been included on a mission with the boss himself.

They passed numerous large and stately homes, pausing in front of a beautiful mansion at the intersection of I and 13th Streets. Pinkerton stuck two fingers in his mouth and gave a loud whistle, though the sound was nearly eclipsed by yet another boom of thunder that sounded a second later. Pinkerton stood back from the house, rubbing his chin in his customary way, as he took stock of their environs. Mrs. Greenhow lived in a dignified three-story brick building with carefully tended landscaping. A veranda extended off of the elevated first floor, which was accessed by a flight of stairs in the center of the exterior.

The trio followed as Pinkerton walked to the side of the house, finding a narrow path that led behind the shrubbery and passing in front of the portico.

"Well boys," Pinkerton addressed Lewis and Bridgman once the group had assembled behind the bushes. "Those windows are a bit too high to peer into from this level." The rain let up for a few brief moments. "No matter." He shed his shoes and then motioned for Lewis and Bridgman to bend down. In a moment, a shoeless Pinkerton stood on each man's shoulder. Rain dripped off of Pinkerton's hat, adding to the deluge that soaked the men underneath him. Pinkerton edged up to peer between the Venetian blinds. No hint of gaslight was discernible in the fading light outside. "It doesn't appear that anyone is home," he whispered loudly.

"Shh!" Hattie commanded, too occupied with watching someone stroll down 13th street to notice that she just chastised her boss. Pinkerton climbed off the men and all of them bent down, hiding amongst the branches before them. It was too dark for Hattie to discern anything about the person, but the lack of a skirt and his walk made her think it was a man. She heard him climb the steps and then ring the bell. Presently they could hear the door close and a beam of light illuminated the bushes directly behind them; Hattie assumed it was more lightning until she realized someone inside had lit a lamp.

Pinkerton resumed his perch and peered in. "I believe that's Captain Elwood, of the Union army. He looks nervous," Pinkerton added, but then fell silent. Hattie could not hear any of what was happening inside, but Pinkerton's hands were cupped around his eyes in an attempt to read their lips. "He's pulled out a map of Virginia. The miscreant." Pinkerton added a few more choice words, which were probably not of the nature for a lady's ears, but luckily another clap of thunder sounded. "They've gone."

"Gone?" Bridgman asked, his eyes on the vacant porch. "Gone where?"

"Out of the room. They've must have walked upstairs." Pinkerton got down, but they stayed at their perch. An hour, perhaps more, went by in silence before they detected movement again. A vague rectangle of light fell on the sidewalk as the front door opened. Hattie heard the couple murmur their goodnights and then what sounded like a kiss.

As night had fallen, the operatives did not have to worry as much about being seen and they maneuvered themselves to get a better look. Elwood's legs descended the front steps, and they watched as he walked down 13th Street in the same direction he had come. Pinkerton, still without shoes, set off behind him.

The three remaining members of the agency exchanged bewildered looks. "What now?" Lewis asked. "Should we head back to the office?"

"You go," Hattie told them. "I'm going to see if she has any more gentlemen callers tonight."

Hattie lingered for another hour or so, finally leaving after the last light had been extinguished at the Greenhow residence, retiring to the small room she shared with Kate, wet, tired, but elated.

The next morning, Hattie arrived to the office early, only to find Bridgman and Lewis already in the Old Man's inner chamber. Hattie pulled a package wrapped in brown paper from her reticule and marched in.

"Ah, Miss Lewis," Pinkerton swept his arm around in a welcoming gesture. "I was just telling these gentlemen what happened when I took off after Mrs. Greenhow's visitor." As the men occupied the only chairs in the room, Hattie stood and listened as Pinkerton recounted how he'd pursued Captain Elwood at a distance, until the man disappeared into an office building at the corner of Pennsylvania Avenue and Fifteenth Street. "I had just opened the door when I felt the tips of a bayonet pointed at my chest. 'Halt or I'll fire,' the bayonet wielder shouted."

Pinkerton went on to say that, as his eyes adjusted, he saw the shapes of four sentries facing him, wearing Union uniforms. He immediately felt the futility of trying to explain who he—the man standing in his socks, with water dripping down every inch of his mud-splattered clothing—really was. "One might have more readily imagined that I had been fished out of the Potomac than I was the chief of the secret service of the government."

The men gave a hearty laugh as Hattie smiled.

Pinkerton gave Captain Elwood his alias but refused to answer any other questions. He didn't want to give the probable traitor any more information than necessary. After they'd put him in a prison cell with a multitude of drunken men, Pinkerton became friendly with the guard and asked him to pass on a note to Assistant Secretary of War Scott.

The guard agreed and soon Pinkerton was escorted to Scott's home. Pinkerton gave up Elwood, and Scott agreed that Greenhow was a dangerous character and must be kept under surveillance.

Pinkerton put his arms behind his head and leaned back in his chair. "And if we detect that she is trying to convey any intelligence to the enemy, we have authorization from the assistant secretary of war to arrest her immediately."

"Yes, sir," Lewis replied. "Shall we set on a course of 24 hours outside her home?"

Pinkerton nodded before readjusting his position and picking up his pen. Lewis and Bridgman rightfully took that as a sign to take their leave, but Hattie remained.

"Sir?" she asked.

"Hmm?" Pinkerton replied.

"I just wanted to deliver these to you." Hattie set the brown parcel on his desk and left the room, hiding a tiny smile behind her hand. As the Old Man's hearty laugh filled the office, Hattie no longer felt the need to hide her grin.

"Miss Lewis, what was in the bag?" Bridgman asked.

"Oh, just the Old Man's shoes," Hattie said as she sat in her desk and got ready for the day's tasks. "I thought he might need them."

. . .

99

Word eventually reached Pinkerton and Co. that Elwood had been escorted directly from Scott's house to Fort McHenry, where he used a penknife to slit his own throat.

Hattie felt sorry for the man: the more she tailed Rose Greenhow, the more she saw the woman as a seductress who used men as pawns to garner information. Several prominent men from the House of Representatives and Senate would call on her in the evenings, not that Hattie ever witnessed this. She had daytime duty, as Pinkerton felt that the nighttime surveillance should be conducted by a man, both because it was dangerous and because it wasn't ladylike to be observing what he termed "illicit affairs." At any rate, Hattie enjoyed her duty: the pleasant spring air made for a good excuse to be outside, and Hattie would often sit on a bench across the street from Greenhow's mansion, pretending to read.

One morning Bridgman came into the office unusually early, before Hattie had left. He was visibly angry and declared it was time to "arrest the whore." He'd seen Senator Wilson, the man who had replaced Jefferson Davis as chairman of the Senate Committee on Military Affairs, being received by her the previous night.

Pryce Lewis waved his hand. "If being intimate with Mrs. Greenhow was a federal offense, our prisons would be full to the brim by now."

Pinkerton, who had come out of his office to retrieve a file, paused. "What would Mrs. Greenhow want with a known abolitionist like Wilson other than his knowledge on army movements?" He nodded at Pryce and Bridgman. "I think we have enough. We'll arrest her tonight." He started back before pausing at Hattie's desk. "Miss Lewis, I believe we will need your presence as well. Greenhow residence, eight o'clock sharp."

"Yes, sir." Hattie could barely keep the pleasure out her voice.

The operatives gathered once again outside of Greenhow's home at the appointed time. This time the night was clear, a pleasant breeze rustling the shrubbery Hattie had become acquainted with a fortnight ago. They watched as yet another well-dressed man exited the home and then made their move. A liveried servant answered the door. Pinkerton barged past him, Pryce and Bridgman, as well as John Scully, on his heels. Hattie stepped over the threshold a bit more cautiously.

A dark-haired woman in a splendid blue silk gown appeared behind the servant. Hattie recognized her as the one she'd been following for the past few weeks. Up close Rose's features were finely lined, but she still had traces of what must have been a beautiful face in her younger years.

"Mrs. Greenhow, I presume?" Pinkerton's words were more of statement and less of a question.

"Yes. Who are you?" She got close to Pinkerton and peered up at him.

Hattie wondered if she was at all aware they had been tailing her. It did seem as though she recognized Pinkerton. As the two stood contemplating each other, Hattie marveled at their contrasting traits. Rose Greenhow had all the airs of an immaculately dressed Southern belle, albeit an aged one; Allan Pinkerton's unruly brown whiskers and ill-fitting uniform lent him a disheveled appearance. Although Rose's war-time proclivities went against the typical Southern ideals, she was heralded as a Confederate championess while Pinkerton was almost as staunch an abolitionist as John Brown himself.

"Major E.J. Allan," Pinkerton finally replied. He did not bow. "I have come to arrest you."

"You cannot enter my home without a warrant."

"I don't need a warrant—I have verbal authority from the War and State Departments," Pinkerton told her before marching to a bold watercolor in an elegant frame placed prominently in the front hallway. He pulled the painting down and ran his hands over it. Rose stepped forward but Pinkerton paid her no heed. "Miss Lewis, please detain Mrs. Greenhow in the parlor."

Hattie wondered if Pinkerton had meant for her to use force, but Mrs. Greenhow consented, though somewhat reluctantly, to lead the way to the parlor. She sat herself on a settee and gestured for Hattie to sit in one of the elegant armchairs she must usually reserve for her gentleman callers. The two sat in awkward silence, Rose watching Pinkerton and his men ransack her house.

As Bridgman and Pinkerton came into the parlor, Rose got up from the couch and glided toward the fireplace, her hoop skirts swishing. She extracted a piece of paper from a vase on the mantle and then flung it at Pinkerton. "You would like to finish this job, I suppose?"

Pinkerton pocketed the note without reading it. The action and his silence made it clear that he thought Rose eminently guilty. He nodded at Hattie before continuing his search.

Hattie probed her mind for a subject to converse with Rose. Timothy Webster, although reticent by nature, could become the most loquacious man when his role demanded it. However, Rose already knew their true purpose in being at her home and Hattie saw no use for a disguise. The constant opening of drawers and doors throughout the house kept the awkwardness out of the silence.

"You there," Rose said, sitting straighter and adjusting her skirts as Pryce Lewis entered the room.

"Madam?" Pryce inquired.

"You are from England?" The surprise was obvious in her voice.

"I was born in Wales. Now I am from Chicago." He sat in the armchair across from Hattie. Pryce had all the mannerisms of an aristocratic Englishman, from his lush sideburns to his carefully cultivated accent. "Mrs. Greenhow, there is another room upstairs—"

She held up her hand before he could finish. "My daughter Gertrude's room. She passed away this March. I couldn't bear to move any of her things."

Pryce handed her a handkerchief, and Rose carefully dabbed at each eye before handing it back to him.

Hattie finally had something to say. "I'm sorry to hear that."

Rose began to pull at her collar. She reminded Hattie of a little bird, always fluttering. A bird that must have been racked with nervousness, knowing her evidence of her guilt was probably hidden in every room in the house. "It's awfully warm in here." She pulled out her fan and flapped it near her face for good measure. "I don't suppose you would let me upstairs to change my dress."

Hattie was about to refuse as Pryce replied, "I can let you leave for a few minutes."

Rose gracefully arose from the couch as Hattie glared at Pryce. She followed Rose up the stairs and down the hallway. Rose must have heard Hattie behind her, but she shut the door in her face. Hattie heard the rustling of papers and then a clattering of what sounded like an iron stove.

I knew it, Hattie thought. *She's destroying evidence.* Rose must have had papers hidden underneath her skirts, but Pinkerton and Pryce were too gentlemanly to search her body. Hattie tried the doorknob, but found it locked. "Madam?" Hattie began banging on the door. "Madam, your time is up!"

Pryce appeared. Hattie indicated the door, and he shoved at it with his full weight. The door burst open on a near-naked Rose. He paused and Rose reached for a revolver on her nightstand and then aimed it at Pryce's face. He made no move as he stared down the muzzle. Hattie, still in the hallway, echoed his stillness, afraid of startling Rose into pulling the trigger.

Hattie's heart leapt into her throat as Rose readjusted her aim. "If I had known who you were when you came in, I would have shot you dead!"

Pryce affected a smile. "Madam, in order to fire that pistol, you first have to cock it."

Hattie breathed an audible sigh of relief as Pryce walked forward and fetched the pistol from Rose's startled grip.

Hattie stepped into the room. "Since you've already started the task, I will ask that you finish undressing." She nodded at Pryce and he left the room. Rose bristled, evidently weighing a refusal, but she relented and began handing Hattie garments one by one until she was stripped down to her linens and boots. Hattie ran her fingers across the fine garments, looking for any hidden papers. Of course, she could not find any remainders of evidence.

After Rose finished, Hattie retreated to the hall while the suspected spy redressed and then followed her back down the stairs.

Pinkerton announced that he was going back to the office to make a full report of what they'd uncovered so far to the War

Department. He asked Hattie to finish cataloging the items they'd found. He also left Bridgman, Scully, and Pryce to guard Rose.

Rose sat down to tinkle on her ivory-keyed pianoforte while Hattie sorted the documents on the dining room table. Many were letters from prominent Yankee men, including one from an Oregon senator who "desired a visit as soon as possible." More than a dozen were letters from the married Senator Wilson declaring his love for Rose. One, written on stationary belonging to the United States Congress, stated that he knew "nothing that would soothe me so much as an hour with you. And tonight, at whatever cost, I will see you." Hattie picked up the letter, pinching it between two fingers, as if its sordidness was contagious, and put it into the "Political" pile of correspondence. John Scully came in to peer over Hattie's shoulder. She was about to ask him to help her when he espied Rose's liquor cabinet. After a brief inquiry into its contents, he declared, "Men, we've had a hard day. I think it's time to reward ourselves." He pulled out a bottle of brandy and poured it into three crystal glasses.

"Miss Lewis?" he asked, holding up another glass.

Hattie shook her head.

The men imbibed, Scully pouring them new glasses when they ran dry. Hattie ignored them. Presently they began slurring their words. When they lurched into the parlor, Hattie heard the music cease. She crept to the doorway, not wanting to miss Rose's reaction. Pryce sat in the same chair he'd occupied not too long ago, although this time with much more unsteady movement.

Rose watched them for a moment before rising from the pianoforte. "Look at your wretched selves," she commanded. "Don't you know better than to be in nothing but your shirtsleeves in front of a lady?"

Make that two ladies, Hattie corrected Rose silently.

Rose continued her tirade. "You have made me a martyr, on par with Marie Antoinette or Mary Queen of Scots. Would you get drunk at their courts? What I am saying?" she cackled. "Of course, you would. Your manners would be horrifying if you were a Southerner, but, being as that you are all slaves of Lincoln, I should expect no better."

The men exchanged glassy eyed glances but did not reply.

"That abolition despot must have you trained like dogs to attack ladies such as myself."

John Scully managed to focus his eyes on Rose's bosom. "That may be so, but here's to nice times we will have with you, Marie Antoinette… in your bedroom tonight." He raised his glass, but no one returned the gesture.

"That's it." Hattie stepped into the room. "You are all a disgrace to the business that you conduct, and I will be having a word with Major Allen about what has transpired this evening." She glared at each man in turn before marching back into the dining room to gather the evidence.

"Hattie, wait." Pryce stood at the threshold between the two rooms. "The men were just having a bit of fun. Scully didn't mean anything by it."

"She might be a Rebel spy, but she is still a lady and we should treat her as such."

Pryce pulled off his hat and fiddled with it. "You are right. And he should have never said anything. If it's any consolation, I don't think he knew you were in the room."

"That makes no matter."

He stepped forward. "Will you not tell the Boss?"

Hattie sighed. She was still exasperated with him for his earlier negligence with Rose. He stopped swaying and gave her a pleading look. Although the men had clearly been out of line, she wasn't sure if Pinkerton would appreciate her tattling on fellow operatives. "I suppose I can let it go this time," she relented. "But don't ever let it happen again. With anyone."

Pryce nodded before putting his hat back on. "Thanks, Hattie."

"I'm going to get going." She shouldered the parcel full of documents.

Pryce nodded at the rest of the piles. "I'll get the men to clean and sort the rest of this out. We'll bring it to the office in the morning."

"Thank you. Goodnight."

"G'night."

. . .

105

When Scully brought the rest of the evidence in the next morning, he looked even worse for wear than when Hattie left him last night.

"Is this it?" Hattie asked as he dumped the contents of the bags on the evidence table. She swooped around the table like a mother hen examining her nest. "There seemed to be more last night."

Scully exchanged a glance with Pryce, who adopted the same sheepish look. Hattie was growing to hate that look.

"We found some ashes in the fireplace this morning," Pryce finally offered. "Mrs. Greenhow might have burned some papers last night."

"However did you—wait, let me guess. You men got even more drunk and passed out."

Scully refastened the empty bag and put it under the table. "That's none of your business."

Hattie walked up to him and stared into his face, ignoring his wan complexion. "It's my business when you go and muck with a case. Especially one so important to our cause."

"Hattie," Pryce reached out to touch her shoulder. "We all make mistakes. We've been under a lot of pressure lately and wanted to celebrate."

Hattie shrugged off his hand and was about to continue to chew them out when Pinkerton entered the room. "Ah," he said, rubbing his hands together, "at last, Mrs. Greenhow's guilt is laid out for the world to see."

Hattie folded her arms and glared at Pryce and then Scully.

Pinkerton used his detective senses to pick up on the animosity flowing through the room, dividing Hattie from the other operatives like the Mason Dixon line between the North and South. "What is it?"

"Nothing, sir," Pryce replied. "It was a long night and my men are a mite tired."

Pinkerton nodded. "The replacements arrived in the morning?"

"Yes, sir, right on time."

Hattie wondered what they had thought upon arriving to see the men who were supposed to be guarding the suspect passed out.

"The General has already given permission for some of his Sturgis Rifles to assist us in guarding Mrs. Greenhow." Pinkerton stated. The men of Sturgis Rifles were McClellan's own body-guards. "Great work last night, men. And Miss Lewis," he added, turning to her.

Hattie gave him a half-smile. She could see the begging expression on Pryce's face, but ignored it and went back to her desk. It was awfully tiring sometimes to be a woman in a man's world.

CHAPTER 16

MARY JANE

SEPTEMBER 1861

*M*ary Jane's new place of business was a gray stucco house on the corner of Twelfth and Clay Streets, at the top of Shockoe Hill. She paused at the entrance to glance down through the trees, catching a glimpse of the slave auction blocks in Shockoe Bottom and the jails of Lumpkin's alley beyond them. She steeled herself, remembering the reason why she was now standing outside the home of the Confederate President. *There can be no slave jails if there are no more slaves.*

She walked around the eastern side of the house to find a door underneath the portico, correctly assuming that was the servants' entrance. A housekeeper in a pristine white uniform greeted her and introduced herself as Mrs. O'Melia. She looked to be in her middle forties, with a kind, round face. "What's your name?" she asked in a thick Irish accent.

"Mary," she replied, omitting her customary second name just in case.

"We already have one Mary," Mrs. O'Melia replied. "We'll just have to call you 'Little Mary.'" She wiped her hands on a towel and opened the door wider. "Mr. Garvin?" she called in a louder voice.

"Yes, Mrs. O'Melia?" a black man with graying hair appeared from the side of a nearby building.

"Mr. Garvin, can you bring Little Mary's bag to her quarters?" She flashed Mary Jane an apologetic smile. "I'll show you around the big house, but right now I've got to get Mrs. Davis her tea. We've been a bit short-handed lately, so I'm glad that you are here."

Mr. Garvin walked into the room and picked up Mary Jane's bag before exiting again. He led her to a two-story log cabin, stating that it housed the servants' living space. Once inside, he directed her through a small hallway. "Normally you'd have a roommate, but, as Mrs. O'Melia said, we're short staffed as of late."

"What happened to the rest of the help?"

Mr. Garvin flashed a brilliant smile. "A lot of them left when they heard the Union army was at Manassas."

"They fled to freedom?"

He nodded. "I believe the Yanks are now calling them 'contraband.' But at least they ain't returning them." Mary Jane gave him a tiny smile, not sure what Mr. Garvin's aim was in telling her this. In her opinion, most slaves, excluding herself of course, fell into two factions: those who were so devoted to their masters that they would never willingly leave them, and those who would run at the first opportunity. Mr. Garvin could be baiting her with the intent to tattle later to Mrs. Davis, but somehow Mary Jane didn't think so. She wasn't sure if it was the articulate timbre to his voice or the gentleness in his brown eyes, but she had an inkling that she could trust Mr. Garvin.

He paused outside a tiny room, gesturing for Mary Jane to enter. The room was bare except for two pallets laid out on the wood floor and a small dresser in the corner.

Mr. Garvin spoke from the hallway. "There's a flushing toilet in the big house, but we don't have those luxuries here."

Mary Jane set her bag on the dresser next to the washing-up

bowl and then followed Mr. Garvin back to the mansion. "How many servants are there total?"

"Right now about nine, but there's work enough for around twelve most days. I heard tell that the Davises owned hundreds of slaves on their plantation back in Mississippi. Only two of them followed them here: Jim Pemberton and his wife Betsy."

Mary Jane avoided a mud puddle. "Are most of the people who work here slaves?"

Mr. Garvin opened the door of the main house. "Most are, although there are others who are paid for their services, including freedmen and white immigrants like Mrs. O'Melia, and Miss Catherine, the nurse. I belong to Mr. Thompson myself. He hired me out to be Mr. Davis's coachman."

Mary Jane nodded in recognition. It was customary practice in Richmond for slave-owners to let newcomers rent their slaves until they bought or hired new servants. Miss Lizzie had offered Mary Jane in the same way—the Davises would be paying the Van Lews for the use of Mary Jane. Miss Lizzie promised Mary Jane that she would give her the money she had earned, after, in Miss Lizzie's words, "the whole affair was over."

Mr. Garvin tipped his hat to Mary Jane before he walked back outside.

Mrs. O'Melia greeted her once again. "All right, Little Mary, let's get you acquainted." As she led her to the front of the house, the housekeeper regaled Mary Jane with the story of how she had been visiting friends in Richmond from Baltimore when the war started and she was unable to cross the lines to get back home. Alone in a strange city and separated from her children, she prevailed upon Mrs. Davis, who offered a job instead of a pass.

Mrs. O'Melia obviously took great pride in her position and pointed out to Mary Jane little details in the décor of the circular main hallway, such as the large plaster statues painted to look bronze and the wallpaper that mimicked white marble. She caught Mary Jane's startled glance at a portrait of George Washington prominently displayed in the state dining room.

"Mr. Davis has a great respect for the man. He's said multiple times that if Washington were alive, he'd be on the side of the Confederacy."

Mary Jane wanted to ask her if she believed that was true. Coming from Maryland, Mrs. O'Melia could veer either way, or, as Mary Jane was beginning to suspect, she held no particular allegiance to either side and remained loyal as long as she was employed.

Mary Jane went over to examine the gray granite fireplace. "It's cast iron," Mrs. O'Melia stated proudly, thumping it with her knuckles.

Mary Jane was beginning to suspect that a lot of the adornments in the Executive Mansion gave off a grand surface impression that belied what they were underneath. *Like Mr. Davis himself attempting to equate himself with Washington.*

Mrs. O'Melia led Mary Jane through the parlor, showing her how the pocket doors could separate it into two "twin" rooms if need be. "Mrs. Davis is in the room the Davises call the 'snuggery.'"

Mary Jane followed her into a smaller room lined with scarlet wallpaper. An elegant woman sat primly on a gold and red brocade sofa. Her pink dress contrasted greatly with her olive complexion and, as she focused her brown eyes on her new servant, she reminded Mary Jane of some of the mulattos, or "quarter-breeds" that she knew.

Mrs. O'Melia curtsied. "Mrs. Davis, may I present your newest maid, Little Mary."

Mrs. Davis nodded a greeting. "You are from Miss Van Lew?"

"Yes'm," Mary Jane said. Knowing her place, she did not meet Mrs. Davis's eyes and instead stared down at the white wool carpet.

"It was very good of her to offer us your services," Mrs. Davis continued.

"Yes'm," Mary Jane repeated, recalling the shyness most new maids exhibited upon arriving at the Van Lews. There, Mr. John and Miss Lizzie, as well as old Mrs. Van Lew, would ask the servants questions or carry on conversations with them, but Mrs. Davis acted as if Mary Jane was not even in the room when she informed Mrs. O'Melia that they would be having company, a Mr. and Mrs. Chesnut, over for tea that evening. "We will be served in the parlor after supper. You can have the new girl assist."

"Yes, ma'am," Mrs. O'Melia replied.

This unfamiliar behavior continued when Mary Jane served the Davises the evening meal. Mrs. O'Melia had instructed her to stand in the corner when she was not clearing plates or delivering food from the kitchen. Mary Jane did as she was told, and it was as if she had disappeared into the shadows. When Mrs. Davis mentioned Mary Jane's arrival, she did not bother to introduce her to Mr. Davis, simply stating that "a new maid had arrived." Mr. Davis kept his austere blue eyes on his obviously much younger wife, and nodded, the somber expression on his gaunt face remaining unchanged.

Mrs. Davis set her fork down. "I'm still not sure it's enough, though, with so many of the help gone now and good maids hard to find."

"Don't forget that everything is double the price now, Winnie." Mr. Davis wiped his mouth. "These Richmonders are a tough lot. We don't want to look extravagant in their eyes."

"No, but a woman has to have help. With the baby coming, the work will be all that much more come December."

Mary Jane didn't bother to cover the shock on her face with the mention of such a private matter in front of her. It didn't matter— the Davises obviously thought their slaves were invisible as well as deaf and dumb and paid her no heed unless they needed a refill. *All the better to spy with*, Mary Jane mused.

Mr. and Mrs. Chesnut arrived after dinner and were escorted to the West Parlor. Mary Jane resumed her role of server/shadow, doing her best to blend in with the gold-embossed wallpaper.

Once they were seated and the tea had been served, Mrs. Chesnut stated, "If what they say is true, and that every Southerner is the equal of three Yanks, we could be a match for twelve Union men right now." She gave a gay laugh.

"Yes," Mr. Davis ventured, "From what I've seen in my experience so far and in the war in Mexico, we will do all we can do with pluck, dogged courage, and red-hot patriotism." His tone did not match his enthusiastic words, however. To Mary Jane, it was almost as if he spoke by rote and did not necessarily believe in what he said.

"Do you think the war will continue on for much longer?" Mrs. Chesnut asked him.

He nodded.

"Oh, but Jeff, don't you think this war is already about played out?" his wife cried.

"No, Winnie, I don't. We are in for a long, bitter fight. We must not be fool enough to doubt the willingness of the Yanks in battle. Instead of them accepting defeat, Manassas seems only to have roused them—we have bruised their egos."

Mary Jane was cheered that even the leader of the Confederacy acknowledged the doggedness of the Union, but she did not think that this was the type of intelligence that Miss Lizzie or Mr. McNiven would be looking for.

Mrs. Davis took a thoughtful sip of her tea. "If they hate us so, why don't they just let us go?"

Mrs. Chesnut answered, "They say that slavery is so horrid for the Negroes, but they don't see that we are offering a better life than they would have had otherwise. Their intellect is far inferior, they aren't cut out for much more than menial labor."

"Not to mention the North is the one who profited the most from our cotton," Mr. Chesnut added.

Mary Jane kept her eyes on the floor through most of the exchange, not wanting to meet the eyes of any of the conversationalists. But no one looked up to see her reaction on the topic of slavery. *Most likely they didn't think her reaction was one worth noting. Or else maybe they thought her inferior brain couldn't process what they were saying.*

"Yes, it's always about money with the Yanks, isn't it?" Mrs. Chesnut agreed.

"Still, they don't fight for the fun of it, and once the war is no longer profitable for them, they will be ready to give in," Mr. Chesnut predicted.

Just then, two little boys ran into the room.

"Jeff Jr. and little Joe," Mrs. Davis set her teacup in the saucer. "Say goodnight to Mr. and Mrs. Chesnut."

"Goodnight, Mr. and Mrs. Chesnut," they called in unison. One of them looked to be about four and his brother was probably about half his age. They ran to the fireplace and placed kisses upon the white marbled women flanking each side.

"They do that every night," Mrs. Davis commented with a tone of motherly pride.

"Adorable," Mrs. Chesnut agreed.

A white servant came into the room. "I will take them upstairs now, Miss." Like Mrs. O'Melia, her accent was heavily Irish.

"Thank you, Catherine," Mrs. Davis replied.

The conversation continued in much the same vein. The Southerners did not veer too much from chiding the Yankees and exalting their own way of life. Mary Jane marveled at their foolishness: the Southern ways would not last through the

war if the Union army was as dedicated to avenging their stung pride as Mr. Jefferson said they were. *One can only hope,* Mary Jane thought after the Chesnuts had left and the Davises had retired. She crossed her fingers briefly before resuming her duty cleaning up after the Confederate president and his guests.

CHAPTER 17

LORETA

OCTOBER 1861

*L*oreta left Front Royal for the headquarters of General "Shanks" Evans but was told there were no officer vacancies. Again she found herself without a regiment, and nothing to do but wait to see if anything should turn up. As she set up camp with the Confederates who were stationed southeast of Leesburg, she was ordered to the office of Captain De Caulp. Loreta immediately recognized the name: De Caulp had been her late husband William's commanding officer and it was he who sent the fateful letter informing Loreta of his death. The tragedy of their first encounter notwithstanding, meeting him as Harry Buford greatly amused her.

Captain De Caulp, a handsome man in his early 40s, had no idea that the dapper young man standing before him was not who he said he was. He seemed to take an interest in Harry and asked him several questions about his background. Again, Loreta was forced to make up a story on the spot, telling him that she belonged to the Mississippi regiment. This seemed to satisfy him and the captain pulled a bottle of whiskey out from his pack and offered some to Loreta. She declined with a pat of her stomach. "I never drink anything strong: it doesn't agree with my constitution."

Captain De Caulp poured himself some, saying, "A drink of the right kind of liquor now and then is a good thing, I think. Here's to the Confederacy," he said, raising his glass. He swallowed the contents without blinking an eye. Loreta watched, thinking that he was one of the most good-looking men she'd ever laid eyes on.

"Lieutenant Buford, you are more than welcome to turn in here if you haven't been assigned to quarters."

Oh, if only I weren't in the disguise of a soldier! "Thank you, sir, but I have my own tent."

"Well, be sure to visit often. I'll be glad to talk with you." Loreta couldn't have agreed more. De Caulp nodded toward a map on the table. "Seems like we're all in need of a good night's sleep tonight, though."

Loreta focused her mind, trying to block out sinful thoughts of De Caulp. Even though she was a woman at heart, with all the needs of the female sex, there were other, more important things she had to accomplish first. "Are there Feds in the area?"

"I've heard tell that General Stone's troops have crossed at Edward's Ferry."

Loreta nodded. "Well, I guess that means I best be heading to my tent." Loreta put her hat on and then bowed. The masculine movement combined with the heaviness of her hat brought her back to reality. "Thank you again, Captain De Caulp. Goodnight." Loreta strode back to her tent, shoving her womanly desires deep into her boots. She found her slave Bob fast asleep and shook him awake to tell him to be up by 3 am. "And be sure to cook plenty of provisions. I expect we'll need them, as I can feel that something's about to happen."

Only the white of Bob's teeth were visible in the dim light. Although Confederate laws prohibited him from participating in battle, his appetite for other soldiery duties such as marching, cooking over a fire, and digging trenches was nearly equal to Loreta's. Bob never spoke much of anything but sometimes Loreta caught him whistling at work. She supposed it was better than working as a field hand, or maybe it was the fact that he took a special joy in witnessing the white soldiers having to obey their superior officers just as a slave would a master.

Loreta and Bob arose early the next morning. Presently the two began to hear the crack of gunshots.

"If I'm not mistaken, the time for fighting's coming soon," Loreta told Bob.

"Yessa, Massa Harry."

After having a hearty breakfast, Loreta left Bob and pushed in the direction of the gunshots, up Ball's Bluff overlooking the Potomac River. At the top was a thick growth of trees and it was impossible for Loreta to discern which man belonged to which army. The woods seemed to be alive with soldiers. Colonel Burth and his 18th Mississippi regiment advanced on the left of the line while Lieutenant Colonel Janifer and his Virginians held the center.

Loreta spotted a group of Rebels that seemed lost. "Where's your officer?" she shouted at a private.

He shrugged in return.

Loreta cast her eyes around the line, and, spotting a gap, shouted at the men in the company to follow her. The line again complete, it seemed that there was little to no maneuvering to be done. Loreta set about keeping the men together to hold the line. The fighting continued without interruption for three taxing hours until at last the Confederate forces succeeded in overpowering the enemy near the end of the chilly October day. As the sun went down and the day became even more gray, the enemy suddenly broke. Instead of marching as an organized army, they became a confused mob running towards the edge of the cliff and the river below. The Confederates rushed after them, hooting and hollering the banshee shriek of the Rebels. Loreta's sense of satisfaction overwhelmed her and she joined in the shouting as she ran, feeling no need to deepen the pitch of her voice. They pursued the Feds through the woods to the top of the bluff. General Evans gave the order to "drive them into the river or capture them." Complying, Loreta advanced the company she'd taken command of, but as they neared the edge, she called them to a halt. The Union soldiers, backed up against the cliff with enemy weapons pointed at them, began plunging over the cliff into the cold waters of the Potomac below. Watching the helpless wretches reminded Loreta of the stories her father used to tell her about Indians pursuing buffalo over ravines.

"Shall we shoot at them?" one of the men asked.

Loreta cleared her throat and, in Harry's voice, stated, "That would be favorable work, but I think they are badly whipped." She glanced down below at the river. In the twilight, she could just make out men in dark uniforms floundering in the wide river. Her comrades around were whooping in victory. She gave an involuntary shudder. Despite the fact they were her foes, they were still human beings. And she was still a woman with no heart to bear the ruthless slaughtering of men. Hours before, these same Feds had fought valiantly and now there they were, suffering a slow death in freezing water. She turned away from the fiendish shouts of her men, blinking back tears. For the first time since she put on her uniform, she was thrown off guard and might have done something foolish to betray her secret. But then she caught a glimmer of silver in the little ravine directly below her. A Yankee sergeant crouching in the narrow crevasse was reaching for his pistol. If she hadn't seen him, he might have shot her. Loreta leveled her musket at him. "No, you don't! Drop that and come up here."

He gave an audible sigh before tucking the pistol back into his belt and scrambling up the side of the cliff. When he got closer, Loreta folded her shaking hands across her chest. Harry's voice affected a bravado that Loreta did not feel. "If I wanted to do the dishonorable duty of murdering a prisoner, I would shoot you in a heartbeat."

"I don't care whether you do or not," the sergeant answered in a sullen tone. He watched the waters below, and then, pointing with a shaking finger, stated, "There goes my colonel."

Loreta watched the man he indicated, who was attempting to swim across the river. "What is his name?"

. . .

"Colonel Devens of the 15th Massachusetts."

The two watched as the colonel struggled against the current of the river. Loreta fervently hoped he would reach the other side safely. She had seen enough death for the day.

Other men did not seem to be as strong as swimmers as Colonel Devens and the night air was filled with the shouts of drowning men.

Soon after she'd directed a soldier to take her prisoner to Captain De Caulp's tent, a man dressed in the uniform of lieutenant approached her. "Sir, I heard that it is you I must thank for taking command of my unit."

"Where were you?"

"The Feds had taken me prisoner, but I made my escape in the confusion of their defeat."

Loreta narrowed her gaze in scrutiny. The lieutenant avoided her eyes and instead focused on the river. This and the sheepish tone to his voice led Loreta to believe the man was lying to her. He probably found a way to slink to the rear of the line to stay out of danger. He was just another dandy officer who strutted about the city streets in his uniform, the type of man who liked to show off by bullying the soldiers in their command but who panicked the moment a gun was fired. *He ought to be court-martialed and shot*, Loreta concluded to herself, but, knowing the hierarchy of a soldier's life, she told him to report to the commanding officer to explain himself.

She watched him as he sauntered off, grateful for at least a temporary distraction to the tragedy that was taking place below her. The Confederate higher powers will probably believe his lies, but hopefully someday he would pay for his betrayal. That man, and others like him, were a disgrace to the uniform. They felt themselves so superior to colored men, but Loreta knew a great many darkeys who would have fought more bravely than they, if given a chance. Bob especially.

CHAPTER 18

HATTIE

OCTOBER 1861

*H*attie and the other Pinkerton operatives continued their investigation of Rose Greenhow, unraveling the secrets of her underground spy network. So far they had implicated a dentist, a banker, even a former clerk in the Department of the Interior. Greenhow had friends in high places in Washington City and Pinkerton's largest fear was that she would be released from house arrest.

When Hattie uncovered a note from Eugenia Phillips, wife of a former congressman with the unfortunate name of Philip Phillips, Pinkerton had her and her adult daughters arrested and confined with Greenhow. Although the women were forbidden to have contact with each other, they joined in chorus to sing "Dixie," and other songs rebellious in nature. The women continued to insult their captors, even complaining about Hattie using a gas light to read her newspaper when on guard in the evening.

Hattie showed Mrs. Greenhow some of the things the papers had written about her. Rose was particularly amused by the cartoons featured in *Harper's Weekly* under the inauspicious title, "How to Deal with Female Traitors." Some of their suggestions to keep the women in line included "Let them see but not touch all the latest novelties in Hats, Dry Goods, etc." and "Make them wear very unfashionable uniforms."

"They don't think much of women, do they?" Rose asked.

"No," Hattie replied. She folded the paper before tucking it under her arm. She decided to take advantage of Rose's conciliatory tone and press further. "Did you have many other females working for you?"

Rose waved her hand. "Nice try, Miss Lewis, but I refuse to incriminate anyone else."

"Don't you understand you might be tried for treason?" she replied. "They might lessen your sentence if you give us more names."

"I am a widow and a mother. Only the Union would serve to persecute such a victim of their worthless cause as me. But let them come, I am ready for them," she said, looking up at Hattie with her black eyes. As if she had foretold what happened next, the doorbell rang.

Hattie answered it, Pryce Lewis appearing in the hallway behind her. The two men on the portico introduced themselves as Edwin Stanton, aide to secretary of war Cameron, and Colonel Thomas Key, an aide to General McClellan.

"We've been asked by our respective bosses to check on Mrs. Greenhow and Mrs. Phillips," Colonel Key stated. He handed a pass over to Hattie. It had been signed by the secretary of war himself and Hattie admitted the two men into what the papers had dubbed "Fort Greenhow."

Hattie led them into the parlor, where Greenhow was knitting, her needles clicking together angrily. She dropped them and stood when presented with her guests.

"Good evening, Mrs. Greenhow," Stanton said warmly. "What have you done now to bring down such a wrath by the abolitionists?"

"That's not funny, Stanton," Greenhow said, her eyes narrowing. "If you are not here to help me out of this confinement, then I'm done with this conversation."

"I will see what I can do." He turned to address Pryce and Hattie. "I find it odd that the government seeks to employ Pinkerton operatives to guard a lady's house."

"It's no oddity: Mrs. Greenhow has created a vast spy network that we are only on the verge of uncovering," Pryce returned, a challenge audible in his voice.

"Spy network?" Mrs. Greenhow laughed a guttural laugh, placing a gloved hand over the lace décolletage of her gown, as if to remind the room that she was still a lady. "These men, and woman, continuously degrade me and treat me with utter disrespect."

"Is that so?" Colonel Key asked, standing and glaring at Pryce.

"It is not, indeed, but our orders are to keep her under lock and key, as a protection to both our government and our soldiers in the field," Hattie explained.

Pryce had been angered, however, and demanded to see their pass. Colonel Key pulled the now wrinkled paper from his breast pocket and handed it over.

"This concerns Mrs. Eugenia Phillips—and it does not give either one of you men proper authority to see Mrs. Greenhow." Pryce returned the note. "I can either lead you to Mrs. Phillips' room or escort you to the door, but your conversation with Mrs. Greenhow is now concluded."

Stanton stood. "What right does a detective have to order us out?"

Hattie had been wondering the same thing, but Pryce remained undaunted. "I have authority from Pinkerton, who has been hired by your boss," he nodded at Colonel Key, "to keep watch on Mrs. Greenhow."

"We'll see about that," Stanton replaced his hat and stalked out of the living room.

A few days after the incident, Pinkerton told Pryce and Hattie that the Phillips women were to be released and sent South.

"They spit on Union soldiers," Hattie stated upon hearing the news. "Like Greenhow, they wouldn't hesitate to conspire against our government if given another chance."

"What can I say?" Pinkerton asked. "Stanton worked for their release. And further," he locked eyes with Hattie before moving on to Pryce. "Stanton has lodged a complaint with the war department regarding the 'chaperoning' of Rose Greenhow."

"That's fine, Boss," Pryce said. "I'm tired of babysitting would-be women traitors. Put me back in the field."

And me, Hattie wanted to add.

"Stanton's a fool," Pinkerton replied with a wave of his hand. "We answer to General McClellan, and I think I've made it clear that Rose Greenhow is shameless in her conduct and will continue to try to undermine the Union whenever possible." He held up a slim piece of paper. "This is a message one of the Sturgis Rifles that act as her door guard gave me. Mrs. Greenhow bribed him to pass it on to another of her contacts."

"Did you get the contact's name?" Hattie inquired.

"Yes," Pinkerton said with a wry grin. "It was Charles Winder, brother of Richmond's provost marshal."

"The woman has no shame," Hattie murmured.

"Yes," Pinkerton said, tossing the note into a drawer. "And that's why she needs to stay put."

CHAPTER 19

MARY JANE

OCTOBER 1861

The silence of the servants at the Davis household sometimes made Mary Jane want to scream. They were trained to be aware of their master's and mistress's wants at all times, to think for them and know what they might demand before they demand it, delivering the unrequested goods all without one word from either servant or commandant. As Mrs. O'Melia told Mary Jane, it would be a miserable failure if Mr. Davis ever had to ask Mr. Garvin for anything. But all the same, Mary Jane wanted the help to have at least a hushed voice, or some autonomy over their circumstances.

Mary Jane was hired to serve at Mrs. Davis's parties and to help her out when her personal maid, Betsy, was occupied. Betsy was always by her mistress's side and, with the combination of Mr. Davis falling ill in late September and Mrs. Davis halting her elegant affairs—she claimed it was to save money, but Mary Jane suspected the *Richmond Examiner's* harsh criticisms had something to do with it — Mary Jane had little to do. She convinced Mrs. O'Melia that she was an excellent housekeeper as well, so she was assigned to clean Mr. Davis's office.

The fact filled Mary Jane and all of her contacts with glee, but with Jeff Davis convalescing, no major work was going down. Mrs. Davis herself received the cabinet members and dignitaries at the door, deciding whether their business required an interview with the bed-ridden president, or if it was something she could handle in the parlor.

One such visitor that did not warrant a sojourn upstairs was Mr. Chesnut. Mrs. Davis ordered Mary Jane to serve them coffee in the snuggery.

As soon Mary Jane entered the little room carrying a tray, Mr. Chesnut banged his fist on the table, startling her. He was clearly adamant in making his point. "As soon as England recognizes us as a sovereign state, all of our problems will be solved. And cotton is the way to do it, Varina."

Mary Jane set down the tray and wiped a napkin over a bit of spilled coffee. She served a cup to Mr. Chesnut and then to Mrs. Davis, who took an approving sip and then placed her cup carefully in its saucer. "I heard the British are favoring the North simply because they are opposed to slavery."

"Once their economy starts to suffer because there is no cotton, they will change their mind about the practice. Cotton is our gold mine and the surest way to win England over. But with all the slaves withdrawing up North, we have no one to pick our crops."

"I don't disagree with you," Mrs. Davis replied in her soft manner. "I just think as of now we have more important matters to worry about. We need our men in battle now, not in the fields."

Mr. Chesnut, his coffee untouched, muttered something about women not knowing the first thing about war.

Either Mrs. Davis did not hear him or she chose to ignore his comment. She bestowed a patient smile on him. "Now, Mr. Chesnut, how do you like your coffee?"

. . .

Despite the paucity of information that was available to Mary Jane that fall, she progressed her mission by gaining the trust of both Mrs. Davis and the rest of the servants. Mr. McNiven continued his daily deliveries of his baked goods and Mary Jane managed to convince Mrs. O'Melia to let her be the one to greet him. No one else was usually around when his wagon pulled into the driveway outside the servants' entrance and they could speak freely.

One day he told Mary Jane that Miss Lizzie had found a new way to keep abreast of Mary Jane's progress. "She wants to meet with you, weekly if possible, at Miss Thompson's shop. She's a seamstress located down the hill. Mrs. Van Lew says to hang your red petticoat on the line a few hours beforehand to let her know of your plans."

"But how will I convince Mrs. Davis that I need to go to a seamstress?"

McNiven shrugged. "I'm sure you'll figure it out."

The opportunity came sooner than Mary Jane thought. As Mary Jane delivered Mrs. Davis's tea, her mistress pulled up the hem of her petticoat. "I wish I could get a new dress, but the Richmonders would use that as an excuse to say I'm being 'extravagant' again." She had said this more to herself than Mary Jane and, consequently, looked surprised when Mary Jane told her she knew of a good seamstress who could repair her dresses.

"She kin also do alterations, ma'am," Mary Jane continued. "Instead of buying new dresses, she kin change the style of yer old ones."

"You might be right," Mrs. Davis conceded, tucking a loose curl behind her ear. "The righteous old biddies of this town can't possibly look down upon re-purposing old dresses, can they?"

Mary Jane wasn't sure if she was addressing her, but she replied, "No'm," anyway.

Once Mrs. Davis had entrusted Mary Jane with her expensive though simply decorated gowns, a new way of reporting intelligence formed. Mary Jane did as Mr. McNiven suggested, hanging something red on the clothesline whenever Mrs. Davis had something to take to the seamstress. Miss Lizzie would meet her there, and though her narrow face would droop each time Mary Jane had nothing to report, Miss Lizzie would fill Mary Jane in on what was occurring on her end. It was clear that Miss Lizzie had greatly expanded her underground network of spies and couriers. She'd managed to make contact with a guard in one of the warehouse prisons, saying that she expected to receive escaped Yankee prisoners at her home any day.

"What about Wit—Mrs. Mary? You are going to house them right under her nose?"

"Not under her nose," Miss Lizzie corrected. "Above. I don't know if you ever noticed it, but there is a small room in the attic."

Mary Jane shook her head in disbelief.

"See?" Miss Lizzie's eyes were shining. "If you didn't know it was there, Mary will never know. They will arrive at night and stay up there until arrangements can be made to get them across the lines to freedom."

As she left the seamstress shop, Mary Jane admitted to herself that Miss Lizzie's determination to aid the Union was as strong as her own, however foolish Mary Jane thought this latest plan was. While she waited to cross the street, she saw a white man in a large hat standing beside the curb.

"I'm going through the lines tonight," he said in a gruff voice.

Bewildered, Mary Jane tried to see if she recognized him, but the large hat covered his eyes. He had a scar that led from his ear to his chin.

Mary Jane took on her slave voice. "Sawry, suh, I'm not shuh what you mean."

"Yer sure you don't, nigger?" he asked as a wagon passed them.

Mary Jane hurried across the street, nearly colliding with a carriage, glad the package in her hands had prevented her from exercising her instinct to slap him.

The next day, as she was running an errand for Mrs. Davis, she saw that same gruff man, this time dressed in a Confederate uniform, leading a handful of troops down Main Street, confirming what Miss Lizzie had advised her yesterday: *Trust no one.*

CHAPTER 20

HATTIE

NOVEMBER 1861

*D*ue to Pinkerton's intervention with the War Department, Hattie and Pryce Lewis were once again attending to Rose at Fort Greenhow.

Pryce told Hattie over tea that Timothy Webster had managed to infiltrate the Knights of Liberty. They were an underground group of Copperheads—Northerners who opposed the war—that were planning an uprising to take place in Washington City. Two days ago, on the same day President Lincoln had called for a national day of thanksgiving, Pinkerton agents and local police officers had raided the Knights' headquarters and arrested the entire group.

"Don't you wish you could be helping the Union in some other way?" Hattie asked Pryce.

He shrugged. "I'm really an operative at heart. This war is a temporary offshoot to my journey. I'm going to own my own agency one day."

"But the rebels—"

Pryce shrugged. "It's not my country."

Hattie wanted to slap him, but she held her hands close to her side. She wondered what Allan Pinkerton, the famed abolitionist, would have done if he knew one of his own operatives had such apathy toward the Cause. Someone rang the bell and Pryce left the kitchen to answer it. A few minutes later he returned with a cake.

"What's that?" Hattie asked.

"A holiday fruitcake for Rose. A delivery man just dropped it off." He took a penknife from his pocket and cut into it. Instead of the expected fruit and pastry, the innards of the cake were made of paper. Hattie extracted a wad and unfolded it. "Confederate bills."

Pryce picked out a folded sheet of paper and unfolded it, his eyes quickly scanning the contents. "Details of an escape to Richmond."

"Why that..." Hattie struggled to keep her language ladylike.

"Tart?" Pryce asked, a smile in his eyes.

Hattie rolled her eyes, momentarily forgetting their earlier animosity.

"I have an idea," Pryce said. He headed toward the front door and donned his overcoat and hat. "I'll be right back."

In a few minutes, he returned, brandishing a beautifully decorated holiday cake. "I wouldn't want Mrs. Greenhow's appetite to suffer because we ruined her other dessert."

Hattie found one of Rose's expensive ceramic serving trays and transferred the new cake onto it before adding the remains of the tainted one. "Shall we deliver this to Mrs. Greenhow?"

"Indeed, we shall." Pryce replied, grabbing a silver cake knife and server.

"Mrs. Greenhow," Pryce called from outside her room. "We had a special delivery this morning for you."

Rose opened the door, expectation written all over her face. *Clearly she knew about the cake,* Hattie surmised. "We found the other one unsuitable," she told the spy. "So Mr. Lewis bought this cake for you instead."

"We think you'll find the ingredients more agreeable to your palette," Pryce added.

Rose's features filled with fury. She seized the serving tray from Hattie and then pushed past her to hurl the entire thing down the stairwell. The three of them watched the cake smash into the wall while the serving tray shattered into a million tiny pieces. Without a word, Rose turned and headed back to her room, slamming the door behind her.

"Guess she doesn't prefer fruitcake to treason," Hattie commented before heading down the stairs to clean up the mess.

A few days later, Hattie was surprised to hear that her guardianship of Fort Greenhow would be at an end. Pinkerton had finally convinced Secretary Cameron to transfer Rose to the Old Capitol Prison. Rose was given only a few hours to pack. Pryce and Hattie thoroughly examined each item before allowing Rose to put it in her valise. When her carriage arrived to transport her to her newest confinement, her final words to Hattie were that she hoped that in the future she would have a "more noble employment than that of guarding defenseless women."

While Hattie agreed with her on the employment aspect, she would never have called Rose Greenhow defenseless. She simply waved to Rose and then turned to supervise the boarding of the mansion's windows.

The first thing Hattie heard when she arrived at the I-Street office the following morning was arguing. Pinkerton's voice was firm while the other's, slightly familiar to Hattie, was raised in protest. She could just discern the shapes of two figures through the frosted windows of the inner office. When she heard the door open, she pretended to be occupied with papers on her desk.

"Ah, Miss Lewis, just the woman we needed. Could you come in here, please?" Pinkerton's stocky body stepped aside as Hattie walked into his office. Timothy Webster paced rapidly alongside the bookcases in the back. Pinkerton gestured for Hattie to sit. "Mr. Webster has just returned from Baltimore."

Hattie nodded. "I heard of your success with the Knights of Liberty."

Webster stopped his pacing and stood at Hattie's elbow. "I don't need a nurse."

Pinkerton sat heavily behind his desk. "I've told you, your information is too valuable for you to fall sick again." He turned his gaze from Webster to Hattie. "Tim's been suffering from attacks of rheumatism. Now that the Knights of Liberty are no longer a threat, I'm sending him on to Richmond. I want you to accompany him to be his caretaker. Not to mention that single men seem suspicious, but a man who is committed to one woman will seem trustworthy to almost anyone."

Hattie bit back her rebuttal as she thought of her own husband, whom not many people would call trustworthy.

Webster folded his arms across his chest. "Boss, I've told you, I work better alone. A one-sided story is easy to fib your way out of, but when you add another person, you have to corroborate every detail so you don't get tripped up."

Pinkerton stood up. "This is a non-negotiable. Miss Lewis will pose as your wife."

Timothy turned to Hattie. "This isn't secretarial work or looking after a Rebel prisoner. We'll be behind the lines, cavorting with the enemy. You'll be endangering your life."

Hattie drew in a breath, insulted by his insinuations. She didn't want either man to think she wasn't up to the task Pinkerton was proposing. "I'm not afraid," she replied.

"Miss Lewis will be a great asset to your mission," Pinkerton added. "She has lived in the South, albeit under different circumstances than the role she will play. She can garner information from the ladies who accompany the men you will be courting. You will leave tomorrow."

Webster gave a deep sigh before offering Hattie his arm. "Seeing as how we're to be husband and wife, we better start getting into the role."

She gave him a shy smile as she accepted his assistance and rose out of her chair.

"Have you any further commands, then, Boss?" Webster asked.

Pinkerton's shrewd gaze fixed on the would-be couple. Hattie dropped Timothy's arm. "No, Tim. I have no other commands, other than for you to take care of yourselves. And each other."

Webster buttoned up his winter overcoat. "I'll try to do that, sir."

CHAPTER 21

MARY JANE

DECEMBER 1861

*M*rs. Davis had given birth to a son, William Howell Davis, nicknamed Billy, in the beginning of December. To her credit, she still planned a gathering at the mansion to celebrate the holiday a few weeks later.

The morning of the party, Mrs. Davis was dismayed to hear that the busts and friezes she had ordered from Europe had been seized by the blockade. "I'll have to cancel it: I cannot have such important guests seeing an empty ballroom," she wailed as she wrung her hands in distress.

They had opened the doors that separated the parlors so that it was one big, still vacant, room. Mary Jane paused her dusting of the mantel. "I have an idea, Mrs. Davis." Mary Jane walked out of the room and returned with several trinkets that had been made by soldiers and given to the First Lady throughout her many hospital visits.

Mrs. Davis pawed through the items and picked up a wood carving. "I suppose it's better than nothing," she consented. "And they can't possibly say anything about my spending on these. Let's put this statue over the fireplace."

Mary Jane did as she was told. She was so busy in her decorating that she forgot about Mr. McNiven until she happened to glance at the clock on the mantle. "The bakery truck!" she gasped before she hurried outdoors.

Mr. Garvin, the coachman, was standing beside the truck, holding a tray of muffins. He winked at Mary Jane when she arrived, gasping for breath.

"Don't you worry about nothin' Little Mary," Mr. Garvin said with another wink. "Mr. McNiven and I go way back."

Mary Jane gave him a tentative smile, unsure if he knew the real reason why Mary Jane made it her mission to meet the baker every morning. Mr. McNiven handed her a loaf of bread, but did not say anything else.

The guests that evening included the Chesnuts, Secretary of War Judah Benjamin, Mrs. Davis's sister, Maggie, and various other associates that Mary Jane didn't recognize. They gathered in the large parlor to enjoy eggnog, port, and ginger snaps, their gossip centering on the recent incident of the Union navy seizing passengers from a British mail ship off the coast of Cuba. Two of the captives had been newly appointed Confederate envoys to England and France. Mr. Benjamin and Mr. Chesnut were convinced that the incident would be the impetus they needed for England to take up arms against the North.

Even though the hour was late when Mrs. Davis finally dismissed her servants, Mary Jane was still fretting over the possibility of England joining the war and knew that sleep was not going to be forthcoming. She took the leftover port with her to the outbuilding.

Mr. Garvin was sitting on the steps of the servants' quarters, smoking a cigar. "How was the party?" he asked Mary Jane in between puffs.

She sat next to him on the steps. "It was a party."

He picked up the cup next to him, dumping out the water and holding it out to Mary Jane, who filled it with port.

Mr. Garvin took another puff on his cigar before asking, "You learn anything good to report to Mr. McNiven?"

Mary Jane's eyes widened against her will.

Undaunted, Mr. Garvin continued, "I know all about Mr. McNiven's, shall we say, 'underground' activities."

Mary Jane stood up and looked around the garden.

"It's all right, we're safe out here." He set down his cigar on the steps to take a sip of port. "In the big house, no. You must watch out for Mrs. O'Melia and the children's nurse. We're not sure if they would report anything to the Davises. But here, we are all friends. Some of them in there," he indicated the outbuilding behind them with his thumb, "are planning to run when they get the chance. And most of them aided the ones that already left."

"Did McNiven help too?"

Mr. Garvin shook his head. "He did before the war, for sure. Helped my wife and son escape when they was still slaves under another master. But now that Mr. McNiven's attentions are otherwise occupied, he doesn't want to do anything that would look suspicious to the rebels." He picked up his still smoldering cigar and examined it. "Mr. Davis gave it to me as a Christmas present," he stated before putting it back in his mouth.

"That was... kind of him," Mary Jane said, for lack of anything else.

He shrugged. "Kind enough."

"Are you still here because of your loyalty to Mr. Davis?"

"No," he let out a breath of smoke. "I reckon I'm here same as you."

Mary Jane gave him a sidelong glance, trying to ascertain his true meaning, but it was so dark that his expression was masked.

"Mr. McNiven ain't the only acquaintance we have in common. Did you know I used to work for the Van Lews?"

"No," Mary Jane gasped out. "I don't think—"

"You wouldn't have remembered me. You were but a baby when I got my freedom. But I knew your ma. She too wanted to leave, but

139

Miss Lizzie wouldn't let her. Miss Lizzie wanted to oversee your education herself."

Mary Jane nodded. "She sent me up North when she couldn't teach me anymore."

"And what did you think of Liberia?"

Not for the first time Mary Jane wondered how Mr. Garvin knew so much. She put her hand on the railing and traced her finger up and down the simple design. "I hated it. Much as I hate what the South stands for, I missed America. They brought our forefathers here, tore them apart from their families in Africa, and enslaved them and their descendants. Now that some of us want to be free, they don't know what to do with us. Their best solution is to send us back, not to let us make a home for ourselves here. Not to let us be free in our adopted country. So I came back to try and make that happen."

"Someday, little girl, someday we will all be free. And with your and my assistance, maybe that someday will come sooner rather than later." He stamped out his cigar on the steps. "If you ever need any help, remember you've got friends."

Mary Jane wanted to inquire more about her mother, and if he knew anything about her paternity, but she was afraid of Mr. Garvin's answers. "What happened to your son and wife?" she asked instead.

He drained the rest of his port. "My wife died a long time ago. My son was a freedman up North, but he risked all that to come back and be part of Mr. McNiven's courier service."

Mary Jane tightened her grip on the railing. "They could arrest him or worse, have him hanged."

He stood up. "He knows that. But he's real stubborn, my son. He won't listen to nobody but that inner voice inside of him. Reminds me of you in that way." He tipped his hat to her. "G'night, Miss Mary Jane," he said before going inside.

CHAPTER 22

BELLE

JANUARY 1861

The incident over the whiskey made headlines. Belle was pleased to read that the "bloody fracas" had occurred between rivals for her "stimulating donations and sweet smiles." Belle's mother, however, had a different take. "It's unbecoming of a lady to be a spy. Not to mention dangerous." Still worried over her daughter's safety, Mother arranged for soldiers on leave for the holiday season to accompany Belle to the various parties and celebrations.

Belle thoroughly enjoyed the season—especially the brief flirtation with the older Dr. Cherry, who had proposed to her shortly after the holiday. Belle told her friends and family they would be married next February, more out of boredom than any particular conviction. But what she really wanted was for spring to come, and, with that, the continuation of the war. She was restless and had grown weary of being under her mother and Mauma Eliza's never-ending guard. At least the war provided the pleasure of peril, as well as both grief and joy.

Her cousin James, on leave from the army, offered to chaperone her and Dr. Cherry for a day of riding in mid-January. But as they came to a clearing, a gunshot sounded, and though it was barely audible from their distance, it spooked Fleeter. He began galloping away. Belle shouted at him to stop, pulling hard on the reins, but Fleeter kept going, taking Belle deeper and deeper into the Valley, and closer to the Union lines. Belle managed to look back once during a break in the trees but did not see her cousin or Dr. Cherry following her.

When Fleeter finally slowed to a canter, Belle heard a voice shout, "You there!" She sighed to herself upon catching sight of a few Yankees standing guard underneath a pine tree.

"I'm terribly sorry," Belle said in a breathless voice. "My horse was frightened and ran away with me on him." She patted the sweaty steed. "I beg you to permit me to return to my friends."

One of the men walked up to Fleeter. "You have a beautiful horse." Belle's grip tightened on the reins—she'd heard of Yankees stealing horses at their whim. The young man continued, "And you yourself would have made a beautiful captive, but we would never think of detaining you." He glanced up at Belle and she noticed his kind brown eyes. "Are your friends with the Rebel army?"

Belle nodded.

"It is no matter." He nodded at his companions. "May we have the honor of escorting you back? That is, if you promise those cowardly rebels won't take us prisoner," he added with a wink.

Belle managed a tiny smile at the Yankee. *How dare he say cowardly and Rebel in the same sentence!* "A pass would have been just as well. But if you insist on becoming my escort, I shall do you the honor of accepting."

The Yankee mounted his horse and fell in line with Fleeter and Belle as another soldier trotted just behind them. As soon as they got back into Confederate territory, Dr. Cherry and James approached. All four men were startled, each of them glowering at each other.

"Here are my 'cowardly Rebel' friends whom you were afraid of meeting," Belle told the young man before turning to her cousin. "James, may I present to you two Yankee prisoners?"

The young man's astonished gaze fell on Belle. "May I ask the name of our beautiful captor?"

She touched her skirts as if to curtsy while seated. "Belle Boyd."

The young man drew in his breath. "Are you none other than the Rebel spy we've heard so much about?"

"I am indeed," Belle replied, pleased that her reputation had finally preceded her. Belle accompanied Dr. Cherry and James as they escorted their newfound prisoners to headquarters.

"That seems a bit heartless, even for you, Cousin," James told her after the Confederate officer in charge had decided to hold the Yankees for questioning.

"All's fair in love and war," Belle replied, thinking that perhaps the Yankee would learn that her friends were not so cowardly after all.

That incident was the only one to liven up Belle's winter. When the Yankees once again occupied Martinsburg, Belle's mother decided she would be safer with her aunt in Front Royal, especially given Belle's spreading reputation. Mother was able to obtain passes for them to travel from the Union provost marshal, an old family friend, and, in late January, Mauma Eliza and Belle took a carriage to Winchester. As soon as Belle stepped aboard the train that would take her to Front Royal, a blue sleeve reached out to grab her arm.

Belle was about to raise her voice in protest as a short man with sideburns demanded, "Am I in the presence of Miss Belle Boyd?"

"Yes."

The man's eyes traveled from Belle's boots to her bonnet. "I am Captain Bannon, assistant provost. I have orders to detain you."

"But sir, we have travel passes." Belle dug them out of her bag and showed them to the man.

"Ah." Captain Bannon's face dropped in confusion. "These are from the Provost himself."

"Yes sir." Bannon realized that Belle's pass superseded the orders he had been given and let her proceed to her seat unmolested.

It was almost dark when the train arrived. Belle was dismayed to find that the bridge spanning the Shenandoah River had been destroyed and the only ferry operating at that hour was one run by Union soldiers. Belle produced her pass again and, despite being exhausted by the day of traveling, managed to arrange passage to Front Royal.

Her uncle had managed the Fishback Hotel for years, and, in his absence, the duties fell to Belle's aunt, Mrs. Fanny Stewart. Belle had expected her be waiting up for her to arrive, but when Belle stepped into the front room, she noticed a fleet of federal officers.

"Where is Mrs. Stewart?" a tired and hungry Belle demanded.

A man with a droopy mustache approached her. "I am Captain Keily, Miss…?"

"Boyd. I am Mrs. Stewart's niece."

Keily bowed. "Please to make your acquaintance. You will find Mrs. Stewart in the back cottage."

Belle narrowed her eyes. "And why is that?"

"Front Royal is now under the Union control of General James Shields. He has commanded the use of your aunt's fine hotel as his headquarters."

Belle faked a smile. "In that case, please give the general my regards and tell him I hope he finds his stay welcoming."

"Will do, Miss Boyd."

Belle did an about-face as Mauma Eliza followed her outside, carrying her bags. She struggled to keep her balance on the narrow brick walkway that led to the back cottage.

Although she'd heard distasteful gossip about the fifty-one-year-old General Shields and his preference for young females, Belle decided to make his acquaintance anyway. When he paid a call on her aunt, Belle chatted with him, finding him to be a polite Irishman with a good sense of humor.

After exchanging pleasantries about the hotel accommodations and the town in general, Belle asked if he could grant her a pass to

Richmond. Shields laughed. "I would not dare trust a beautiful woman like yourself to the Rebel's tender mercies." He helped himself to more cake before adding, "Luckily we will have annihilated them in a few days, and then you can wander wherever you please."

"Oh?" she asked.

"Indeed," he continued, spilling a crumble of cake onto his whiskers. "We will be meeting tonight at your aunt's very own hotel to plan TJ Jackson's and his army's demise."

Belle put a hand to her mouth. "I see." She let her eyes travel the length of his coat. "I don't suppose you'd have any buttons to spare for a little Southern girl like me?" A Union officer's button would be a nice addition to her collection.

Shields ripped one off and handed it to her before rising from the table. "I best be getting going. The best laid plans and all." He tipped his hat to her before he left the cottage.

That night, Belle stole out of the cottage and glided up the brick walkway to the hotel. She made her way to an upstairs closet, which was positioned right above the drawing room. A small hole had been carved into the wood floor a long time ago and now Belle lay down to put her ear over it. Below her she could hear the men greeting each other before getting comfortable in their seats. Finally, the men began discussing their intentions. She heard someone mention that Stonewall Jackson was making his way toward Richmond.

"McClellan too, is coming in," another voice replied.

Belle listened carefully, at times halting her breathing so she could hear every word. She wished she could sit up to write the information down, but in doing so, she might miss something important. She forced herself to memorize every minute detail, trying to ignore how hot it was in the closet and the ache in her body from being in its cramped position for so long. Shield's cigar smoke crept its way through the tiny hole to assault Belle's nose and twice she had to pause her listening to sneeze and then wipe her nose on her uncle's scratchy old coat.

The men finally said their goodbyes and adjourned well past midnight. Belle waited until the last chair scraped the floor and then got up and stealthily made her way back to the cottage, stretching out her sore body once she made it to the brick walkway. The cool night air felt like heaven after the stuffy, mothball-scented closet.

She knew this was the most pertinent information she had managed to gather thus far, and, likewise, Colonel Turner Ashby, commander of the 7th Virginia cavalry and the head of General Jackson's intelligence committee, needed to be informed of it as soon as possible. Luckily Belle had garnered a pass to go beyond the lines from Captain Keily earlier in the week.

She pulled at the stays of her corset, unlacing it as fast as she could, and stepped out her skirts. In mere moments she was redressed in her male garb. She tiptoed to the stables and chose a horse. She had heard that Colonel Ashby was staying with an acquaintance of Belle's aunt about fifteen miles away.

Although she was stopped twice by Union officers, they let her go after just glancing at the pass and she arrived without incident at Ashby's lodgings at about three in the morning. No lights were on at the house, and it took a few minutes of Belle banging on the door to arouse someone.

"Who is it?" a male voice finally called from an upstairs window.

Belle backed up from the porch to peer at the speaker, but it was too dark to discern who it was. "It is I, Belle Boyd. I have intelligence for Colonel Ashby and must speak to him at once."

"Wait one moment." The speaker disappeared from the window and reappeared at the front door. "Come, come," the man said, motioning to Belle. Once inside, he asked how she came about looking for Colonel Ashby at this hour.

"I have no time to tell you of that. I must see Colonel Ashby now."

"Good God!" someone called from the top of the stairs. Belle turned to see that Turner Ashby, dressed in a nightshirt and wiping the sleep from his eyes, was making his way down. "Miss Belle, is that really you or am I dreaming?"

"Yes, sir, it is me and not a ghost." She pulled a paper out of her bag. "I'm sorry to disturb you and your kind hosts at this hour, but you must know that the Yankees are setting a trap for General Jackson's troops."

Ashby took the note from her and scanned it, his weary eyes growing wider. "Good God," he repeated. "I need a pen and paper!" The host nodded and disappeared further into the house. "Thank you, Miss Belle, for this information. But you should be getting home now. I'll take it from here."

Now that the excitement of reaching Ashby had worn off, so had Belle's adrenaline and she was anxious to head back to the warmth of the cottage. She took her leave of Ashby and then remounted her horse. She had not gotten very far in her journey when it began to rain. A crack of lightning lit up the landscape around her. That it was void of Yankees was the only pleasant thought Belle had as a loud boom of thunder quickly followed. The next time lightning flashed, Belle caught sight of a rifle barrel staring her down. She stuck her hand into her pocket, but her pass was not there. She was too fatigued to remember the countersign, and felt panic mounting as thunder sounded again, closer this time.

"Let the boy pass," a deeper voice commanded. Belle glimpsed an officer standing behind the soldier. "I know him."

The soldier turned to give his reply, but Belle had already started galloping away. When the first light of dawn arrived, Belle was asleep in her bed, dreaming of the praise she was sure to receive from Stonewall Jackson himself once he caught word of her bravery that night.

CHAPTER 23

HATTIE

JANUARY 1861

*H*attie and Timothy Webster met in the office early to go over their mission before they left for Richmond at the end of January.

"Mr. Webster—"

"I suppose you ought to call me Timothy now since we're supposed to be married."

"Timothy, then. What exactly is the nature of our mission?"

He reluctantly related the real reason that Hattie was to accompany him. When he wasn't infiltrating the Order of the Knights of Liberty, Webster had become a trusted Rebel courier and frequently made trips from Southern locales such as Memphis and Fredericksburg, bearing correspondence for Copperheads up North. On his most recent trip, he had journeyed from Pinkerton's office in Washington City back to Virginia. He stopped, as he frequently did, at a hotel run by John Miller, a known Rebel sympathizer. Miller arranged for a canoe to ferry Webster across the Potomac. Two women and three children had also paid to cross, but the canoe could not dock and Webster carried all of the passengers and their baggage through the freezing cold water to get to the boat. The canoe trip took over three hours, all of which Timothy said he spent trying to huddle against the wind in his wet clothes. In addition, once they got across to Virginia, they discovered that the landing spot had been destroyed by Union boats, and Timothy and the rest of them had to sleep on ground covered by frost. "As you can imagine, the experience triggered a drastic effect on my own health."

"I'm sorry to hear that. That was a kind thing you did, bringing the women and children to the boat."

He gave her a half-smile. "I had to keep up my guise as a Southern gentleman."

Hattie returned his grin. "Something tells me that you would do the same thing under your own identity." She straightened her face back into operative mode. "What will be our assignment in Richmond?"

"You will do your best to ferret information from the Southern belles you encounter. As for me, it will be more of the same. I've been entrusted by several high-ranking Confederates as a courier. That allows me both to travel throughout the South as well as pass on those same messages to the Boss," He tugged his uniform sleeves down. "On my previous trip to Richmond, General Winder asked me to carry messages back to his son in Washington City."

Hattie's brow furrowed. "The son of the Richmond provost marshal is in the Union army?"

Timothy nodded. "General Winder confided in me that he wants him to desert as soon as possible. He'd have him stay in jail the duration of the war, or," Timothy smiled at the recollection, "he said he'd rather his son suffer death in the most dishonorable way possible than serve the United States in a war against the South."

Hattie shook her head. She was still sometimes taken aback by the contempt the rebels held for their former country. "Do you think he will desert?"

Timothy scratched at his beard. "I don't think so. I think the younger Winder ultimately will remain true to his country, despite the discord with his father. Besides, his salary as captain is the only income he can provide for his wife and son. He's approached McClellan and asked to be relocated to California. Pinkerton, however, wants him arrested—he says there is no parallel short of that penultimate traitor, Benedict Arnold."

"I'm not sure I'd go that far—it sounds to me like the son wants to please his Confederate father and his country, but can't do both. Benedict Arnold committed treason for a more nefarious purpose. Besides, is there any evidence that he will give up information on the Union?"

"No." Timothy reached for something under his desk. "Not yet, anyway. But if anyone knows how to supply counterintelligence, it's Winder." Timothy replaced his stovepipe hat with a wider-brimmed one.

"What is that?" Hattie asked, pointing to his new headpiece.

"It's a secession chapeau."

"A what?"

"A Confederate officer's hat. My contacts in Memphis bought it for me." He handed her a carpetbag. "Did the boss tell you how we are getting to Richmond?"

"He mentioned something about hiring a boat to take us across the Potomac."

"Yes." His blue eyes flashed with an emotion Hattie couldn't discern. "I don't suppose he mentioned your disguise, though."

"Disguise?"

He nodded at the carpetbag and Hattie took out the contents: a man's shirt, pants, and overcoat.

"There will be fewer questions about two men crossing than a man and woman. Once we get to Fredericksburg, you can change and we'll take the train into Richmond."

"How will we pass through the lines?"

Timothy pulled a piece of paper out of his pocket and showed it to her. It was a pass signed by the Confederate secretary of war, Judah Benjamin.

"My, you have indeed infiltrated the enemy government."

Instead of replying, he tipped his Southern-style hat to her.

. . .

Hattie and Timothy set off for Leonardtown, Maryland, arriving at a boarding house kept by a contact of Timothy's named Mr. Miller.

"Just so you are aware," Timothy said, his hand on the door of the carriage, "he's pretty vocal about his secessionist viewpoints. I usually stop to chat with him, but, circumstances being as they are," he nodded toward her masculine garb, "I will try to avoid that today."

Hattie picked up her carpetbag.

"Mr. Webster!" A short man with a balding head greeted them. "You've brought a companion."

"Yes, Mr. Miller, this is Mr.—"

"Lawton," Hattie supplied. It was the first name that popped into her head.

"Ah, nice to meet you." Hattie felt a tingle of nerves as his eyes traveled up and down her form. She pulled her kepi hat down a little further on her forehead. She was regretting her and Timothy's decision not to glue any facial hair on her, for that way she could have at least hid a bit of her face.

Luckily Mr. Miller was distracted by the appearance of another man. The newcomer was tall, with a heavy beard and mustache. The man's eyes darted to Hattie first and then to Timothy before he turned to Mr. Miller. "Can I speak to you in another room?"

As the two men walked through a door off the lobby, Hattie raised her eyebrows at Timothy. He scratched at his beard and then shrugged.

When Mr. Miller came back alone, he told Timothy that the man asked the quickest route to Richmond, and Mr. Miller supplied that Timothy might be able to help.

"He seemed to be quite nervous, wouldn't you agree?" Timothy asked.

Mr. Miller shrugged. "He has cause to be, I suppose."

Timothy tilted his head. "A Yankee deserter?"

Mr. Miller leaned forward, Hattie and Timothy following suit. "He says he worked as a surgeon for the Union army, but he's a Southerner and quit his commission in order to join our side." Hattie straightened, trying not to cringe at the words, "our side," as Mr. Miller continued, "He also mentioned that he is carrying messages for Judah Benjamin and, accordingly, is anxious to deliver them as soon as possible."

Timothy nodded. "He can accompany us if he wants. What's his name?"

"He said it was Dr. Gurley."

Hattie could almost see the thoughts churning in Timothy's head. She knew he wanted to get his hands on those messages for Secretary of War Benjamin and wondered what his plan would be.

"I will make the arrangements to get you all to the boat tomorrow," Mr. Miller added.

"Thank you," Timothy replied. Hattie echoed the sentiment.

Mr. Miller pulled out his ledger. "Separate rooms then, gentlemen?"

"Yes, please," Hattie was eager to get to her room, if just to take the bindings off her chest for a few minutes.

"I think I will take a short walk before dinner," Timothy patted his stomach. "It helps me work up an appetite."

"Would you like company?" Hattie asked after Mr. Miller had handed them their room keys. She figured Timothy's "walk" had something to do with Dr. Gurley's dispatches.

"No, I'll be fine," Timothy replied as the two walked out of the lobby. "I'm sure you're probably tired after a long day of traveling and would like to... freshen up?" He whispered the last two words and Hattie smiled at him gratefully.

Mr. Miller formally introduced Dr. Gurley to Hattie and Timothy at dinner.

"Rest assured Mr. Webster here is quite familiar with the countryside and will help get you to Confederate territory safely," Mr. Miller said, rising from the table.

"Whatever your reasons are for wanting to get to Richmond," Timothy added as Mr. Miller left the room.

Dr. Gurley's eyes wandered about the room before returning to Timothy. "Thank you."

Miller appeared, brandishing a bottle filled with amber liquid and four glasses. "Kentucky bourbon," he stated. He poured a glass and then handed it to Dr. Gurley. "The best, although now it's hard to come by down South."

As he began to pour the other three, Timothy advised him to served just a bit to Mr. Lawton. He rattled the ice in his glass and then pointed at Hattie, intimating that "Mr. Lawton" had trouble handling his alcohol. Miller filled each one to the brim anyway.

Dr. Gurley drank the glass in one gulp and then set it on the table. "Indeed it is good bourbon." He rose and nodded at Hattie and Timothy. "I will meet you two gentlemen on the morrow, then." He tipped his hat to the landlord. "Mr. Miller, thank you for your hospitality, but I must be heading to bed now."

"G'night, Dr. Gurley," Mr. Miller replied, pouring himself another shot. "You two need to drink up, now," he said, waving his glass at Hattie.

She took a cautious sip. The bourbon tasted faintly sweet, but mostly it burned as she forced it down her throat.

Mr. Miller was well into his third glass when Timothy finished his first one. Hattie's was still nearly full. She gave an apologetic smile to Mr. Miller. "I'm trying to take it easy." She had just gotten the words out when Dr. Gurley burst back into the room.

"I've been robbed!" a hatless Dr. Gurley shouted, his face gone pale. "Someone broke into my room!"

"Now, sit down, Doc," Miller said, kicking out the empty chair.

Gurley remained standing. "My room's been ransacked, but the only thing taken was the dispatch to Mr. Benjamin." He glared at the hotel keep. "What kind of place are you running here, Miller?"

Miller poured him a refill. "Clearly whoever it was knew that you had information for the Confederate government. You're lucky they didn't arrest you for deserting."

Dr. Gurley's eyes shifted guiltily to Timothy, who raised his glass of spirits at the elder man. "It don't matter to me what your circumstances are, but at least you had the guts to leave them abolitionists."

Gurley turned his glance to Hattie. She murmured in agreement.

Timothy continued in sotto voce, "When you arrive in Richmond, I'll introduce you to Mr. Benjamin and you can tell him personally of whatever was in those papers."

154

Dr. Gurley fell into his chair, taking a long gulp of bourbon. "I didn't actually know what was in them. They were given to me by the secessionists who brought me here. As they were sealed, I didn't open them."

Timothy waved his hand. "Perhaps the people who gave them to you had second thoughts on your loyalty, you once being in the Union army and all, and retrieved them themselves."

Hattie hid her smile by taking another sip. Although Timothy's reasoning made no sense, it seemed to reassure Gurley, who finished his second glass. Her partner's lack of concern meant that he knew the whereabouts of those papers. Not only had he prevented their arrival in Richmond, there was no way for the Confederate secretary of war to receive his message. She wondered who had broken into Gurley's room, however, as Timothy had not left the table all night.

She had no further chance to reflect, however, for Timothy soon rose from the table, claiming that he had to get a decent night's sleep for their journey tomorrow. "And you men should do the same," he told Hattie and Dr. Gurley.

Dr. Gurley was already in the lobby when Hattie arrived the next morning. He made a few expletives as he checked his bag, probably making sure the papers were really gone.

He stood up. "Oh, Mr. Lawton, I didn't know you were behind me." He made no apologies for his bad language, and Hattie wondered if he would be rightfully embarrassed had he known he'd spoke such obscenities in front of a woman.

She offered her condolences for the theft of his papers as Timothy entered the room. "If you want to stay and see if Mr. Miller will investigate, you can. But my companion and I must leave today."

Dr. Gurley gave his bag a small kick. "No, no, that's okay. If the message was that important, the secessionists will find another way to get that information to Mr. Benjamin."

. . .

155

The trio took the coach to a house owned by a Mr. Gough, whom Timothy appeared to know well. Mr. Gough invited them in for supper, telling them that, weather permitting, he could take them across the Potomac that evening. Hattie looked anxiously at the gray clouds gathering above them.

Mr. Gough was evidently not so concerned about the possible storm, for, after a hearty supper, they boarded his boat. Hattie curled into a corner—the rest of the deck was crammed with boxes of various sizes. Mr. Gough told them they contained medicine, weapons, and other goods that were getting harder to come by in the South because of the Union blockade.

It took several hours to cross the wide Potomac and they reached Virginia around midnight. When they arrived at the spot that Timothy named as Monroe's Creek, they were greeted by a Confederate officer. He nodded at Mr. Gough, obviously familiar with the man. Timothy produced the pass from Secretary Benjamin and handed it over. "I'm a courier. And these are my associates, Mr. Lawton and Dr. Gurley."

The man nodded and handed back the pass to Timothy, who pocketed it. Timothy glanced up and down the creek before asking, "Where are all the rest of the docks?"

"We had orders to destroy all docks and boats anywhere there were no pickets placed. It's to prevent the slaves from running away —a fortnight ago we captured more than a dozen trying to escape."

Timothy nodded.

The soldier helped them carry the boxes of supplies to the home of a Mr. Woodward, a partner of Gough's who obviously played a part in his shipment of Union goods into Rebel territory. They slept for a few hours in their clothes, and at dawn, parted ways with Dr. Gurley. Woodward promised to secure the deserter a pass to board the train to Richmond.

Timothy and Hattie started off on foot for the station. The morning was cool and cloudy but mercifully it was not raining. After about half an hour of walking, Timothy stopped at an abandoned farmhouse. "You'll be wanting to make the transition to Mrs. Webster before we get to Fredericksburg." His eyes flashed again. Hattie had the brief notion that Timothy's eye color changed with the territory—she could have sworn they were blue when they left the Union, but now they appeared as gray as the Southern sky above them that morning.

Hattie had never been so grateful to don a corset and petticoat in her life; no matter how constraining she'd once thought they were, they were nothing compared to the bindings she had worn to keep her curves hidden under her jacket and pants.

"How did you manage to confiscate Dr. Gurley's papers?" she asked when she came out of the farmhouse.

"I have another contact who travels in and out of the lines. I took the chance that he was in Maryland and found him on my walk. It was he that snuck into Gurley's room."

"Is your contact another Pinkerton operative?" Hattie paused at a fork in the road.

"Not exactly," he replied, motioning her to follow him down the path on the right, "but I'm confident he will get those papers to McClellan."

They arrived in Richmond at nine o'clock in the evening. The first thing that Hattie noticed when she disembarked was the pungent odor of tobacco that hung over the city. They hastened to the Monument Hotel, where they were to stay for the duration of their mission. A military officer came to Webster's side, watching intently as he wrote, "Mr. and Mrs. T. Webster" in the registry. Webster placed his hand on Hattie's elbow and stepped back as another man who had also been a passenger on the train carefully signed the registry. As Webster picked up their baggage, Hattie noted that the military officer was copying the names from the registry onto a ledger.

Just then another man dressed in a gray suit entered the hotel lobby and, after casting his eyes around the room, walked up to the fellow train passenger. He whispered something into the passenger's ear. The newcomer's eyes kept darting around the room, Hattie noticed. She cast her own eyes downward, but his gaze did not seem to linger upon her. Finally, the two men left the hotel. Hattie was standing close enough to the door that she could watch them walk hurriedly down the street, the train passenger's arms behind his back.

After the men were out of sight, Hattie turned to Timothy to inquire, "What was that about?"

He walked toward the stairs. "I believe it means that man is under arrest."

"Arrest?" Hattie stumbled a bit on the first step. "For what reason?"

Timothy paused to gesture toward the lobby, and presumably, the registry. "My suspicion is that he signed a home address from the North."

Hattie took a deep breath. "Is that enough to warrant his arrest?"

Timothy was occupied with unlocking the door to their room and did not reply until they were inside and the door had been shut. "You have to remember that we are amongst the enemy, and most of the people around here would hang any Northerner on sight."

Though Hattie's stomach was a ball of knots, she was determined not to let her partner know of her apprehension. Her eyes surveyed the room from the desk and chair to the large wardrobe in one corner of the room to the lone bed. Timothy saw her gaze and gestured toward the bed. "It is yours."

"No." Hattie replied. She was under no false notion that her duty was as important as Timothy's. She was only there as his accomplice and that did not necessitate a good night's sleep in a comfortable bed. Still, Timothy insisted and built himself a nest on the floor out of extra blankets he found in the wardrobe. Hattie lay awake long after Timothy's snoring commenced, listening to the sounds from both inside the room and outside, wondering just exactly what she had got herself into.

CHAPTER 24

LORETA

FEBRUARY 1862

*I*t was becoming increasingly apparent that if the South was going to achieve independence from the Union, it would be through a long and bloody war. The terrifying scene at Ball's Bluff had made even Loreta think twice about whether she could continue on as a soldier, but she was still determined to prove herself worthy in the cause for Southern independence. Upon hearing that the Federals were attempting to capture river ports in Tennessee, Loreta, accompanied by Bob, headed that way.

By the time Loreta and her slave reached the Cumberland River, Fort Henry had already been captured by the Union. Everyone knew Fort Donelson would be the site of the next attack and Loreta and Bob were immediately put to task constructing fortifications for the purpose of defending the river. It was tough work conducted in brutally cold conditions, but most of the Rebels were in good spirits, confident that they would be able to defend the stronghold in the way that those at Fort Henry could not. For her part, Loreta was pleased to come upon her old friend Major Bacon, toiling away a few men down. They'd exchanged pleasantries, filling each other in on their adventures since Martinsburg. Major Bacon stated with pride in his voice that he had recently become engaged to a young woman from Leesburg. Loreta wished them good tidings before the hard work made it too difficult to talk much more.

By late afternoon, the Union gunboats were visible on the river below them. "Massa Henry, them Feds look to have quite a large force," Bob gasped out before tossing a shovel full of dirt behind him.

Loreta dug her blade into the ground. "Indeed Bob, but they haven't met as fine and gallant fighters as our forces here."

Major Bacon, obviously overhearing their conversation, ventured to say, "Those Feds need this position. They will stop at nothing to gain it. And the darkey's right," he said, nodding at Bob. "The odds won't be in our favor."

"Still," Loreta stood up, "There's not much we can do now but make this the most impregnable fort those blue bellies have ever seen."

Loreta's enthusiasm waned as the evening wore on. Both Bob and Major Bacon were much better excavators and each could toss two shovels of dirt for every one of hers. The Battle of Manassas, her first battle as Harry Buford, had taken place on a pleasantly warm day in July. She'd been naïve and eager, and hadn't yet experienced the horrors of war seen at Ball's Bluff. Now that thirst had been replaced by misgivings. It felt unseasonable, that war shouldn't be conducted in winter time, and as her comrades continued building the fortifications, she had a feeling that she was being shut in a prison from which there was no escape.

Finally, she cast her shovel aside. Even Loreta was willing to admit there were some, though few, things that men could do better than women and digging trenches in a ground white with hoarfrost was one of them. She righted herself, clutching her aching back with her blistered hands.

"Hey, what say you?"

Loreta glanced back to see a young man standing behind her.

"Tired much?"

Loreta dropped her hands by her sides. "Just winded."

"I won't tell General Floyd you're shirking your duties if you do me a favor."

"What's that?"

"Go on picket duty for me tonight in the trenches. I want to take French leave and go see my girl in town."

Loreta nodded.

It turned out Loreta was even less suited to lie in the trenches in the freezing cold than she was at digging. This she blamed less on the fact that she was a woman and more that she had grown up in semi-tropical climates: first Cuba, and then Texas and New Orleans. But Loreta's pride would not grant her permission to give in, despite the storm that formed overhead, causing the snow and sleet to come in horizontally, stinging her face. She endured, convincing herself that she was no better than the other men in the trench. Their moans turned into cries and then shouts, as the soldiers begged for water, for medicine, for anything to take their minds away from the wind and biting cold.

Loreta folded her arms around her and bent her head, trying to escape the wind. She focused her mind on the stories of her child-hood heroines, most of all Joan of Arc. It was Joan's doing that she was there. All of her life she tried to find an opportunity to prove herself and could scarcely believe it finally had presented itself. She thought that perhaps she would have been a good wife and eventually mother, had William lived. But he hadn't and there had been nothing holding her back from becoming a soldier. She'd been fortunate to be at the right place at the right time to participate in the Battle of Manassas.

Not so fortunate now, though. Loreta came crashing back to a sorrowful reality of aching limbs. Her body seemed to be frozen everywhere. The minutes stretched into hours and the memories of her husband seemed like a thousand years ago. She felt like lying down and giving in to the cold and the wind, wondering if eternity would be warm and sunny. Just when she thought she would totally succumb to her misfortune, the soldier she had relieved returned and she was able to climb out of the entrenchment to seek shelter.

The next day, Valentine's Day, Loreta found herself in the midst of yet another battle. The air was thick with bullets humming fast and furious, severing tree branches, shattering fence rails, and slamming into wagons. Soldiers to the right and left of Loreta fell to the earth. When she heard a bullet whizz by at close range, she thought that the end had finally come and searched herself for the telltale sign of blood.

But the words, "I've been hit!" belonged to Major Bacon.

Loreta tried to catch him as he fell, but his solid body was too much to bear. She sank to the ground with him, her clothing stained with his blood.

"Damn the Yankees! They have killed me," he gasped.

"No, my friend," Loreta replied, touching the hole in his uniform in nearly the center of his chest, knowing that a Minié ball must have lodged in his heart. "You will live to see yet another dawn."

Bacon's body went into convulsions and then he was still. Loreta sat beside him for an unmeasurable amount of time until she became aware of the chaos around her. At the whoosh of yet another bullet, Loreta realized she must leave her fallen friend in order to save herself.

CHAPTER 25

HATTIE

FEBRUARY 1862

Timothy woke Hattie up early the morning after they had arrived in Richmond. The dark circles had disappeared from under his eyes and his countenance seemed refreshed. Hattie felt just the opposite. In silence, they riffled through their respective bags, pulling out their attire for the day and then parted to dress in the hall bathrooms. They re-adjourned in their room before heading downstairs for breakfast. Timothy dug something out of his bag and held it out to Hattie.

"What's this?" she asked, accepting the object, which appeared to be a brooch. "Oh," Hattie said as recognition stirred a desire for her to fling it at the wall. The black and white cockade had come to be an unofficial badge that secessionist women wore in support of their cause.

"If you are to be successful in the role, you must look the part," Timothy said as he adjusted his string tie in the mirror.

After breakfast, Hattie and Timothy went out for what would appear to observers as a leisurely stroll to the post office. Hattie's grip tightened on Timothy's arm as she noticed a man in a Confederate officer's uniform on the other side of the street. Timothy seemed to take no notice of the man as he began whistling, slowing their pace. A few moments later, Timothy stopped to peer into a store window. Hattie looked to see if the man had passed them, but he had also paused, standing parallel to them across the road. Timothy pulled Hattie into the store.

"Is he following us?" she asked once the door had shut. Timothy looked at the clerk, who was writing in a ledger and paid his new customers no heed. Timothy held one finger up to his lips briefly before nodding. The two operatives stalled in the store for a while, Timothy plopping hats on Hattie to try on. They would have made for a passable married couple had anyone else been in the store or the clerk actually noticed them. After approximately fifteen minutes, Timothy declared that they must be going. The clerk finally looked up, seemingly startled that he had customers. Timothy tipped his hat and the clerk followed suit.

Outside, Hattie noticed the officer was sitting on a bench reading a newspaper. She tried to convince her racing heart that this was a perfectly normal thing to do on a pleasantly sunny day. Timothy turned her back in the direction in which they had come. Hattie avoided glancing backward until an intersection gave her the opportunity to do so, at which she spotted the man a few paces behind them. She was now positive they were being shadowed. Timothy must have recognized this fact as well though his face betrayed nothing of what he was thinking.

Timothy led Hattie back to the dining room of the hotel, where he ordered her a sherry and himself a whiskey. He lit a pipe and opened up the paper as Hattie gazed around the nearly empty room. After a few minutes, three men in Confederate uniforms entered and took seats at the bar. Their conversation was loud and easily overheard.

One man, clad in an extravagant officer's coat with gold lace detail said, "I agree with you in principle: it will not do to let a

Southern man set foot on Kentucky soil until the Northern troops disregard the neutrality of that State."

Hattie refrained from wrinkling her lip. She immediately hated everything about the man, from his gaudy get-up, to his large stomach that he seemed content to fill with just liquor, to the fact that he seemed to thoroughly enjoy listening to himself talk. But most of all, she hated that he was a Southerner.

At this, Timothy carefully folded his paper and got up to saunter toward the bar. "Pardon sir, but I couldn't help overhearing your comment. Will you permit me to ask of you a question?"

Hattie sipped her sherry as she watched the trio of officers turn toward Timothy, expressions of mild curiosity on their faces, as the shortest man replied, "Why of course."

"Do you not suppose," asked Timothy, "that Kentucky will allow the Northern army to march through the state without instigation?"

"Not by a jug-full," the older man in the garish uniform responded. "The moment that blue devil Grant crosses the Cumberland river, Kentucky will rise in arms in Southern solidarity."

"And if she doesn't," Timothy mused heartily, "she will prove herself unworthy of any true Southern man's respect!"

At this, the older man's face lit up. He placed his hand on Webster's shoulder as he asked, "May I inquire from where you hail?"

"I was born in Tennessee and raised in Maryland," Webster stated evenly. "I've newly arrived to your fine city direct from Baltimore."

This seemed to please the men as they repeated "Baltimore!" and reached to shake Timothy's hand in turn. Hattie marveled at the ease at which Timothy had inserted himself into the welcoming arms of the enemy.

"I am always glad to meet a Baltimorean," the old man added, "Despite Maryland's poor decision not to secede, I know there is many a true Southern man in that city. May I now inquire of your name, sir?"

"Timothy Webster."

"And a devilish good name at that," the old man said. "My

friends call me Doc Burton." He gestured to his companions. "Allow me to introduce you to Colonel Dalgetty and to Captain Stanley of the Arkansas Rifles."

As if he suddenly remembered her, Timothy indicated Hattie. "And that's my wife, Harriett Webster."

Hattie raised her cup of sherry as Doc bowed toward her. Timothy turned back to the trio. "Gentlemen, I am pleased as pie to know that there is still hope for the fair state of Kentucky." He raised his glass. "To the health of Kentucky!"

One of the other men echoed the gesture, saying "Death to the Yankees!" Webster met each man's glass with what must have been forced enthusiasm, although Hattie couldn't discern anything amiss from her vantage point. She raised her glass again in solidarity, but the men paid her no heed as they clinked their glasses together. "Down with the rebels," she said to herself.

Timothy invited Doc and his companions to dine with him and Hattie. As they were digging into their afternoon meal, Hattie noticed a new man enter the room. She covered her gasp of recognition with a sip of her sherry. Now that she caught a closer glimpse of the man who had been following them, she realized that it was the same one who had arrested the Northern man in the hotel lobby the other night. Hattie's eyes followed him as he went to the bar.

"That fellow is one of the safety committee," Doc commented casually as he refilled his glass.

"Is he looking for someone in particular?" Hattie asked, trying to keep her voice neutral.

"I reckon," replied Doc. "He's always looking for someone. And, thank goodness he is—he does a great deal of good for our cause. A Union man stands no chance around here if the safety committee spots him. They'll hang 'em just on suspicion."

Hattie gave Doc a flirtatious smile. "Indeed, Mr. Burton, I believe in hanging every Union man that comes skulking around these parts. And without a trial."

Timothy shot her an appreciative look from across the table, but Hattie could detect something else lying below the surface. Fear perhaps? Her heart was still racing and it seemed as clear as the crystal on their table that the man from the safety committee was following them.

"Doc." Timothy leaned in. "Will you introduce us to that man? I'd love to show my appreciation."

Doc gave a loud whistle. When the man at the bar looked over, Doc beckoned him to their table.

"Burton," the man said in a gruff voice. "How goes it?"

"Not bad, not bad. I wanted to introduce you to my new friend. This here's Timothy Webster and his wife—"

"Harriet," Timothy supplied.

The man tipped his hat to Hattie and then Timothy. He looked to be in his late 30s. With his dark hair and eyes, he might have been attractive but for a large paunch above his belt. "How do you do, Mr. Webster?"

"I could be better, considering I've heard the Yanks are crawling all over Tennessee as we speak."

"Is that so?" the man replied.

"Tim here's originally from those parts," Doc put in. "He's just returned from Baltimore."

Hattie watched the man's face for any hint of recognition, but his expression was inscrutable. He met her eyes. "And where do you hail from, Mrs. Webster?"

"Kansas."

"Ah." Again the man gave no hint as to what he was thinking.

Doc laughed. "I know you too well, Wes. But I'm going to vouch for my new friends here. Just because they're new in town doesn't mean they're Northerners."

The man attempted a smile but it didn't reach his eyes. "No?"

"C'mon," Doc replied. "Take a break from your duties and sit down with us. You'll see you couldn't be more wrong if you think these two are spies."

The man did as he was bid, introducing himself as Captain McCubbin of the Confederate Military Police.

"Is there an active Union underground of information in Richmond?" Timothy asked.

"Yes," McCubbin replied, helping himself to a bite of chicken with his fingers. "We are working to uncover them, but they seem to be highly organized and elusive."

Timothy nodded. "Those blue devils usually are."

McCubbin swallowed his meat before replying. "Indeed." He stood up from his chair. "I must be going now. Duty calls." He reached out to shake Timothy's hand. "Nice to meet you, Mr. Webster." He tipped his hat to Hattie. "Mrs. Webster."

"G'night, Captain," Hattie replied, discreetly wiping sweaty hands on her skirts as the man left the room.

Hattie soon excused herself as well. When she got back to the room and shut the door behind her, she took a deep breath. It had been a close call, but it seemed they had convinced McCubbin of their authenticity. *For now, at least,* Hattie told herself as she undressed.

CHAPTER 26

MARY JANE

FEBRUARY 1862

Jefferson Davis had initially been appointed president under a provincial government, but last November, he and his vice-president, Alexander Stephens, were elected for a term to last six years under the Constitution of the Confederate States of America.

Mr. Davis's official inauguration speech was scheduled for February 22, George Washington's birthday. The day dawned gray and thunderous, fitting weather for such an occasion, at least in Mary Jane's opinion.

Mary Jane was not invited to attend the ceremony, but Mr. Garvin, as the Davises' coachman, accompanied Mr. Davis and told Mary Jane afterward how the muddy streets were filled with people. "Businesses had been ordered to close and the trains ran overtime. It seemed all of the Confederacy had gathered at the Washington Monument in Capitol Square to witness their President be sworn in." Mr. Garvin went on to tell her that Mrs. Davis had been dismayed by the arrangements he had made for her arrival. He'd ordered four more Davis servants to walk beside the carriage, two on each side, dressed in black suits and white gloves.

"As though it were a funeral?" Mary Jane asked.

Mr. Garvin grinned. "When Mrs. Davis demanded to know why they walked so slow, I replied, 'That's how we always does it for funerals and sich-like,'—as if I didn't know the difference."

"What did she do?"

"She told the men to go back to the house and change their clothes before resuming their normal tasks."

"Was she angry?"

"Nah. I think Mr. Davis was amused, but it seemed to dampen Mrs. Davis's spirits."

"Did Mr. Davis say anything about slavery in his speech?"

The smile disappeared from Mr. Garvin's face. "No. After he accused Lincoln of being barbarous for imprisoning what he called 'peaceful citizens and gentlewomen' for opinion's sake, he then stated that the Confederacy has made no act to impair personal liberty or freedom of speech."

"A lie if I've ever heard one."

"Indeed. But the Southern crowd seemed pleased—their ending applause was louder than even the storm." Mr. Garvin heaved a heavy sigh. "And now the Confederate Government is official."

"But at least they suffered a great loss with Fort Donelson."

"Yes." A hopeful spark gleamed in Mr. Garvin's eyes before it extinguished as abruptly as it had appeared. "I heard that the Confederates have been driven out of most of Tennessee."

Mary Jane clasped her hands together. "Praise the Lord the same will happen to Richmond soon."

Mr. Garvin nodded before bidding Mary Jane goodbye.

That evening, the Davises hosted a reception. The mansion's front hall overflowed with well-wishers waiting for their chance to speak to President Davis. Mary Jane's job was to escort them as quickly as possible into the west parlor, where they were introduced to Mr. and

Mrs. Davis by the President's staff. After Mr. Davis greeted them warmly and his guests expressed earnest wishes for the welfare of the Confederate States, they were then escorted through the central parlor back to the hall and out of the mansion. The Armory Band was stationed on the lawn and filled the air with the notes of Confederate pride songs such as *Dixie* and *Maryland, My Maryland.*

CHAPTER 27

HATTIE

FEBRUARY 1862

*T*imothy soon became a fixed part of the Richmond Confederate Contingency. He wined and dined with important Confederate leaders in an effort to continue the guise of Rebel courier. He'd tour the surrounding camps with his secessionist friends, returning to the hotel late at night to fill out detailed reports regarding troop numbers and movements. He always informed Hattie of the information he'd gleaned.

"What about you, Hattie?" he asked as he was preparing to meet some of his Rebel friends, including Doc Burton, for drinks. "Have you been able to gather anything?"

"Not anything of use. These women will gossip about practically anything, such as getting new fabric from the blockade, the high prices of food, even the weather, anything but the war."

He raised his eyebrows at her. "Is that so different from Chicago?"

"From the women I knew, for sure."

"I know you were great friends with Miss Warne." Hattie felt a tightness in her chest upon hearing Kate's name. "Did you socialize much else?"

She sat on the bed. "Not really. I leased a room in a boarding house, but I didn't really talk with the other boarders often."

He settled into the desk chair. "Pinkerton hinted once that you had an intriguing back-story. I've come to realize that we know very little about each other."

"What of your family?"

He threw back his head and laughed. "I do know that you are a master at changing the subject. I have a wife, Charlotte, whom I've been married to for over twenty years, and two children: one son and one daughter. My son is almost 18 and wants to join the Union army, but Charlotte won't think of it. She says it's enough to fret over losing one man in the war." He sighed. "But of course there's plenty of wives and mothers who are worried about multiple loved ones… on both sides." He stood up, placing his customary hat on his head. "I'd better leave for another suffering dinner with those secessionists." He shot her a grin. "Although I'd probably find your conversation much more entertaining. Maybe someday you'll tell me about your background?"

"My story is not that interesting."

"Oh, but I'm sure that it is. There must be some explanation for the sadness behind those brown eyes."

Startled at his insight, Hattie cast those same brown eyes downward. "Mrs. Atwater invited me to dine with her and a few other wives tonight." She'd managed to garner the friendship of Mrs. Atwater, the wife of Captain Atwater, who was also staying at the Monument, but, as she told Timothy, hadn't been able to pick up any intelligence of worth from her or her associates.

That night proved to be no different. Hattie met up with Mrs. Atwater and her companion Mrs. Mary Chesnut, whose husband was an aide to Jefferson Davis, in the dining room.

As they were served dinner, Mrs. Chesnut told them that last week her husband had two of their slaves arrested for stealing whiskey, but when he'd then heard that they had spent the next few days lying on a cold prison floor without blankets or suitable covering, asked that they be released. She glanced about the room before leaning forward. "He then told the slaves to escape and even gave them money for shoes to run away with."

"Oh," Mrs. Atwater put a hand to her mouth. "What did you do?"

"I told him that he just aided in a felony, but he replied, 'Woman, what do you know about law?'" Mrs. Chesnut gave a tinkling laugh and Mrs. Atwater joined in.

"Did you hear whether the slaves made it to freedom?" Hattie asked.

"No," Mrs. Chesnut returned. "John hired two more to take their place, so I suppose all is well."

Mrs. Atwater wiped her mouth with her napkin before replying, "I'm surprised more darkeys don't try to escape, what with the Yanks so close and all."

"You'd think, to hear all those abolitionists talk, all the Negroes in the South would be marching over the border. But we've barely lost any," Mrs. Chesnut replied.

Hattie pushed her plate away as Mrs. Atwater harrumphed, "They expect from us Southerners a virtue they themselves never exhibited. The Northerners sold their slaves down river to pick more cotton for their mills."

"And they expect their freed colored to work and behave as a white man would," her friend added.

"But of course we know that will never happen." Mrs. Atwater set her fork down. "Why, Mrs. Webster, is something wrong with your food? Your face has gone terribly white."

"I think something at dinner did not sit quite well with me." *Make that multiple somethings.* She removed her napkin from her lap and rose from the table. "I think I will retire to my room and hope that I feel better in the morning." She walked off, part of her regretting that she would have no chance to glean anything of value from the wives. But the other part could not stand to listen to their hateful conversation anymore.

. . .

"Anything new to report?" Timothy asked when he returned to the room that night.

Hattie sat up in the bed, carefully pulling the sheet over her chemise. "Besides the prejudice these women exhibit to the very source of their livelihood? No."

"I'm sorry." Timothy sat down in the desk chair to remove his boots. "I can't stand their talk any more than you. But the good news is that I've been given a pass to head south to Kentucky. I should be able to pick up a good amount of information on Confederate movements, as well as the state of the railroads down there." He began undoing his tie. "Will you be okay here on your own?"

Hattie nodded.

Timothy retreated behind the wardrobe to change, as was their custom. He returned with the blankets and pillows he used to make his roost on the floor. "About your background—"

Hattie reached over to turn out the light.

Timothy's voice had a hint of resignation. "G'night, Hattie."

She lay back on the pillows. "My husband beat me." As comfortable as she had gotten with Timothy, she felt better about talking with the light off, especially as she would not have to see the sympathy that was sure to form in Timothy's kind eyes as she told the story of her marriage and how she came to be under Allan Pinkerton's employ.

"I'm sorry, Hattie," Timothy stated when she finished. "But I am grateful to your brother for rescuing you. There are many in this world who have no choice but to endure that kind of cruelty."

"I know," Hattie said softly.

As she tried to fall asleep that night, she couldn't help but wonder about the fate of Mrs. Chesnut's escaped slaves. She did agree with one thing those women had spoken about: she too was surprised that more slaves didn't try to escape over the border.

Timothy left early for his journey the next day. Hattie went down to have breakfast in the lobby, where she noticed Mrs. Atwater was reading the *Chicago Tribune*.

"Why do you read such Northern trash?" Hattie asked her.

"Because I find it amusing to read the slander they report about us Rebs," she told Hattie. She tapped a headline regarding possible Southern movements. "Besides, this here tells us that there are spies in our midst."

"Spies?" Hattie asked, her heartbeat accelerating.

"Oh yes, there are spies everywhere, how else would they know what type of defenses exist in Richmond?" She leaned in conspiringly. "Do you recall Mrs. Morton's story?"

Hattie shook her head.

"They were living in Washington City when the war started. Mrs. Morton was under suspicion of being a Southern sympathizer, can you imagine? They set that rat Pinkerton onto her."

The mention of her boss jogged Hattie's memory: Pinkerton had Scully and Lewis investigate the house. Although they didn't find anything incriminating, the government exiled the entire family anyway. The Mortons evidently had relocated to Richmond.

"But enough discussion about the war." Mrs. Atwater placed a gloved hand over Hattie's. "I know that Mr. Webster will be out of town these nights. My husband and I are hosting a tea this evening and would love for you to attend."

Hattie's smile was authentic. For weeks she'd been attempting to infiltrate the ranks of Richmond society. So far the ladies had proved unfruitful, but perhaps there would be something to be gained from associating with the fine Southern gentlemen of the Confederate capital.

Hattie took great care in dressing for the tea, choosing her best petticoat and dress, a green and yellow striped calico print. After arriving at the Atwaters', Hattie soon realized that having tea was really a euphemism for downing bourbon aperitifs. When Mrs. Atwater introduced Hattie to her husband, Hattie could tell from his lingering gaze that he would be easy enough to charm. She waited until he was on his second glass of bourbon before inquiring about his purpose in Richmond.

"I oversee the Tredegar Iron Works," he replied. He took another swig of bourbon. "Of course, I'd rather be at the front, killing Yanks, but duty necessitates."

Hattie knew that Tredegar was the largest iron manufacturer south of the Mason Dixon line and assumed that it supplied munitions to Confederate troops. "Oh, I'd love to see where our Rebel guns are made," she said sweetly, adding an eye bat for effect.

He placed an arm across the fireplace, causing him to be closer to Hattie than polite society would approve of. "Of course, I'd be happy to escort you. Would tomorrow work for you, knowing your husband is away on business?"

"That would be delightful," Hattie stated, taking a casual step back.

Atwater dropped his arm as his wife sauntered over. "Caroline, I've just invited Mrs. Webster on a tour of the iron works."

Mrs. Atwater placed a hand over her bosom. "Why, Husband, I've been asking you to take me on a tour for weeks now."

Hattie reached out to squeeze Mrs. Atwater's hand. "I wouldn't dream of going without you."

Atwater cleared his throat. "It's settled then. Tomorrow morning at nine, we will pick you up at the Monument and proceed to Tredegar together."

Hattie straightened her shoulders. "Wonderful."

But when Captain Atwater met her in the lobby of the hotel the next morning, he greeted her with sincere apologies that he had been summoned on another mission. "To see a test of an underwater boat, what they've been calling a submarine," he added.

"Oh, I'm sure I would enjoy that very much," Hattie replied.

Atwater's eyes lit up. "Would you? Mrs. Atwater had no interest and insisted on staying home."

Hattie clamped down her obvious enthusiasm at seeing the Confederate secret weapon. "Well, that is as long as there would be no danger."

"None at all," Atwater assured her. "And I'm sure there will be other ladies present at the waterside."

Hattie seated herself in the carriage across from Atwater and one of his servants. Atwater asked Hattie several questions about her background, which she answered as best she could while the servant remained silent, his eyes cast downward.

When they arrived at the designated spot on the James River a few miles south of Richmond, Hattie noted the abundance of men in Confederate uniforms. As Atwater had predicted, there were quite a few well-dressed women milling about. A weather-beaten dinghy sat in the middle of the flowing river in front of them.

The crowd hushed as a man in civilian clothes stepped onto a platform. He introduced himself as William Cheeney, and began informing the crowd of what they would see. He gestured to a floatation device located near the shore and told them that the submarine was just below. The float had been painted a dark blue, "to match the surface of the water," Cheeney explained. Hoses affixed to the device would supply air to men while they were in the submarine and also while they were submerged outside of the boat. According to Cheeney's description, the submarine would be directed to approach an enemy ship. The navigators—a crew of only three—would then leave the vessel suited in full diving gear and attach explosives to the side of the target. At first, Hattie felt relief: the whole thing sounded far-fetched—like something out of a novel. Cheeney directed their attention to the barely discernible floating apparatus, which had now reached the dinghy in the middle. Cheeney explained that the divers were attaching under-water magazines containing gunpowder. Assignment completed, the crowd stared in bewildered silence as the float moved away from its mark.

Hattie was still watching the maneuverings of the floating device above the submarine when she heard a deafening sound. To the crowd's delight and Hattie's secret horror, the dinghy had exploded. Cinders of what had once been wood and cloth drifted toward the astonished onlookers on shore while the remains of the dinghy sank into the river.

After the roar of the crowd died down, Cheeney explained that the underwater vessel was a prototype. A larger submarine was nearing completion and would soon be targeting the federal gunboats that guarded the mouth of the James River. "The South will be able to move freely, trading cotton and tobacco with England, without the fear of Northern blockades."

Hattie bit the inside of her lip as she realized the lethal implications these submarines could have on the Union. If they took out the blockade, the Confederacy could then turn their weapons of destruction up river to Washington City. *She had to somehow pass this information up North, but how?* Timothy had already left on his courier mission. She was so deep in thought that she did not notice the gray uniformed man shaking hands with Atwater. He lifted his chapeau off his head as Atwater introduced him. "Mrs. Webster, may I present Major Lawton."

Hattie could not prevent her mouth from dropping open in recognition. The man, formerly known as Captain Lawton, the one who featured a prominent place in Hattie's dreams, bestowed a dazzling smile. "*Mrs.* Webster?"

Hattie recovered herself as best she could and offered her hand. "Indeed."

"Have you two met before?" Atwater asked.

Major Lawton's hands were soft as he held Hattie's hand to his lips for the briefest of seconds. "A long time ago. Would you be of relation to Timothy Webster, the Rebel dispatcher?"

Hattie tucked her now free hand into her skirts. "He is my husband."

"Ah," Lawton said. The two once staunch abolitionists stared at each other as the Southern sun dropped lower in the sky. Although nearly four years had passed since Hattie had last seen him, he looked as handsome as ever, as if he had just stepped out from her imagination. Hattie tried to read what was written behind Major Lawton's brown eyes, but he remained inscrutable. *Did he know she was a spy? If so, would he give her away? If not, did that mean he supported the Confederate cause?*

Atwater, as oblivious to the undercurrents flowing beneath him as the ill-fated dinghy had been a few minutes ago, remarked about the staggering possibilities of Cheeney's new submarine.

"Indeed, it presents a great threat to the Union," Major Lawton replied in an ambiguous tone.

Atwater held out the crook of his arm. "I should be escorting Mrs. Webster back to the Monument now."

Hattie curtsied toward Lawton before allowing Atwater to convey her back to the carriage.

"I look forward to speaking with you again, Mrs. Webster," Lawton called. Hattie glanced back to see his expression, but he was facing the water.

When she returned to her room in the early evening, she had written page after page of notes and accompanied them with drawings, trying to recall everything Cheeney had spoken about. She concluded by suggesting the navy employ some sort of way to drag the water if the blue floating device was spotted. This would serve to destroy the tubes that supplied air to the men within the submarine.

Hattie met the Atwaters and a few other acquaintances that night for dinner. The talk, of course, centered on the submarine, but Hattie was hardly listening. Her thoughts floated from finding a way to inform Pinkerton about the plans to blow up the federal ships to Major Lawton and what he had been doing on Confederate soil.

They were finishing up the main course when a new man entered the dining room.

"Major Lawton!" Atwater called. "What a pleasure to see you twice in one day."

He introduced him to his wife. "Major Lawton was at the viewing I was telling you about earlier."

"Ah," Mrs. Atwater replied, holding out her hand to Lawton. "The... what did you call it, dear?"

"Submarine." Atwater supplied.

"Indeed I was," Major Lawton sat down in the empty chair next to Hattie. "Mrs. Webster, it warms my heart to see you again."

Hattie met his dark eyes once again, noting in the abundant candlelight that the lines at the corners of his mouth were deeper than she had once drawn. She resolved to fix her sketch when she returned to her room that night. She figured that once again

Lawton would be a fleeting presence before he disappeared. Although she longed to explain her presence in Richmond, she knew that doing so would possibly put her, and Timothy as well, in danger. *And what exactly was Lawton doing in the Confederate capital, anyway?*

The talk at the table turned to war, as it always did once the men got a suitable amount of whiskey in them.

"They say the Feds are concentrating their efforts on Tennessee," Lawton said. Despite the determined tone of his voice, Hattie had a hard time believing that his convictions could change so easily. She pushed her dessert around her plate with her fork, the fluttering in her stomach from being once again so near to Major Lawton meant that she was unable to eat another bite.

As if one unit, the men rose for their after-dinner cigars. Lawton grabbed for Hattie's hand and placed something in it as he bid her farewell.

Hattie waited until she was back in her room before unfolding the slip of paper. "I need to speak with you," Lawton had written. "Do you have a suitable disguise to meet with me? I'll be on the street bench outside the sweet shop on Main."

Hattie threw on the male clothing she'd worn to cross the Potomac. She put her ear to the door to make sure the hallway was silent before cautiously opening it and peering both ways. After she was sure the coast was clear, she made her way to the stairs.

If Lawton was surprised to see Hattie dressed in male attire, he didn't show it as he patted the bench next to him. She sat enough distance away that they would not be touching, but could still converse in low voices. Despite their earlier relationship, she did not fully trust that he was not a Confederate, and she also did not necessarily trust herself in keeping her cool.

Lawton began by saying, "We have to get information to Washington City about what we saw today."

"You are not with the Southern cause, then?"

Lawton held his hands out, palm up. "How could you believe that is so? Did I not risk my life and limb to help John Brown and your brother cross the country and rescue twelve slaves from a life of torture?"

"And myself."

He relaxed his arms. "Yes. I do not forget the reason you ran."

She nodded. The tone of his voice was even, holding no hint of emotion that she could pick up on.

"And I am familiar with your new husband's underground activities as well," he continued.

"If that's the case, I suppose you also know he is not my husband."

Lawton grinned, his teeth bright in the lamplight of the street. "I have met the real Mrs. Webster. Charlotte is a devoted wife, though perhaps not as pretty as you."

Hattie chose to ignore the compliment. "I've made sketches of the submarine. I have contacts in Washington City."

"Yes, we must get the plans to Pinkerton. He'll be able to pass them on to General McClellan."

"How did you—"

"I told you, I'm familiar with the Union Underground. I'm also aware that Timothy is currently away on a mission. In his absence, I must return through the lines tonight if we are going to get those papers into the right hands. Where are they now?"

"No."

Lawton clearly did not expect this reply.

"Mrs. Webster. Carrie—"

Her given name sounded foreign to her. "It's Hattie, now," she corrected him. She'd changed it upon arriving in Chicago, lest her husband come looking for her.

"Hattie then. Do you not trust me?"

She gazed at him. He looked as sincere as ever, and she knew he was the same person that saved her from an abusive marriage all those years ago. But Hattie had also been treated cruelly by the most important men in her life: first her father and then her husband.

His expression was still inscrutable, but there was a tenderness in his voice as he spoke. "You know I was there when Aaron was shot."

Hattie took a deep breath at the mention of her brother's name. "No, I was not aware of that."

"I was. I even attended the hanging. He died like a man."

Hattie nodded, never having believed Aaron would act any other way when faced with death. "How did you escape?"

He shot her one of his easy-going grins. "I have my ways. But Hattie, if you think I would ever abandon the cause those men died for, that your brother died for, then you don't know me at all."

Hattie, thinking again of Aaron and his blind, if not foolhardy, devotion, blinked back tears.

"Hattie…" Lawton reached out a hand as if to touch her, but then thought better of it and dropped his arm by his side. "You must believe me."

She finally consented. "All right, Major Lawton, you've convinced me." She stood. "Now we need to figure a cover for two men, neither of whom are her husband, arriving at Mrs. Webster's hotel room in the dead of night."

"Hugh," he said in a barely discernible tone, causing Hattie to lean in toward him. "Pardon?"

There was that grin again. "Now that I've officially earned your trust, you can call me Hugh." He got up from the bench and laid a jocular arm around her shoulders. "I think I've had too much to drink," he declared loudly. He leaned heavily on Hattie, his lips next to her ear. "And that's my real name," he whispered.

Hugh kept up the ruse of being drunk as Hattie escorted him to the hotel. Luckily there was no one around. Once they'd arrived at her and Timothy's room, Hattie handed over her intelligence on the submarine.

"These are fantastic," Hugh said, looking over her sketches.

"It's a living," Hattie replied.

"You do a great service to your country, you know. I'm sure Pinkerton and McClellan will agree when I deliver these." Hugh put his hand on the door.

"Thank you."

He looked for a moment like he would much rather have stayed. "Hattie—"

She drew in a deep breath. "You'd better go now if you want to get through the lines before morning."

He nodded. "I hope someday to meet you again. Perhaps not

with you under the guise of Mrs. Webster, though. And perhaps not with you dressed in men's clothing."

For one brief moment, Hattie let go of her reserves. She walked over to Hugh and undid the tight chignon she'd worn under her kepi before embracing him. He wrapped his arms around her, burying his hand in her hair. After a moment entwined, he pulled away with a sigh. "Till we meet again," he said and then closed the door behind him.

Hattie, blinking back tears, retrieved her sketch book and began a new drawing, this time incorporating the look of love that Hugh's eyes held before he walked out of her life again.

CHAPTER 28

BELLE

MARCH 1862

*B*elle threw herself into the Front Royal social scene. She quickly recognized that the women there were not her biggest fans, though she continued to tell of her adventures despite their lack of enthusiasm. The midnight rendezvous with Colonel Ashby had increased her already overflowing confidence in her abilities as a spy. When she heard about a position for a courier in Winchester from her cousin James, Belle volunteered straightaway. She went into her aunt's hotel to locate her latest pet, Lieutenant Hasbrouck, a tall, thin redhead.

"We are friends, aren't we, Lieutenant?" Belle demanded when she caught sight of him.

"Why, of course, Miss Belle. Why do you ask?"

"Auntie has asked that I pay a visit to one of her friends in Winchester who has fallen ill." Belle placed a pale hand on the man's sleeve. "Will you accompany us through the lines?"

"Today?"

"I'm sure Colonel Shields will grant you permission if you tell him it is a favor to me."

Lieutenant Hasbrouck agreed and went off to find his superior.

Lieutenant Hasbrouck had been assigned some business and disembarked from the carriage near the federal camp outside of Winchester before the carriage continued with Belle and Mauma Eliza to town.

Winchester was a contentious area and frequently vacillated between rebel and federal control; it had once changed hands thirteen times in one day! The town was currently under Union control, but Belle was pleased to see that the women of the town refused to bow to their authority. Despite being outlawed, they continued to wear secession cockades and "Jeff Davis" bonnets, gingham hats that had been supposedly designed by Varina Davis herself. The Union soldiers didn't like them because the wide brim concealed most of the wearers' faces from their would-be Yankee accusers. Belle even spotted one woman, after a Union officer passed her on the street without tipping his hat, spit on him. The Yankee went about his business, not noticing the wad of spittle that dripped down the back of his coat. He had to zigzag most awkwardly in order to avoid being targeted by women evacuating soiled chamber pots onto the street.

Belle was not sure who or what her mission was supposed to involve, but James had arranged for her, accompanied by Mauma Eliza, to meet her contact at the home of Mrs. Winslow, an old friend of Belle's mother.

The woman, her daughters, and other neighbors of obvious secessionist sentiments were in the living room, repairing Confederate uniforms.

"Rumor has it that Stonewall Jackson is on his way toward Front Royal," one of the ladies commented.

"Front Royal?" Belle asked. "I just left there."

The woman nodded. "Lord knows we wouldn't mind him returning here and freeing us from these Yanks."

The other women murmured their agreement and Belle spent a pleasant enough evening sewing and chatting about the Southern cause. No other visitors came, and Belle went to bed wondering how she would complete her mission if she didn't know exactly what it entailed.

The next morning, she rose early. The house was quiet and she was surprised to find Colonel William Denny standing in Mrs. Winslow's kitchen. Colonel Denny was familiar with both Belle's father and cousin and Belle had become casually acquainted with him.

He bowed. "Miss Boyd."

"Colonel Denny," Belle replied, a question in her voice.

He bent over to retrieve something from his pack. "I need you to take these letters to the Confederate army outside of Front Royal. This package," he continued, passing a brown parcel to her, "is of great importance."

Belle stacked the letters and the parcel in a picnic basket.

"Lastly," Colonel Denny said, "it is imperative that this letter gets to Stonewall Jackson as quickly as possible. It needs to arrive carefully and safely to him or another high-ranking Confederate. Do you understand?"

Belle bowed her head. "I do and will obey your orders with great haste."

Colonel Denny tipped his hat to her before exiting the house.

Before she and Mauma Eliza left, Belle took stock of the information Colonel Denny had passed her. She folded the most important one, the letter to Stonewall Jackson, into a tiny square, intending on keeping it in the palm of her hand. The large package seemed too conspicuous in her basket, so Belle gave it to Mauma Eliza to enfold it in her skirts, knowing that the Yanks would never search a darkey.

Belle was too preoccupied with arranging Colonel Denny's missives to pay much notice to the servant who had entered the living room, ostensibly to dust, but who also watched the exchange between her and Mauma Eliza.

189

. . .

Belle's next task was to arrange a way to return to Front Royal as she had gotten word that Lieutenant Hasbrouck had been detained on his business. She and Mauma Eliza went to the florist shop, where Belle purchased a fine bouquet to send to Winchester's provost marshal, Colonel Fillebrown, whom she had heard was susceptible to flattery. She wrote a message asking if he might pause his grand duties to write out a pass for Belle to get through the lines. The pass came via Fillebrown's aide-de-camp in less than an hour, accompanied by a note from the colonel himself thanking Belle for the sweet compliments.

Belle and Mauma Eliza secured a carriage and had made it as far as the picket lines outside of town when a repulsive-looking Yankee with greasy black hair and bad teeth stopped them. "We have orders to arrest you."

Belle's fingers tightened around the letter in her palm, but she forced herself to swallow back her fear. "On what reason?"

"We've heard that you have suspicious letters on your person."

Belle blinked hard, suddenly recalling the servant in Mrs. Winslow's living room that morning. The soldier leaned in and gave instructions for the coachman to travel to Colonel Beal's head-quarters.

"Miss Belle—" Mauma Eliza began in a panicked voice as the coachman turned his horses around.

"Shh, Mauma, let me think a bit." Belle paused before opening the picnic basket, pulling out a rose she had intended on sending to Lieutenant Hasbrouck. She placed the handwritten card with the words "Kindness of Lieutenant H," under the twine holding together the packet of letters before unfolding the creased letter to Stonewall Jackson.

When they arrived at headquarters, Colonel Beal immediately demanded to see the letters. Without hesitation, Belle reached into her basket and pulled out the packet that Denny had deemed of least importance.

Colonel Beal ripped open the card. "Kindness of Lieutenant H? What is the meaning of this?"

190

Belle fanned herself with the letter to Stonewall Jackson. "It is for Lieutenant Hasbrouck. It is of no consequence."

Beal dug his fingers under the twine and pulled. Letters of various sizes and a few magazines spilled onto his desk. He picked up a copy of a rebellious news journal and held it between his thumb and forefinger.

Belle attempted a smile as she fanned herself more rigorously.

"What is that?" Beal demanded, pointing at her fan/ letter to Stonewall Jackson.

"This?" Belle asked. She held up the wrinkled missive, the address facing her. "It is nothing." She waited for his reply, thinking fast. There was no way she was going to let Beal's beady eyes note the intended recipient. She would have to rip it up and swallow it the way she'd heard Rose Greenhow once did.

But Beal's gaze refocused back to the letters scattered on his desk. He picked up Belle's hastily scrawled card and ordered one of his guards to fetch Lieutenant Hasbrouck.

"What of these traitors?" the remaining guard asked.

Beal threw up his palm. "Be gone with them. What harm could a young lady and her darkey do?"

And with that, Belle and Mauma Eliza left Colonel Beal's office, Belle clutching her makeshift fan in her hand and the important package still buried within Mauma Eliza's skirts.

CHAPTER 29

LORETA

MARCH 1862

*A*fter the disaster at Fort Donelson, Loreta made her way to Memphis, Tennessee where she was pleased to encounter the dapper Captain De Caulp once again. He invited Harry to go with him and a few other officers to a local saloon. Loreta decided to use the opportunity to ferret information as to the captain's romantic notions.

"Why, my intended resides right here in this fair city," Captain De Caulp announced. "Would you like to meet her? I can arrange for her to be accompanied by a friend if you'd like."

"A friend for that dandy? What purpose would that serve?" The remark had come from the man on the other side of De Caulp, who had been introduced as General Peters. Loreta knew of his reputation: he evidently had a greater fondness for whiskey than he did his own reputation, and consequently spent more time in the cups than at the front commanding his unit.

Loreta set her mug down on the table, attempting to match the general's aggressive tone. "You would be surprised at how many girls appreciate a refined man."

"Are you implying that I am not a refined man?" General Peters rose from his chair with some difficulty and loomed over Loreta.

Loreta had spent enough time amongst the male species to discern that most men with exalted family names who thought themselves great were usually not, and that patriotism was a very thin disguise for egotism. A man who is a true gentleman will continue to act gentlemanly even in the dispiriting midst of warfare, but one who merely claims to be a gentleman will soon reveal the scoundrel concealed within at the earliest sign of strife. Loreta could see that the soldier standing before her would be the latter type—a lackey to his superiors, a bully to those who served under him, a coward during battle, and a thief when given the opportunity.

Loreta did not wish to indulge in his drunken insults, but at the same time, she had no wish to get into a brawl with him. She'd quickly learned at camp, where petty jealousies were even more pronounced than they had been at her all girls' boarding school, that a bully delighted in antagonizing one he didn't think would fight back.

Loreta replied, "See here, sir, I don't want to have anything to do with you, so if you would please go away and let me be. Otherwise I will make it worse for you."

The general's eyes narrowed with inebriated passion. "What d'ya mean 'worse' for me? I can lick you and a dozen more like you." He began swinging his arms wildly. Loreta instinctively backed away as Captain De Caulp stepped in. "I think Harry and I will adjourn for dinner." He grabbed his jacket off the stool. "You men have a good night." He put a comforting arm around Loreta and guided her out of the saloon.

The simple, nonchalant contact from the captain had a not-so-simple effect on Loreta's insides. She thought back to her contention that she'd met every kind of gentleman. *Scratch that*—she never before had met the likes of Captain De Caulp.

. . .

194

After a pleasant supper at a nearby restaurant and the resultant cigars—or cigarette in Harry's case—Captain De Caulp grew impatient and begged Loreta to meet his intended. Not being able to think of a valid excuse, Loreta finally agreed and the two set off down the boulevard.

When they arrived, a servant greeted them and showed them into the parlor. Loreta took a tentative seat, folding one leg over the other perpendicularly, the way she'd observe other men do at such an occasion.

Two young ladies soon entered. As De Caulp seemed more enthusiastic in his greeting to the petite, towheaded Miss Margaret Miller, Loreta tried to converse with Miss Emmeline Carter, a brunette with large, fawn-colored eyes. Miss Carter soon proved herself very reticent and bashful and, as Loreta herself was far from ease, conversation proved incredibly cumbersome. Soon Miss Carter left the room and returned with a darkey bearing a tray of apples. Loreta was grateful for the distraction, for De Caulp and Miss Miller, who hitherto had been in the corner, deep in conversation, came over to enjoy the apples.

"Let's see who can eat their apple the fastest!" Miss Carter commanded.

They each began to chew the fruit down to the core. De Caulp was the winner, Loreta noted, wiping juice off her chin with the back of her hand.

"Now we can read our fortunes." Miss Miller twisted her core in half and then counted the seeds within. "I got five."

"Oh, that means a marriage is in the works for you, Maggie!" Miss Carter announced.

That's the most I've heard her speak all night, Loreta thought.

De Caulp gave Miss Miller an earnest look, which, Loreta noted, she deliberately ignored, rolling her eyes to the ceiling.

De Caulp had three seeds in his apple, which Miss Carter said foretold bad luck. Loreta shifted her eyes to see Miss Miller's reaction. Instead of looking sympathetically at De Caulp, Miss Miller met Loreta's gaze squarely. "How many seeds did you have, Lieutenant Buford?" she asked.

"Four."

She put her hand on Loreta's arm. "That implies a great surprise is in your future."

Her forwardness surprised Loreta, but she was quickly seized with an idea and assumed Harry's best smile before giving Miss Miller a wink.

De Caulp cleared his throat. "Margaret, do you mind if I talk to you?"

Miss Miller gave Loreta's shoulder a squeeze before dropping her hand. De Caulp attempted to seize it, but she folded her arms in front of her as she followed him into the corner.

"What do you suppose they are talking about?" Loreta asked Miss Carter, crossing her fingers out of sight. Miss Miller certainly did not seem to care as much for De Caulp as he did for her.

Miss Carter, clearly resorting back to her shy ways in the absence of the apples seeds, shrugged.

Loreta sat down, watching the couple in the corner. Miss Miller still had her arms crossed, her head and neck held in a stiff posture. Loreta could hear a pleading tone in De Caulp's voice but she couldn't discern what he was saying. His voice rose in protest as he threw out his hands. Miss Miller shook her head.

De Caulp appeared beside Loreta, his voice resigned. "Are you ready to leave, Lieutenant Buford?"

Loreta jumped from the couch. Miss Miller and Miss Carter escorted the two to the door. When Miss Miller bid them farewell, she grasped Loreta's hand with more strength than their brief inter-action had justified and bid her to call again as De Caulp's frown deepened.

Loreta's assumption that her ploy had worked was confirmed when she asked De Caulp what was wrong.

"We had a falling out," he said, a fervent tone in his voice. "She stated she 'did not, could not, and would not, love me.'" He stopped in the street and faced Loreta. "Do you suppose some other fellow is cutting me out?"

Mainly me, Loreta thought, but she threw an arm about his shoulders. "Don't spend too much time thinking about one girl, Captain," she replied. "I'm sure there are plenty of other belles that would fall at your feet."

"Thanks. And, seeing as we're friends, you can call me Tom."

"And I'm Harry."

Tom nodded. "Ain't women damned deceitful things?" he continued. "A fellow has to give a girl so much attention, buying her all kinds of little presents. It takes a sight of trouble and women are so fickle a species that it is almost impossible."

Loreta sighed loudly as a sign of solidarity, but inwardly she was thinking that she would like some male attention and little gifts, especially if they were from Tom. "We ought not to complain about women being what they are. After all, our mothers were women."

Tom shot a grin her way. "True, true. A good woman is better than the best of us men. I suppose we'll have to put up with it."

They'd reached the hotel, and Loreta gave Tom a playful swat. "I wouldn't give up on all women, just Miss Miller."

He nodded. "G'night, Harry."

"Night, Tom."

As Loreta was making her way back to her room, inspiration again overcame her. Grabbing a quill and a sheet of paper, she wrote Tom a letter from the widow Loreta, stating that she was in the area and remembered the kindness he extended when William died. *I'm all alone in a strange city and was hoping to meet up with a friend. Do you suppose we could have dinner?* She named a different hotel and suggested that he come by to visit the next day. She sent Bob down to the front desk to have the letter delivered to Tom's room, making the slave promise not to say who it was from.

Loreta rented another room at the Gayoso Hotel and spent the day purchasing a dress, parasol, and all the trimmings of a well-dressed woman, including the biggest bonnet she could find in order to hide her short hair. The clothing felt foreign and greatly constricting. Loreta summoned a Negro female with hot water so she could bathe and remove her mustache glue. She then used powder to lighten her swarthy complexion. When she was done, the darkey helped her get dressed. "I've forgotten how hard it is to breathe in these things," she gasped as the negress tied her corset.

"Yes'm," replied the darkey.

"Can you also curl hair?" Loreta asked, patting her short coif.

"Yes'm."

"It's desperately important I look my best tonight. I'm about to meet my future husband."

The darkey said nothing as she got to work, coiling the front of Loreta's hair with tongs heated over an oil lamp. Loreta gazed in the looking glass, shocked to see a woman staring back. "I'm beautiful again," she said aloud.

"Yes'm."

Loreta, who had forgotten the darkey was still there, dismissed her with a wave of her hand.

Tom seemed as equally pleased with Loreta's appearance when she entered the dining room that night. As he kissed her hand, he stated, "William always talked about his gorgeous wife, but I had no idea his exalted words would be so inadequate."

Loreta blinked several times, as if to hold back tears. "Oh, my poor William. I've been so lonesome and afraid since his death."

Tom extended a handkerchief to her. "I'm sorry to hear that. I trust his inheritance finds you able to survive?"

Loreta delicately wiped at each eye. "I have enough to get by. My father also put me back in his will after hearing of William's death, although Lord knows what will happen to his investments now that I'm the only heir." She carefully sat in the chair Tom held out for her, unaccustomed to the weight of her skirts. "God rest both of their souls. And tell me about you, Captain De Caulp." She was careful to not call him by his first name. "What have you been doing since last I've heard from you?"

He took a seat across from her and began to explain what company he was in and that he was in the area because they were expecting the Federals to make a move.

"The Yankees?" Loreta put a hand over her décolletage, noting that Tom's eyes followed her movement. "I shall fear for my life."

"Never. I would never let those blue devils harm a woman."

"Of course you wouldn't." Loreta put a flattering hand on his arm, searching for a way to change the subject. "Do you have a girl you will write to while you are at the front?"

"I did, but I'm afraid she is unworthy of my love."

"Oh, how could she?" Loreta dusted off long forgotten powers of coquetry, channeling the masterful Miss Boyd. "I would consider it a most desirable position if I were to be your pen pal."

Tom's face brightened. "Would you now? I would be delighted to have a beautiful woman such as yourself to write to. Have you a daguerreotype I could carry around to remind myself of your face?"

Loreta nodded, digging through her reticule to retrieve one. "I'm sorry it's rather dated—I haven't found the time to sit for a new one."

Tom accepted the proffered picture with an eager hand. "Thank you. I could send one of me to your room if you'd like. The talk is that the Union army is planning to attack Corinth, Mississippi, and I will most likely need to leave for the front soon."

Loreta didn't tell him that she would have no need for his picture as she intended to fight the Yanks by his side, but she replied, "I shall have a hard time forgetting your face, but please do send one to me."

Loreta never received the picture as the next day Harry and Tom, accompanied by Bob, set off for the field. Heavy spring rains had deteriorated the roads and their progress was slow.

Loreta's heart was glad to be near Tom again, and she wished she could reveal herself to him, knowing that to do so would mean giving up her chances at glory. She realized, however, she could get Tom's true opinion of Loreta. "What did you get up to last night?"

"I met up with an old friend's wife."

"Oh?" Loreta put a hint of impropriety in her voice.

Tom glanced at her. "It's not like that. Her husband died, leaving her a widow. And, from what she says, a hefty amount of inheritance." He looked wistfully toward the horizon. "I intend to marry her as soon as I am able."

"You love her?"

"Indeed."

That was enough confirmation for Loreta and she decided to drop the subject, thinking the more he spoke about her, the more tempted she would be to drop the charade of Harry Buford. They had to halt in a small village called Monterey located halfway between Corinth and their destination: a little meeting house just outside the federal picket lines called Shiloh Church.

CHAPTER 30

HATTIE

APRIL 1862

*T*imothy returned a few days later. He'd first gone to Fredericksburg to deliver the Confederate messages, making detailed reports on the troops assembled there before crossing the Potomac at Monroe Creek to drop off said information to Pinkerton in Washington City.

"The Confederate troops are in rather dire straits, with sickness and low morale," he told her. "They've passed a conscription law, meaning that Southern men are being drafted. I've heard people in Virginia speculate that—with their men gone off the plantation—the slaves are going to rise up in rebellion."

Hattie sat up in bed, thinking again of Aaron and Major Lawton. "John Brown would finally be avenged."

"But of course they won't. I'm surprised more slaves don't leave, what with the Union army only miles away. I wish they would."

She gave him a wistful smile. "Someday they will all be free."

He opened his carpetbag and began to unpack. "Anything of note happen here while I was gone?"

Hattie was pleased to tell him that, for once, she had made her own progress. She filled him in on the submarine demonstration and about Major Lawton leaving to deliver the information to Washington.

Timothy nodded. "I had heard that Lawton was in town. But how did he know to contact you?"

"He's an old friend of my brother's."

"Ah," Timothy said slowly. "I didn't make the connection to John Brown before." He nodded to himself. "Lawton's a trustworthy man. He'll be able to get that intelligence to Pinkerton and McClellan. What they do with it from there is not our job, I guess." Webster's tone carried an uncharacteristic bitter note to it.

"What's wrong?"

Timothy sat heavily in a chair. "President Lincoln and General McClellan are at odds with each other. McClellan may be the head of the Army of the Potomac, but politically he is a democrat and, while I wouldn't say he is pro-slavery, he is not exactly against it."

Hattie gasped. "How could that be?"

Timothy's shoulders drooped. "I don't know. McClellan wants more and more power, but Lincoln, probably rightfully so, refuses to give it to him. And Pinkerton, for reasons still unknown to me, refuses to see the general for what he is." Timothy paused to take a long sip of water. "McClellan is excusing his lack of offense on the fact that the Union army is outnumbered, but I can't see how he could possibly think that. In my last report, I put the Confederate forces at around 60,000, yet McClellan claimed they were 200,000, a gross exaggeration."

"Why are the numbers so off?"

"Either the Boss is amplifying the intelligence we give him, or McClellan is lying."

Hattie lay back and stared at the ceiling. "Neither way helps our cause."

"No." Timothy took a long breath. To Hattie, it was not quite a sigh, more of an attempt to get more air in his lungs. "Despite their radically different views, it seems the Boss will back McClellan right into a Southern victory."

Hattie watched as he took yet another long sip of water. "Timothy, are you feeling all right?"

He gave her a sheepish smile. "I'm just tired from the trip is all. A long night's rest will set me right."

"You should take the bed tonight. I'll sleep on the floor."

He set the glass of water on the table and retrieved the quilt he used from the closet. "I would never. You take it. G'night, Hattie."

"Good night, Timothy."

Hattie woke up in the middle of the night to the sound of labored breathing. "Timothy?" she called out in the darkness.

"Hattie," he gasped. "Can you possibly get me a glass of water?"

She retrieved the glass as well as a washcloth, wetting both of them in the hallway sink. When she returned, she knelt beside her partner. "Timothy, you're burning up!"

"It's my rheumatism," he gasped out. "It started after I helped those women cross the river last winter. I guess it's come back to haunt me."

Hattie insisted that Timothy move to the bed and he was too weak to argue. She spent the night in his nest on the floor, snatching sleep in between refilling his water glass and re-wetting the washcloth before placing it back on his forehead.

Timothy stayed in bed all the next day while Hattie fetched the doctor, who confirmed what Timothy had told her. "Inflammatory rheumatism. His joints have swelled to the point where it is difficult for him to walk."

She glanced at the sleeping patient. "Will he get better soon?"

"It is difficult to say." The doctor picked up his bag. "The symptoms come and go on their own, but it is something that will most likely occur off and on for the re of his life. The best you can do is keep him hydrated and make sure he gets plenty of sleep."

"Thank you, Doctor." She escorted him to the door and then grabbed the water glass by Timothy's bedside. As Hattie left the room, she nearly walked straight into a man standing in the hallway. "Oh, sir, I'm sorry."

"Mrs. Webster, it is entirely my fault." He extended his hand. "We've met before, albeit briefly. I am Captain McCubbin. I will be your neighbor now."

"Of course," Hattie said. He was the same man that followed them around Richmond their first morning. She placed a clammy hand into his.

"Is everything all right?" McCubbin asked as he released his grip. "You seem to be in quite a worry."

"It's no matter, really." She held up the water glass. "I was just going to get a drink for my husband."

He tipped his hat to her. "I will leave you to it. G'day, ma'am."

She watched him walk into his room before she retrieved the water.

Timothy woke up when Hattie shut the door behind her. Predictably, he was none too pleased when Hattie told him that a member of the Confederate military police had taken the room next door.

"What do you think that means?" Hattie asked.

Timothy grimaced. "It's probably a bad sign. Perhaps you should return to Washington City and get help."

Hattie shook her head vehemently. "I can't leave you here. We will wait for you to get better and then we will go together." Her mind drifted to Hugh Lawton. If he were here, he would know what to do, but Hattie hadn't heard from him since he left Richmond and even Timothy didn't know how to contact him.

Timothy took a deep breath. "Hattie, just so you know, Pinkerton was afraid this would happen. That's why he had you come on this mission—to be my nursemaid."

Hattie picked at a thread on her skirt. "It's just the same. I'm here now."

Timothy took her hand in his. His grip was weak, his hand cold. "You are better than that. Pinkerton will see that once he receives the information about the Confederate submarine." It was obviously painful for him to talk, and Hattie admonished him to get some rest.

"No," he sighed. "You should be out in the field, not in here taking care of me."

"You will be on the mend soon," Hattie promised. "And then we can both leave here and be back on Northern soil."

Resigned, Timothy lay back. "Just a little longer," he said before he fell into an unsettled sleep.

But even after two weeks of Hattie's constant care, Timothy's health had not improved enough for them to travel. One afternoon, after she'd fallen asleep in a chair with Timothy breathing laboriously beside her, she was awakened by a knock at the door. She opened it to find fellow Pinkerton operatives Pryce Lewis and John Scully. She gestured them inside and then shut the door as quietly as possible.

"What are you doing here?" she hissed with a glance at Timothy's sleeping form.

"The Old Man sent us here. We haven't heard any dispatches for weeks."

"Of course you haven't," Hattie said. She moved toward the bed to reposition Timothy's sheet.

"Ah," Scully began to laugh. "Are we too busy playing love games to serve our country?" he asked, a condescending tone discernible beneath his Irish accent.

"Hush up," Hattie commanded. "It's not what you think."

"Wha—?" Timothy awoke with a start, sitting up straight in bed. His eyes briefly focused on his colleagues before his gaze grew feverish again. He managed to say, "Pryce? John?" before he fell back onto the pillow.

"Tim," Pryce began as Hattie soaked the washcloth in a nearby bowl.

"Now do you see why we haven't been able to communicate?" she demanded. "He is very ill." She placed the cloth on his forehead before turning to the operatives. "You shouldn't be here. You are endangering our cover."

Scully stepped forward, a scowl on his face, but Pryce held up his hand. "The Old Man wanted us to give you this letter." He handed it to Hattie.

"We'll take our leave now," Pryce said with a nod at Hattie.

Just then there was another knock at the door. She glared at her comrades, intending to communicate just how much trouble they'd caused, but they avoided her eyes.

Hattie dropped the letter in a desk drawer before she went to answer the door. "Captain McCubbin," she exclaimed, a bit louder than necessary. "What brings you here?"

"I wanted to check on Mr. Webster's health." His observant eyes landed on Pryce and Scully. "Hello, who's this?"

"Pryce Lewis." He moved forward to shake McCubbin's hand as Hattie wondered if it was a good idea to use his own name.

John Scully did the same, stating that they were businessmen on their way to Chattanooga to discuss a cotton contract.

"They are old friends of mine from Baltimore," Webster added in a weak voice.

"Ah," McCubbin said, obviously catching Webster's implication. "In that case, have you gentlemen reported to General Winder?" he asked as Hattie bit down a rush of nerves.

"No, sir," Pryce replied. "Our permission to travel was granted by Major Beale. We didn't think it was necessary to report to the provost marshal."

"Of course it is necessary to report to Winder," McCubbin stated, spittle flying out of his mouth. "All persons crossing the Potomac must report. I'm giving you official notice."

"Sure thing, sir." Pryce nodded at Scully and the two men exited.

They returned less than an hour later. McCubbin had thankfully left after Hattie reassured him Timothy was recovering from a minor illness.

"No problem," Lewis stated after Hattie had let them back into the room. "Winder told me he was glad to meet any friends of Captain Webster's."

"You need to leave Richmond as soon as possible," Timothy managed to gasp out.

"Boss," Scully replied. "Lewis just said—" he paused and fell silent as a hard knock on the door reverberated through the room.

Hattie went to the door to find that McCubbin was back. This time he was accompanied by a young man in a Rebel officer's uniform.

"Sirs?" Hattie inquired.

McCubbin removed his hat. "Mrs. Webster, I'd like to introduce you to Mr. Chase Morton."

Hattie curtsied before inviting them in. "Captain McCubbin has returned, Timothy," she said.

She couldn't help notice that Scully was avoiding the rebels' eyes. He stepped toward the door and put his hand on the knob, as if he couldn't wait to leave the room. "I must take my leave of you now, Mr. and Mrs. Webster. I can see you have company." He fled down the hallway, leaving the door open behind him.

The room fell into a shocked silence until finally Pryce spoke. "I apologize for my companion's rudeness." He retrieved Scully's coat, which, in his haste, he had left draped over a chair. "I shall go find him and admonish him for his behavior."

"No need for admonishment," the man named Morton stated. "It is clear from your friend's reaction that he recognized me." Morton nodded at McCubbin, who left the room. "And that you recognize me as well," Morton turned his gaze to Pryce.

Hattie's eyes met Timothy's as she handed him a glass of water. She could tell they both were wondering the same thing: who was this Morton and what was his relationship to Lewis and Scully?

"I do not recall ever having seen you before today," Pryce replied. After months of working with the nearly inscrutable Pryce, Hattie could just detect the waver in his voice.

"You don't recall raiding my family's house in Washington and searching through my mother and sister's things?"

Hattie kept her outward expression neutral, but inside she was fuming. *Of course—Morton was the son of Mrs. Morton, the suspected spy that Scully and Lewis had banned from Washington City!* Morton would not have forgotten the faces of the operatives who had accused his mother of being a spy and who had searched through his family's possessions, looking for evidence.

McCubbin burst back into the room, a downtrodden Scully at his side. Another man in a general's uniform smelling of whiskey entered the room. *Provost Marshal Winder*, Hattie supposed.

"Ah, Mr. Lewis," Winder moved forward as if to shake his hand. "How goes Mr. Pinkerton?"

Hattie's gaze once again connected with Timothy. His was pained with more than fever. They were clearly in agreement that their cover had been blown by Pryce Lewis and John Scully. The rebels escorted the two men out of the room as Hattie and Timothy sat in shocked silence, not daring to say anything in case someone was listening.

McCubbin returned to their room the next morning. He barely murmured a word of greeting to Hattie before he pulled a chair beside Timothy. "Strange events that occurred last night, wouldn't you say, Webster?"

"Strange?" Timothy paused to cough. "I don't quite get your meaning."

"Those men, are they friends of yours?"

"I would say more acquaintances," Timothy corrected.

"Spies are more like it. Can you believe it?" McCubbin's gaze was locked on Timothy's, waiting for any sign of betrayal. But Timothy, even in his poor health, gave no sign of recognition. "They were here to deliver a letter. Did they give it to you?"

Timothy's gaze focused on Hattie. "Wife, do you know where that note was?"

She got up to retrieve it, trusting that Timothy knew what he was doing. Hattie handed it over to the detective, who pocketed it and then, after a terse goodbye, strolled from the room.

After he left, Timothy fell back onto his pillow, his reserve spent. "Hattie," he gasped, "You must leave as soon as possible."

"I will not."

His breathing grew even more difficult. "We are in grave danger. You need to leave Richmond before the axe falls."

"I can't." She placed her hand over his waxy, cool one. "We must remain here and hope for a favorable outcome."

Scully and Lewis were put on trial for sedition against the Confederate government. Webster was summoned as a witness and gave testimony from his bedside, stating that both men had been friends of the Southern cause and were not Union spies. But they were found guilty, anyway. Hattie read aloud a newspaper with the headline "Yankee Spies to be Hanged" to Timothy. The article contained both facts and fiction about their apprehension, stating that "the proof of their connection with the secret service of the enemy is most positive." Because they were both British subjects, they were appealing to their government, banking on the Confederacy's determination to gain favor with England to stay their execution. But, as the article claimed, "this will avail them little."

"Now will you leave?" Webster asked when she finished reading.

Hattie was about to refuse again as their door burst open. She rose from her vigil at Webster's side. "Who are you?" she demanded.

"I am Philip Cashmeyer," the man replied. He shook out a paper. "Under the orders of General Winder, you are both under arrest. I am to convey you to Castle Godwin."

The silence in the room was deafening. Hattie refused to give into her instinct to cry out her denial. Instead, she said in a voice as calm as she could manage, "I'm sorry for the misunderstanding. But to take Mr. Webster now would be the death of him. As you can see, he is in no condition to travel."

"I'm sorry as well." Cashmeyer's gaze dropped to the floor. His obviously apologetic manner revealed that he was one of the rebels whom Timothy had cultivated a friendship with. "My orders were to retrieve him, dead or alive." He whistled and two Confederate officers immediately appeared in the doorway, their bayonets directed at the inhabitants of the room.

"My wife is innocent of all charges. You cannot mean to condemn her to my fate," Timothy declared in a halting voice.

"Nonsense, Husband," Hattie moved toward him. "I intend to accompany you."

Cashmeyer nodded. "My orders are for both of you."

"What are the charges?" Timothy demanded.

"I'm afraid I am not privy to that information," Cashmeyer replied, opening the door. Hattie bent forward to help Timothy to his feet as Cashmeyer and the soldiers watched.

CHAPTER 31

LORETA

APRIL 1862

General Sidney Johnston ordered his Confederate army of Mississippi to attack the Union army of the Tennessee stationed at Pittsburg Landing on April 6th. The Yankees were not expecting them. As the Rebel army rushed out of the woods into their encampment, men half-dressed in blue uniforms sleepily reached for nearby rifles. In only a few minutes the Confederates took possession of the camp and Loreta sat down to consume a still-hot breakfast that a Federal officer had been forced to abandon.

She had just finished eating when Tom De Caulp came upon her. "Well, Harry, now that you have been fortified with a healthy breakfast, what are your plans for the rest of the day?"

Loreta could feel her face grow hot and put the bowl down. "Sir, I am anxious to do my share in battle, and request to be placed where there is ample chance of combat."

Tom nodded. "There's still plenty of fighting to be done and we will wait to see what action we can bring about."

In short time, the command was given for them to advance and Loreta experienced an unfamiliar anxiousness. She had never worried about her own fate in battle before, but for the first time, she fretted for the safety of another. She forced herself to bury her feelings of uneasiness so that she could fight with even more vigor than ever. Though Tom couldn't have known the man beside him was the same woman he'd pledged to write to, Loreta was determined to win his praise.

The Confederates rushed through the lines with unfaltering perseverance. To Loreta, it seemed they cut the Federals down as methodically as a mowing machine sheared grass. Before long, much of the enemy lay on the ground in every position imaginable. The wounded who could still speak begged the assiduous rebels for help, to no avail. Loreta glanced down as she passed over a deceased Yankee, his eyes wide open, staring at eternity.

Upon spying a crowd of Confederates gathered around a fallen man in an officer's uniform, Tom shouted at one of the men standing helplessly, "Who lies there?"

"General Johnston," the soldier replied.

"Is he dead?"

The man merely shook his head and waved at them to continue on.

In the late afternoon, a rider came up to Tom shouting "Halt! We have orders to halt!"

"Halt?" he repeated. "Who gave this order?"

"General Beauregard, sir."

"Where is he stationed?"

"Shiloh Church."

Tom scratched at his beard. "Is the general aware that the Yanks have been pushed all the way back to the landing? One more blow and this will be another victory for the rebels."

The man turned his horse and called, "These are the orders, sir," before riding off.

Tom shot a bewildered look at Loreta, who shrugged.

They retreated back through the Union camps, which were

nearly abandoned. After Tom's men took prisoner the few Yankees they found lingering, the men in his unit began rummaging through the cache left behind, confiscating boots, clean shirts, and even Federal dollars, which were plentiful in the tents.

Loreta sat by the campfire to eat her second ample meal of the day.

"You Rebs don't know what you have in for you." Loreta looked up to see that the voice had come from an exceedingly dirty Yank in an equally soiled uniform. He sat nearby on the ground with his arms tied behind him.

"Is that so?" Loreta spoke with a mouthful of gruel. "What say you?"

"I say nothing to slaveholding coots."

A plan popped into Loreta's head. She set her bowl down. "If you must know, I own no slaves. They forced me into the army. The first opportunity I have to desert, I will." She placed a hand over her heart. "Or if they take me prisoner, I'll be glad to pledge an oath to Union."

The Yank smiled an oily grin. "You might have such an opportunity sooner than you think."

Loreta picked up a loaf of bread and walked closer to the man. "How so?" She broke off a piece of bread and stuffed it into the man's mouth before tipping her canteen toward him.

Water and crumbs dripped from the man's mouth as he told her that the Feds were expecting General Buell to arrive that night with reinforcements.

Loreta did not bother to reply. She dropped the bread beside the soldier and immediately went into Tom's tent. "Sir, I have information from one of the prisoners that the blue devils are expecting more men to arrive this evening."

Tom sighed. "I knew it was a mistake not to press forward."

"Sir, with your permission, I'd like to get closer to the Union lines to try to get an idea of their movements."

"Harry, while I commend your fortitude, that's an exceedingly dangerous proposition. The colonel would never agree to it."

"The colonel does not have to know."

Tom finally consented, knowing that if the rumor was true, the Confederates would possibly lose their advantage.

Loreta approached the riverbank by keeping close to the ground and frequently pausing when she heard a noise, at times crawling under bushes to avoid being seen. As Tom had predicted, the Feds crowded at the landing above had no means of crossing the river, and, had the Rebs pursued them, could have pushed their advantage and caused a repeat of Ball's Bluff. It angered her that General Beauregard had allowed the opportunity to inflict another crushing defeat upon the enemy slip by.

Loreta watched in disgust as a steamboat arrived with fresh bluebacks. She crept on her elbows and knees to get a better view as yet another boat appeared and more enemy troops unloaded. She was close enough to smell the steam and hear the bells directing the troops to disembark. She was about to report back when she saw a smaller boat pass by. This one only had two officers in it. She shielded her eyes against the moonlight to get a better view, recognizing one of the men from his picture in the newspaper articles on Fort Donelson. She could hear the pitch of their voices, but the splashing of the oars and the chirping of the crickets beside her made it difficult to discern what they were saying. Loreta grabbed her pistol and took aim. General Ulysses S. Grant had been declared the hero of Fort Donelson, and half of her wished that he not be declared a hero ever again.

But the other half of her would not let her pull the trigger. It was too much like murder. She watched as the boat floated out of range. When the general boarded one of the gunboats, Loreta rose from her position, her knees aching, her shoulders lowered in defeat.

Tom was predictably disappointed to hear about Loreta seeing the Yanks' reinforcements arrive, but he convinced her that she could not go to headquarters with her report, assuring her that General Beauregard would be well aware of their arrival. "You should get some rest now, Harry. Something tells me tomorrow will be a difficult day of fighting."

Loreta left, her reluctance doubled—not only was she upset that she couldn't tell the general what she saw, but also because she would have given anything to be able to linger in Tom's tent. But she knew that Tom was right: she risked being arrested if any high-ranking officer knew that she'd been behind enemy lines without the general's permission. Not to mention that would put Tom in danger for having given his friend Harry consent to do so.

Loreta tossed about all night. Her agitation was soon replaced by regret that she couldn't bring herself to shoot General Grant.

Loreta rose at dawn to the ominous sound of Federal gunboats firing. The Union army, which had been nearly annihilated just the day prior and who should have retreated in defeat according to the rules of war, managed to recover its lost ground and assume the offensive. By two o'clock, Loreta knew the day had been lost.

"It is useless now," she confessed to Tom as they withdrew into the woods. "We should have pursued them yesterday."

"It is not up to us, we were following the general's orders."

"Indeed. Soldiers may lose their lives, but generals lose the war." Loreta had not sooner gotten the sentence out when a Minié ball hit the ground beside Tom. Time seemed to slow as she watched her beau's body rise into the air and then land nearby with a sickening thud.

"Tom!" she screamed with a woman's voice, rushing to his side. He was still breathing, but barely. "Tom, Tom, Tom," she repeated as she checked for bullet wounds.

His eyes stared up at the sky. "Harry, you've got to get out of here."

"Not without you." She attempted to lift him to his feet, but he was considerably heavier than her.

"My leg is broken," he gasped. "I can't walk."

Loreta looked back to see bluebacks advancing on them.

Tom turned his face to the side. "Harry, you've got to go."

"Drop him and run!" another Confederate called. "The Yanks are coming. He's as good as dead anyway."

When Loreta refused, the man grabbed her arm, jerking her

away from Tom. When she glanced back, she saw Tom raise his hand briefly before letting it drop again.

Although the Yanks were victorious, they did not push the Confederates back much further than Shiloh Church. The battle was over by dusk, and Loreta resolved to go back to find Tom. She found Bob at camp, who had managed to confiscate a horse. The steed carried a branding of "US" on its quarters and the saddle was made of fine leather—an officer's horse.

"I found him in the woods without a rider," Bob stated.

"Thank you, Bob." Loreta mounted him, accepting Bob's proffered lantern, and filled her canteen before going back to where she had last seen Tom. As if to add to the day's miseries, the sky opened and rain began pouring down. The bodies in the field lay so close together that Loreta had to tie her new horse to a tree and walk among the slain, searching for her beloved. Occasionally she would come upon a man who was still alive and, after offering him water, called out to the ambulance corps, "Over here!" The men with stretchers would eventually arrive and carry the wounded off. They were Confederate, but Loreta noticed they would occasionally pick up Union men as well.

When her canteen was halfway empty, she resolved to save the rest for Tom. She heard a woman's voice and marveled that they would send nurses to the battlefield, but as they crept closer, Loreta saw they were ladies in civilian clothes. Like her, they shone their lanterns onto to reveal the faces of the bodies as they stepped over them.

Loreta thought she had an inkling of where they had been when the Minié ball hit, but with the rain and the darkness, she could not get her bearings. It was as if she were trying to find a four-leaf clover in a field of grass. She was exhausted from the battle and after an hour of searching in the pouring rain, had to force herself to quit before she became yet another body on the ground. She had just started for her horse when she heard one of the ladies emit an unearthly scream. Loreta watched as the woman sat down on the muddy ground with a dead man's head in her lap and cried, "Oh my Samuel, my poor husband." She stroked his hair as she repeated, "My darling," over and over. Her companions rushed over to kneel beside her, wrapping their arms around the anguished woman. Loreta could stand it no longer and mounted her horse, vowing to return once again in the morning to search for her own loved one.

CHAPTER 32

MARY JANE

APRIL 1862

*M*ary Jane had just arrived at the Big House for the day's work when a courier ran into the dining room. Jefferson Davis was already seated, ready to receive his breakfast.

"Shiloh is lost!" the courier shouted. He bent over to take in a breath before continuing, "Our troops are retreating."

Mr. Davis stood up. "How can that be? News last night was of a sure victory."

"Sir, General Sidney Johnston… was," the courier gulped. "Lost."

"Lost? As in taken prisoner?"

"No sir." Mary Jane raised her eyes to see a forlorn look on the young man's face.

"As in dead, sir. And the number of lost troops is the greatest we've seen. On both sides, it appears."

Mr. Davis sat down and buried his stricken face in his hands.

The courier left him alone. Mary Jane, unsure of what to do, fetched him a cup of coffee.

He looked up at her when she put the saucer and cup in front of him. "Has Mr. Harrison awoken yet?"

"No suh, I don't believe so." Burton Harrison was Mr. Davis's personal secretary and had a room on the third floor of the mansion. "Do you want me to rouse him?"

Mr. Davis nodded and Mary Jane went to find Mr. Garvin in order to get Burton Harrison presentable.

CHAPTER 33

LORETA

APRIL 1862

*A*fter yet another sleepless night, Loreta rose to find that the Confederates had been ordered to retreat back to Corinth, Mississippi. Loreta volunteered for burial duty, thinking that it would give her one last chance to locate Tom's body and give him a proper goodbye. But still she could find no trace of him.

They dug large trenches with garden hoes and laid the boys on top of one another. There was no time to dig individual graves, nor were the gravediggers in the right state of mind to do so. One of them carried a small notebook and would copy down names of any soldiers that were recognized by their comrades, but most of them went into the ground unidentified. They were covered by as many blankets as could be found, and, after a brief prayer, the men commenced covering them over with soil.

Presumably the Feds were burying their own as well, but every once in a while, a shot rang out. As no bullets landed, at least not near the diggers, Loreta did not pay much attention to the gunfire. But when they had nearly finished their mournful duty, a shell landed behind Loreta, and she was thrown to the ground.

A nearby soldier helped her to her feet. "Are you all right?"

Loreta glanced down, noting the man who had been next to her had been propelled into the mass grave. He made no motion to get up. Another soldier commented that "he'd thought they'd been done but this new one needed more dirt."

Loreta felt sick to her stomach. At first she assumed it was from the shock of what just happened, but then she realized her right arm had gone numb. The soldier who had picked her up noticed as well and helped her back up on her horse, and then began leading it back to camp. The next hour was agony—every time the horse made a sudden movement, the pain in her arm heightened. As they neared, Loreta's anxiety grew. She knew that she would need to be examined by a surgeon, who would possibly discover that Harry Buford was not who he said he was.

By the time they reached camp, Loreta's arm and wrist were so swollen that the surgeon had to cut the sleeve off her coat. He brought a vat of cold water for her to soak her wounds in, but it gave little relief. The surgeon pulled it out to examine it, Loreta gasping in pain. He gingerly held her wrist in his hands and turned it over.

"Such delicate bone structure," he said, looking up from his attendance into her face. "Your mustache seems to have come loose as well, Lieutenant."

Loreta could tell by the tone in his voice that he had discovered her secret. At that point all the fortitude and valor that Harry had exhibited in the last year had disappeared. All she wanted to do was to allow her arm to heal, and if she had to do that as a woman, then so be it.

"All right, you've discovered my secret," she told him. "That doesn't change the fact that I am wounded."

The doctor sat back for a moment. "How did you come about—"

"Please," Loreta commanded, her voice shaky with pain.

The doctor shook his head, obviously disagreeing with her choice to deceive the Confederate army, but his duties came first. "Your shoulder has been dislocated and much of your hand and arm, including your pinky, has been lacerated from the shrapnel."

"Tell me you won't amputate it, sir."

"The wounds will not require amputation." The doctor managed a tiny smile. "I'm sure you would have come up with quite a story, however, if you were a woman with an amputated arm." He applied dressings to the open wounds and then put her arm in a sling. "I believe that will do it for now," he said, rising.

Loreta got painfully to her feet as well. Despite his words, she did not fully trust that the doctor would not reveal what he'd discovered. Not to mention there was nothing keeping her there now that Tom was gone and she had been wounded. "Please sir, is there any way you can secure a pass for me to travel to New Orleans? I want to go home."

"New Orleans is quite a long way from here. I suggest you stay in Corinth until you are healed."

"Sir, I need to get away as soon as possible." She gave him a pleading look, hoping to appeal his sense of chivalry.

It seemed to work as he nodded. "I'll see what I can do."

In her haste to leave the area, she temporarily forgot about Tom. She fell asleep on the train, the sheer exhaustion of the past few days overcoming the pain in her arm. She awoke when the train arrived at Grenada, Mississippi, and disembarked, still in her now ruined soldier's uniform. The station was in a state of chaos, with people waiting to receive the wounded or corpses that had been managed to be removed from the battlefield.

"Please sir," a woman touched her good arm and shoved a tintype of a young man in Loreta's face. "Do you know my Bernard?"

As Loreta shook her head, she was accosted by many more women carrying pictures of men of various ages. The pain in her shoulder mounted as Loreta had no choice but to witness the grief of these poor souls upon not hearing news of their loved ones. She guessed that some of those boys being inquired about were back in Shiloh in the mass graves that had been hastily dug and she was filled with shame and sorrow. "I'm sorry," she said, pushing past the crowd, cradling her bad arm close to her.

CHAPTER 34

HATTIE

APRIL 1862

*H*attie and Timothy were conveyed to Castle Godwin, a former Negro jail in what was called "Lumpkin's Alley." They kept up the ruse of being married, and were allowed to stay together, sharing their second-floor cell with a few other men and women who had been accused of passing information to the Union.

Timothy was charged with being an enemy alien to the Confederate States and of lurking around their armies and fortifications. He was put on a trial, which lasted a few days. Because of his poor health, he only occasionally attended in person. He was there the day that Lewis and Scully testified, telling Hattie that Lewis had insisted he had never met Webster before the incident in the hotel room. Scully, however, had made a full confession, including identifying all of them as Pinkerton operatives. "Including you," he told Hattie with a sigh.

She nodded, knowing that even the Confederates would not execute a woman. Timothy, however, was another story. On Friday, April 25, Timothy was escorted from his cell by armed men as Hattie looked on helplessly. When he returned at dusk, thrown back into the room by the same men, he related to Hattie that he had been taken to City Hall where the official verdict of his case had been read to him. "Guilty," he said, his voice as stoic as ever. "They sentenced me to death. I'll be the first spy to hang since Nathan Hale during the Revolutionary War."

"Oh, Timothy, surely Mr. Lincoln will be able to exchange you for a Confederate spy and you can return home."

"When they asked me if I had any last requests, I asked to be shot by a firing squad instead of dying a traitor's death."

She took his hand in his and they sat in silence. After what felt like an eternity, but was in reality probably less than an hour, a guard entered. "I'm here to move Mr. Webster to the condemned cell."

Hattie rose. "Oh, please, sir, can he not stay here?"

The man held the cell door open. "I have my orders."

The days, the last of Timothy's life unless Hattie could help it, dragged by in a monotonous blur. Even his Rebel guards managed to take pity on them and allowed Hattie into his cell for a few minutes a day. She tried her best to clean it, but the smell of decay and dying men was not something she could wash away. Every night she prayed for her friend, but she searched her mind for something more she could possibly do to save his life.

CHAPTER 35

MARY JANE

APRIL 1862

$\mathcal{M}$ary Jane was dusting the bronze busts in the hallway when Mrs. O'Melia answered the door. The man standing there introduced himself as a prison guard. "I bring a request to Mr. Davis from a Mrs. Webster, held of late in Castle Godwin."

Mary Jane was aware the Websters were a husband and wife team that had been arrested on suspicion of betraying the Confederate government.

Judah Benjamin had just exited Mr. Davis's office and overheard. "You can tell that damned traitor that the President of the Confederacy is too busy plotting the Union demise with Bob Lee to pay the wife of a Union spy any heed." He marched past the bewildered prison guard, who then cast a helpless look at Mrs. O'Melia.

Mrs. O'Melia's face softened in sympathy. "That poor woman," she muttered to herself. She tapped a hand on his chin before telling the guard she'd be right back. She disappeared into the interior of the house and came back a few minutes later with Mrs. Davis.

"How can I help you, sir?" Mrs. Davis asked.

"Ma'am," he bowed. "I'm sorry to bother you, but I brought a missive from Mrs. Webster, a prisoner who pleas to save her husband." He handed a piece of paper over to her.

Mary Jane moved her dusting to just inside the central parlor so she could read the expression on Mrs. Davis's face. She read the letter quickly before handing it back to the guard. "It's a terrible fate to suffer, but it's also a terrible thing they've done, spying on our government like that."

"Yes'm," the prisoner guard agreed. "I understand."

"In this case, I don't think I can offer much assistance. Matters of state are first men's work, and then God's."

"Thank you anyway, ma'am." The guard tipped his hat and then left.

Miss Lizzie had been incensed upon hearing of the arrest of Mrs. Webster and a few other "good ladies of Richmond" who were being held prisoner. "It's no good, I tell you Mary Jane, no good at all."

Mrs. Thompson, the seamstress, paused in her examination of a crumbling hem. "If they are arresting women now, it will only be a matter of time before they get to us."

"Nonsense," Miss Lizzie snapped. "What right do they have to suspect an old spinster, a widow seamstress, and a servant?"

"Slave," Mary Jane corrected her. "I am not paid for my services."

"Not in money." Miss Lizzie raised her eyebrows. "What news do you have for us today, Mary Jane?"

She told them of the prison guard's visit.

"Typical," Miss Lizzie shook her head. "If Varina Davis had any sense, she would have divorced that traitor long ago."

Mary Jane, thinking of Jeff Davis's ill health and daily anxieties, did not reply.

"I hear that they are going to make a public spectacle of the hanging," Mrs. Thompson stated.

"A warning to the Richmond Underground," Miss Lizzie added.

Mrs. Thompson nodded. "They're building the gallows on the city's former fairgrounds at Camp Lee."

"That poor Mrs. Webster." Miss Lizzie nodded resolutely. "I must pay her a visit and offer her my service."

CHAPTER 36

HATTIE

APRIL 1862

They allowed Hattie to say goodbye the morning of Timothy's execution. Timothy's form had grown even more ashen and gaunt than it had been before the trial. She hugged him to her, careful of his frail body. She tried not to let him see the tears that had formed, wanting to show him that she could stay strong, even in this, the face of his death. "I'm sorry," she said once she was sure her voice would be steady.

"Me too," Timothy said. "I'm sorry you are being punished." Hattie had been found guilty of "conspiring with an alien enemy" and was sentenced to a year's imprisonment. She attempted a smile. "It's all part of the job." She'd meant it to be funny, but, after the sentence left her mouth, she realized her mistake.

When Timothy didn't reply, Hattie's next words caught in her throat. "I will send word to your wife as soon as I can."

"No." Timothy's words were firm. "Not until after you've been released. You cannot compromise your identity as Mrs. Webster."

Hattie nodded, wondering if his family had any notion as to what had happened. *What was going to happen.* It was possible they had no idea their husband and father was about to be put to death. Perhaps they were under the impression that Webster was still undercover, working to expose Confederate plans in favor of the Union. *If only...*

Timothy must have caught sight of the wistful look on her face. "Don't you worry about me. I'm not afraid to die a martyr to my country. Have you ever passed through a tunnel under a mountain?"

Hattie nodded, thinking of the time she'd accompanied Lincoln on his journey, before the war began, when she had been filled with hope and ambition.

Timothy continued, "My passage, my death may seem dark and ominous, but beyond is light and bright."

Hattie lost the battle with her tears. They slipped down her face as she thought about the great man the Union would lose when Timothy died.

"Mr. Webster?" a voice inquired. Both Timothy and Hattie turned to see a brawny man dressed all in black beside the open cell door. "I am Captain Alexander. I've come to escort you."

Timothy used the crutch they had provided him to get to his feet, carefully balancing himself as he leaned in to Hattie. "Tell Major Allen that I can meet death with a brave heart and a clear conscience." He kissed Hattie on the forehead. "Goodbye my friend."

Captain Alexander offered Timothy his arm, but he politely refused, instead hobbling out of the room, and Hattie's life, on his own.

Hattie did not move from her bed all day. In the late afternoon a guard announced that she had a visitor. She sat up in bed and told the guard to allow the visitor in.

Hattie did not recognize the older woman with the crafty blue eyes. "Yes?" she asked, cautious that it was a Confederate woman there to gloat over Timothy's death.

"I am here to bring news of your husband."

Hattie stood. "Did you attend his execution? Did they allow him to die like a man by a firing squad?"

"No. He was hanged, and I'm afraid the noose slipped."

Hattie took in a hopeful breath, but the woman held up a gnarled hand as she continued, "the first time. When they prepared him again, he told the crowd, 'I suffer a double death.' But he died bravely, no matter what you might read in the papers tomorrow. They are determined to vilify him as a traitor. They left him hanging for half an hour. When they finally took him down, some of the spectators cut pieces of the rope to keep as souvenirs."

Hattie nodded, the tears threatening yet again. She wished the Richmonders could have known the type of man Timothy had been. Enemy or not, he deserved as much respect in death as he did in life.

The woman offered Hattie her handkerchief.

"Mrs. Webster, the body of your husband has been brought back to the prison." Once again the black-coated Captain Alexander had appeared without warning. This time he was accompanied by a large bloodhound, whose coat was predictably pitch-colored. "Ah," the captain said, turning his eyes to Hattie's visitor. "Miss Van Lew can escort you to the viewing if you'd like."

It seemed to Hattie that Miss Van Lew's eyes turned cold and icy. "That's quite all right," she said in a haughty tone. "But I would ask if it would be possible for Mrs. Webster's sentence be carried out in my home."

"I think you've done quite enough for our Yankee prisoners of late, don't you agree, Miss Van Lew?"

"No," the old woman replied. "It's never enough."

Captain Alexander kept his beady black eyes on Miss Van Lew's back as she left the cell. "Mrs. Webster?"

Hattie followed him to a room in the rear of the prison. Timothy's lifeless body lay on a table. There were rope burns around his wrists. She reached out to touch one of the bruises on his neck. "I am sorry, Husband," she said aloud. After a moment, she turned to Captain Alexander. "How will he be buried?"

He shrugged.

"I'm going to purchase him a metal coffin. Could it be arranged for his body to be sent North?"

"I doubt it," the captain replied. "He angered a lot of higher-ups in the Confederate government in his betrayal. I don't think they are inclined to do him any favors."

Hattie sighed, thinking his statement was a testament to Timothy's skill as a spy: he'd earned their trust and respect, and their resentment was born out of embarrassment. Hattie said one final, tear-filled goodbye to her friend before Captain Alexander escorted her back to her cell.

CHAPTER 37

LORETA

APRIL 1862

*L*oreta stayed in Grenada for a few days recuperating until her fever had subsided. The pain in her arm was still overwhelming, but she was resolved to continue on to New Orleans, only stopping for a few hours when the aching became too great to remain on the train.

Loreta felt almost too unwell to keep up appearances, especially considering her uniform had been badly battered and her mustache was the worse for wear. Almost as soon as she returned to the city of her youth, a large man in a police uniform commanded that she come with him, telling her that she was under arrest.

"What are the charges, sir?" she demanded in a tone that she hoped covered her anxiety.

The officer did not reply, and she soon found herself in front of Mayor Monroe, whose squinty eyes were fixed on the arrest papers in front of him. "Lieutenant Buford, you are under suspicion of being, in fact, a woman." He finally looked up, gazing at Loreta with interest. "You are ordered to change your apparel immediately."

His pompous manner angered Loreta. "Sir, you will have to prove that I am a woman first."

Loreta saw with delight that her challenge seemed to disconcert the mayor. He pushed back his wild dark hair, revealing a receding hairline. She took a seat as he left his desk, summoning someone from outside his office. Loreta watched Monroe scratch at his long beard that was more gray than black as he conferred with the unseen person. He nodded and bid his conspirator adieu before returning. "I'm confining you to prison until we can decide who you really are, once and for all."

Though horrified at the sentencing, Loreta was still unwilling to give herself up as a female, and left the office without another word.

She was taken to the Parish Prison. Luckily a guard summoned the prison doctor, who set Loreta's arm and redressed her wounds. He was a quiet man and promised not to inform anyone of the fact that she was female, especially after Loreta gave him some money for his services. But a few days later, the local paper printed a story of a woman arrested in a soldier's uniform. A guard let her read the article, which was almost an afterthought, taking up only a small portion of the interior of the paper. The article did not state either her real name or her alias. She folded the paper, and then looked up, startled.

"Is this true?" she asked the guard, pointing to the headline claiming that Union gunboats had broken through the Confederate defenses on the lower Mississippi.

"That's the rumor," the guard replied. "If it's true, it won't be long before the Yanks occupy the city. Most of our troops were called to hold the forts. We don't have much defense left."

Loreta's fear of being taken as a soldier prisoner by the Yankees overcame her indignation at Mayor Monroe. She'd been operating under the premise that the best way to keep a secret was to not tell anyone, but perhaps now was the time to reveal. "Is it possible for you to let the Mayor know I'm ready to confess?"

The guard walked closer to her cell and peered at her. "Are you really a woman?"

She nodded, and the guard left immediately. He returned a few minutes later and unlocked her cell, stating the mayor was ready to see her.

Mayor Monroe was sitting behind his desk in the same position as she had last seen him, but this time he held an expectant look on his smug face. "Well, miss, I'm told you are ready to confess."

Used to spinning stories, Loreta again told partial-truths: that she had decided to pose as a soldier in order to write a history of the war, giving her name as Mrs. Mary Ann Keith. She gestured to her shoulder. "This is from Shiloh, where I fought heroically for our side."

The mayor waved his hand. "Seeing as how the Union is set to occupy the city at any moment, you are the least of my worries." He ordered her to pay $10 and not to fall on the other side of the law again.

As Loreta made her way out of the office, Monroe summoned his personal secretary to ask about news of the federal fleet.

Loreta paused in the doorway as the secretary took her former place in front of the mayor's desk. "I believe they are now making their way up river," he stated.

"We won't go lightly," Monroe declared. "Mr. Baynes, can you see that the flag of the venerable state of Louisiana is poised above the courthouse? I'll be damned if they try to raise the flag of the Union anywhere in the city."

"Yessir." The secretary hurried past Loreta. As she left Mayor Monroe's office, she couldn't help admire the man's tenacity, her punishment and fine notwithstanding.

Now that she'd been released, Loreta pondered what to do. She had no family and no friends left in the city and was still suffering from the pain in her arm. She began walking, her path taking her right in front of her old boarding school. Seized with an idea, Loreta went in, telling the clerk at the desk that she was looking for an old friend. The clerk helped her locate Nellie Jones, the girl she had stolen William from all those years ago.

Loreta headed straight to the address the clerk had given her and knocked at the door. If Nellie was surprised to see her old roommate in a soldier's attire, she did not say so. She'd probably read the newspaper and connected it to Loreta. Nellie had always been quicker than most of the other girls at their school.

"I need you to lend me a dress," Loreta stated simply.

Nellie agreed, as long as Loreta left her steps immediately and never contacted her again, adding, "You needn't worry about returning the clothes—I have much more appealing ones."

When Nellie returned from the inner reaches of the house with the requested clothing, she asked, "Whatever happened to William, anyway?"

"He died," Loreta said, accepting the dress. "G'day, Nellie."

"G'day, Loreta Velazquez. Or Mary Ann Keith. Or whatever your name is."

Loreta headed to a nearby boarding house and secured a room, registering herself with her real name to avoid confusion with the newspaper article. The hotel clerk glanced up from the registry to Loreta's battered uniform, his eyes narrowing at the dress stuffed under her arm. Loreta pulled out a wad of money and threw it at him before heading upstairs.

"I hope you enjoy your stay, Miss Velazquez," the clerk called out in an astonished voice.

Loreta changed into Nellie's dress, the garment again feeling foreign. She pulled on a battered bonnet as she heard shouting in the hallway. Opening the door, Loreta inquired of a young man outside what was happening.

"The Yanks are coming!" he replied.

Loreta shut the door to finish dressing as quickly as possible and then headed to the levee.

She had never seen such a sight as the one that greeted her

when she arrived at the banks of the Mississippi. Hundreds of wagons, carts, and boards with wheels—anything that could be rolled along—stretched along the horizon. They were stacked with bales of cotton. Slaves hurriedly unloaded them and then threw them into a pile. They then made a teepee of pinewood surrounding the cotton and poured a bucket of whiskey over it before lighting it. Loreta watched as they worked tirelessly, sweat pouring down their black faces. She could feel the heat from the flames from her vantage point and could only imagine how hot it would be in the midst of the burning piles. *Like hell itself.* Still the slaves worked, and she wondered what for—the Yankees represented their salvation and here they were, endeavoring to burn the material that they themselves had labored over picking and what the Yankees would give anything to procure. Once they ran out of land for the burning piles, they began to pile the cotton on flatboats and lit the cotton on fire before pushing the boats out into the water to drift down the Mississippi. A funeral pyre consisting of thousands of precious dollars in both cotton and liquor.

Through the blaze and smoke, the federal fleet made its way into view. The gunboats that had fought their way past Fort Jackson and St. Philip were even grander than the ones that Loreta had glimpsed at Shiloh. One by one the vessels dropped anchor. The water outside the levees was higher, elevating the ships to a level in which their guns could point downward at the city streets. The sight gave her a greater understanding of both the federal government's power and the weakness of the Confederacy. "They can fire at any building at will," Loreta said aloud.

"Or they could just destroy the levee and flood the city," another curious observer replied. "I think our game is all but lost."

"Not yet," Loreta said as she started away, a trace of Harry's swagger still visible underneath her skirts.

Even though her identity had been discovered and she could no longer fight, she still longed to do her part to win independence for the South. It was true the Yanks had greater power, but perhaps there was more than one way to win this war. She reasoned that her greatest success thus far had been that she had been under the guise of Harry Buford for over a year, and, save for her confession, no one but the doctors had discovered her true gender. And, having some expertise at being in disguise, she focused on a new tactic: becoming a spy.

CHAPTER 38

BELLE

MAY 1862

*B*elle awoke one morning a few weeks after her Winchester adventure to a commotion below her window.

Mauma Eliza informed her that it was the Yankees that were making all the "fuss in de street." Still clad in her chemise, Belle rushed to the window. Indeed, the avenue was filled with men in blue coats. She was about to run outside when Mauma Eliza stopped her with her thick arm, hollering to put some clothes on.

Belle impatiently posed at the bedpost while Mauma Eliza tugged at her corset strings. "Can't you go any faster?" Belle demanded.

"No, Miss Belle. Why are you so anxious anyway?"

"I need to find out where those Yanks are headed."

When Belle was finally dressed and out the door, she ran into the hotel and found a Yankee scout she'd become friendly with.

"What's happening?" she cried.

"The Rebel army is approaching," the scout replied. Belle managed to refrain from crossing herself as he continued, "No one had any idea Stonewall was so close."

I did. Belle remembered the talk in Mrs. Winslow's sewing circle.

"He's supposedly less than a mile outside Front Royal." The man nodded his head toward the chaos outside. "Colonel Shields has ordered his men to burn the depot stores."

"What if the rebels arrive before you can burn them?"

"Then we fight," the man said, the muscles underneath his mustache twitching. "If, God help us, we retreat upon Winchester, we'll burn the bridges after we cross them."

A man entered the lobby just as the scout was leaving. Belle was dismayed to see that it was Charles Dunham and could not keep her lip from curling. She had met the reporter for the *New York Herald* shortly before her Winchester trip and found him to be extremely repugnant, as if Dunham's only joy in life was to insult young Confederate women.

Belle pushed past him to leave, but he stopped her by grabbing her arm. "What's the matter, Miss Boyd?"

"Nothing much to speak of," Belle edged out of his grasp and made to leave. But she paused at the threshold to tell him, "The rebels are coming and you best prepare yourself for a visit to Libby Prison."

Dunham's face went white before he rushed to the staircase.

Belle knew she should get back to the cottage and prepare, but she couldn't help herself. She slowly walked up the hotel stairs to stand outside the Yankee reporter's room. She spotted him hurriedly throwing papers into a bag. "Where are you planning to go, Mr. Dunham?"

He glanced up. "I'm not sure, but I think it's best if I skedaddle now."

Belle's gaze fell on his room key, still stuck in the door. Dunham's focus had returned to his packing. Stealthily, Belle closed the door and turned the lock before dropping the key into the pocket of her apron.

. . .

As Belle headed outside, she saw a few men she recognized as Confederate sympathizers standing in a huddle, jeering at the few Yankees who were still on the street.

Belle approached them. "Is there one among you who would be willing to relay information of the Yanks' plans to General Jackson? It is of vital importance."

Each man refused to meet her eyes. "Sir," she said, turning to Mr. White, a man she knew to use any opportunity to denigrate the Union. "If we don't pass on this intelligence, Stonewall might run into a Yankee trap."

"Indeed, it is of great consequence," Mr. White concurred. "But if any of us were to be caught by the Yanks, we would be hanged."

"A small sacrifice for the greater good of our country," Belle replied as she narrowed her eyes.

"So says the lesser of the sexes," another man hooted. "Why don't you go yourself?"

"I will," Belle said before turning on her heel. The dress Mauma Eliza had put on her that day was royal blue. Yankee colors, Belle thought, as she ran in the direction where Stonewall Jackson's troops were supposed to be coming from. She had not gotten very far when the gunshots began to sound. The Union soldiers had erected artillery on the hill just outside of town and were lighting cannons pointed at Main Street. When Belle spotted the gray uniforms of the Confederacy advancing on the other side, she realized she was trapped between the two armies. The rebels on the front line took aim and began to fire. Belle felt the bullets whizz past her ears but she kept her pace until she felt a tug on her skirt and glanced down, expecting to see a stray dog nipping at her heels. Instead she was confronted by a large hole in her petticoats: a bullet had penetrated her skirts, but, luckily, had not reached her person.

Belle ran faster as renewed adrenaline coursed through her veins. She had not another thought but of her mission to reach General Jackson. As she got closer to the Confederate line, she tore her bonnet off her head and waved it in a circle, calling for the rebels to press toward town. The men started running forward, shouting triumphantly, some of them cheering her by name as they passed her.

Belle paused, watching the men heading toward Front Royal. There did not seem to be as many of them as she had thought. She sank to her knees, fearing that she had just sent them toward their deaths. *There was no time to delay,* Belle reminded herself as she rose. She continued, a bit slower this time, toward the hilltop on the outskirts of town where the gray coats had seemed to be emerging from. Presently, Belle heard hoofbeats and looked up to see Henry Kyd Douglas, a native of Martinsburg only a few years older than herself, approaching.

"Good God, Belle, you look a fright."

"Henry," Belle gasped, trying to catch her breath. "Tell Stonewall to charge down the hill and he will be able to capture every last Yankee haunting Front Royal."

"Are there so many Yanks in the town still?"

Belle opened her hands as though counting and flexed her fingers several times instead of replying. *Hundreds.*

Henry caught her meaning and tipped his cap. "Well, I'll be damned." He turned his horse around. "Aren't you just the girl to dare to do such a thing!" He shouted this last remark over his shoulder as he began galloping back in the direction he'd come from.

"Remember, should anyone ask, you did not meet with me today!" Belle called to Henry's retreating back. She blew a kiss into the air in Henry's direction. In short order, she heard the unworldly Rebel yell sounding as more men headed in the direction of the town. Belle ducked behind a tree as she heard the beats of dozens of horses, watching as the Confederate cavalry rode right past her.

Belle sat under a tree to rest her throbbing legs for an hour or so. As the sun dropped lower in the sky, she headed back to the nearly empty town, her steps much more labored than they had been when she had set out that morning. A few federal officers still roamed through the Fishback hotel. Belle kindly offered them some lemonade and inquired if they had any news. Sadly, they did not.

In the end, the Confederacy was, once again, indomitable, and the Union retreated, attempting to burn the bridges exactly as the

Yankee scout had declared they would. However, the Confederate cavalry reached the bridges in time to save them from becoming uncontrollable conflagrations.

Henry Kyd Douglas arrived on horseback with his regiment to declare any remaining Federals in Front Royal prisoners of the Confederate army.

"Henry!" Belle called as she caught sight of him. He stopped his horse in front of her.

"I have something for you." Belle stood on her tiptoes to pin a bright red rosette to his coat. "The color is the blood red of succession," she told him, "and it looks quite fair on you."

"And I have something for you too." He passed her a sheet of paper before he rode off.

Belle quickly scanned the note and then held it against her heart before she read it again, slower this time, mouthing the words. It was addressed to her and written by none other than Stonewall Jackson:

Miss Belle Boyd,

I thank you, for myself and for the army, for the immense service that you have rendered your country today.

Hastily, I am your friend,

T. J. Jackson, C.S.A.

The short note became Belle's most valued possession.

CHAPTER 39

LORETA

MAY 1862

*L*oreta scoured the papers, reading with glee the exploits of Mayor Monroe, her recent nemesis, when he was asked to surrender the city. Monroe had declined, professing his loyalty to the Confederate States of America. He'd also refused to lower the Louisiana state flag from the courthouse, the same one he'd ordered raised in Loreta's presence. Federal naval officers had then been ordered to take it down and raise the Union flag in its place.

Loreta's next order of business was to befriend Eugenia Phillips, a Richmond exile who was known to have conspired with the legendary Rose Greenhow. When Loreta informed Eugenia that she too wished to become a spy, the older woman broke into a wide smile and told her that they could use her now more than ever.

Accordingly, Loreta began accompanying Eugenia to dinners and balls, borrowing fancy gowns from Eugenia's adult daughter. At one dinner, Eugenia introduced Loreta to a civilian friend of hers, Mrs. Taylor, a widow who was anxious to return to England but was currently staying at the same boardinghouse as Loreta.

"This whole war is having the most turbulent effect on my nerves," Mrs. Taylor told Loreta, taking a casual sip of sherry.

"Have you heard about poor William Mumford?" Loreta asked.

Mrs. Taylor shook her head.

"He pulled down that wretched Stars and Stripes from City Hall, intending on returning it to Mayor Monroe."

"But a mob ripped it to shreds," Eugenia added. "That beast General Butler arrested him and now he's in the Parish Prison, awaiting trial."

Loreta did not think it was necessary to add that she had recently spent time there as well.

"But that's not the worst thing General Butler has done since he's come to power," Eugenia continued. "Have you read his latest proclamation?" Both ladies shook their heads and Eugenia called in her servant to fetch it. "Officially it is known as General Order #28, but Butler's calling it 'The Women's Order.'" Eugenia cleared her throat and then read aloud:

As the officers and soldiers of the United States have been subjected to repeated insults from the women (calling themselves ladies) of New Orleans, in return for the most scrupulous non-interference and courtesy on our part, it is ordered, that hereafter, when any female shall, by word, gesture, or movement, insult or show contempt for any officer or soldier of the United States, she shall be regarded and held liable to be treated as a woman of the town plying her avocation.

"Can you believe it?" Eugenia asked, putting the paper down. "He hints that we are not ladies at all."

"What a barbarian," Loreta replied. "He's likening us to prostitutes and practically giving permission for his soldiers to rape the women of New Orleans."

"Oh my, oh my," Mrs. Taylor said, fanning herself with her napkin. "This is just terrible. Now I know I must return to England as soon as possible."

"They are just idle threats," Eugenia said. "They cannot possibly enforce such sadistic treatment of women." She ended the night by inviting both women to a party she was giving the next day.

"Aren't they giving a procession for a fallen Union soldier tomorrow?" Loreta asked. The route would take them right under Eugenia's balcony in the French Quarter.

"Indeed they are. You should probably reschedule," Mrs. Taylor told her hostess.

Eugenia gave a dismissive wave of her hand. "There is no need for that. This is New Orleans, after all. It is rare for a day to go by without some sort of procession."

Accordingly the women met again at Eugenia's apartment the next day. Eugenia insisted on hosting tea outside on the balcony.

The newest gossip was over Mayor Monroe's arrest for protesting Butler's order.

"At least someone is willing to defend our honor," Loreta commented, remembering the mayor's determination.

"Honor?" another woman sneered, turning to Loreta. "Aren't you one to talk, going about parading as a soldier."

Loreta was about to deny the accusation when Eugenia threw her head back and laughed. "Loreta, was that you? I never put the two together." She put a gloved hand over her chest, catching her breath, before looking at Loreta with admiration. "I was right, we could use women like you."

Loreta straightened the hem of her dress. "It was nothing, really." She had started to tell of her battle adventures, but Eugenia's black servant appeared on the edge of the balcony. "I's sorry to inarupt but Mrs. Phillips, there be some men lookin' for you's at the door."

"Did you tell them I'm occupied at the moment?"

"Yes'm, but they's insistin'."

Eugenia rose. "I'm sure I won't be long."

But the men were already making their way through the living room. "You are all under arrest," one of them declared.

Loreta's heart sped up when she recognized the speaker as the detested General Butler himself.

"Whatever for?" Eugenia asked, stepping forward.

Butler walked over to her and stared her down, his droopy eyes and triangular mustache giving him the appearance of an old, overweight beagle. "You women are breaking the law."

"By having a party? Are you going to outlaw having fun in our fair city now?"

"You were laughing during a funeral procession," Butler sneered.

Eugenia returned his glare with a bewildered look until understanding dawned. "I was laughing at something one of my companions said."

"You can tell that to the judge." He put his hands on his wide hips. "I know exactly who you are, Mrs. Phillips. I will imprison you for now, but I expect that either you or Mrs. Greenhow will be my undoing and will someday be responsible for my murder."

"You are wrong on that account," Eugenia spat back as one of Butler's soldiers began leading her out. "We usually order our Negroes to kill our swine."

Loreta could not contain the giggle that slipped out and, consequently, while Butler consented to let the other women go, she was also placed under arrest.

Loreta was none too happy to be back at the Parish Prison, but the assistant provost marshal, who was tasked with arraigning her, treated her kindly.

He introduced himself as Deputy Steward. "I don't agree with Butler's proposition," he told her helplessly, "but I have my orders."

Loreta had absolutely no desire to go back to jail, and pretended to be a devoted Federalist. "I did not know what Mrs. Phillips stood for when I accepted her party invitation. Had I known about the funeral procession, I would have stood at street level to pay my respects to our fallen soldier."

Steward grabbed a napkin to wipe up the tea he had dribbled at Loreta's declaration. "Is that so? It is rare we get women in here expressing Union sentiment. They'd rather spit on us in the streets."

"Oh no, sir. I was happier than a clam to see the federal flag being raised once again in New Orleans. It won't be long before the Stars and Stripes wave from every rooftop in the South." Loreta reached behind her and crossed her fingers, hoping the movement would suffice for retribution if she ever had to confess to denouncing the cause that she loved.

Steward tilted his head. "Have you taken the oath to the Union?"

Loreta had not and did not intend to. She changed the subject instead. "You see, I am of Northern birth—my father was from New York—and, as I was caught down here with the blockade, could not return."

"Have you any family?"

"No sir," Loreta replied truthfully. "I am a widow." She then told him that her husband had been an Englishman and left her with a large sum of money and property. "But those wretched rebels robbed me of everything." She reached into her reticule and drew out a handkerchief. She studied the officer as she dabbed at her eyes.

Her crocodile tears had the desired effect. Steward got to his feet, saying, "I think I can convince General Butler to drop the charges against you." He left the room and returned a few minutes later.

"Mrs. Phillips is to be brought to Ship Island for her indiscretions, but I have better news, for you, Mrs..." he glanced down at his paperwork. "Williams. General Butler has agreed to release you as long as you promise to be more considerate when out in public."

"Oh, yessir. Thank you." She rose to leave.

"And Mrs. Williams, don't hesitate to call on me if there is ever any way I can help you."

"Thank you again, sir," she said, leaving the office feeling light on her feet. Not only had she avoided arrest, but she'd managed to make the assistant provost marshal as an ally as well. She was sorry that Eugenia was to be imprisoned, but she knew that her friend would have approved of Loreta's manipulations for the cause they shared.

. . .

Loreta ran into Mrs. Taylor in the lobby of their boardinghouse the next day. After exchanging what little information they had about Eugenia, Mrs. Taylor informed Loreta that she had secured passage to return to England. Struck with inspiration, Loreta asked if she could borrow her foreign identification papers.

"Whatever for?" Mrs. Taylor asked.

"They would assist me a great deal." She told Mrs. Taylor of her latest plan, brought on by a letter she'd received that morning from one of William's old comrades, who was now a surgeon in Mandeville, located on the other side of Lake Pontchartrain. Loreta leaned in. "It is still under Confederate control and Dr. Childs told me that his hospital is low on medicine, especially quinine. As summer is almost upon us, he is worried that the malaria epidemic will wipe out the few Confederate soldiers they had left in the area. If I had your papers as authentication, I could secure a pass to Mandeville."

"But I don't understand how you would be able to help the situation there."

Loreta glanced around the lobby before whispering, "The federal hospitals have plenty of quinine. I could use the provost marshal's recommendation to get a job as a nurse." She left the rest of the plan up to Mrs. Taylor's interpretation.

Mrs. Taylor nodded as she dug through her carpetbag. She handed Loreta a certificate that gave her place of birth in England and her address at the boardinghouse.

In the next few months, Loreta managed to make a few trips back and forth across Lake Pontchartrain, and even once to Mobile, delivering the much-needed medicine and conveying Confederate correspondence. She was pleased that once again she could help the cause, although she knew that to do so under Butler's beagle snout was inviting a great amount of risk.

With that mindset, she assumed she'd been caught when Dr. Childs presented her with a letter addressed to his hospital, but with Loreta's name on it. "What is this?" she asked, flipping it over. The return address was in Memphis.

"I'm not sure, I didn't open it," Dr. Childs replied.

Loreta's trepidation at being found out quickly turned over to joy. "It's from Tom!"

"Tom?"

"Major De Caulp."

"Why is my old commanding officer writing you?"

"He and I…" Loreta did not feel like trying to explain the situation to Dr. Childs. Clearly Tom had wanted to get in contact with her and used any New Orleans connections he could. "I must go to him."

Dr. Childs took the letter and scanned it. "Most of Tennessee is under Union control now and it's probably only a matter of time before Memphis falls. It's highly unlikely you could get a pass to go there."

Loreta felt her heartbeat, which had been hammering away at the astonishing news, slow. It seemed desperately unfair that, now that she knew her beloved was alive, she would be prohibited from seeing him. She thought for a moment before asking Dr. Childs what they did with the uniforms of the soldiers who have perished at the hospital.

He knitted his eyebrows. "We try to return them to the families of the deceased, provided we know where to send them. The others we store. Ailing soldiers often request replacements, especially the boots."

"Where do you keep the extras?"

Dr. Childs led Loreta to a basement storeroom. She dug through a pile of old uniforms until she found a coat and pants that would fit her frame. Dr. Childs sighed. "This should be where I tell you to not do this, but even I can see any effort I would make to prevent you from leaving would be futile."

"Indeed," Loreta replied, shouldering the uniform. "This whole time I thought that Tom was dead. Nothing you or anyone else could say would prevent me from going to him. Not even General Butler or the United States government can stop me now."

CHAPTER 40

MARY JANE

JUNE 1862

*T*he Confederate White House had been quiet these past few days. Rebel intelligence had informed the government that General McClellan was continuing his offensive by marching his army through the peninsula formed by the York and James rivers. For a few days in early June, it seemed that an attack on Richmond would be imminent.

"Let them come," Miss Lizzie had stated at the seamstress shop. "I have prepared a room for General McClellan to stay if he so chooses."

Mary Jane could not help but smile. "What about your sister-in-law, Mary? Something tells me she would not be so pleased to have McClellan as a houseguest."

Miss Lizzie shook her head. "Mary's gone. She'd said that she didn't want her children raised by 'damned Yankees,' and took the girls to her family's estate."

Mary Jane's mouth dropped open. She recalled Miss Lizzie's nieces, two sweet young girls who definitely had not inherited their mother's disposition.

"But John brought the girls back to the Church Hill house, and now I help supervise them."

"Do they know of your secret room?"

"Not yet. But perhaps someday I will fill them in on all that happens in our home." Miss Lizzie waved her hand. "And now, Mary Jane, what of the going's on in the Davises' home?"

Mary Jane had not much to report besides the changing of Judah Benjamin's title from Secretary of War to Secretary of State.

Mrs. Thompson looked up from her sewing. "Why'd Davis do that? I thought he doted upon that old Jew."

Mary Jane bristled, wishing that derogatory term hadn't slipped so easily from the seamstress's tongue. "When they were debating over the Conscription Act, Benjamin suggested that the Confederate army employ slaves as soldiers. He thought they could win their freedom by serving the South. It was vastly unpopular, and although many in Congress called for Benjamin's complete resignation, Mr. Davis wouldn't hear of it." Despite herself, Mary Jane had looked favorably upon the portly Mr. Benjamin. He often tried to distract the president with his humorous outlook on the blunders of the Confederate generals of late. All but those of Bob Lee, who had taken over the Army of Virginia after Joe Johnston had been wounded. Both Benjamin and President Davis had nothing but praise for Lee, calling him the Confederacy's most able general.

"They have no choice but to keep soldiers in their army by force," Miss Lizzie stated.

"Indeed," Mary Jane agreed, scooping up Mrs. Davis's newly hemmed dress.

When Mary Jane returned to the house, she found Mrs. Davis in a state of panic.

Mrs. O'Melia confided that a courier had come, informing the Davises that their plantation in Mississippi had been raided, their possessions stolen and their remaining slaves confiscated.

"Disaster follows disaster," Mrs. Davis muttered as she sat in the snuggery. She began rocking as Mrs. O'Melia and Mary Jane exchanged frightened looks. "First the death of our great friend and loyal commander, Sidney Johnston, and then the evacuation of my family from New Orleans, and now this." She reached over to touch the satin drape. "McClellan might as well come now and finish the job. This dreadful way of living depresses more than I can say."

Mr. Davis entered the room. "Winnie," he said sharply.

His wife stopped her murmuring and looked up. "What is it, Jeff?"

He sat down next to her and clasped her small hands in his large, thin-fingered ones. "If our cause succeeds, we shall not mourn over personal deprivation any longer."

"You're right, of course Husband," Mrs. Davis replied, retrieving her hands from his grip. "Someday we Southerners will all laugh at how vain we were."

Although Mary Jane knew that Mrs. Davis had a different definition of vanity than herself, the slave couldn't help but hope that Mrs. Davis was right.

CHAPTER 41

BELLE

JUNE 1862

*A*lthough Belle's feat at the Battle of Front Royal further solidified her heroism in the South—the papers there hailed her as the "Secesh Cleopatra"—she made an enemy of the Northern newspapers, and especially Mr. Dunham. After Belle had locked him in the hotel room, he attempted an escape through the window but the Rebel army caught sight of him shimmying down a drain pipe and captured him. When he spotted Belle on the street, he threatened her, saying it was her fault he was now a prisoner and that he'd make her rue the day she did that to him. As General Jackson considered him an "innocent journalist," he was released only hours after he'd been taken prisoner. When Dunham returned North, he wrote an article in which he called her an "accomplished prostitute who'd passed the first freshness of youth."

Rumors had been circulating for weeks that Lincoln had finally persuaded General McClellan to take action and Stonewall Jackson had therefore abandoned the Shenandoah Valley to try to recapture the Virginia Peninsula.

The new Federal commander in Front Royal, General Nathaniel Banks, also decided to establish his headquarters at her aunt's hotel. Belle intended to weave him under her spell much like she had his counterpart, General Shields. She took careful care getting dressed before she went to call on him for the first time: accessorizing her dark green dress with a hat covered in Confederate buttons and her gold palmetto pin at her breast, a nod to South Carolina, the first state to secede from the Union.

Her plan appeared to work; after they exchanged pleasantries upon meeting, Belle asked if the general could grant her a pass to travel to Alabama to visit her cousin.

The general tilted back and let out a big belly of a laugh. "But what would Virginia do without you?"

"Why General, whatever do you mean?"

"How can your native state do with your absence? We have heard about your daring during the Battle of Front Royal and beyond. It caused the defeat of my own army, but it still was admirable."

Belle fluttered her lashes. "So you will grant me a pass."

"Of course not," the general replied, turning back to his papers, the genial facade disappearing. "I would prefer to keep you in your aunt's cabin where I can watch over you."

Belle, at first not sure if she'd heard him right, folded her arms across her chest, but the general refused to look up. With a harrumph, she left his office.

As she navigated the brick walkway back to the cabin, she reflected on the conversation. She supposed she couldn't blame the general; after all, she was a great danger to his army, perhaps the greatest of them all.

Now that she was stuck in Front Royal, at least for the time being, Belle resumed her role of being a flirtatious spy and managed to coax a Union private to give her a pistol. He told her he was an admirer of her courage in defending her mother from the German. Belle planned on presenting it to Stonewall Jackson when she had the chance.

Although she had her share of admirers and hangers-on, she recognized that some of the men who pursued her might have ulterior motives. She confronted such a man one day as she was waiting on a bench for the Union provost marshal, intending to inquire about another pass. Although his face was much less worn than her father's, the man's uncombed hair and beard were a premature gray. His eyes, which kept darting around the room, looked to be black as pitch, however.

Belle had seen him a few times previously about town. Each time had resulted in an admonishment from General Banks about leaving the cabin without his permission.

She acknowledged the black-eyed man with a slight nod. "I suppose you came to report me again."

"Miss Boyd." His low voice contained a hint of an English accent. "Are you aware that we have a mutual friend?"

"I'm sure you mean General Banks." Her own voice carried more than a hint of accusation.

He smiled an oily smile. "I was referring to Eugene Blockley."

Belle searched her memory. "The shoemaker?"

The man nodded before bidding her adieu, leaving Belle wondering as to his purpose in mentioning Blockley, whom she knew vaguely. He owned a shop in Front Royal, but, upon thinking more about it, she recalled seeing a man who resembled Blockley on the street during her trip to Winchester. After she was once again denied a pass, she left the office feeling slightly worried that Banks, Blockley and now this other man might be tailing her.

The next morning, Belle sat by the window in the cottage's parlor, warming herself in the June sun. She caught sight of a Confederate soldier standing next to the provost marshal's tent. She grabbed her white bonnet before strolling into the courtyard and venturing over to the handsome soldier to inquire his name.

He bowed. "C.W.D. Smitley."

"My, that is quite a mouthful."

The Rebel man smiled. His neatly trimmed brown beard had hints of red that glimmered in the sun.

"Are you trying to get a pass?" Belle asked, nodding toward the tent.

"Indeed. I've just been paroled, and now I'm hoping to head south to Richmond."

"Good luck. I tried to get a pass just the other day, to no avail."

"Well, let's hope I'll be more fortunate than you."

Belle fiddled with the ribbons on her bonnet. "When would you leave?"

"Not until late this evening."

"In that case, you must dine with my aunt and me tonight."

"I'd be honored." Smitley tipped his hat.

"Will six o'clock give you enough time to pack? We're just in that cottage over there," she said, pointing.

"Six o'clock will be perfect." Belle thought for a moment she saw his eyes twinkle, but then decided it had just been a trick of the sunlight.

After getting word that General Banks was out on duty, Belle decided to call on the Dahl women to invite them to dinner. She chose these particular sisters for a few reasons; besides the fact that Emma, the older one, was betrothed to a Confederate soldier, they were both plain-looking and dull in personality. They also usually complied with whatever Belle commanded.

Sarah Dahl, who was a year younger than Belle, answered the door.

"What happened to your maid?" Belle asked.

"She ran away." Sarah opened the door a little wider. "Are you even supposed to be wandering about town?"

"Probably not. Listen, Sarah, this is important: I want you and Emma to come to dinner tonight. And make sure you ask plenty of questions about what happened during the Battle of Front Royal."

Sarah rolled her eyes. "I think everyone in the town has that story memorized."

"Maybe so," Belle admitted. "But not Mr. Smitley."

"Oh?" Sarah peered down at Belle. "Who is this Mr. Smitley? Is he handsome?"

Belle waved her hand. "Just do as I asked, if you don't mind. And tell Emma to do the same."

Sarah gave a deep sigh before agreeing.

"Six o'clock," Belle reminded her before Sarah shut the door.

As soon as Belle returned to her room, she scrawled a missive to Stonewall Jackson, updating him on the Union's command of Front Royal. She called Mauma Eliza in to help her get ready.

Mauma Eliza's eyes widened upon spying the white muslin dress that Belle had laid out. "Lawdy, Miss Belle, this here an evenin' gown. I thawt y'all was just havin' dinner."

"Yes, Mauma," she replied, fingering the blue ribbons on the dress. "But clothing has a great deal to do towards making us all appear what we would like the world to take us for. I may be a spy, and perhaps a tomboy, but I'm also a young woman now."

Mauma Eliza eventually complied, muttering under her breath how folks have too many other things to be worried about than their clothing.

Dinner went exceedingly well, with Sarah and Emma Dahl playing their parts to a tee. Not only was Belle able to brag of her exploits in front of Mr. Smitley, but the Dahl sisters were so monotonous that Smitley's eyes barely fell on them.

When Mauma Eliza began clearing the meal, Belle pulled Smitley aside to ask if he would be able to deliver a letter to General Jackson when he set out on his journey.

Again, that twinkle appeared. "I will do so with utmost fidelity," Smitley replied. He peered over Belle's shoulder. "In fact, I should be going soon. It's getting dark, which is the best time to slip through the Union lines."

"Will you call on me when you return?" Belle asked with a little sway in order to show off the fullness of her skirts.

"Of course." He again tipped his hat and then returned to the dining room to take his leave of Belle's other guests.

After the Dahl sisters had left, Mauma Eliza demanded to know what she had given "dat man."

"A letter for Stonewall. He's on his way to Richmond."

Mauma Eliza grasped Belle's arm. "Miss Belle, that man ain't no Confederate. I seen him talking to dat Union man with da black eyes. He's a spy."

"No, Mauma," Belle insisted. But her blood turned cold as she recalled the odd twinkle to Smitley's gaze. She shook off Mauma Eliza's hand. "Mauma, quick, we have to send a message about him."

"How?"

Belle put her arm under her chin and thought. "Through the underground, of course. But we can't use you this time. Send George in." Mauma waddled off as Belle sat down to write a letter to Henry Kyd Douglas of the Confederate cavalry. She described Smitley's coloration and build, whom he claimed to be, and his intended destination. She folded the note several times and then held it in her hands for a moment, wondering how to disguise it. She opened a desk drawer and dug around, her fingers closing in on an old pocket watch of her uncle's. After a moment of thought, she used her knife to open it and remove its innards, replacing them with the folded note. The watch didn't quite close, but someone would have to look really close to realize that. Belle knew that George would be unlikely to be questioned since the Yankees assumed all darkeys were on their side. She instructed George to have Douglas read the note on the spot and send her a reply.

Belle spent the next few days feeling as though she were one of the ill-fated coils she'd removed from her uncle's pocket watch. Ever since the confrontation with the man with the black eyes, Belle had been nervous about getting caught. Now there was a letter addressed to Stonewall Jackson carrying intelligence that was probably at this moment in Union hands. Every day that went by was agony as she waited for the coil to spring out of control.

CHAPTER 42

LORETA

JUNE 1862

*O*nce again dressed as Harry Buford, Loreta managed to make it through the Union lines to Memphis. The going was rough—at times she found herself crawling through the underbrush, brambles scraping at her face and hands. When she finally reached Confederate lines, she found a picket and told him she had escaped from a New Orleans prison camp. He whistled at the officer in charge, who rode out from the woods and dismounted, scanning her very closely. Loreta stood as tall as she could while knowing her masculine appearance was scanty at best. She tried smoothing her mustache, but touched only skin and realized she'd must have lost her fake facial hair somewhere along the way.

She decided to appeal to the officer's basest desires. "Sir, I've been walking since last evening without food or sleep. I'd love some breakfast." She pulled out the flask of whiskey Dr. Childs had given her before she left. "Would you like a drink?"

The officer's eyes widened as he accepted the flask. He took a long drink before handing back the practically empty bottle. He then motioned for Loreta to follow him, leading her through the woods to their camp. Breakfast had already been set, and the captain offered Loreta a place at the table. The meal was as meager as Loreta's threadbare uniform, but it was the most she had to eat in days.

After breakfast the other soldiers, having heard the news that Loreta was an escaped prisoner, plied her with questions. She filled them in on the capture of New Orleans and what she had seen of their troops on her recent journey. She then showed the captain her arm and told him she was in need of medical care. He directed her to the hospital. Loreta, eager to see Tom at last, even if it was as Harry Buford, set off accordingly.

It had not just been a ploy to be under the same roof as Tom. Although she would have marched through hell to be near him once again, the arduous traveling had taken its toll on Loreta's injuries, and, after a brief examination, Dr. Hay admitted her to his ward.

After she was settled, her arm re-wrapped, Loreta inquired after Tom.

"You must have some rest," Dr. Hay chided her.

"No, I must go to him now."

Dr. Hay indicated the room next door. "He is there, but he too is sleeping. If you give me your name, soldier, I will convey your message."

Loreta had nearly forgotten she was still dressed as Harry. "Tell him his old friend Lieutenant Buford is next door and is eager to pay his condolences at his earliest convenience."

Loreta tried to console herself that it would only be a matter of time before she could lay eyes on her long-lost love again, but it was of little help since even then she would not be able to express the depths of her feelings as Harry Buford.

When she was finally permitted to go to him, Captain De Caulp seemed quite glad to see his friend. "Harry, my brother in arms," he said weakly.

Loreta rushed to his bedside, trying not to cry. She touched his hand for a brief moment and wished she could hold it in hers. "I thought you had died."

"I almost did. I was parched for water and shrapnel had hit here," he indicated a spot to the right of his chest with shaking fingers. "And my leg was broken. But they were not mortal wounds and I lived to see more days."

"How did you end up here?"

"A cavalry regiment nearly trampled me after the retreat was called, but I managed to cry out. A good Samaritan Yank picked me up on his mount and took me back to the Union camp. I never caught his name," he said with more than a trace of regret. "In the morning I was well enough to escape and found a Confederate camp, and they brought me here."

"Are you well healed?" Loreta thought she might know the answer, based on Tom's frail frame and the nearby tureen filled with both pus and blood.

"Mending every day," was Tom's meek reply.

"And what of your lady friend? Does she know of your fate?"

"I have written to all of the contacts I know in both New Orleans and Memphis, begging them to tell her I'm here." He turned to face the wall. "I'm not sure why she does not come to me."

Loreta's fragile heart nearly cracked as she realized he was crying. She sat silently until Tom composed himself, wiping his eyes with his sheet and turning back to face her.

Despite his obvious sorrow, Loreta wanted more confirmation that he was truly hers. "You are still in love with her?"

"Yes, I'm still hoping to marry her as soon as we are in contact again. As soon as the doctors pronounce me safe to travel, I will find her."

"Have you heard that New Orleans has fallen to the Union?"

"I know." Tom took a deep breath. "I would rescue her from the heavy jowls of General Butler himself if need be."

"I think you've done enough fighting for the present. You deserve to have all the rest you need."

"I don't plan on leaving the army unless it is necessary for my health, and even then it would be with great reluctance." He began coughing. Loreta held the tureen under his chin but he waved it away. "I am determined to get married, even if it costs me my commission. Each day that goes by that I don't see her, the hole in my heart grows deeper."

Loreta's voice was so choked with emotion she could hardly utter her next words. "What if you could see your lady right now?"

The color seemed to immediately return to Tom's cheeks. "I would give everything I own. Indeed, I would steal the stars from the heavens if I could see Loreta again."

Just hearing her name from Tom's lips filled Loreta with a strange combination of glee and anguish. She got to her feet, bidding him goodbye before he could see the turmoil his words had caused. She hurried back to her room hoping he was too drained to notice how abrupt her departure had been.

Tears sprang to her eyes, blurring the floor in front of her and she stumbled the rest of the way to her bed. Although they were tears of joy, the doctor thought that Harry was in great pain and forbade him to leave the room for at least a day.

Loreta tried her best to soothe her aching heart, telling herself that it would not be long before their union and she would never have to feel that degree of angst again.

After she awoke the next morning, she penned a letter to Tom from Loreta, stating that she had arrived in Memphis and would see him as soon as possible. She asked Dr. Hay to deliver the letter right then. She gave Tom a few minutes to process what she had written before entering his room again.

Upon spying her at the door, he spoke with renewed energy, "Ah, Harry, look here." He waved the note. "She has come, my friend, she will be here soon."

Loreta entered. Her face was red and her hands were shaking, but Tom did not seem to notice. She was convinced that his love was wholehearted, but that did not mean he might not forsake her when she told him the truth of her identity. She had spent time enough among men to know what their true opinion of a woman's place was, and it certainly was not on the battlefield.

She had been resolved to tell him, but now that the time was upon her, she scarcely knew how to begin. She pulled a chair next to his cot, speaking low for fear that others might hear. "Captain, before your sweetheart returns to you, I have something to tell you."

Tom gave her a startled look, evidently fearing whatever it was she had to say would burst his bubble of excitement.

Loreta removed his letter from her coat pocket. "I believe this belongs to you."

He turned the paper over with obvious confusion. "I sent this in care of my beloved. However did you get it in your possession?" He gave her a weary look, probably wondering if he'd lost another girl to the likes of Harry Buford.

"Captain, you said last night that each day you don't lay eyes on Loreta, the wound in your heart gets more severe."

"Yes," he replied with a touch of impatience.

"Well, I'm here to say it's at least one day less than you think."

He continued to stare blankly, obviously not comprehending Loreta's meaning.

She reached over and took the tintype of herself out of his bedside drawer. "Take a good look at that and tell me if you haven't seen someone that looks like her in recent days."

He touched the picture tenderly, still not understanding.

Loreta's heart was nearly ready to burst. "Do you not think the picture holds a bit of likeness to your friend Harry Buford?"

Finally his face was filled with understanding. He looked deep into her eyes before sinking back to his pillow, gasping for breath.

"Tom?" Loreta begged. "Are you okay?"

He held up a finger, still trying to get air, and then rose up again. "Can it really be possible?"

"Yes." Loreta grabbed his hand. "It is me, your Loreta, in the flesh and blood. It was I who fought by you at Shiloh, whose heart broke when she saw you fall. I am here now and I won't ever leave you again."

His silence was so prolonged that Loreta feared that she had lost him by confessing. "Do you despise me now that you know my secret?"

"No," he said, squeezing her hand. "I love you more for what you have done for our country."

Tears again filled Loreta's eyes.

He put his hand under her chin, turning it upward so she could meet his eyes. "Is it really possible that you have been so far from me, yet so near as well?"

"Yes, my love," she checked to make sure that no doctors were near. "I love you, Tom."

"We will marry straightaway then," he whispered. He was breathing heavily again, and, despite her elation at his reaction, she reminded herself that her beloved was still sick. She did not want her revelation to cause any more toll on his health than was strictly necessary. "Please get some rest." She held his hand to her lips and kissed it. "We can talk more in a few hours."

"Yes, my love," he whispered before succumbing to slumber.

Loreta breathed a deep sigh of relief as she went back to her chamber. It had all felt like a dream: she had a new fiancé in whom she had confided her secret and who loved her more rather than less for it.

Doctor Hay was in the room when she returned. She held up her hand before he could again admonish her for getting out of bed. "It is fine, Doctor. I am much on the mend. In fact, I think I'm ready to be released."

The doctor shook his head. "No, lieutenant, I think you could use a few more days. Are you so inclined to get back onto the battlefield you would put your health in danger?"

Loreta hid a smile. "I don't think my beloved would approve of me going back to the battlefield so soon. Or ever again, for that matter."

He gave her a searching look. "The Confederate army has instituted dire consequences for deserters."

"Don't worry, Doctor. I'm not talking about deserting, necessarily." She changed the subject. "How do you like Captain De Caulp?"

"I think he is a fine gentleman. Why do you ask?"

"I was with him at the Battle of Shiloh, where he behaved like the hero he is."

"Ah," Dr Hay replied. "I knew you were acquainted, but didn't know you had fought together. That explains your close relationship."

Loreta smiled again to herself, thinking that it didn't quite explain it, but the doctor's answer was satisfactory. "Do you think he will be well enough to be released presently?" She held her breath, knowing that Dr. Hay would probably not consent, but he surprised her by agreeing.

Dr. Hay flipped through some paperwork. "He had a hard time recovering at first, especially with the onset of his illness, but, providing nothing occurs to threaten his health as of late, I think he should be ready in a few days." He eyed her carefully before consenting, "If it pleases you, I can write your discharge papers now."

"Oh, yes, that would indeed please me greatly. Thank you, Doctor."

"Good luck, soldier."

CHAPTER 43

BELLE

JULY 1862

*B*elle, still too anxious to sleep for more than a few hours at a time, was sitting out on the balcony of the cottage when she heard hoofbeats of what seemed like dozens of horses. She got to her feet to watch the soldiers in bluecoats approach. The officer in front raised his sword and the squad halted. The chirping of birds and the panting of the horses were the only sounds as the men stared up at Belle. A carriage was brought from the back of the hotel to the front of the cottage, but still no one said anything. She sighed, guessing that the carriage was probably meant for her.

"Miss Belle," Mauma Eliza called from below. "de Provo' is here and dere's two older men wid him."

Belle's knees were weak. The hammering of her heart caused her to feel off balance and she grasped the railing as she made her way downstairs.

She immediately identified the men standing in the front room as Front Royal's provost marshal, Major Maginnis, and Major Francis Sherman. The man on the other side of Maginnis turned. Belle's gasp was audible as she saw the other man was the one with the black eyes. He pulled a letter from his coat pocket and flipped it open, holding it just in front of Belle's face so she could read it:

Direct Cridge to come immediately to Washington and bring with him Belle Boyd in close custody, committing her on arrival to the Old Capitol Prison. Furnish him such aid as may need to get her safely here.

It was signed by C.P. Wolcott, the Union's assistant secretary of war.

Belle met the man's black eyes. "I suppose you are Mr. Cridge?"

"Yes." He tucked the letter back into his pocket. "I work with the Pinkerton Detective Agency."

"Never heard of them," Belle swished past him to sit down on the couch, hoping her heartbeat wasn't audible to the rest of the room.

"But we've heard of you," Cridge said, seating himself opposite of her. "Allan Pinkerton has got quite the file on you already. And he's informed Mr. Stanton, the secretary of war, of your... actions," he paused and raised a sleek eyebrow, "Surely you've heard of Mr. Stanton?"

Belle nodded.

"He has advised us to imprison you."

"On what charges?"

Cridge stood. "It was I who sent Smitley to incriminate you. Now if you will excuse me, I must gather some more evidence."

Belle rose as well, realizing that there were papers that could be construed as traitorous in her room. "Sir, please permit me to make sure the upstairs is in suitable condition for a *gentleman*." She spat out the last word so Cridge would not mistake that she thought him the furthest thing from. Cridge did not reply and Belle rose, hurrying to her room. She could hear the detective's heavy shoes pounding up the stairs. He entered the room right after Belle, pushing past her to search through her drawers, tossing out undergarments and petticoats, before heading over to her desk. Belle was relieved to notice that it was empty of most of her dispatches—Mauma Eliza must have gotten rid of them while they were talking downstairs. After briefly examining the pistol given to her by a Union soldier—the one she was planning on presenting to Stonewall Jackson—he pocketed it along with other various papers.

Satisfied, Cridge turned to Belle. "You must be ready within the hour for the journey to Capital Prison."

Mauma Eliza made a low noise from the hallway and held a handkerchief up to her face.

Belle adopted a pleading tone. "Can my maid accompany me?"

"You mean your slave? No."

Mauma Eliza's cries grew louder and she enveloped Belle in her enormous bosom.

"Within the hour," Cridge restated as he left the room.

"I'll be alright, Mauma." Belle freed herself from her embrace. "Come, help me pack."

They hurriedly threw the garments Cridge had strewn around the room into Belle's trunk and then headed back down the stairs, Mauma Eliza openly weeping the entire time. Belle said a tearful goodbye to her before Cridge motioned for the soldiers waiting outside to load Belle's trunk onto the awaiting carriage. Soldiers and Front Royal citizens crowded the courtyard and the walkway. Some of their faces appeared sympathetic while others looked downright hostile. "Serves you right," Belle heard Mr. White—the same self-proclaimed Confederate who'd refused to deliver her message to Stonewall Jackson during the Battle of Front Royal—say. Although she felt like breaking down into tears, Belle steeled her heart, not willing to betray any scrap of emotion to her hypocrite neighbors and the enemy soldiers. She took her place inside the carriage while Cridge installed himself in the driver's seat. Belle heard the crack of the whip and they began to rattle away. Belle moved the curtain back, hoping for one more glance of Mauma Eliza, but the cavalry had surrounded the carriage on both sides. *There must be at least 50 of them!* Belle marveled. Was she that much of a threat?

Maybe they were so numerous because the local Confederate cavalry were at this moment planning to rescue her. Their fearless leader, Turner Ashby, had been killed in June and perhaps they were hoping to exact revenge by attacking Belle's escorts. The thought briefly cheered Belle and prevented her from completely breaking down. Her sorrow eventually turned to anger as she recalled that Cridge never replied to her inquiry as to what she was being arrested for. Wasn't this the Union that was so anxious to fight for the rights of slaves, and yet here they were, imprisoning her without the due process of a hearing or trial?

The conveyance halted. In her past exploits, she had grown quite familiar with the terrain surrounding Front Royal and recognized that they were atop a high hill on the way to Winchester. She saw a familiar tree, but the limbs Belle had once appreciated for their sturdiness seemed to be reaching out to her. *A tree suitable for hanging traitors,* Belle thought before she pulled the curtain shut.

The carriage and its cavalry escorts arrived at General Julius White's headquarters outside of Winchester just before dark. Cridge escorted Belle into General White's tent. The general bowed deeply as Cridge left.

"What do you intend to do with me?" Belle demanded.

"Tomorrow you will travel to the commanding officer in Martinsburg, and he will know more of your fate. You will be able to rest here tonight."

"I have acquaintances in Winchester. Surely you will permit me to stay with them?"

"Oh no, Miss Belle," White replied, not unkindly. "I cannot consent to that."

"I've never slept alone in a tent, and here I would be at the mercy of your men. How can I endure such a punishment in the hands of my enemies?"

"Rest assured your ladyship will be in perfect comfort and security."

Belle wrinkled her nose, trying to think of another reason she could not stay, but gave up.

General White then led her to a dinner table decorated with fine silver and china. *Too fine for an army.* Belle examined a porcelain plate depicting Daniel Boone as she recalled stories of Yankees looting goods from Rebel homes. She did not have much of an appetite and picked at her food in silence.

After the plates had been cleared, General White summoned for a servant to show Belle to her tent. She hadn't had much sleep for days, and now that the axe had fallen and her fate had been somewhat decided, Belle was able to fall into a deep sleep.

She was awoken in the night by what sounded like musket shots. A bugle resonated in the distance, soon accompanied by drum beats. Belle lit a candle and opened the flap to the tent. The camp was in chaos as officers, half asleep and tugging at their suspenders, mounted horses and rode to their posts. *The Confederate army is here to rescue me!*

Belle was gleeful as she took in the scene. A man rushing by shouted at her to put out her candle. "We don't want to signal the rebels!"

Belle ducked back into her tent, and briefly considered not putting out the light, but eventually consented. She did not want to make it worse for herself if the rebels were not actually coming.

And indeed, they didn't. In the light of morning, General White informed Belle that a cow had wandered away from its farm. A soldier, not being able to discern the shape, commanded it to halt and then fired when it didn't obey. Other sentries had followed suit, hence the multiple gunshots Belle had heard. When they discovered the sentries' mistake, the other soldiers had all retired to their tents. The offending soldier had been assigned to carry a heavy log around camp all the next day.

"And what of the cow?" Belle asked.

"The cow was returned to his farm, unscathed," the general replied.

After breakfast, Belle was again commanded to return to the carriage and Cridge took his place at the helm. When they arrived in Martinsburg in mid-day, Belle asked the commanding officer there if she could visit home. The officer seemed to be considering, but Cridge replied, "Impossible." He turned to the officer. "This girl is a known spy and will only cause more trouble if left alone to her own devices."

"But this is my hometown," Belle protested. "My family is here."

Cridge sneered. "I know. I will be paying a visit to your mother's house myself, to see if you have any more evidence hidden away." He turned back to the officer in command. "See to it that she has a tent. The train pulls out at two in the morning."

Not long after Cridge departed, another carriage pulled up and a woman in full mourning dress got out. Despite the heavy black veil disguising the figure's face, Belle recognized her walk. "Mother!" she cried, forgetting herself and where she was.

"My dear child," Mother replied after a long, heartfelt embrace. "What is to become of her?" she asked the commanding officer.

"She will lodge here in a tent for a few hours before the train leaves for the Old Capitol Prison in Washington City."

"Won't you please allow her to come home for a little while?" Mother begged.

The officer hesitated. "I cannot allow for that. I suppose I can send guards to a hotel and you may stay with her there."

"Oh, thank you, kind sir," Belle replied.

CHAPTER 44

LORETA

JULY 1862

*L*oreta rented a room in the Gayoso Hotel, the same hotel that she and Tom had dinner at so long ago, so she could make preparations for their marriage. Both of them wanted a small, quiet affair, especially considering the circumstances. Not to mention Loreta's recent arrests, which she held back from telling Tom for the time being. They did inform Dr. Hay of the circumstances in order that he could be a witness. The doctor was not as surprised as one might have predicted, confessing that he knew something was "off" about Loreta.

Loreta purchased several dresses as part of her trousseau, choosing a smart gray dress trimmed with blue ribbon to wear during the ceremony. They were married in the parlor of the Gayoso in front of a few soldiers from the hospital. In the end, the couple declined to consummate their marriage that night, thinking it wisest to wait until Tom had recovered a bit more.

The morning after the ceremony, they were just about to depart for breakfast when there was a knock on the door. Loreta opened it to find the desk clerk.

He seemed agitated as he shifted his weight from one foot to the other. "Ma'am, we are evacuating the hotel. The Yankees are marching toward Memphis as we speak."

"The Yanks are coming?" Tom asked, coming to the threshold. "But we just got married."

"I'm sorry, sir, but the Union army doesn't wait for a convenient time to invade."

Tom nodded as he shut the door. He began packing his army-issued knapsack.

Loreta asked him to untie her corset.

"Why?"

"So I can put my uniform on."

"Loreta, you are a married woman. You can no longer keep up the guise of being a soldier."

She turned to face him. "I'm going with you. We are going to fight side by side just like we did at Shiloh."

"I was almost killed at Shiloh, remember?"

"And you are still not quite recovered. I can make sure you are protected."

"No. You have served your country well enough, but we both know what life is like in camp. You cannot continue to risk endangering your reputation, nor mine." The corners of his mouth turned upward, lessening the sting of his words. "I'll fight twice as hard this time, for the both of us."

"What will become of me?"

"What about your family?"

Loreta shook her head. "I can't go back to New Orleans."

"And your inheritance?"

Loreta shook her head again. She'd spent the last of the money William had left her on her trousseau, and her father had written her out of his will a long time ago.

Tom sat on the bed. "You will go to Richmond. I have a house there. It's not large, but it is comfortable. You can make it into a home so that when I return we will live out our lives together." He patted her hand. "And we can finally be together the way God intended."

Loreta assented, seeing it futile to argue now that Tom was officially her husband. It was true she should not be living a soldier's life anymore. She helped him to finish packing and kissed him goodbye before shoving the rest of her woman's clothes into a carpetbag.

CHAPTER 45

BELLE

JULY 1862

*B*elle did not have much recollection of departing from her mother nor the train ride to Washington City. She vaguely recalled Cridge sitting across the aisle from her, but not much else. She remained in a sort of half-awake state, doing the minimum to get by, but not much else. All she could think about was how she was leaving her family and friends, her material pleasures—indeed, everyone and everything that she loved, to the will of the enemy.

Belle had once spent a winter in Washington City, and the city had changed little, despite how much the country around it had. The Capitol building was still unfinished and Belle recognized many of the beautiful houses which she had spent time in as a debutante.

The jail of Belle's final destination had once housed members of Congress during their sessions. Now the brick exterior hid its inmates: smugglers, blockade runners, and political prisoners alike. *And a Confederate spy,* Belle thought to herself upon arriving.

She was immediately presented to William Wood, the superintendent of the prison. Belle found him to be a short, ugly man in an ill-fitting uniform. "So this is the celebrated Rebel," he confirmed with a flash of his strange hazel eyes. "I am beyond pleased to welcome a woman of your reputation."

Belle nodded, unsure of how to interpret his statement.

He continued, "Whatever you desire, ask and you shall have it."

Belle curtsied and thanked him, thinking perhaps prison life wouldn't be as horrifying as she predicted.

Wood led her to her cell, informing her that Rose Greenhow's old cell was on the floor above hers. He promised Belle that she would most likely not be there for long, especially if she became a model prisoner. He placed a small pamphlet on the bedside table before leaving, shutting the door gently behind him.

Belle picked up the pamphlet and traced her finger over the title: *Rules and Regulations of the Old Capitol Prison.* She flipped through it, her eyes falling on a tenet stating she was to have "no communication whatsoever with fellow prisoners." She let the document flutter to the floor before glancing up at the cracked ceiling. She'd read of Rose's imprisonment—the Virginia newspapers had carried stories of starvation and mistreatment of Mrs. Greenhow for months. Belle had thought she'd receive similar treatment, and hoped the Southern newspapers would also make her a martyr. She had not been prepared for a somewhat kindly superintendent and a room that was not so different from the one in her aunt's cottage. But perhaps if she did not act the "model prisoner," she'd receive harsher treatment.

She heard the march of boots outside her door. Finding it unlocked, she opened it to see a sentry standing adjacent to her quarters. "Sir," she commanded.

"Yes, Miss Boyd?"

"I'd like for this fireplace to be lit."

"But it's the middle of July."

"Superintendent Wood told me I could have whatever I desired and I desire a fire to warm my chilled bones and brighten up this dreary room."

The soldier looked up and down the empty hall. He sighed to himself before entering and did as Belle wished.

"Anything else?" he asked in a sarcastic tone when he had finished.

"I would like a rocking chair."

The soldier shook his head as he left. Belle went to the window, noting that it offered a view of Pennsylvania Avenue. She recognized one of the houses across the street as belonging to John Floyd, the secretary of war under the previous President James Buchanan. During the winter she had spent in the city, Belle had attended many a party at that house, bedecked in beautiful dresses with her hair neatly pinned. Compared to her memories of the boisterous parties, at which her voice was probably the loudest of them all, the room seemed eerily silent, the crackling of the fire the only other sound besides Belle's own breathing. The silence was mercifully interrupted when the rocking chair was delivered.

Belle expected a meager dinner of bread and water, but the meal included fresh vegetables as well as meat and potatoes. After dinner, Superintendent Wood knocked on her door. He was accompanied by a man he introduced at Lafayette Baker, who called himself the chief of detectives.

Belle invited them to sit before stating, "I thought a man named Pinkley was the head of the Union secret service."

"Pinkerton?" Baker waved his hand. "No. He'll be lucky if he's not kicked out of Washington City entirely for all the mistakes he's made. I'm authorized under Secretary of War Stanton." He unfolded a small notebook and leaned forward, his bushy eyebrows furrowed. "I've come to get you to make a full confession of what you've done to our cause. As we've got plenty of proof against you, you might as well acknowledge what you've done." His voice held the twang of a frontiersman.

"Sir," Belle said. "I have nothing to say."

"Ain't you tired of your prison already?"

Belle shook her head. "I will make my statement when you have informed me on what grounds I have been arrested and given me a copy of the charges against me. But not until then."

Baker dumped a document on her lap. Belle picked it up, holding it between two fingers. It was a copy of the Oath of Allegiance to the United States of America.

Baker began to expound on the implications of Belle's supposed crimes and finished by saying the South's cause was hopeless. "Won't you now take the oath of allegiance? Secretary Stanton has sent me here to ensure that you do."

Even through Belle's anger, she saw that the men had left the door standing open. She thought of Rose's time in prison, and how her vocal denouncement of the Yankees had ended up in the paper. Seized with the sudden desire to emanate her idol even more, Belle declared loudly, "Tell Mr. Stanton that Miss Belle Boyd has stated that when she commences the oath of allegiance to the United States Government, her tongue may cleave to the roof of her mouth." She took a breath before adding, "If I ever sign one line that will show to the world that I owe the United States Government the slightest allegiance, I hope my arm falls paralyzed by my side."

Baker's lower jaw dropped. He gave her a long penetrating look with his colorless eyes before stating, "If this is your resolution, you'll be here until you are dead. Serves you right."

Belle raised her head and met his gaze. "Sir, if it is a crime to love the South, its cause, and its esteemed president, then I am a criminal. I am in your power, do with me as you please." Her voice escalated in sound with every word. "But I fear you not. I would rather lie down in this prison and die than leave it owing allegiance to such a government as yours." It was time for the crescendo. "Now leave the room for I am so thoroughly disgusted with your conduct towards me that I cannot endure your presence any longer."

"*Bravo!*" Both Wood and Baker's heads turned as cheers echoed up and down the hallway. As intended, Belle's fellow prisoners had overheard her tirade.

Superintendent Wood turned to Baker. "I think we've had enough for tonight. The lady must be tired after her long journey."

"We will continue this presently," Baker sneered before leaving, banging the door shut behind him.

Belle paced anxiously around the room. She could feel the presence of past senators, who might have stayed in the very room she was now imprisoned in. Perhaps John C. Calhoun had written his statements favoring the states' right to secede here. Or perhaps Henry Clay had brainstormed the Compromise of 1850 while staring into her fireplace. Some solution that was—by allowing California to join the Union as a free state while at the same time strengthening the Fugitive Slave Act to please the South, it only delayed the inevitable. *What if they had decided to fight it out then and there, way back in 1850?* The conflict would have been over already, Belle figured, and she'd be married to a nice Southern man, not completing a prison sentence in the Northern Capital. *But there's no use in dwelling on what might have beens.*

The combination of her stressful pacing and the activities of the past few days exhausted her. As she lay down in the cramped bed, the earlier exchange with Baker replayed in her head. She was quite pleased with the outcome: though Baker had left furious, Superintendent Wood had appeared bemused. Belle closed her eyes and recited lines from a poem her father used to read to her:

Stone walls do not a prison make,
 Nor iron bars a cage;
 A free and quiet mind can take
 Those for a hermitage.

CHAPTER 46

HATTIE

AUGUST 1862

*M*ore and more prisoners taxed the already overcrowded Castle Godwin. At the end of the summer, Hattie was informed that she was being transferred to the newly appropriated Castle Thunder. The latest addition to Richmond's military prisons was located a few blocks from the notorious Libby Prison and consisted of three buildings. Hattie was installed in the former Whitlock's warehouse, along with about 100 other female prisoners, mostly women like her who were accused of being spies or "suspicious characters" as well as escaped slaves.

Hattie's new roommate was a loquacious older woman who introduced herself as Mrs. Francis Abel Jamison of New York. After asking Hattie to call her Frankie, she revealed that she had followed her husband to war and had fought for the Union in the Battle of Bull Run, but after he was killed, she had left the army to become a nurse. Finally, she concluded by stating that she'd been in prison since October of last year.

"Under what pretense?" Hattie asked.

"I was still in male disguise, so they arrested me." She puffed out her chest. "It took them a while to figure out that I was a woman."

Frankie could curse like a man and often directed her vitriol at the guards, who were not quite sure what to do with her. Hattie was more amused by her than anything else. As the weeks dragged by, Frankie tried to suss out "Mrs. Webster's" story, to no avail.

One day as Frankie was telling another one of her stories, a guard dropped a packet on the floor.

Frankie paused her diatribe to demand what was in the packet.

"Letters for Mrs. Webster," the guard remarked.

Frankie raised her eyes at Hattie. "From your family?"

Hattie shook her head as she picked up the packet and untied the ribbon. There were six envelopes in all, addressed to her at Castle Godwin, and dating back to April.

"Who is Major Lawton?" Frankie asked, picking up one of the envelopes.

Hattie snatched it back. "An acquaintance of my husband's."

She easily opened the first one, for the seal had already been broken. The single page inside contained multiple creases, evidence that at least one other pair of eyes had read it. Hattie scanned the letter before letting it drop to the floor. "It doesn't make any sense."

Frankie picked it up and began reading.

My Dear Auntie,

I am sorry for not writing before, but I was not sure whether you would be able to receive my letters. The Yanks scour all letters addressed to Richmond, especially to prisoners. You'll be happy to hear that my sister, your niece, Susannah, is on the mend.

Yours affectionately,
Hugh Lawton

. . .

Frankie set the letter down. "What's wrong with that? It sounds like your niece is doing better."

"I don't have a niece, nor a nephew for that matter."

Frankie narrowed her eyes. "So this supposed nephew or, acquaintance of your husband..." She picked up the letter again. "Where have I heard the name Lawton before?" A look of understanding came to Frankie's face. She went to the door of their room and opened it, looking out to see that there were no guards in the vicinity before she walked back and dug her fingers between her bosom, muttering to herself.

Hattie watched her, bewildered both by the mystery letter and Frankie's actions. Her roommate finally pulled a tiny bottle out of her décolletage. She put the letter on the desk and turned her back toward the door, blocking what she was doing to anyone outside of their cell. Hattie stood and watched over Frankie's shoulder as she uncapped the vial and smeared a cream-colored liquid onto the paper. Soon words appeared in the blank space at the bottom of the letter.

My Dear Mrs. Webster,

I have heard about the dire circumstances of Mr. Webster and I want to extend my sincerest apologies. Rest assured that our previous activities resulted in stopping our enemy's naval attempts. I hope that your fate has not turned you against such future activities, and if not, I look forward to working with you again. I also want you to know that our authorities are attempting to secure your release.

The signature remained unchanged.

Frankie and Hattie turned to each other. "How did you—" they both started at once.

"Well, well, well." Frankie stated. "You are definitely not what you claim. You were aware of your husband's activities as a spy for the Union?"

"He wasn't my husband," Hattie finally admitted. "And why do you have that with you?" She gestured toward the vial Frankie had curled in her hand.

Frankie cocked an eyebrow. "I too am a Union spy. Sometimes the best way to avoid suspicion is to act as dubiously as you can."

Hattie didn't think it necessary to retort that Frankie had apparently done a poor job of avoiding suspicion, seeing as she was currently in prison.

"I've heard the name Lawton before." Frankie whistled a low note. "He's a fine man, in multiple ways."

"He's—"

"I know, I know. He was an acquaintance of the man who wasn't your husband." Frankie picked up another letter off the floor. "Let's see what else he had to say."

Hugh's next correspondence contained terse remarks regarding the leadership in Washington City, stating that "the men in charge are never in agreement." Consequently, he was having a hard time obtaining clemency for Hattie.

"By men in charge he must mean McClellan and Lincoln," Hattie mused.

"McClellan. What an ingrate," Frankie said. "And his lackey Pinkerton, he only served to confirm McClellan's whining."

"Pinkerton was my boss."

"That stooge?" Hattie cringed at her coarse words as Frankie continued, "Why'd you work for him?"

Hattie knitted her eyebrows. "You didn't?"

"Nah. Pinkerton's not the only one claiming to be in charge of Washington City's detectives." She nodded at Hugh's letter. "And with the kind of mistakes he's been making, his good friend McClellan shouldn't be head of the Army of the Potomac for much longer."

"Pinkerton's a good man, and a good boss."

"He might have been a good detective, but he's terrible at gathering military intelligence." Frankie paused and tilted her head. "I think someone's coming."

Hattie hurriedly gathered up the packet of letters and stuffed them under the mattress while Frankie replaced the vial into its hiding spot between her breasts.

"Dinner is served," the guard outside called roughly.

"I wouldn't exactly call a bowl full of boiled beef and month-old bread, 'dinner,'" Frankie returned, winking at Hattie as she did so. The guard opened the door, stepping aside for a black man to deliver the buckets stocked with their meal.

After Frankie shoveled her food down, and Hattie forced herself to eat what she could, they decoded the rest of Hugh's letters. They were filled with more updates on the war, filling Hattie in on the progress made in Tennessee and McClellan's defeat by the newly appointed commander of the Army of Northern Virginia, Robert E. Lee.

"Now there's a gallant man if I ever laid eyes on one," Frankie commented.

"Lee? He's a Confederate."

"He nearly was Union, and I rue the day he chose them over us. I would have left my husband for him quicker than you could say, 'Southern gentleman.' But you're right, he was on the wrong side of the war," Frankie added, as if that was the only reason she and Lee hadn't realized their true potential. "Now about you and Major Lawton…"

Hattie faked a yawn. "The events of the day have me exhausted."

Frankie waved Hugh's last letter. "I think I have enough solution left to translate one more." She accordingly wet the paper and then leaned closer, frowning. "There's nothing else written." She tossed the letter at Hattie, who read the visible version.

My Dear Auntie,

As I haven't heard from you, I can't help but fear the worst. News from Richmond has become scarce, and I am concerned for your safety. I know that you cannot get word to your family about your welfare, but I wish for you to know that I think about you daily and will be anxiously waiting your release.

Yours affectionately, as always,

Hugh Lawton

. . .

His words needed no translation and, after tucking that letter on top of the others under her mattress, Hattie slept well for the first time in a long time, dreaming of the day when she and Hugh would be united at last.

CHAPTER 47

BELLE

AUGUST 1862

*D*espite the ban on socializing, Belle quickly made friends with her fellow captors. The few who hadn't heard her outburst on that first night soon learned about her through prison gossip, and they slipped her little presents of candy, flowers, and even tiny Confederate flags that had been smuggled into the Old Capitol prison.

In typical fashion, she won the hearts of even her guards: the sentry who guarded her door during the day permitted her to sit in the doorway of her room and sing. The sentry barely batted an eye when Belle sung tried-and-true favorites such as "Dixie" and "Maryland, My Maryland!" Despite the best efforts of the music teachers at Mount Washington, her voice was forever tuneless but she sang as though she was pouring out her soul with every word. Prisoners of both Northern and Southern sentiments seemed to be transfixed by the melancholy sound of Belle's voice.

The nighttime sentry, however, was not so amused, especially when other prisoners began joining Belle's singing, shouting the words, *She spurns the Northern Scum,* at the top of their lungs.

"You girl," he sneered when his patrolling brought her to her doorway. "Stop that singing."

Belle rose from her rocking chair conveniently positioned just inside the door. "I shan't do so and you can't make me."

He stared her down. Belle saw that he was a young man, perhaps even younger than herself. She grabbed a nearby broom and swept at the path just recently tread by the sentry, singing the stanza even louder than before.

The sentry walked away, muttering to himself about "damned rebels."

Belle, being the only woman in the prison, had the room to herself while others shared a cell with up to ten other men. The loneliness began to weigh heavily on her. She was used to gallivanting all over the Shenandoah Valley—remaining indoors was the most torturous part about the prison. She prevailed Superintendent Wood to let her walk in the prison yard accompanied by a guard, but even Wood could not grant her this simple request, claiming it was ordered by the secretary of war himself that she stay confined inside.

The only instances she was allowed out of her room were Sunday mornings, when Wood would pace the hallways, calling, "All ye who want to hear the Lord God preached by Jeff Davis, go down to the yard, and all ye who want to hear the Lord God preached by Abe Lincoln, go to Room 16." The other prisoners would clamor to be near her in the courtyard, and those that lost out would doff their hats upon making eye contact with her or reach for her hand as she passed by them. Belle would touch them briefly, as though she were a queen walking among her subjects.

Belle's window faced I-Street. Whenever she heard soldiers marching, she quickly rushed to the window, sometimes interrupting her own singing, to taunt the boys in blue walking by, shouting inquiries as to where they were coming from or where they were off to.

The reply was nearly always the same: "Hush you damned rebel or I'll shoot you."

"Then shoot me," Belle would command. "What are you doing, marching down the street when there's a war to fight and Stonewall's waiting for you on the other side of the Potomac?" Sometimes she would instigate things further, telling them that all they had left after being driven out of the Shenandoah by the men of Virginia was to pick on defenseless women. The fact that their abusive and derogatory language was better suited to a brothel than a public street further convinced Belle that these Union soldiers were no gentlemen.

New captives would arrive daily. Their presence was usually announced by one of the prisoners whose window faced Pennsylvania Avenue, shouting "Fresh Fish!" The seasoned prisoners would then all crowd around the window and watch the reoccurring scene of a new enemy of the state being escorted by a sentry or detective into the Old Capitol Prison. One day Belle was astonished to see that the newcomer was none other than Clifford McVay, one of her former beaus from before the war. She'd heard that he'd been wounded during the Peninsula Campaign. His fellow comrades had left him for dead, and, having recovered from his wounds, he became a federal prisoner.

Her favorite sentry happened to be on duty the evening he arrived. As McVay was escorted to the cell directly across from hers, Belle stood in the open doorway and sang "My Southern Soldier Boy" in the most seductive tones she could manage. Belle was pleased to see McVay pause just inside his open door. As she began the final stanza, Belle held up one arm and, with the other, slipped off her right glove and held it between her fingers before dropping it to the floor. She peeked to make sure the guard's back was turned. As McVay watched, Belle wrapped a note around a marble. She began a new refrain as she bent down, making sure McVay caught a view of her décolletage and then rolled the marble across the hall.

McVay stopped it with his foot. He finally broke Belle's gaze to pick up the note and read it, his lips forming a smile. He winked at Belle as he left his place by the doorjamb just as the sentry passed by. A few minutes later, he reappeared and held up the marble before sending it back across to Belle. Belle unwrapped the slip of paper. She had written, "I'm glad to see you are making a recovery."

McVay had written, "I'm glad to see *you*," in return. He signed it "Clifford."

Belle and Clifford continued their marble rolling for the next few nights, their notes becoming increasingly more familiar with each return. It became a sort of game: they'd roll when the sentry's back was turned. He'd hear it and quickly look for the offending noise, but by then the marble had made it to its destination.

After three nights, Clifford asked Belle for her hand in marriage. Belle refused, and the same the next night. It was a Southern tradition to refuse a man twice before accepting. The morning of what Belle assumed would be the third and final proposal, she demanded an appointment with Superintendent Wood.

"What may I do for you, Miss Boyd?" he asked when she entered his office.

"I am going to be engaged to a Rebel officer and would like to speak with you about my trousseau."

If Superintendent Wood was surprised to hear of her impending betrothal, his facial expression did not betray it. "Your trousseau?"

"We wished to be married as soon as possible, and circumstances being as they are, it is very difficult to secure proper wedding attire." Belle handed him a list of her desired items: a gown with white lace and pink ribbon trim, an underskirt with beaded ruffles, and a velvet cloak.

Wood looked over the demands. His hand was placed over his mouth but Belle detected the hint of a smile. "I'll see what I can do for you, Miss Boyd."

. . .

That night another admiring prisoner sent Belle a sugar loaf. One of her least favorite guards was on duty, but when Belle asked if she could deliver the cone of sugar to Clifford, he gave his consent.

Belle marched across the hall and knocked on the door. Clifford answered. Belle gave him a deep curtsy, rotating her shoulders for optimum décolletage viewing. When she rose, she held out the proffered sugar loaf.

The sentry was immediately at her side. "What do you think you are doing?"

"Giving a gift to my love, just as you said I could," Belle replied.

As Clifford reached out to accept the sugar, the sentry hit his musket against Belle's hand, causing her to drop the loaf. Refined sugar sprinkled all over the floor as Belle held up her sore hand to her lips, tears forming in her eyes.

"Keep your hands off of her!" Clifford shouted.

Belle faced the guard. "You said—"

"You did not tell me that he was your love. It's bad enough there are Rebel scum like you two. The last thing we need is for you to produce more of them."

Belle started to bend forward to retrieve what was left of the fallen loaf but the sentry blocked her with the bayonet of his musket. "Go back now, or I'll break every bone in your body."

Belle folded her arms over her chest, enjoying loud protests from Clifford and his roommates. The guard pinned her against the wall, his bayonet stuck through the lace sleeves of her dress like a dart. Belle felt a sharp pain in her upper arm. She began to scream, prompting the prisoners to shout even louder. More guards rushed to the scene. One of them shoved her attacker away while another released Belle. She touched her arm where the pain was and her hand came away with blood. Shocked, Belle screamed again. The guard nearest her ripped open her sleeve. Belle tried shoving him, but he was a large, solid man. "Quiet, girl, I'm trying to see where the blood is coming from."

Belle yanked her arm away and stepped back to examine herself. The bayonet had sliced a small wound shaped like a half moon through her upper arm. The scar that eventually formed after it healed became Belle's favorite testament to her work during the war.

The next morning, Belle was awakened by Superintendent Wood's shouting. She tried to focus as she overheard her name.

"What was that?" she asked, coming to the door with a sheet thrown over her sleeping outfit.

"You are to be sent through the lines to be turned over to General Dix starting tomorrow. You've been set free."

"How?"

"Prisoner exchange. Rebels for true union men. Seems the Confederates have one of our women spies among them, so it's an even trade." Wood walked off.

"Miss Belle?" Clifford was standing in his doorway.

Belle tightened the sheet around and strolled over. "Yes, Cliff?"

"I never did get to ask you in person to marry me. I was going to ask you agin' via marble last night but then that," Clifford's hands tightened and he took a deep breath. "I was fixing to kill that man if he hurt you any further."

"Oh no, Cliff. You would have ended up in solitary confinement, or probably worse."

"Will you wait until I can get out of here? Then we can have a proper wedding."

"We probably can't have a proper wedding until after the war is over." Belle chose her words carefully, not wanting to commit to marriage now that she was going to be set free. Cliff was a handsome, dashing man, but he was still a prisoner and Belle was sure she had many more adventures ahead of her. After Belle left the Old Capitol Prison, she never saw Clifford McVay again.

A crowd of well-wishers and reporters had gathered outside the Old Capitol Prison the morning of Belle's release. Belle used her now-perfected queenly manner to wave at them as she made her way to her carriage.

"God bless you, Miss Belle," one woman shouted. She used the hand of the babe in her arms to blow kisses to Belle and the prisoners who had been released with her. The carriage proceeded to the riverboat, the *Juaniata*, which set sail down the Chesapeake Bay toward Virginia. Belle could see Union ships all down the Bay, preparing an attack on Richmond, Belle assumed. Despite the presence of the enemy all around them as well as onboard, the ex-prisoners on the *Juaniata* were in a jolly mood and the afternoon and night was filled with singing. Belle joined in many of the songs. When the ship headed up the James River, a Confederate flag proudly waving outside someone's home came into view and someone called for "three cheers for Jefferson Davis." Belle's ebullient calls were louder than any of the men's.

She stayed in Richmond's finest hotel, the Ballard House. When she arrived in her room, she found a brown package sitting on her bed. The card on top read, "Complements of Superintendent Wood." Inside was every piece of the trousseau she'd requested.

CHAPTER 48

MARY JANE

SEPTEMBER 1862

*D*espite the cheering news of Union successes in the deep South during the early summer, in late August, the second Battle of Manassas ended with a Confederate victory.

The Davises decided to host a ball in honor of the occasion. Mrs. Davis declared that it was important to let the belles of Richmond see that there were still eligible men available. Mrs. Davis's young sister, Maggie, insisted that there were absolutely no suitable bachelors left during dinner one night. "There are some towns where the only males left are younger than 16 and older than 65," she stated, twirling a piece of brunette hair in her finger.

"That cannot possibly be true," Mrs. Davis retorted.

"Yes, sister, you're right. There is the occasional invalid and amputee to add to the mix."

Mr. Davis looked up from his plate. "If you had to choose between a man with an empty shirtsleeve and a man who stayed home to grow rich from the war, I would say you should take the hero with the empty sleeve."

This time Mrs. Davis borrowed sabers from soldiers to decorate the parlor walls, and masked the worn damask couches with bright slipcovers in red and white. She draped every remaining surface with Confederate flags and even commissioned a local artist to draw the Stars and Bars in colored chalk on the linen rug covering the parlor floor.

In a world where unprecedented carnage and destruction had become the new normal, the Southerners' sense of humanity seemed to be restored, at least for a few hours. As Mary Jane watched the soldiers—many of them in the empty shirtsleeves and legless pants Maggie had predicted—twirl women dressed in patched gowns and homemade palmetto bonnets, she marveled at how careless they seemed, clinging to a past that didn't want them anymore. *Like Nero hosting a ball while Rome burned.*

As the night grew late, the dancers completely annihilated the chalk flag: the blue, white and red pigments becoming affixed to the ladies' slippers and men's boots and then scattering in a sudden gust of wind.

CHAPTER 49

BELLE

SEPTEMBER 1862

*A*lthough Richmond held many social and fashionable attractions, Belle longed for home. Martinsburg was again in Confederate hands which meant that travel would be safe enough. She sent word to her father, who arrived promptly to escort her. He had been given leave from the army and indeed he looked sickly: thinner, his age showing with each painful step he took using his new cane.

They arrived back in Martinsburg to the news that Lincoln had issued a preliminary Emancipation Proclamation after the Battle of Antietam, warning the Southerners that the slaves of the Confederacy would be "thenceforward, forever free," if the states did not return to the Union by January 1.

After reading the latest headline, Belle's father folded the paper and tossed it across the dining room table. "So the war indeed is about them."

The weary tone in his voice made Belle's anger swell. "It was always about them, though the Yanks would have you believe it was about preserving the country. And besides Father, Lincoln can declare everyone free until he is blue in the face. It means nothing to the Confederacy. We are ruled by our own president."

He nodded. "Indeed."

Belle set out the next morning for Stonewall Jackson's headquarters. She wore her favorite riding habit: it was cut close to show off her curves and Rebel gray in color. She carried a gold saber knot intended as a present for the general in her bodice, underneath her palmetto brooch.

Belle rode the eight miles from town, her anxiety mounting. She hoped that General Jackson would remember meeting her as well as praise her for the deeds she had done for the South. After she arrived at camp, she told an aide that Belle Boyd was there to see the general.

More uneasy minutes ticked by until at last Stonewall stepped from his tent. "God bless you my child!" he exclaimed, placing his hands on her head as though he was a priest. "I was horrified to hear of your imprisonment." His hands dropped back to his side.

"Yessir, although I was happy to serve in the name of the Confederacy."

"Ah, but Miss Boyd, if our army evacuates the area, you will once again be in danger. Take heed, it will be worse if the Yankees capture you again. You should travel deeper South. Take the time to drink in all of the beautiful scenery our great country has to offer."

"Will you send word if you have to leave?" Belle asked, hoping to have a place in the general's thoughts.

"Indeed I will, but you must hasten back home now. God bless you," he said again.

On the way back to Martinsburg, Belle saw a young soldier painfully stumbling along the road on bare feet. She quickly removed her own leather ankle boots and handed them down to him.

"You're wasting your pretty boots," another soldier called. "We won't be pullin' them off his dead body to send them back to ya."

Belle glared at the speaker. "If my shoes rest his poor young feet only a little while, I am repaid." She turned back to the boy. "You're not old enough to be away from your mother."

"Yes'm," the boy replied. He held up the boots and grinned. "Thank ye, miss."

Belle rode the rest of the way home barefoot.

A few days later, Belle received a letter from Stonewall Jackson, telling her that Martinsburg was no longer safe for her. He advised her to go visit family further South, signing his letter, "Truly your friend, TJ Jackson." Belle heeded his advice and left for Knoxville.

CHAPTER 50

LORETA

OCTOBER 1862

Soon after Loreta arrived in Richmond, General Winder declared that he was placing the city under martial law. He forbade liquor to be sold, and residents were forced to give up their weapons. He employed a group of men, who quickly became known as Winder's Plug Uglies, to enforce his laws.

While Loreta was mostly unaffected by these new circumstances, she chafed at life as a housewife. The Richmonders had heard of her arrest and refused to socialize with her, fearing the Plug Uglies would accuse them of being a suspicious person. Consequently, Loreta was relentlessly bored.

Tom's letters were her only solace. He was posted in Corinth under General Braxton Bragg. At first his descriptions made her miss the action of a soldier's life even more, but his later writing took on a bitter tone. The recently passed amendment to the Conscription Act, or as Tom called it, the Twenty-Slave Law, had created a lot of tension among the Confederate soldiers, who began referring to the conflict dividing the nation as a "rich man's war, poor man's fight." The conscripted soldiers, forced to battle when they had no wish to do so, were deserting every day. Those that were caught were whipped and sometimes even shot. Tom called General Bragg an "inhumane tyrant," complaining that none of the soldiers ever had enough to eat and coffee and whiskey had been outlawed. The last letter Tom sent related that the Yankees were advancing toward Corinth and he was worried because the starved troops were in no condition to fight.

And then everything went silent. After not hearing from him for a few weeks, Loreta tried to make inquiries with the Richmond authorities as to her husband's whereabouts, but could not get any information.

When a uniformed soldier appeared on her doorstep one afternoon, Loreta's heart leapt into her throat. She invited him in with trepidation, expecting him to tell her that Tom was dead. As the soldier opened his mouth to speak, it seemed to Loreta that time slowed down.

"I'm sorry?" Loreta asked. "Can you repeat that?"

"I am here to place you under arrest."

It took a moment for Loreta to reset her brain. When she finally replied, it felt as though her mouth was full of sawdust. "Whatever for?"

"You have been accused of being an alien enemy."

"But I've just recently arrived in Richmond."

"Exactly."

As the soldier escorted her to the headquarters of the provost marshal, Loreta figured it was just a simple misunderstanding. General Winder was out, so Loreta pleaded with his assistant, playing on the fact that she was an innocent woman.

The assistant marshal laughed. "That's not what I've heard, Mrs. De Caulp. Or should I refer to you as Lieutenant Buford?"

Shocked, Loreta sat back, realizing her fate had been sealed.

They sent her to Castle Thunder. The man in charge there was

Captain Alexander, a well-toned brute who had the reputation of favoring prisoners who had the means to bribe him. After introducing herself to the captain, Loreta cooed over his black bloodhound, bending over to pet him.

"His name's Nero," Alexander told her, pride obvious in his voice.

"He's very charming," Loreta said, straightening and surreptitiously wiping her hands on her skirts. "Now, Captain, I'm here to see about arranging for the finest prison suite you have."

"I think it can be arranged… for the right price." Alexander held out his hand.

Loreta turned away, feigning deep anguish. "You don't understand. My husband's missing, and I am but a poor woman."

"And a suspected traitor," Alexander added.

"Oh, but sir, that is not true. In fact, I've risked my life multiple times for the cause." She relayed her story, from living through moments of near-death on the battlefield, to being a courier in New Orleans, to nearly losing the man she loved.

Captain Alexander finally relented and gave Loreta a private cell. He also granted her permission to roam the prison freely. The first full day she was there, she received an invitation to Alexander's "citizens' room." She entered it to find a sort of game room, complete with second-hand billiard and card tables. She strolled to an empty chair at a poker table and told the dealer to cut her in.

"With what money?" he replied.

Loreta took off her boot and emptied it on the table. A few Confederate dollars and coins came out. She shoved one of the coins into the center of the table and glared at the man who spoke.

He shoved his unruly blonde hair out of his eyes before reaching a thin arm across the table. "Charles Dunham."

She shook his hand with a touch of Harry's finesse. "Loreta De Caulp."

He pointed his thumb at the other men and introduced them before asking why she was there.

"I'm not sure," she said, picking up her cards. "It could be any number of reasons." She used the down time in between raising and calling to repeat the story she'd told Captain Alexander.

"Where is your husband now?" Dunham asked when she'd finished.

Loreta looked down at her cards and frowned. "I believe he is dead. His injuries were the type that would have slowed him in battle." She shoved the rest of her dollars to the middle of the table. "Raise."

"What was his name?" Dunham asked. He furtively reassembled his cards before putting them face down on the table. "I have a lot of connections and can make some inquiries as to his fate when I am finally released."

"Captain Thomas De Caulp."

Loreta watched his lips move as he repeated the name. He looked at his cards again and then sprinkled his own coins into the pile. "I'll see you and raise you ten more."

The only other player left in his game put his cards down. "Too rich for my blood."

Loreta's hand was terrible, but she had no intention of folding. "I'll see your ten and I call." She nodded at Dunham, who flipped an ace over. She revealed a pair of sevens. Although they had both been bluffing, the pot went to Loreta. As she leaned over to collect her money, she couldn't help notice Dunham staring at her. She dropped her new booty into her shoe before bidding the men good-day.

The next afternoon, Loreta was summoned to Captain Alexander's office.

"Mrs. De Caulp, can I talk freely?" he asked as he pushed a pile of paperwork aside.

"Of course, Captain," Loreta said, taking the seat he proffered her.

"I wanted to warn you about the man you've been seen with recently."

"Mr. Dunham?"

Captain Alexander nodded. "Or Sandover Conover, James Wallace, or any of the other aliases he uses."

Loreta leaned forward. "I don't understand."

"The man is a reporter and writes under multiple names. Although he claims he is a Southerner, he writes articles for newspapers on both sides. He's even used one pen name to outright argue against things he himself has written."

"Why would he do that?"

Alexander heaved his large shoulders. "Who knows? No one is quite sure to which side he pledges his allegiance. That is, if he has any loyalty at all."

"I had no idea."

Alexander reached over to pet Nero. "Neither did General Winder until the Union called for his arrest. Our informants in Washington City passed on his dossier, which included the pen name he uses to write for the *Richmond Examiner*. Somehow he is able to travel back and forth through the lines indiscriminately."

Loreta stood. "Thank you for the warning, Captain Alexander. I will be more cautious in my interactions with him from now on."

Alexander held up his hand. "That's not the only thing I wanted to speak with you about. I've been thinking about what you told me about your exploits in New Orleans."

Loreta sat down again. "What about them?"

"It sounds to me like you have great talent as a spy."

Loreta beamed, pleased her work had finally been noticed.

"If you want, I can write you a letter of introduction to General Winder," Alexander continued. "I believe that you would be a great asset to his core of secret service detectives."

"Oh yes sir, please do." Loreta bestowed a wide grin upon the prison commander. "Nothing would please me more."

Two weeks after Loreta entered Castle Thunder, Captain Alexander came in personally to tell her that she had been released.

Even Nero's ears perked at Loreta's sigh of relief. "General Winder must have finally realized he had no reason to keep me prisoner."

"He's requested to meet you, actually," Captain Alexander replied. "He must have received my note."

"I'll go right away," Loreta declared.

Captain Alexander stepped into her cell. "Just be careful, Mrs. De Caulp. The old man has a reputation being so adept at double-dealings you won't realize for weeks that you've been deceived."

Contrary to the captain's warning, Loreta found General Winder to be a rather pleasant looking gentleman, with bright white hair and a kind face.

Loreta curtsied and began to introduce herself, but Winder held up his hand. "No need to exchange pleasantries. I know who you are as surely you are familiar with me."

Loreta sat down. "Yes, sir."

His voice was low and gravelly, reminding Loreta of Nero's growl. "I'm told you are looking for employment."

Loreta folded her hands. "I am anxious to continue my service to the Confederacy."

"Is that so?" his gray eyes looked skeptical. "Are you aware that your slave escaped North after Shiloh?"

"Bob?" Loreta looked down and, noticing her knuckles turning white, released her hands and flexed her fingers. "I didn't know that."

"And your husband, Mrs. De Caulp. Do you know where he is?"

She looked up. "No, sir."

The left side of his lip curled. "If you want to prove to me that you are capable of reconnaissance, the first thing you need to do is locate the whereabouts of your husband."

Loreta nodded and stood, marveling at how quickly General Winder's pleasant demeanor had completely disappeared. As she took her leave, she realized she was more than a little afraid of him.

CHAPTER 51

HATTIE

DECEMBER 1862

*H*attie's situation in Castle Thunder grew even worse. The prison commander, Captain Alexander, was horribly abusive to those he didn't favor. Although Hattie and even Frankie managed to stay out of his way, they were forced to witness the wrath of his anger when he ordered men to be hung by their thumbs in the courtyard. At night Hattie would try to cover her ears with a pillow to drown out the screams of men being whipped or beaten.

She wrote to everyone she could think of, from Jefferson Davis to Judah Benjamin to General Winder, to no avail. She even penned a few letters to Kate, knowing that she'd never be able to get them North. As she'd received no more letters from Major Lawton, she feared he had finally been captured, or worse, hanged.

Finally, in December, the captain informed both Hattie and

Frankie that their release had at last been secured and that they, along with a few other prisoners, were to be escorted back to Washington City by boat the very next day.

Hattie had never been so pleased to see an American flag as she was when she saw one flapping in the breeze on the boat that would take them across the Potomac.

She spent the entire crossing restless. She'd been in Confederate territory since she crossed the wide river with Timothy almost a year ago. As far as she knew, her friend's body still lay behind her, buried in an enemy land. Her main objective now that she was free was to avenge Timothy's death, but she had no idea how to go about doing so. She supposed she would resume her position at the Pinkerton Detective Agency, but, considering that the Confederates knew her as Mrs. Webster, she would not be able to work undercover in the South anymore. Which was just as well, as she was not anxious to go back any time soon.

Frankie soon became seasick and sought refuge below deck. Hattie refused to be confined anymore and relished the cold winter air at the bow of the boat. As they approached land, Hattie, catching sight of people waiting at the wharf, felt lonely: there wouldn't be anyone there to greet her. She had no family to speak of, and most of her co-workers had been executed or jailed.

But as soon as she disembarked, an almost empty carpetbag in her hand, she saw a familiar figure standing on the dock: Hugh Lawton.

She dropped her bag and ran straight into his embrace. After what seemed like an eternity, he held her at arm's length. "Hattie, I'm so sorry. I wanted so badly to visit you in prison, but I couldn't get a pass."

It was all so overwhelming: finally being back on Union soil and seeing Hugh standing before her, that Hattie had a hard time focusing. "It's okay, Hugh. I understand."

"You're not mad at me?"

"Of course not. You could have been killed for associating with a Union spy. There are enough dead and guilty men at my feet. I don't need any more." She meant the comment to be light, but her voice choked up at the end.

They began walking down the dock, hand in hand.

"I love you." He said it so casually that at first Hattie wasn't sure if she heard him right.

"What?"

"I've loved you since I helped you escape from your husband all those years ago."

She stopped to face him. "Why didn't you say anything?"

"I knew I was going to go along with John Brown's raid and your marriage wasn't officially ended. Once you decided to stay in Chicago, I didn't know if we'd ever meet again. And then, after Timothy... well, I thought you might hate me."

"Why would I hate you?"

"I tried to get you out of prison, but I didn't know how. After we tried... we tried to save Timothy..." For the first time since she'd known him, Hattie saw Hugh's finely sculpted plaster crack. He enveloped her in his arms, burying his face in her hair. "I'm so sorry, Hattie. I love you."

"I love you, too."

He pulled away to look into her eyes. "Do you?"

Hattie met his gaze. "I do."

His grin filled his face. "What shall we do now? My Southern instincts are telling me that I should ask your family permission for your hand in marriage, but I know that's not necessary in your case."

"My husband..." Hattie said softly.

"He's dead."

"How do you—"

Hugh pulled out a piece of paper from his inside jacket pocket. "Antietam. He had fought for the Confederates. I made some inquiries once I heard you were being released."

"You checked up on me?"

"And I bought you this." He again reached into his pocket and pulled out a tiny ring. He got down on one knee. "Carrie Stevens, or Hattie Lewis, or whatever your name is... will you marry me?"

"Yes, I will, Hugh Lawton."

"Then come with me." He took her hand and started back for the boat.

"Where are we going?"

"The captain can marry us."

"Now?"

"I waited all of this time for you to be released—I'm not going to let you get away now or ever." He paused walking. "Is that okay?"

She laughed. "Yes, let's get married."

Frankie was exiting as the two stepped onto the boat. She put her hands on her hips, still green from her earlier bout with seasickness. "Hugh Lawton, what are—"

"C'mon," Hattie told her as they breezed past. "You can be our witness."

Half an hour later, after they'd once again stepped onto the dock, Frankie and the new Mrs. Lawton looked around, both wondering what would happen next.

"I'd like to meet with Allan Pinkerton," Hattie stated. "There're some things we need to discuss." *Namely Pryce Lewis and John Scully.* To Hattie's knowledge they were both still in prison in Richmond.

Hugh shook his head. "I'm sorry to say that, with McClellan's firing from the Army of the Potomac, Pinkerton returned to Chicago."

"And Kate Warne?"

Hugh furrowed his brow. "Some of his operatives stayed on to work for Lafayette Baker, but I think Mrs. Warne went with Pinkerton."

Hattie bit her lip, thinking that all of her friends had indeed abandoned her. As if he could read her mind, Hugh touched her cheek and stated, "Hattie, you have me now."

"Well I'd like to meet with Stanton," Frankie announced. "I'd like to ask the secretary of war why it took so long to set us free."

"I'm sorry for that," Hugh started walking up the dock. "We've been trying to negotiate your release for months. You were supposed to be exchanged for Belle Boyd, a Confederate spy, but she was released in August."

"That strumpet?" Frankie inquired. She folded her arms across her chest. "It's not what I would call an even exchange."

"C'mon," Hugh strode forward. "I'll buy you both some lunch. I'm sure you're starving for a decent meal."

CHAPTER 52

LORETA

JANUARY 1863

*T*he more Loreta thought about Winder's challenge, the more determined she became to demonstrate her abilities as a spy. She just needed to find Tom.

The solution came in the form of a letter dropped on her doorstep. There was no return address, Loreta noted as she ripped it open and scanned for the signature. It was from Charles Dunham, the dubious journalist she'd become acquainted with in Castle Thunder. He wrote that he had returned to Washington City and urged her to come there as well. He ended the cryptic note by stating he had information on her husband's whereabouts.

Loreta tossed the letter aside and ran to her room to begin preparations to go North. She thought about resuming the disguise of Harry Buford, but with both McClellan's and Lee's armies converging in the area, Loreta soon realized that she would be better off dressed as a woman.

The first hurdle would be crossing from Virginia into Union territory. After traveling to the edge of the Potomac, she found an old negro man with a boat and offered him $25 in Confederate money to take her across.

The man's eyes widened. "This sum risky bizness, traveling 'cross this here river. You's got soldiers on both sides who won't hes'-tate to shoot. *And* you's got cold weather and strong waves."

"I need to get through the lines. I've got something for them Yanks."

"Why, miss, you gone aid them in freein' us colored folk?"

Momentarily taken aback, Loreta quickly recovered herself. "Yes, sir," she lied smoothly.

"I suspect you's be back in a few days with the whole Union army at your back for the purpose of settin' all us slaves free." The darkey's blind faith in Loreta tugged at her heart, but she figured that, sometimes, lying was as necessary as fighting. "Yes, sir," Loreta replied. She waved the bill under his nose and he grabbed it.

It took three hours to get across to the opposite shore. The negro pulled hard at the oars, but it was hard work in the bitter night air. The woolen shawl on Loreta's shoulders was no match for the wind and she longed to take over the rowing for a bit, just to get warm. Instead, she sat like a proper lady, shivering in the hull of the boat. By the time they reached the Maryland side, Loreta was numb from the cold and her legs were stiff from the cramped position she had been sitting in.

She thanked the old man and then turned away.

"You shuh you gone be okay?" he asked.

Loreta narrowed her eyes. She'd heard about negroes attacking women, and, although the old man seemed kind, she decided to discourage any thought he might have in that regard. "You should probably get back as fast as you are able. If you don't you might find yourself in the hands of abolitionists."

The old man opened his mouth and then shut it.

He probably thinks abolitionists are the same as cannibals, and who wouldn't hesitate to use him as substitute beef.

"Lawd miss, I don't want dem to catch me fo shuh." With that he darted off, clutching the money Loreta had paid him for his services.

Loreta made her way into Washington City and checked into Brown's Hotel. In the morning she sent a note to Dunham at his place of business, the *Daily National Republican* newspaper. He paid a call on her that afternoon.

"Mrs. De Caulp," he said, bowing toward her.

She nodded a greeting before getting right to the point. "You said you have news of my late husband."

Dunham sat down with the back of the chair in front of him, his legs spread wide. "He's not late."

"Pardon?" She took a seat on the bed.

"Your husband is not dead. He defected to the Union."

Loreta had the notion that she might fall off the bed. She put a hand on the wall to steady herself.

Dunham, studying her face, continued, "Although I'm not sure that it's the proper thing to call him your husband, seeing as he was already married when you met him."

Loreta had trouble catching her breath and Dunham fetched her a glass of water from the end table before sitting back down. "Do you want to hear the rest of it or have you heard enough?"

"Just give me a minute," she said, taking another sip of water. She set it down and then sat as straight as she could on the soft bed. "You may continue."

"Captain De Caulp's real name is William Irving, originally from Pennsylvania. He claimed to Union officers that he was in Atlanta on business when the war started and was conscripted to serve in the Confederacy."

"But he willingly volunteered at the beginning of the war. He served at Ball's Bluff, long before the Conscription Act." Loreta put a hand under her chin. "And why would he change his name?"

Dunham shook his head. "All I know is what I read in the Union report that they took after he deserted. You know they are offering to pay Confederate deserters who swear the Federal oath of allegiance. Perhaps he needed the money."

A memory of the look on Tom's face after she told him her inheritance had been depleted returned to Loreta. She readjusted her skirts. "Tell me more about his other wife."

"He has a two-year-old son. My guess is that he didn't know he had one and intended on somehow profiting from the war down South—without the burden of a wife. That accounts for the name change." Dunham shrugged. "Maybe finally getting word that she had given birth was the impetus for him to desert and come North."

Half-numb from shock, she felt no bitterness or sorrow, only curiosity. "But it doesn't make any sense. What about me? Where do I fit in?"

The corners of Dunham's mouth turned downward. "Mrs. De Caulp... if I should still be calling you that. There's one last thing you need to know."

She sighed, wondering if there was anything else he could say that would be more startling than what he'd already told her.

"The reason you came to be arrested in Richmond was because your... husband gave your name to General Winder as a fraud. He was probably hoping that the Confederate government would forgive his betrayal if he provided them intelligence."

This was the last straw for Loreta. She recalled the shrewd look on Winder's face when he'd asked about her husband. "Thank you, Mr. Dunham, for all of your information." She rose from her chair. "It has shed much light on the fate of Captain De Caulp. But, seeing as how I've had a long journey, I'm quite tired."

Dunham replaced his hat and also got up from his chair. "I was just trying to be helpful. As a journalist, I am privy to much information."

"Yes, I can see that." She walked over to the door and opened it. "Good day, Mr. Dunham."

He pulled a piece of paper out of his coat pocket. "I also found William Irving's last known address before the war started." He opened her hand and placed it in her palm. "Just in case you were curious. It's in Georgetown, right near our fair city of Washington."

Loreta stared at the address long after he had left. Her head was still spinning with all the information Dunham had provided, one word taking precedence over all the questions she still had: *why*.

Why had Tom lied to her about everything? Why had he married her if he already had a wife? Why had he claimed to be a Union man while serving two years for the Confederacy? And why had he given her name to the Confederate authorities? Loreta suspected she knew the reply to all her questions would be the same. As Dunham predicted, he probably did it all for money.

She squeezed the paper in her hand. There was only one man who could possibly tell her the true story, and that was Tom De Caulp himself.

Loreta tidied herself the best she could before making her way to Georgetown, finding the address she was given with little problem. A woman answered the door.

Loreta, realizing this was her rival for her husband's affections, studied her. She wore a plain calico dress with a tattered belt loosely tied across her wide waist.

The woman, as if sensing Loreta's resentment, put her hand on her hip. "Can I help you?"

"I need to speak to Tom—William Irving."

"My husband is not home," the woman responded.

Loreta, suppressing the urge to declare that he was her husband too, asked instead if she knew of his whereabouts.

"He's enlisted with the army." A child began to cry from inside the house. "I'm not sure where he's stationed at this point." The woman's hand tightened on the doorknob. "May I ask what this is in regard to?"

"It is no matter," Loreta replied, her voice hoarse. She could tell that the woman's patience was growing thin and made no inquiries as to what battalion Tom had joined. She bid the woman good-day and returned to the sidewalk in defeat. She had thought she could turn Tom's mind to his former loyalties with both his wife and government, but it was clear that, for whatever purpose, Tom had made his decision.

Loreta walked back to her hotel room feeling as though she were at a crossroads. Her first husband had died and her second had placed both herself and the cause she loved in peril. Her past arrests had made continuing life as a soldier even more of a difficult feat than before, and she had no money to support any more adventures, not to mention that the Confederate secret service thought she was a traitor, thanks to Tom. She paused at a bridge overlooking the river. *It could be so easy to end it all.* She placed a cautious boot on the banister, wondering if she could really go through with flinging herself into the cold waters of the Potomac below.

Just then she overheard a man's voice raised in protest. "Give it back!"

Loreta looked up to see a white man pulling a carpetbag away from a Negro.

"Suh, it's my's. I's won it fer and skwer," the darkey replied.

The white man clenched his fists. "We both know you ain't won nothin' yet."

His opponent, clearly deciding that whatever was in the carpetbag wasn't worth the fight, let it go. "Maybe not yet, but someday."

Loreta drew in a breath as she recognized the darkey as Harry's former slave, Bob. He had gained weight and his clothing looked new.

"Someday we'll all be in hell!" the man shouted as he made off with his prize.

Loreta silently watched as Bob sauntered down the street in the opposite direction of his opponent. He started to whistle before he was out of earshot, seemingly undaunted by the loss of whatever was in the carpetbag. Loreta marveled that she had never seen Bob, or any Negro down South for that matter, exhibit such confidence with his place in his world.

Loreta returned her foot back to the ground, realizing that Bob had abandoned her just like Tom. Just so he could go North.

Let them all go North, she thought as she resumed walking. *Let the Union figure out what to do with their good-for-nothing spoils of war.* If Tom wanted to raise his son in a world full of freed black men, so be it. But she would never stoop so low herself, nor would any of the men she knew back home.

CHAPTER 53

MARY JANE

JANUARY 1863

The Emancipation Proclamation officially took effect at the beginning of the New Year, but most Virginians paid it no heed. Its main impact in Richmond was that slaves fled North in greater numbers than ever. The amount of staff at the Confederate White House continued to dwindle. Mary Jane was not surprised when Mr. Garvin told her he planned on leaving as they walked back to the house from McNiven's truck one day.

"It's gotten too dangerous here," he asserted. "I think Mr. Davis suspects there's information leaking from this house. You should consider going North too."

"I can't. Not yet," Mary Jane replied.

Mr. Garvin conceded with a nod of his head. "I was hoping you would say that. The Richmond Underground will need your eyes and ears more than ever."

"I am aware. Miss Lizzie thinks there are great plots underfoot to rescue the Confederacy from their inevitable defeat."

He nodded. "I will still do what I can from the Union side."

"Mr. Garvin." Mary Jane took a deep breath. "I've been wanting to ask you about my father."

Mr. Garvin patted her arm. "Sometimes things are better left unsaid."

Mary Jane's voice firmed. "You know who he was, then."

He looked off to the horizon. "There were rumors at the time. And I've heard some things since then that convinced me that they might be true."

"Who, then?"

He shook his head. "I don't think——"

"Mr. Garvin, please. I would like to know."

He rubbed at his chin. "Not now. Tonight. Meet me on the porch of the outbuilding after you are dismissed."

"Yes sir." Mary Jane crossed her fingers briefly, hoping that nothing would occur to make Mr. Garvin change his mind.

True to his word, Mr. Garvin was seated in his customary spot when Mary Jane returned from the mansion. He patted the seat beside him and began by saying, "You and your mother came from the Richards' when you were just a baby. Mr. Richards was old Mrs. Van Lew's brother."

"I know." Mary Jane had always been under the assumption that her father was Mr. Richards himself or possibly his son.

Mr. Garvin was lost in his recollection and didn't seem to hear Mary Jane. "While many assumed that your mammy had been sent away because Mrs. Richards didn't want her husband's mistress around, I had heard a different story." He paused before continuing, "Old Man Van Lew often paid a visit to his brother-in-law's plantation to hunt and fish."

The blood running through Mary Jane's blood seemed to freeze. "No."

He put his hand on top of Mary Jane's. "It makes sense. Miss Lizzie had always given you special treatment, having you baptized and then married in her church. I think that both Mrs. Van Lew and her daughter wanted to raise you under their own roof."

Mary Jane pulled her hand away. "You are saying that Miss Lizzie is my sister?"

Mr. Garvin took a deep breath. Unable to meet Mary Jane's eyes, he stared off into the distance. His normally cultured voice seemed to lose its polish when he spoke again. "I'm not sayin' I know dis to be fact. They's always ben just wha' I say—rumors. I'm just sayin' it's an explanation." He finally looked at her. "I'm sorry if this upsets you."

"He… my father, didn't want me to be free."

"No," Mr. Garvin agreed. "He wouldn't let any of us be free. But Miss Lizzie did. You have to remember that. She wanted the best for you. Always wanted that."

"Look at me, Mr. Garvin." Mary Jane waited until his gaze finally settled on her. "I'm still doing her bidding, risking my life at this house. I've always been a pawn in her game."

"Miss Lizzie's game is freedom, girl." Mr. Garvin's voice dropped to a low growl. "That's the ultimate game, and don't you forget it. What I tole you tonight don't change anythin' about whatcha doin' here."

Mary Jane's chest rose in protest, but quickly sank again. Mr. Garvin's words had only confirmed what she herself had suspected for years. It wasn't his fault she was who she was, not anyone's fault but Mr. Van Lew's. "Thank you."

He stood. "I should go pack. I've got a long journey ahead of me." One side of his lip curled upward. "And something tells me you do as well. Someday."

CHAPTER 54

HATTIE

MARCH 1863

*H*attie soon settled into Hugh's Georgetown townhouse. It was refreshing to be able to be herself, as Mrs. Lawton, instead of living under the guise of a lie. She no longer had to test every word in her head before she spoke to make sure she did not give anything away. When she walked down the street, she did not have to take stock of every person she passed, wondering if they had any ulterior motives. Although she did it often anyway—it was hard to turn off the detective part of her brain.

Hugh still made frequent trips through the lines, and Hattie worried for him every time.

He had been gone for a few days on a mission when Hattie received a telegram from Secretary of War Stanton, requesting that she come to the War Office. Hattie did so immediately, her heart hammering, thinking it could only mean that something had happened to her new husband.

"Ah, Mrs. Lawton," Stanton said when she entered his office. "I asked you here today in regard to this." He handed Hattie a telegram, which she accepted with shaking hands. He looked at her over the top of his wire-framed glasses. "Tell me what you think I should do."

Hattie sank into a chair, overcome with relief. The telegram was from Pryce Lewis, still in Castle Thunder. He was asking for $100 in gold coins in order to retain a lawyer.

"The lawyer's name is Humphrey Marshall from Kentucky." Stanton pulled at the long beard that obscured his chin. "He signed on to be a Confederate General, but had to resign his commission because they couldn't find a horse to hold his weight!" He laughed, a sound that seemed incongruous with his solemn features. "Lewis thinks that Marshall could get both him and Scully out, but I'm inclined not to pay the money since I believe they are the ones truly responsible for Webster's death."

Hattie handed him back the telegram. "I don't believe that Pryce Lewis ever used evidence against Timothy. He says Scully did, though."

Stanton nodded. "I'll send this on to Pinkerton. Maybe he'll put up the money." He tucked the paper into a pile and then folded his hands in front of him. "Also, Mrs. Lawton, I wanted to know if you ever thought of resuming your former work."

"Sometimes," she replied truthfully.

He sat forward. "Excellent." He waved his hand at a passing associate in the hallway.

"Yes sir?" he asked, stepping into the room.

"Could you bring me the Antonia Ford file please?"

The clerk disappeared for a moment, returning with a rather large file. Stanton flipped it open. "Miss Ford is a young miscreant that seems intent on giving Union intelligence to the Confederates. Rather like Belle Boyd. Have you heard of either?"

"Just in passing," Hattie replied. "I was supposed to be exchanged for Miss Boyd."

Stanton set his glasses down in front of him and looked thoughtful. "Yes, if only those Confederates would have cooperated, we could have gotten you out a lot sooner." He ran a hand through his thinning brown hair. "Miss Ford lives in Fairfax—"

"I'm sorry sir," Hattie's apprehension overtook her social refinement. "I don't mean to interrupt you, but I can't go back there." She grasped her reticule handle. "Not so soon."

"It's no matter." Stanton replaced his glasses. "We are in need of a woman to befriend Miss Ford and get her to confess her contemptible dealings. Someone with Union ties that doesn't mind getting a little underhanded."

Hattie leaned forward. "I know just the woman. Have you ever heard of Frankie Abel Jamison?"

CHAPTER 55

MARY JANE

APRIL 1863

*R*ichmond had become a miserable place to reside, even in the Confederate White House. The war was nearing its third anniversary and the Confederacy was floundering. Because the inland town was far away from trade routes, prices for what once had been considered necessities like flour and bacon had risen at a staggering rate.

In what was perhaps an ill-advised move, President Davis declared a day of fasting and urged Richmonders to spend the day praying for the cause instead of eating. It was spoken throughout the servants' quarters that this might finally be the Confederacy's undoing.

Mary Jane could picture Miss Lizzie's lined face light up with glee upon hearing Mr. Davis's request that his already gaunt citizens give up their sustenance for a day. But she wouldn't get to see her mistress's pleasure in person: ever since Mr. Garvin left, Mary Jane had been avoiding Miss Lizzie. She told Mr. McNiven during one of his deliveries that it was too risky to go to meet her at the seamstress's now that all the servants were leaving.

"Are you in danger?" he demanded.

"I don't think so," Mary Jane answered truthfully. Although Jefferson Davis had admitted to Judah Benjamin he thought the Yankees were paying his servants to run away, his behavior toward Mary Jane had not changed. Nor had Mrs. Davis's. "But I don't want any of us to fall under suspicion."

Mr. McNiven nodded. "I will let Ms. Van Lew know. She worries about you constantly."

Mary Jane forced a smile. "Tell her I'm fine, just a little wary is all."

While Mr. Davis had never been exactly what Mary Jane would call robust, his health continued to decline that spring. He'd often complain of headaches or stomachaches, and Mrs. Davis had to treat his swollen left eye with drops of mercury every evening. On days when he stayed home to work, Mary Jane would wait to clean his office until after he'd returned to his bedroom to nap. She would memorize whatever she saw in the myriad of papers on his desk and then code it in her quarters before passing it on to McNiven the next day.

One day in early April, Mrs. O'Melia asked Mary Jane to run an errand for the household. "Normally Phebe would, but seeing as she's escaped, I need you to do it."

Obligingly, Mary Jane, shopping list in hand, headed to Capitol Square. Right after she'd crossed Broad Street, she heard the sound of glass breaking. As she got closer she could see that the square was filled with people shouting. Mary Jane stopped short, ducking behind a building when she saw that they were brandishing weapons such as knives and hammers, some of them even holding stones in their hands. It was far enough away for her to feel safe, but close enough to discern that the townspeople were chanting, "Bread or blood!"

As if on cue, pandemonium suddenly erupted and the crowd, mostly women from Mary Jane's vantage point, broke into stores by clobbering the locks with a hatchet or smashing the windows with rocks. They stole whatever they could get their hands on, from food to clothing to jewelry to brooms, loading them into the hundreds of awaiting carts and wagons. Mary Jane was about to leave for safety's sake when she heard horse-hoofs coming up Seventeenth Street. She flattened herself against the doorframe upon recognizing Mr. Davis's gaunt frame in front of a troop of soldiers.

After he passed, she crept a bit closer to see if he would have any luck ending the riot.

At first no one paid the president any heed, but then the Public Guard began arresting some of the mob, leading them into their walled cart. Those who remained stopped their raiding and grew somewhat subdued. Mr. Davis stepped onto a bench and waved his arms. Most of the crowd paused to stare.

"What has caused such a lawless act?" he asked in a loud voice.

"We are starving, sir," one woman shouted.

He gestured to her arms, which were full of boots and candles. "Those will not feed your family."

"Get us back into the Union!" a man's voice called. "We are tired of the Confederacy's depriving us of basic needs."

Mr. Davis dug into his pockets and pulled out a wad of cash. "This is all I have, but I will give it to you." He threw it up into the air as people dropped their goods to retrieve the money.

Mr. Davis cupped his empty hands around his mouth and called in his loudest voice, "You have five minutes to disperse or you will be fired upon." The soldiers who stood guard around him fixed their bayonets.

Mary Jane decided to leave at that point. The crowd must have decided to heed the president's orders as she did not hear any gunshots on her way back to the Confederate White House.

That evening, select members of the Confederate Cabinet met with Mr. Davis in the executive dining room to discuss the bread riot. The new Secretary of War, James Seddon, urged Mr. Davis to keep the "god-awful disorderliness" of a few people out of the papers. "We wouldn't want the Yanks to hear of our misfortunes here in Richmond," Mr. Seddon insisted.

Another Cabinet member concurred. "The Yanks themselves were the ones who probably started it all in the first place."

As she walked to the outbuilding that night, Mary Jane speculated that hearing of the riots over bread might boost morale in the Union—the starving Southerners surely couldn't keep up their war effort for much longer. As she passed the spot on the porch where Mr. Garvin had always sat, she heard his words in the wind: *Miss Lizzie's game is freedom, girl.* She supposed he was right: Miss Lizzie had arranged for Mary Jane to be educated up North, and when she had come back down South, her head full of free thoughts, Miss Lizzie had sent her to Liberia in hopes she'd find peace there. What Miss Lizzie didn't realize was that Mary Jane had always wanted more than what even her liberal mistress could provide.

The next day Mary Jane hung a red petticoat on the line and, toting one of Mrs. Davis's dresses, made her way to Mrs. Thompson's.

Miss Lizzie's appearance was even more haggard than usual: her hair was unwashed and her clothing stained. Mary Jane couldn't decide if it was another calculated move or if she really had become that negligent with her grooming.

"Where have you been?" she asked Mary Jane, embracing her with her skinny arms.

"I was there, at the riot."

Mrs. Thompson's hand went to her mouth as Miss Lizzie demanded if Mary Jane was all right. She looked as though she would hug her again, but Mary Jane waved her off. "I'm fine. I want you to make sure you spread the word up North via your contacts in the Underground."

She nodded. "Of course." Her normally pinched face grew even more strained. "Is anything else the matter?"

"No." Mary Jane fought to keep her voice light, but her insides were in turmoil. She wanted to confess what Mr. Garvin had told her, but she couldn't. *Besides, would it change anything about their relationship?* Mary Jane resolved right then that she would never have that discussion. It was possible Miss Lizzie had done what she had for Mary Jane out of a familial love, but could have just as well been because Miss Lizzie always chose to do the opposite of what proper Southern society said she should.

"How are you getting along?" she asked her former mistress, carefully keeping her eyes away from Miss Lizzie's disheveled outfit.

"Fine, fine. The impressment agents have stolen two of our fine white horses, but as I'm keeping the last one in the house with us, they won't be able to seize him."

Mary Jane had to smile despite herself. "Of course you would have a horse living in the house. Is he installed in the attic room?"

Miss Lizzie's face lit up. "No, there are too many Union men hiding in there now. I put the horse in the study. My nieces keep him fed with apples, and he knows enough not to make noise when the neighbors are about. With Winder's 'plug-ugly' detectives always roaming about, it's not safe for man or beast." The light in her face faded as quickly as it had appeared. "I heard that the Davises are in need of help again. The talk of the town is that all of their slaves are deserting. Perhaps we should make arrangements for you to leave as well."

"No." Mary Jane recalled what Mr. Garvin had said about them needing her more than ever. "Not yet. They are having yet another meeting in the dining room tonight."

Miss Lizzie nodded, a bit satisfactorily, Mary Jane thought. She dug something out of her carpetbag and pressed it into Mary Jane's hands. "This is for you."

It was a tiny parcel of sugar. "However did you get such a luxury?" Mary Jane asked.

"Mr. Garvin sent it by way of my brother, John."

Mary Jane tucked it into her skirt pockets. "Make sure to thank him from me."

"Of course. Please be careful, Mary Jane."

"I will."

• • •

Mary Jane returned to find the Davises' house filled with people. The Confederates had somehow triumphed at the Battle of Chancellorsville, a fact that Mary Jane found hard to swallow considering the talk the days prior had been how badly Lee's army was outnumbered.

"That Bob Lee will be our salvation!" Mr. Davis called from the dining room. "Little Mary, can you fetch my best bottle of whiskey from the cellar?"

When she returned with the bottle and as much glassware as she could muster, Jeff Davis insisted on toasting to both Lee and Stonewall Jackson. "God bless him and his wounds," he added before taking a tiny sip of liquor.

"I was not aware General Jackson was hurt," Judah Benjamin stated as he handed Mary Jane his glass to refill.

"Friendly fire, I heard," someone replied. "One of our boys mistakenly hit him."

"Three times!" another man called. "Luckily only in the arm, though they would've done no worse had they hit him through that stonewalled stomach of his."

The celebrations continued long into the night, the Confederates believing that their army had become invincible, General Jackson's minor wounds notwithstanding.

It was the last time Mary Jane recalled the President smiling, for the news a few days later was that General Jackson had developed pneumonia after the amputation of his shattered arm and was in dire straits. Mr. Davis paced the hallways continuously upon hearing the news, and the next morning Mrs. O'Melia confided he had been up all night. Mr. Garvin's replacement was ordered to wait at the train depot while a secretary was stationed at the telegraph office. Mr. Davis wanted to be the first to hear the news, good or bad, on General Jackson's fate.

When the report came that the great General Jackson had died,

Mary Jane thought Mr. Davis likely to keel over as well. He immediately volunteered his house as host for the General's body, but word came that the governor, a long-time rival of the Davises, would be hosting the funeral. It was another low blow for the already downtrodden president.

CHAPTER 56

BELLE

MAY 1863

*B*elle had spent the winter and spring passing from family to family in Tennessee and Alabama. She had just returned to her cousin's home in Mobile when she received a heart-wrenching telegram:

Miss Belle Boyd:

General Jackson now lies in state at the Governor's House.

It was signed by T. Bassett French, the aide-de-camp to the Governor of Alabama.

She'd previously heard that Stonewall Jackson had been shot in the arm by his own men, but also that the wound had been trifling and the general was expected to make a full recovery. She immediately shot off a telegram to Virginia governor John Letcher to verify the awful rumor:

Please telegraph if Gen. Jackson is dead. If so, save me a lock of his hair. Yours truly, Belle Boyd

She could hardly believe the rumor: the general was surely bulletproof, his stamina impregnable. A man such as he would never have been brought down by enemy fire. But sadly, Letcher soon confirmed that General Jackson was indeed dead.

In true military style, Belle showed her mourning by wrapping a black crepe band over her left arm for the next thirty days. She refused to speak of his death to anyone, telling people that her sorrow was inextinguishable, like the sorrow of all the South. Stonewall had been the one to advise her to go on her Southern tour and now all she wanted was home.

But Martinsburg now was part of the new state of West Virginia, the thirty-fifth in the Union. The new state's constitution freed all people born into slavery after July 4, 1863. All others would be freed on their twenty-fifth birthdays.

Belle had strongly opposed the decision and publicly called West Virginia the "bastard state of a political rape." As part of her release from Old Capitol Prison, Belle had been forbidden to cross into Union territory; a return to Martinsburg would violate the conditions of her parole. News that her father was again on sick leave and that her mother, at thirty-seven, was nine months pregnant, only made Belle all the more determined to go home.

CHAPTER 57

MARY JANE

MAY 1863

*M*ary Jane answered the door a few weeks after General Jackson's death to find an elegant looking man with a neatly trimmed beard and a polished uniform standing on the portico.

"General Lee?" she guessed, moving aside for him to enter.

He glanced down at his boots and offered Mary Jane a shy smile. He did his best to wipe the muck from the Richmond streets on the hallway rug, but it didn't stop him from leaving muddy footprints on the cream-colored carpet leading to the snuggery.

"Ah, Bob," Mr. Davis rose when they entered. "Coffee, please, Little Mary." He sat back down, motioning for Lee to do the same as Mary Jane left the room.

General Lee discussed his strategy as Mary Jane returned to serve the two men. "I've had to reorganize our army now that we've lost Stonewall." His voice broke and he looked up. "Jeff, I never believed until he took his last breath that he would be gone. It's made a staggering impact on our boys' morale."

"It's made a staggering impact on all of our morale. But we will get past it."

General Lee nodded. "Thank you," he said to Mary Jane as he picked up his cup.

She returned his nod, thinking that might have been the first time a Confederate had expressed any gratitude for her service.

Lee took a sip as Mary Jane went to her customary place in the corner. "I know that the news from Vicksburg is no good."

"We stand to lose most of the West if Grant doesn't end his siege."

General Lee nodded. "That seems inevitable now." He put his saucer on the table. "What we need to do is try to disable their own capital. We need to make another Northern invasion."

"After Antietam last year—"

General Lee held up his hand. "I know. I plan on moving the Army of Virginia through Pennsylvania." He gave a small smile. "The army can grow fat off of the Union's crops and then we can attack."

Mr. Davis demurred, saying he would call a cabinet meeting to discuss Lee's proposal.

The next day, Mary Jane informed Mr. McNiven of the Confederate's plans to invade the North. He, in turn, handed her a letter.

"Who is it from?" There was no return address on it.

"Your husband." Mr. McNiven tipped his hat toward her. "I will deliver your information straightaway. We can't let the Rebels attack us in our own territory."

That night Mary Jane opened the letter to find that Wilson had left for Ohio to enlist with the Union army's brand-new colored unit. She traced her fingers over the words *Even with all that Miss Lizzie has given to me, I still have the urge to help my country in a greater way. I know you of all people would understand.*

Mary Jane refolded the letter, intending on burning it in the parlor fireplace the next morning. She wiped away a single tear, shed for the things that might have been if circumstances had been different, before blowing out her candle.

A few days later came the news that General Ulysses S. Grant and his Army of the Tennessee had reached the city of Vicksburg, Mississippi. Mary Jane hoped that the likelihood of losing the last stronghold on the Mississippi River would be the impetus for the South to surrender, but they doggedly continued on. His poor health continuing to besiege him, Jefferson Davis met almost nightly with his cabinet in the executive dining room. The discussion centered on how to increase the number of soldiers in the army.

"The Deep South is so against conscription, they are threatening to secede from the Confederacy," Mr. Davis's voice was faded but firm. "With the Union elections looming, a unified South would be the best weapon we'd have to prevent Lincoln's reelection."

"There is another solution besides forcing our good men to stay in uniform," a man in a general's coat stated. "We could employ the slaves."

"Nonsense!" Judah Benjamin hit his fist on the table, silencing the startled debate the general's comment had provoked. "The insult of employing contraband was the lowest blow the Union has delivered to us yet."

The general sat back. "I would think that every secessionist would surely choose to forfeit their negroes rather than become a slave himself."

At that remark, all Mary Jane could think of was getting away. She temporarily tuned out as she imagined running out of the mansion, down the hill, not stopping until she reached Union lines, and leaving those men in the dining room behind forever. She blinked a few times, bringing herself back to reality just in time to hear Stephen Mallory, Secretary of the Navy, state he had an alternate plan.

"There are about 2,000 officers being held prisoner on Johnson's

Island off Lake Erie. If we could somehow rescue these men, they could lead an attack of the Midwestern states."

A stunned silence followed until Judah Benjamin broke it. "I don't think there are that many Federal troops stationed in the Great Lakes. As far as I know, they only have one gunboat up there."

"The *Michigan*," Mallory supplied.

Benjamin's eyes were somewhere above Mary Jane's head, speaking aloud as he hashed it out in his head. "The entire lakeshore from Ohio to New York would be ours. All of that commerce, all of those men returned to arms." He focused on Davis. "Mr. President, this sounds like the best proposal we have at the moment."

Mr. Davis nodded. "You may be right." He turned to Mallory. "Can it be done without interfering with our European negotiations?"

Mallory rubbed at his beard. "I believe so, sir."

Mr. Davis rose from the table. "Then you may start drafting a plan."

The men left, presumably to reassemble at their offices on Capitol Street and formalize a formal plot to attack the Midwest. Mary Jane headed straight to her room to try to counter their plans as best she could.

CHAPTER 58

LORETA

MAY 1863

*L*oreta spent the spring in Washington City lying low. She befriended several Union officers, who paid for her meals and gave her various pieces of information, but nothing of major interest. At last, Loreta decided to call on Dunham at his place of business to see if he had any worthwhile intelligence. When he met her for tea, he told her she had interrupted his writing about the possibility of a prison break in Ohio. Loreta's ears perked upon hearing this and pressed Dunham for more information.

"The South is always threatening such things," he replied. "Every prison houses Union deserters and refugees who could be persuaded to take up arms, not to mention Confederate soldiers."

"You sound almost as if you are in favor of such an act. I thought you had Northern sympathies."

"I do not believe in fighting the devil with fair play and claim the right to use his weapons. The raid would sharpen Northern sympathies and resolve them in ending the war as quickly as possible."

Loreta recalled what Captain Alexander told her at Castle Godwin about not knowing which way Dunham's sympathies lay. "Your aim is to sell more newspapers." The words came out as a statement, not a question.

He nodded, and Loreta marveled that Dunham's skills at deception might even be greater than her own. But the more she thought about it, the more she realized that this could be the impetus to turn the tide of the war. Even if it didn't immediately result in a Southern victory, it might at least result in Lincoln losing the election next year, and the Confederacy could negotiate peace on their own terms. A plan began to form in her mind. "Can you write me a letter of introduction to the head of the Union secret service?"

"You speak of Lafayette Baker. Indeed I will." He put a fresh sheet of paper in the middle of his desk. "Shall I refer to you as Mrs. De Caulp or Ms. Velazquez?"

"Please use the name Ann Williams."

Dunham's expression remained indifferent. "Very well."

Loreta found Baker to be a stern-looking gentleman with gray eyes that reminded her of his Confederate counterpart, General Winder, but with the brawny, leathery skin of a pioneer. She told him about William's death but left out Tom completely. She pleaded with him to find her gainful employment. "Please sir, I've lost everything now. I was so badly treated by the rebels that I fled to New York."

Baker gave a snide laugh. "New York? For a moment there, I thought you'd come from the South."

"Why, no sir. I know that my late husband was a Confederate, but I've always thought that the Union should be preserved and so I went North upon his death."

"Good." He turned to look Loreta straight in the eyes. "We've had a great many problems with Confederate spies running about the city and passing on information. We've arrested most of the native citizens, but more seemed to be coming in through the lines."

"Sir, I can help you with that. Having lived for a time in the South, I might be able to recognize some of those traitors."

Loreta held herself as still as possible, trying not to fidget as Baker's colorless eyes examined her from bonnet to slipper. He began to bombard her with questions. Loreta answered them as quickly as she could, thinking that his questions about her background and employment desires were asked in a less skillful way than Winder would have done. She told him that all of her relatives had fled to Spain or Cuba before going into detail on how she had won William away from her roommate, thinking that Baker would be impressed with her cunning.

Throughout Loreta's long-winded explanations, Baker kept his hand under his full beard. When she finished, he sat back in his chair. "We have been investigating possible Confederate plots to release prisoners." He held up his hand and examined his fingernails. "While we are always hearing of far-fetched plans such as these, I have reason to believe this might be one to keep abreast of."

"Oh yes, sir," Loreta said, leaning forward. "You can send me to Richmond and I will find out what I can about the plot, as well as pick other information that might be of value to compensate for what it would cost the government."

Baker laughed. "The Rebs would capture the likes of you straight away if you attempt to get through their pickets."

"I can get through on my own accord. I just need you to supply me with the means of making the trip and write me a pass so I can make it through the Fed lines."

"Aren't you a plucky little woman?" He scribbled something on a piece of paper. "Here is your pass. But..." he continued, pulling his arm back as Loreta reached for it. "You must not blame me if you're caught. They have a nasty habit of hanging people they catch in the business of spying."

Loreta reached out and plucked the pass from his fingers before placing her other hand over her throat. "I don't think this neck was made to fit in a noose, but I am willing to risk it."

He bent down and Loreta heard a dial spin. After a moment, he set a pile of money on the desk and pushed the stack toward Loreta.

"There's a thousand counterfeit Confederate bills in there as well as a hundred and fifty dollars of real greenbacks."

"If the rebels catch me carrying bogus bills, my punishment will be a mite harsher than for just spying."

"Ah, don't worry. These fake bills pass readily down South, even more so than the real ones. Which lends proof to the fact that the Confederacy is a fake government." He gave another deep laugh as Loreta scooped up the money and offered him a faint smile in return.

CHAPTER 59

BELLE

JULY 1863

*G*eneral Lee's failed Gettysburg Campaign resulted in overwhelming losses, and, although the B and O Railroad seemed to be running continuously, Belle had a hard time securing a ticket as every train carried hundreds of wounded Confederate men into Martinsburg. She finally arrived at her childhood home to find that it had been delegated as a provisional hospital. Belle's father was still on leave, having been sent home due to exhaustion after General Jackson's death and Mauma Eliza had confined Mrs. Boyd to her room. Consequently, Belle had to act as nurse to both her parents and the patients lying in the parlor and hallways of the Boyd home. Medical and food supplies in Martinsburg were scarce, and the town showed the wounds of a never-ending battle. A courier had just relayed the message that the Union army was again approaching the town when Mrs. Boyd went into labor.

Three days later, Belle was not overly surprised to hear a loud knocking on the door, and, a few minutes later, Mauma Eliza announced that "Them Yanks are here agin."

Belle slowly descended the stairs from her mother's room, where she had been keeping her and her new sister company. The man standing on the threshold was young, with a pudgy face and build. "Miss Boyd, I am Major Nathan Goff of the Third West Virginia Infantry."

Belle wanted to remind him that, to her, there was no such state called West Virginia, but she bit her tongue as the young man continued, "General Kelly has received a report that you have arrived home. As he did not credit it, I have come to ascertain the truth."

"Well, surely you can see that the report is true." She halted a few steps above the bottom of the stairwell. "Is there something so peculiar about me returning to my own home to be with my parents in their time of need?"

"Why, there is, of course. Are you not afraid of being arrested?" The major glanced into the parlor and Belle wondered if was aware she'd shot one of his comrades nearly two years ago.

"What grounds would they have? I am no criminal." Belle could hear the baby begin to wail upstairs.

"That may be, but you are a Rebel."

"There are other rebels who remain in this town."

"Yes, but then not so dangerous as yourself. You will do more harm to our cause than half the men could do."

Normally Belle would have been pleased by such praise, but she was too worried that Major Goff would force her to leave her home to pay much attention. Her mother was doing poorly after giving birth and needed constant nursing. The summer was heating up, and the dark circles under her father's eyes were expanding daily.

Major Goff returned after a few days with an order to place Belle under house arrest. He stationed several soldiers on guard around the perimeter and told Belle that her movements would be restricted—she would not even be allowed to go out onto the balcony—but at least she could stay and give her mother the care she needed.

But only a week passed before another soldier rang the doorbell, carrying a message stating that Belle was to be in Washington City by eleven the following morning.

"Sir," Belle's father begged. "My wife is very sick, and Belle's departure might kill her."

"I'm sorry," the soldier indeed looked sorrowful. "But I have my orders from Secretary of War Stanton himself."

Belle plodded up the stairs to share the news with her mother, telling her not to worry, but hardly being able to convince her. Belle had been excited about prison a year ago, but now the whole thing just seemed depressing.

CHAPTER 60

LORETA

JULY 1863

*L*oreta had little trouble getting through the Federal lines with Baker's pass. When she reached the Rebel pickets outside of Richmond, she told the scout that she was on a secret service mission for General Winder. The scout insisted on escorting her directly to General Winder's office.

Winder recognized her straight away. "Well, Mrs. De Caulp, did you end up finding your husband?"

"No sir." Loreta cast her eyes downward to the papers on his desk. She decided not to disclose what Dunham had revealed.

"And why exactly have you returned to Richmond?"

She produced the pass. "I am employed by the Federal government to look into a plot to rescue Rebel prisoners."

Winder gave a deep belly laugh. "Is that so? Most people caught committing espionage don't confess to it so readily."

"Oh, but you see sir, I am what you call a double-agent," Loreta tried unsuccessfully to keep her voice from sounding haughty.

Winder's tone was equally contemptuous. "I find that hard to believe, seeing as we never employed you."

"But won't you now? I can freely move within the Union and communicate with the prisoners we plan on setting loose."

Winder targeted his slate eyes on her. After what seemed like hours of his staring, he finally let out a large breath. "I don't fully trust you, but you do have a point. This plot of ours could end the war immediately in our favor." He stood. "Give me a few days to think about it, make some inquiries. I will send for you when I've made my decision."

Loreta thanked him and left to check into the Spotswood Hotel. She realized that she was already running low on funds, and, as she couldn't see herself convincing Winder to give her more money, decided to exchange the Confederate bills for greenbacks. The exchange rate was very low and she received only a modest sum in return, but it was necessary since most people up North didn't accept Southern graybacks.

As Winder promised, he sent for her in a few days. This time he agreed to let her operate under the Richmond Secret Service. He gave her a special package to take to Ohio and oral instructions to complete her mission. Winder stressed the great importance of the raid, but when she pressed for more details, he remonstrated that she need not know any more than her immediate duties.

CHAPTER 61

BELLE

JULY 1863

*W*hen Belle arrived at Carroll Prison, a group of buildings next to the Old Capitol, she found Superintendent Wood was still in charge. He told her that he would give her the room reserved for "distinguished guests," but the cell was filthy, the smell of dirt and decay clinging to the chipped and broken furnishings in the tiny room.

Although Belle resumed some of the antics she had performed during her last stay in prison, this time she did so half-heartedly. Her father had accompanied her to Washington City, and was reportedly staying with a friend nearby, but Secretary Stanton had issued an order that Ben Boyd was not allowed to visit his daughter. Thankfully she was not searched upon entering the prison, as her father had slipped a gun in her handbag before their tearful goodbye.

She spent most of her time next to the window, where she often attracted onlookers—mostly diehard Confederate supporters with a few other people who wanted to set their eyes on the famous Belle Boyd.

One evening, after she had entertained her fans by singing "Take Me Back to My Own Sunny South," she felt a whoosh of air as something hummed past her ear and struck the wall opposite the window. *The Yankees were trying to kill her!*

Belle grabbed a candle and went to examine the object. Instead of a bullet she found a small Confederate flag. She unfolded the paper that had been wrapped around it. It was from someone who called themselves C.H and claimed to be a Southern sympathizer, and "therefore her friend." The letter also included detailed instructions on how to communicate further with her supposed ally.

Belle refolded the note, wondering if it was a trick, but the following evening she did as C.H. had instructed, offering several oranges to her guard, who gave her a small rubber ball and a sewing kit in exchange. She split the ball into halves, inserting a note into one half and then resewing it. When she heard someone walk by underneath her window whistling an Irish tune, Belle threw the ball as far as she could into the square. Another flag soon flew through the window, this time accompanied by a note informing her of Confederate movements in the western theater.

A guard, one of the more detestable ones, appeared in the doorway of her cell. "What do you have there, Miss Boyd?" Belle tossed the note under the bed. She inserted the Confederate flag into her bodice and walked over to him. Predictably, the guard reached a hand through the bars to seize her flag, but Belle pulled her revolver from her skirts and took aim. The guard stared down the barrel of the gun, his eyes wide and mouth open. Belle cleared her throat as loudly as she could, causing her prison mates to go to their doors and take in the scene. "These are the kind of men General Lee hangs by their thumbs," Belle said in her loudest voice before dropping the arm with the gun by her side.

CHAPTER 62

LORETA

JULY 1863

*L*oreta lingered in Richmond for most of the summer to help set the Confederate plans in place before she again crossed the Potomac. The idea of using the chief of Federal detectives for the advancement of the Confederate cause was a source of delight to Loreta, but she couldn't help feeling that returning to Baker's Washington City office was a bit like walking straight into the lion's den.

After a cordial greeting, Baker got down to business, demanding what she had found out in Richmond.

Loreta fell upon her old ways of telling half-truths, figuring the detective would be able to see through complete lies. "Indeed, there are plans to arrange a great stampede of the Rebel prisons. The Underground has found a way to communicate with the Southern-sympathizing Copperheads up North." She kept her voice neutral, hoping to play down the great raid as yet another idle threat about releasing Confederate prisoners.

She moved on to what else she'd observed in Richmond, intending to fill his head with the minute details she'd acquired about the bread riots, but he waved his hand. "We know all about it. Is there anything else regarding the Johnson Island coup?"

"Not that I know of at this time, but perhaps you could send me to Ohio to try to ferret out the Confederate contact. It will be easier for a woman to be granted access to the prisons. I can see if the prisoners really have the intention to make a break, and if so, if they also plan on attacking the Union."

Baker steepled his fingers and then cracked his knuckles. "While I do believe women are better suited for some tasks, I am not sure if you are the right woman for this particular task."

"Sir, I've the idea to pass myself off as a Confederate. That way the captives will be able to talk plainer to me."

After a pause that seemed to last an eternity, Baker finally consented. "All right. I'll arrange for your travels and supply you with passes and a confidential letter to the prison marshal, but do not let anyone else see it unless you believe it will save you from harm. I don't even want my own detectives to know of you."

"Yes, sir."

CHAPTER 63

HATTIE

JULY 1863

That summer in Washington City felt even hotter than the summer Hattie had spent in the Richmond prison. Hugh had been sent South on another mission and when Secretary Stanton asked if Hattie was ready to take on a mission of her own, she readily agreed. She reported to the War Department where she was shown to Colonel Baker's office.

The door was opened, but the man she took to be Lafayette Baker was occupied, his head bent over a paper. She stood in the doorway and waited, noting that his desk was just about as disheveled as his hair. *Pinkerton would have never approved of such defilement in a detective agency.*

"Mrs. Lawton?" Colonel Baker's deep voice interrupted her thoughts.

"Sir?"

He waved at her to sit down. "I received your name from Secretary Stanton. I'm hoping to send you North to follow a suspicious person." He pushed a blank sheet of paper toward her. "Technically, I've hired her to work for the secret service."

Hattie pulled a pen out of a nearby inkwell and began to take notes as Baker continued, "She mentioned a possible plot to rescue imprisoned Confederate prisoners."

Hattie set her pen down. "Another one?" For weeks the papers had contained information about such goings-on, but none of them had come to fruition.

"Yes, but that's not necessarily what concerns me. This woman mentioned she would pose as a Confederate double-agent, and something is telling me it might not be a farce." Baker went on to describe the woman as small-boned, of Spanish descent, and who seemed uncommonly sure of herself. "I'll arrange for you to follow her to Ohio on tomorrow's train. Make note of who she contacts there. If she is indeed a Confederate spy, I'd like to know."

"Yes, sir."

The woman of Baker's description was easy to recognize. Hattie sat on the train in the seat directly behind her and listened to her converse with a young lieutenant, speculating about the dire situation in the South in regard to inflation and the consequent deprivation of its poorer citizens.

It was midnight when they finally arrived in Sandusky, Ohio. The lieutenant with whom Ms. Williams had acquainted herself hired a coach for the two of them. Another coachman motioned to Hattie, and pointed three fingers downward. Recognizing the signal, Hattie climbed into the coach and was driven to the hotel by another Baker operative.

CHAPTER 64

LORETA

JULY 1863

*T*he first thing Loreta did when she woke the next morning was draw the curtains open to gaze across Lake Erie. She had to squint her eyes to find the little island that focused so largely in her plans. Plans that, if carried out successfully, would do more to promote the cause—not to mention bring her more glory and distinction—than all of the fighting she'd done. She pictured the thousands of brave Confederates imprisoned there, ready to do their bidding and transfer the seat of war from the disadvantaged South to the prosperous Midwest.

After Loreta had dressed, she rang for the chambermaid to take her card to the lieutenant she'd met on the train and let him know she was ready for breakfast.

The chambermaid had a more exquisite air about her than Loreta would have supposed. She had a dark complexion, and large brown eyes that hinted at past tragedies.

"Is that Johnson's Island?" Loreta asked, indicating the small dot in the middle of the lake.

"It is indeed," the chambermaid replied, joining Loreta at the window. "It houses Confederate prisoners." She paused before adding, "I wish they would all just go away."

"Why?"

She turned away from the window. "I am afraid they will break loose sometime and burn the town."

Loreta hid a smile, thinking that was exactly her hope. "There must be enough Union soldiers to guard them."

"I'm not sure on that point," the woman replied before bowing so low that something fell from her apron. "I will see to delivering your card," she said, leaving the room. Loreta was about to call out to her that she had dropped something, but thought better of it when she realized that it was her master key. Loreta pocketed it, thinking she could find a use for it later.

After breakfast, Loreta went to the telegraph office to send coded dispatches to Confederate agents in Baltimore and Detroit, letting them know she had arrived. She then boarded a ferry out to the island. On the way there, her heart began to hammer in her chest. She was no more afraid for her own safety than she had been when bullets whizzed past her on the battlefield, but at the same time, she knew the fate of this magnificent campaign was on her thin shoulders. She mused that her trepidation was not that different from what a general might feel when making the first advance in a great battle upon which the future of his country depended.

After she'd arrived on the island, she displayed her letter from Baker to the commanding office, explaining that she was searching for Rebel spies. The officer nodded and showed her to the gate outside. Loreta watched as the prisoners milled around, recognizing one she had known when she was acting as Harry Buford.

"You there!" she called.

The haggard soldier obliged her by coming to the gate.

She introduced herself as Ann Williams and then motioned for him to follow her out of the guard's earshot. "Are you ready to regain your freedom?"

The man looked around and then said in a low voice, "What would you know of it?"

"On the night of August 21, a group of rebels will capture the steamship *Michigan* and then train its guns on this island. You and your fellow prisoners will use that opportunity to overpower your guards and then escape to the city, capturing all the steamboats you can lay your hands on, before heading on to Canada. The resulting border skirmishes will incite Britain into joining the war on our side."

The man threw his head back and laughed.

Loreta tightened her hands on the wire fence. "If you will not act as a leader, find me someone who will."

"Your plan sounds extremely fantastic. I suppose the end result will be the Confederacy winning the war."

"That's right," Loreta said. "And, although you think it too far-fetched, the cogs have been spinning for months. My instructions came from General Winder by way of President Davis."

The man's smile disappeared. "Is that true?"

"Yes," Loreta said pointedly. "Now are you ready to serve your country again or not?"

Although she'd had to repeat the plan a few times to the young man, Loreta left, satisfied he was prepared. Upon returning to the hotel, she inquired after the young lieutenant, but was informed that he was out. "What room number is he again?" Loreta asked. "I need to leave him a note."

"Four," was the clerk's reply.

Loreta accordingly went to Room 4, furtively checking each side of the hallway before using the chambermaid's key to open his door. She headed straight for the desk and riffled through the papers there. It seemed the lieutenant was on his way to New York to try to quell the race riots that had been occurring there. It was interesting information, but not exactly pertinent to Loreta's mission and she replaced the papers as best she could remember.

As soon as she finished locking the door behind her, she heard a bell boy coming down the hall. She affected her most perplexed look. "Which is the servants' staircase? I must have gone down the wrong stairs."

The boy pointed, and Loreta hurried down the hall. She met the chambermaid outside her room. "Oh, I was just bringing you a cup of tea," the woman said.

Loreta nodded her thanks. "I'll just have time to enjoy it before I need to run more errands. I need to telegraph my husband my whereabouts."

The woman smiled. "Good luck."

CHAPTER 65

MARY JANE

JULY 1863

*A*fter hearing of the possibility of a prison breakout, Miss Lizzie encouraged Mary Jane to find out all she could. Consequently, Mary Jane snuck into Mr. Davis's office to rifle through his files. There she'd memorized all of the details, including where the money was coming from to finance the operations, and the exact date of the *Michigan* seizing. She relayed all of this to McNiven, who promised to send it up North.

The next time she met with Miss Lizzie, she informed her mistress that it was time to begin organizing her escape from the Confederate White House. "After what happened at Gettysburg, Mr. Davis suspects there's a spy in his household. The determent of the prison coup will be the final blow. Even if he doesn't figure out who the informer is, he will be much more careful in the future."

Miss Lizzie nodded. "Winder's sent several of his plug-uglies to search the Church Street mansion. So far they haven't found anything. I even heard they interviewed my sister-in-law, but for now they've taken no action. But I did receive a threatening note from someone." She got to her feet, breathing heavily. "I will make arrangements for your departure. When you are ready to leave, hang a black petticoat on the line."

CHAPTER 66

BELLE

JULY 1863

$\mathscr{T}$hat summer, Belle suffered from a bout of typhoid fever. When she was on the mend, a sympathetic guard informed her that her mother had pleaded with Stanton for her freedom, but the secretary had responded, "She's a damn Rebel. Let her die there!"

Finally Belle received word that her release had been scheduled for early August. As word had gotten out that she would be escorted to Richmond, the same friendly guard delivered her gifts and contraband from Washington City to bring South with her.

One day the guard came in and pulled a flat package out of his pocket breast. "This is from your friend, C.H."

"What is it?" Belle asked. It felt very heavy in her hands, and, as she turned to examine it, she heard coins jingle.

"It's Union gold and some greenbacks. It is imperative that it gets to Judah Benjamin in order to aid in a Confederate plot up

North." He handed a pair of black and brown field glasses. "For your troubles. I'm told they were General Jackson's."

Belle blinked back tears as she accepted them, picturing her hero using them to scout enemy forces.

"And the last thing," the guard said, holding up another envelope. "This is a letter of introduction to vice-president Alexander Stephens, affirming your devotion to the Confederate cause. As if anyone would be in doubt."

"Thank you." She slid the letter underneath her mattress. "Who are you?" she turned to ask the guard, but he had already disappeared.

The morning of her release, Belle packed the glasses carefully along with her clothes into a trunk, but hid the money by tying the bills to her hoops and sliding the gold and letter into her underwear.

Her escort introduced himself as Captain James Minx, a burly man who claimed he used to be Lincoln's bodyguard.

"And now, here you are guarding little old me." Belle couldn't help but feel important. "Where is my father? I thought he was to accompany me back to Virginia."

"I'm told he was too ill to travel," Minx growled.

Belle put her arm on his sleeve. "Please sir, you must take me to him."

"My orders are to deliver you to General Butler in Norfolk, only. And I always follow orders."

Belle's disappointment at not being allowed to see her father was quickly replaced by trepidation at being under the care of "the Beast" Butler, the scourge of New Orleans women. Jefferson Davis had even gone so far as to declare Butler a felon deserving of capital punishment.

She thought the man's dastardly appearance perfectly in line with his reputation. He had a large head that sat upon an equally large neck, his stomach unable to fit beneath his desk. As he turned his droopy-eyed gaze to her, Belle couldn't help but think his eyes crossed each other like the stars on the Confederate flag.

374

"I take it I am in the presence of Miss Boyd, the famous Rebel spy?"

Belle nodded.

"Please take a seat."

Belle locked her shaking arms by her side. "Thank you, General Butler, but I prefer to stand."

"Pray, girl, why do you tremble so? Are you frightened?"

"No," Belle replied, intending to tell him she shook out of anger, not fear, but then changed her mind. "Actually, yes, General Butler. I do feel frightened to be in the presence of a man of such infamy as yourself."

Butler rubbed his hands together and shot her an evil grin. "What do you mean when you speak of infamy?"

Belle stepped forward. "I mean General Butler, that you are a man whose atrocious conduct and brutality, especially to Southern ladies, is so known that even Jefferson Davis has declared that he would have you executed if he ever captured you. Naturally I feel alarm to be around you."

Rage seemed to fill his sagging face and he ordered her to leave. Already halfway out, Belle cursed herself for letting her anger get the best of her when there was so much at stake.

Minx brought her to a nearby hotel, telling her to remain put until she was called for.

The following evening she was taken to the Norfolk provost marshal's office. Her trunk and bonnet box were on the floor and Belle watched as a detective searched her baggage.

"Is this really necessary?" she asked as the detective pulled out a clean pair of undergarments. "I have just come from prison."

The detective did not reply. He held the field glasses in the air as if he'd just seized a fine prize. Which indeed he had. "I'm sure General Butler would appreciate a new pair," he sneered.

Belle had to refrain herself from snatching them back, thinking Butler didn't deserve any possession of Stonewall's. She reminded herself not to antagonize them into searching her person.

As if he'd heard her thoughts, the detective asked, "Do you have any money on you?"

"No, sir. Well, just a few dollars in Confederate currency."

"You can keep that stuff. We have no need for it in this country. What else are you carrying?"

"Nothing, sir."

"Would you swear on that?"

The gold in Belle's drawers caused her to squirm. "Just some letters, sir."

The detective eyed Belle up and down but, in the end, decided not to search her.

When Belle reached Richmond, she sent word to the Confederate authorities about the gold she'd managed to sneak past Butler before checking into the Spotswood Hotel. Almost immediately, a clerk from the State Department came to retrieve it.

Belle had unceremoniously dumped the coins on the nightstand. As the clerk scooped them into a carpetbag, he tried to make conversation. "I'm sorry to hear about your father."

"Yes, but I'm sure his health will improve now that he knows I'm a free woman again."

The clerk paused, his hands frozen in their activity. He flexed his fingers before looking up. "Miss Boyd, do you mean to tell me that you didn't know that your father has passed?"

Belle felt everything grow cold as tears formed behind her eyes. "No." She sank into the nearest chair. "No, I didn't."

"I'm sorry," the clerk said. He didn't seem to know what else to do but go back to his task. Belle sat numb as he finished. He apologized again, placing a conciliatory hand on her shoulder, before he left.

CHAPTER 67

HATTIE

AUGUST 1863

*H*attie had Mrs. Williams followed to the telegraph office by one of Baker's operatives. After the man reported back, Hattie changed out of her chambermaid disguise in order to send a telegraph of her own. She'd acquired enough information to know that Baker had been right—the woman was indeed a double-agent. Luckily the competence of Loreta Janeta Velazquez De Caulp was inferior to her ego.

A few hours later, Hattie received an encrypted message from Baker, which she quickly decoded. He'd received complete details of the plot via the Richmond Underground and the Union now knew everything. Hattie breathed out as she read that he'd sent Hugh to infiltrate the men intending to attack the *Michigan*—Baker was going to do everything he could to make certain the infamous plan would never go through. He ended by authorizing Hattie to arrange for Mrs. Willams' arrest as soon as possible.

CHAPTER 68

LORETA

AUGUST 1863

On the night of August 21, Loreta poured herself a glass of sherry and planted herself at the window with a pair of field glasses focused on the harbor. The *Michigan* was stationed in the bay with its guns trained on the island prison. Any attacking ship entering the lake would therefore have the advantage. Loreta rubbed her hands together in glee, picturing the chaos the rebels were about to cause.

But the time for the attack came and went with Loreta observing no evidence of gunfire. Around midnight, her dismay mounting, she began pacing the floor. Eventually she exhausted herself and dozed fitfully in the chair, her head on the window, oblivious to the pain in her shoulder.

She awoke at dawn. As the sun illuminated the still placid bay, Loreta realized that the plan to save the Confederacy had failed.

Almost as if on cue, someone started pounding on the door. The brief thought that it might be an escaped prisoner lent a quickness to her frazzled muscles.

She opened the door to find the chambermaid, now neatly dressed in calico, a man in a plain suit, and another in a police uniform standing in the hallway.

Without thinking, Loreta attempted to shut the door again, but the police officer stuck out his foot and blocked it. "You are under arrest for committing treason against your country."

"It's no longer my country." Loreta's hand resignedly dropped from the door handle.

"But it is that of your husband's, is it not, Mrs. De Caulp?" The woman—whom Loreta now suspected was not a chambermaid—inquired.

"How did you know that was my name?"

"It's my job to know," the woman said, entering the room. Loreta watched as she folded the clothes that were on the floor before placing them into an awaiting carpetbag.

The plain clothed man crossed his arms across his broad chest. "There is someone I believe you will recognize at the prison we are taking you to."

"Oh?" Loreta asked. "And who would that be?"

"*Mr.* De Caulp. I think it's about time you two got reacquainted."

The woman handed the man Loreta's bag and shot her a sympathetic smile. "If you would follow us now."

Loreta did as she was bid, her heart heavy that she would be forced to be in the same vicinity as Tom, especially now that she had failed in her ultimate mission.

CHAPTER 69

BELLE

AUGUST 1863

*A*fter hearing of the death of her father, Belle wanted nothing more than to return home to Martinsburg. She wrote to every Union high-up she could think of, from Secretary Stanton to Lincoln's personal body guard—an old family friend—to Lincoln himself. None of them responded. Finally she gave up and sent another note to Jefferson Davis to offer her services as a Confederate agent in Europe and included a reminder of the dangers she faced to smuggle "all of that gold under General Butler's crooked nose."

She was rewarded for this latest effort when the same clerk that told her about her father arrived back at the Spotswood bearing introduction letters from Judah Benjamin and dispatches addressed to English dignitaries.

"What's that?" Belle asked as the clerk dropped a heavy carpetbag at her feet.

He smirked. "Gold coins."

"Are they the ones I—"

"No," he replied, his smirk disappearing. "Those were used to fund a failed coup up North."

"Oh." Belle's thoughts turned to her new mission. "How will I get to Europe?"

"The only ships that can get through the ports are the blockade runners. It's going to be a dangerous trip. I would suggest that you not speak to anyone of your true mission and go under the guise of a civilian in case the ship is boarded."

"Yes, but by now everyone knows who I am, even Union officials." Belle took a deep breath. "However, I'm prepared to do what I need to for my country."

Belle traveled to Wilmington, North Carolina to board the *Greyhound*, a light grey steamer that bore the British flag on its mast. The captain introduced himself as "Captain Henry." Although Belle gave her name as "Mrs. Smythe," Captain Henry recognized her anyway, and divulged that he'd known her father well. He became even more esteemed in Belle's eyes when he pulled up his sleeve to display a scar he'd acquired while on campaign with Stonewall Jackson.

Belle gestured toward her shoulder. "I have one from Old Capitol Prison." She showed him the approximate size with her fingers and Captain Henry's kind eyes widened in appreciation.

The night was clear with a waning moon. All lights on the boat were extinguished as the anchor was pulled up around ten o'clock in the evening. No one spoke as the steam began to blow and they got underway. The main deck was covered with bales of cotton upon which men dressed in dark clothing stood with spyglasses trained on the waters before them. Belle knew getting past the blockade would be tense and indeed it was. No one thought of sleep, and the scant passengers, including Belle, sat on deck, silently praying. Any stray movements sent ice water through Belle's veins. She hated that they would not be able to discern enemy boats in the darkness until they were upon them.

When dawn finally started to break, Belle felt her relief rising in time with the sun—the sea was clear from horizon to horizon. Soon after, a thick haze set in, not giving way until around noon when the look-out on the mast shouted, "Sail ho!"

Belle could feel the *Greyhound* speed up, and she rushed to the railing. By squinting her eyes, she could see a gunboat with the letters *U. S.* painted on its hull. It seemed to be gaining on them.

As their ship tried to outrun the enemy, the deck seemed to sway under Belle's gold coin-laden skirts. She bent over the side of the ship, her hands tight on the railing, to empty her stomach. When she'd finished, she noticed the distance between them and the Yankee gunboat had shrunk considerably. All Belle could think of was that she was about to be sent back to prison.

The look-outs tucked their spyglasses into their coats and climbed off the bales only to commence tossing the cotton into the sea. "By damn!" one of the men called as he stared down at the drowning bounty. "That's more of our goods they shalt not get!"

Captain Henry paced up and down the deck, alternating between glancing at his compass and staring at the gunboat growing ever closer. "More steam, fellows!" he called. "We've got to give her more steam!" He clicked his compass shut upon spying Belle. "Oh Miss Boyd, but for your presence on board, I would burn her to the water's edge than let those infernal scoundrels reap the benefit of a single strand of our cotton."

Belle's stomach was still churning along with the waves, but she straightened herself as best she could. "Please, Captain Henry, do your duty and pay me no reference." She took a woozy breath. "Burn her by all means—I am not afraid."

The crewmen had finished with the cotton bales and were now heaving the rest of the contraband over board until the water below surged with medicine, tobacco, and Confederate bills.

Belle, suddenly recalling her own contraband, rushed to the engine room below deck. She dug underneath her skirts to retrieve the hidden dispatches and tossed them into the furnace. She'd just returned above to hear Captain Henry call, "It's too late to burn her now, men—the Yanks are upon us!" He faced the oncoming gunboat and waved his arm back and forth, shouting, "Surrender. We surrender!"

Belle grabbed the banister as something shrieked past her head.

"By Jove!" the captain shouted. "They show no mercy!"

The ship slowed as a voice that seemed to come from the water commanded them to lower their flag. Captain Henry raised a defeated arm to the man on the mast and the British flag began to descend. The goods-polluted waters were now filled with rowboats being steered by men in blue uniforms. Belle retreated to her first-floor cabin, standing just inside the door so she could still hear the commotion as the Yankees began to board.

"Good day to you, Captain," a man's voice called out. "I am glad to see you. This is a mighty fine vessel you have." Belle stepped closer to catch a glimpse of the Yank with such a polite voice. Although he wasn't necessarily the standard of handsome, Belle quite liked his look: brown hair that hung past his ears and eyes so brilliantly blue that she could see them even from her vantage point. The dapper officer clicked his heels together in a manner that might have made Belle giggle under different circumstances before he asked to see the captain's papers.

Captain Henry shook his head. "Good day to yourself, sir, but I cannot say I'm quite as glad to see you. I do not have any papers."

"Ah," the man replied. "That presents a problem, doesn't it?"

Just then Belle caught a movement out of the corner of her eye. A soldier had appeared beside her. "Sergeant of the guard!" His shout was so loud that Belle's ears rang. "Put a man in front of this door and give him orders to stab this woman if she dares come out any further."

Belle's gaze traveled back to the blue-eyed man but he was focused on the captain.

The soldier stepped closer and snarled, "Now ain't ye skeared?"

She turned her eyes on him, narrowing them with hatred as he stuck out his hand to smooth his overgrown mane.

"No," Belle returned. "I've never been afraid of a Yankee."

His hand dropped back to his side. "Do you know that it was I who fired the shot over your head?"

"Oh?" Belle put her own hand on her hip. "Are you the coward

384

who fired on a defenseless ship after her surrender? How admirable of the Federal government to select such an officer as you." She would have gone on in her insults had her attention not been caught by the blue-eyed man, who strode past her without a second glance.

As her adversary began to mount a reprisal, she waved her hand. "That man," she said, pointing at the officer's back. "Who is he?"

Obviously caught off guard, he sputtered.

"What did you say?" Belle demanded.

"Harding. Lieutenant Harding, spelled with an e on the end."

"An e on the end. Like my name," she said dreamily. *How nice Belle Hardinge would look on paper.*

As if he'd heard his name, Lieutenant Hardinge walked toward Belle's room. "Hallo Swasey," he said to the soldier, his tone as affable as ever. "And who do we have here?" he asked as he at last turned those magnificent eyes on Belle.

Belle knew she should introduce herself with her pseudonym, but she couldn't help herself. "*Miss* Belle Boyd."

He bowed and Belle noticed how perfectly his hair fell back into place when he righted.

"Am I to be a prisoner?" she asked in a deferential tone.

"Since I am now in command of the vessel, I beg of you to consider yourself a passenger, not a prisoner."

Belle's grin was genuine as she acquiesced, hoping he would make more agreeable requests in the future. Even if he was a Yankee.

Lieutenant Hardinge disappeared to conduct some business, but he soon returned to Belle's doorway. "The stars are so pretty tonight. Won't you come see?" He held out his hand and Belle placed a gloved hand in his as he led her to the bow.

"That's Orion." He pointed his finger at a constellation before moving it to the moon. "Its light seems to shine directly on you and only on you."

Belle stepped closer and put her hand on his arm. "Where is Virginia?"

"South. We are currently headed to Boston."

"Oh." Belle held her lips together in an exaggerated fashion, noticing Hardinge's eyes focus on her mouth before dropping to her décolletage.

"But don't worry." He met her gaze. "I'll make sure you are granted your freedom."

"And Captain Henry?"

He looked out to sea. "I have my orders. He is to be arrested as soon as we get to shore."

"Of course you must obey your commanding officer." Belle dropped her hand back to her side. "If you don't mind, I'd like to tell Captain Henry myself. We've gotten to be good friends in this short while."

Lieutenant Hardinge nodded. "I have some more things to take care of before I row back to the *Connecticut* tonight."

Belle spied his empty boat tied to the deck, floating in the dark waters below. "Are you leaving so soon?"

"Just for the night. I need to report back to my captain. But I shall stop in to say goodnight."

"I'd like that very much. I will probably be with the captain when you leave."

When Belle arrived at the captain's quarters, she found that Captain Henry was accompanied by two guards. They obliged by admitting her into his room.

Belle curtsied. "Captain, I'm sorry to say that the kindly lieutenant has orders to detain you when we arrive at Boston Harbor."

The captain nodded. "I suspected as much."

Belle walked over to a table where there was a bottle of whiskey and a few glasses. She picked two up and held them out to the guards. "Gentlemen, would you like to enjoy a drink to the captain's health?"

The two men glanced at each other. One of them shrugged and the other stepped toward Belle. "Sure."

In no time the men had drank most of the bottle. Belle held a glass up to her lips but didn't drink anything. Without looking at

Captain Henry, she spoke in a low tone, "In a few minutes time, Lieutenant Hardinge will be here to bid us goodnight. After he leaves, you should sneak away on his rowboat."

She could hear the captain suck in his breath. "I don't—"

She nodded toward the drunken guards. "They won't be much bother. I will take care of distracting the lieutenant."

The captain set his glass down with a clink. "I suppose I would rather escape with my dignity than become a prisoner of the Union." He stood. The guards paid him no heed as his eyes darted back and forth, taking stock of his chambers.

Presently Lieutenant Hardinge arrived.

"Lieutenant," Belle linked her arm through his. "Would you escort me to my room?"

"Of course." If Lieutenant Hardinge noticed his men were on the way to passing out, he made no comment.

Belle nodded a farewell at Captain Henry as they left his quarters.

As they returned to her doorway, Belle noticed Lieutenant Hardinge fidget with the chain of his pocket watch.

"Miss Boyd—"

"Belle."

His face relaxed. "Belle then. And you can call me Samuel."

Belle caught sight of the captain, clad in his overcoat and hat, appearing on deck. She turned Samuel so that his back was toward the rowboat. "What constellation is that?"

"Um..." he cleared his throat before rotating his head. "I'm not sure."

Belle coughed. "This night air is getting to me. I should go inside soon."

"Belle, I know this is very soon, but I was wondering if you could ever think of becoming betrothed to me."

She heard a small scuffling and assumed Captain Henry was climbing into the boat. She coughed again and Samuel tapped her back. "Is it because I'm a Union man?"

"No." She held a fist to her mouth and finished one last coughing spree. "That's not it at all. I'm just a bit congested is all." She perked her ears but heard nothing else. "I will think about your proposal, but I cannot give you an official answer until we arrive in Boston."

He nodded solemnly. "I shall anxiously await your consent, then."

"Goodnight, lieutenant."

"Goodnight."

Belle slipped inside her room before he could notice his boat was gone. *Once again she had outwitted the Yankees.*

Presently she heard a whistle and then shouting. She slipped off her dress, petticoat, and corset before getting into bed wearing just her chemise. A few minutes later there was a knock at her door. Belle opened it a crack.

"Captain Henry has escaped!"

"Are you sure?" She pulled the door wide enough for Samuel to see that she was in her bedclothes. "I just saw him!"

Samuel shook his head, sighing to himself. "I'm sorry to bother you. It is of no concern for a lady. You must get some sleep."

Despite the chaos of soldiers shouting and running about the ship, Belle slept blissfully, dreaming of one of Stonewall's men rowing through an empty harbor back to freedom.

The next morning when Belle awoke, she found Samuel pacing back and forth across the deck, clearly still distraught over the disappearance of Captain Henry.

"You still have not located him?"

"No." Samuel slammed a hand on the railing. "How could I have been so careless?"

"I'm so sorry that happened to you. But," Belle reached out to finger the lapel of his uniform. "I've decided that I want nothing more than to marry you."

When he turned to face her, his solemn expression had turned into a grin that seemed to stretch from ear to ear. "You've made me the happiest man there is, North or South!"

Belle stood on her tiptoes to place a kiss on his cheek. "Forgive me for being so bold, but I feel like I've known you forever."

"And I, you, although I look forward to spending the rest of my life getting to know you better."

"Indeed. And now if you will excuse me, I have some wedding plans to start making."

He winked at her. "Whatever storm lies ahead as my punishment, I know I shall be sailing into calmer waters, thanks to you."

She gave him a little wave and went back to her room to begin making a list of things needed for her trousseau.

Belle took a walk on the deck after lunch and returned to her room to find a letter from Samuel:

My dear Belle,

I am told that I will be put on trial for the escape of Captain Henry. The Admiral says it looks very bad for us. I have already informed my men that I will take all the blame and they shall be spared, for I know that I can weather any storm knowing that you love me and will someday be my wife.

Affectionately,
Samuel

Belle folded the letter and placed it in her desk drawer. How exactly was she supposed to plan a wedding with her betrothed in prison?

CHAPTER 70

MARY JANE

AUGUST 1863

*T*he courier came promptly the morning after August 21 to deliver the news of the failed coup. Jefferson Davis read the missive in the dining room, his face falling more with every line.

"Thank you," he told the soldier before getting up from the table to escort him out of the dining room. Mary Jane, ostensibly dusting in the hallway, caught the president's glance for a brief second before he retreated back into the room, this time shutting the door behind him.

She immediately proceeded to the back of the house and hung a black skirt on the line. Her conviction that she needed to act quickly only grew stronger the rest of the day. Although she acknowledged that it could be her intense fear getting the better of her, it seemed that voices grew hushed when she entered the room, and the other servants' steps became more cautious around her. In the evening, without waiting until she was dismissed, Mary Jane headed to the nearly empty outbuilding and threw what little she owned into a small bag and then walked down the hill to Shockoe Bottom. Heading east on Broad Street, she kept her pace casual as she passed the old negro prison, now converted to one for white soldiers, and turned up Church Street as dusk fell.

The Van Lew mansion was quiet and dark, but Miss Lizzie must have been waiting next to the door because it opened as soon as Mary Jane stepped onto the portico.

"The coup was overthrown?" Miss Lizzie asked when she'd shut the door behind Mary Jane.

She nodded.

Miss Lizzie folded her gnarled hands in front of her. "Praise be to God this war will be over soon." She led Mary Jane to her former room, telling her that she would be leaving before dawn and then bidding her goodnight.

"Goodnight," Mary Jane returned. She set a nightshirt on the bed before calling out a hesitant, "Miss Lizzie?"

Miss Lizzie turned toward her, a hand on the doorknob.

Once again, Mary Jane thought better of making a confession, even though she figured it would be the last time she would see her presumed half-sister for a long time. "Thank you for all that you have done for me."

Miss Lizzie's face relaxed. "Thank *you*, Mary Jane. You've served your country well." She made to leave, but paused before saying, "I will miss you."

"And I, you."

"You should get some rest," she instructed before she left.

Mary Jane finished getting changed and then pulled the covers back on her old bed before climbing in. Often times when she'd slept in that same room, she felt bitterness over her lot in life. But now, her feelings of trepidation for her impending journey were mixed with a quiet satisfaction with all she'd accomplished.

Miss Lizzie came for Mary Jane at what seemed the middle of the night, leading her out the unused servants' door at the back of the house. A farm wagon was attached to two horses, including one of

Miss Lizzie's cherished white stallions. A man hopped off the front of the wagon upon seeing the women approach.

"Mary Jane," Miss Lizzie said in a whisper. "I'd like to introduce you to Mr. Garvin. Mr. Garvin, this is Mrs. Bowser."

If Miss Lizzie saw Mary Jane startle in recognition at the name, she gave no sign.

The man extending his hand was not the same Mr. Garvin that Mary Jane had befriended at the Davises.' Although he had the same kind eyes, this Mr. Garvin was much younger, his dark skin unlined and his frame well-muscled.

He directed Mary Jane to the back of the cart and, in a low voice, instructed her to lie down. Another of Miss Lizzie's servants appeared with a shovel and hoisted something on top of Mary Jane.

"Is that manure?" Mary Jane hissed.

"Yes. We've got to get you through the lines, and this is the best way," Miss Lizzie murmured from the side of the wagon.

Mary Jane gave a sigh of resignation, breathing through her mouth instead of her nose.

Despite her putrid surroundings, the revolving of the wagon wheels lulled Mary Jane into a sort of suspended state of consciousness. She wouldn't call it sleep, but, judging by the position of the sun, a great amount of time had passed before they finally halted.

"You can come out of there now," Mr. Garvin's resonant voice called.

Mary Jane crawled out of the wagon with as much dignity as she could manage. Mr. Garvin offered her a hand, but she declined. Although his nose was wrinkled against the smell, he refrained from commenting on her disheveled state. He retrieved her bag from the front of the cart and gestured toward a flowing stream. "You can get cleaned up there."

"Where are we?" Mary Jane asked when she returned, washed of the most offensive smells and clad in somewhat fresher clothes. It was mid-afternoon, but Mr. Garvin already had started a campfire to warm up food.

He leaned over to stir the fire with a long stick. "We're in Union territory now. You needn't worry about being caught anymore."

Mary Jane sat on the ground across from him. "It was that easy?"

Mr. Garvin flashed her a brilliant smile. "I am quite experienced with running contraband."

"I knew your father," Mary Jane stated. "How is he?"

"We got him out safe as well, and he's currently stirring up trouble in Philadelphia."

She met his grin with a small one of her own. "Is that where we're headed?"

Mr. Garvin poked at the fire. "Miss Lizzie told me to bring you to where your husband is stationed."

"No."

He nearly dropped the fire stick. "No?"

"He was only my husband because Miss Lizzie arranged our marriage. Now that I'm in free territory, I want to make it on my own."

"But Mrs. Bowser…"

"Mary Jane."

"Mary Jane." Once he got the words out, he didn't seem to know what else to say. "You don't love him?" he asked finally.

She avoided his eyes and stared at the fire instead. "I don't think I'm capable of loving anyone."

He set the stick down. "Now I don't think that's true. My father told me all about the fearless woman he'd met at the Confederate White House. I know what you did for the Union."

"That doesn't mean—"

"If you'll forgive my boldness, ma'am," he said as he rose from his seat, coming around to sit beside her. "Some white people say we're an inferior race, that we don't have human sentiments. But they are wrong—we most certainly do. And those sentiments include the capacity to love." He put a hand over hers. "You deserve to experience unconditional trust and affection for someone who has those feelings in return."

Mary Jane's first instinct was to pull her hand away, but something inside prevented her from doing so. "Maybe you're right."

He squeezed her hand before letting go to draw his knees up to his chest, folding his arms on top of them. "You're free now, and your life can be what you make of it. Someday that will be true for all of our brothers and sisters." He met her eyes. "Thanks in part to your bravery, the South cannot hold out much longer. All of our struggles will have been worth it, for they will eventually result in a Union victory."

Mary Jane turned her head to watch the setting sun. "And an everlasting freedom for all of our people."

*=

EPILOGUE

A NOTE ON FACT VERSUS FICTION REGARDING THE CHARACTERS IN UNDERGROUND:

*A*lthough *Underground* is a work of fiction, I attempted to relay the stories of the real-life people the best I could. However, while researching, I quickly discovered that many authors, particularly Loreta Velasquez and Allan Pinkerton, took fictional liberties with their autobiographies, so even their supposed true stories might ring a little fantastical. What follows is a synopsis about the fates of the characters as best we know.

Belle Boyd married Samuel Hardinge in August of 1864. He had been dismissed from the Union navy over the Captain Henry debacle—no longer was he a Yankee. The happy marriage quickly disintegrated when the pair ran short on funds, causing Belle to tell the press that she would have rather been back in the Old Capitol Prison than endure the suffering of poverty. The two finally relocated to England, where Samuel turned to drinking. Although the couple was becoming more estranged, they still had a baby girl in 1865.

Belle wrote her memoirs and published them under the title *Belle Boyd in Camp and Prison*. She also took to the stage to supplement her income, starring in the comedy *The Lady of Lyons*. When Samuel began seeing another woman, Belle decided to take advantage of President Andrew Johnson's promise of amnesty to former Confederates and returned to the United States. She filed for divorce, stating that she was so anxious to be rid of her husband that she would demand no alimony. From then on she claimed to be a widow, although Hardinge still lived.

Soon Belle married another Yankee, a self-proclaimed fan of her theatrical performances. Four children and two stints in an insane asylum followed. When she was forty, she disowned her eldest daughter by Hardinge for being "ruined." To further illustrate her point, she wounded her daughter's lover by shooting him with a revolver.

Although the scarcity of acting gigs had caused Belle to once again become poor, she managed to find money to purchase a plate and high chair for the first grandson of her old servant, Mauma Eliza. Belle died at the age of fifty-six in what is now Wisconsin Dells. Near the end of her life, she was quoted as saying, "I thank God that I can say on my death bed that I am a virtuous woman."

Hattie Lewis Lawton was the hardest character to pin down for this novel. As one of the first women detectives, she clearly had the both the justification and impetus to frequently change her name. Indeed, Allan Pinkerton sometimes referred to her as Carrie Lawton, but Pryce Lewis, in his own memoirs, wrote of a Hattie Lewis. Most of what I could find of her were unsubstantiated rumors: both Rose Greenhow and Elizabeth Van Lew mentioned her in their autobiographies, although Van Lew was not aware that "Mrs. Webster" was actually an operative of the Pinkerton Detective Agency. Not much else is known about her work, especially considering the records of the Pinkerton Agency were lost in the Great Chicago Fire of 1871. I therefore took great liberties in

Hattie's backstory and motivation for becoming a detective. What we do know was that there was a female employee of Pinkerton who operated under the alias H. H. L and who assisted in preventing Lincoln's assassination before his inauguration as well as accompanying Timothy Webster on his fateful trip to Richmond. Mrs. Webster is mentioned a few times in the *Richmond Examiner* as being a prisoner of state who was held at first in Castle Godwin and then in Castle Thunder. There is also a note from Mrs. Wester to Jefferson Davis in which she pleaded to be freed, asking to "go home where I may seek some spot, and unnoticed pass the remainder of my dreary, dreary days." After her release in December 1862, Hattie disappeared from the historical record all together. It is this author's hope that her remaining days were not all dreary and that, someday, someone will discover what happened to Hattie.

Mary Jane Richards Bowser, like Hattie, went by many names. Her baptism record from St. John's Church in 1846 listed her as Mary Jane, "a colored child belonging to Mrs. Van Lew." Most of the other Van Lew slaves were baptized in the First African Baptist Church of Richmond, so it was clear that Mrs. Van Lew and her daughter Elizabeth treated Mary Jane differently from the rest of their slaves, even at an early age. The Richards were cousins of the Van Lews, so it is possible her last name originated from their ownership. Later in life she would tell contradicting stories of her parentage, once claiming that her mother was a Van Lew slave and that "her father was a mixture of Cuban-Spaniard and Negro," although she also one declared that she never knew her parents.

On August 21, 1860, the Richmond Whig reported "Mary Jones, alias Mary Jane Henley, a likely mulatto girl, about twenty years of age, arrested for being without free papers, was committed for nine days. She was sent to the North about nine years ago, by a highly respectable lady of this city, for the purpose of receiving a thorough education, after completing which she went to Liberia." It was not soon after she returned from Liberia that she found herself in the slave jails of Lumpkin's Alley.

Mary Jane did indeed marry Wilson Bowser on April 16, 1861

(the day before Virginia seceded), once again in Saint John's Church. The official record stated they were "(colored) servants to Mrs. E. L. Van Lew." Although there is no other record of their relationship, or intention for marriage for that matter, a Wilson Bowser enlisted with the 27th US Colored Infantry, giving his age as 44 in 1863. If this was the same man, he was more than two decades older than his wife. Soon after the capture of Richmond by Union troops, Mary Jane Richards was teaching former slaves to read and write. She never again used the last name Bowser, although Wilson Bowser was still living at that time.

After the war, Mary Jane traveled North to give speeches about her wartime experiences, using the pseudonyms Richmonia Richards and Richmonia R. St. Pierre. In 1867 she wrote a letter to her employer—she had helped found a freedman's school in Georgia—to inform him that she had married and signed it Mary J. R. Garvin. She continued to argue for equal rights for blacks in both the North and the South until she too disappeared from the records, at the probable age of 28.

Loreta Janeta Velasquez wrote a hotly contested book called *The Woman in Battle*, originally published in 1876. In it she claimed to have participated as Harry Buford in the battles of Bull Run and Shiloh, among others. At first I took her portrayal of her adventures with a grain of salt, knowing it made for a great story, but also that some of her timeline conflicted with known events. However, upon reading William C. Davis's well-researched book, *Inventing Loreta Velasquez*, I realized that Loreta was nothing more than a 19th century con-artist, who probably never saw a battle in her life. Although she declared herself to be the descendent of Cuban aristocrats, she was probably born in New Orleans and resorted to prostitution as a teenager to make ends meet. There is no record of her marrying before Tom De Caulp, who was indeed a Confederate soldier that eventually defected to the Union. His real name was mostly likely William Irving, and he had a son by his first wife, whom he never divorced and who was still living when he married Loreta. In her novel, Loreta claimed he died in battle, a convenient death for the husband of someone who claimed to be devoted to the Confederate cause and who couldn't bring herself to relay his desertion.

After the war, Loreta was involved in various schemes, including gold-mining out West and raising money for a non-existent railroad. She married at least three more times and had a son, or possibly two. She continued to change her story every time she spoke to the press, so it is difficult to discern what was fact from fiction. She died in a mental hospital in 1923 when she was around eighty years old.

SELECTED BIBLIOGRAPHY

Abbott, Karen. Liar, Temptress, Soldier, Spy: Four Women Under-cover in the Civil War. Harper Perennial, 2015.

Boyd, Belle, and Sam Wilde Hardinge. Belle Boyd In Camp and Prison. London: Saunders, Otley, and, 1865.

Davis, William C. Inventing Loreta Velasquez: Confederate Soldier Impersonator, Media Celebrity, and Con Artist. Southern Illinois University Press, 2016.

Enss, Chris. The Pinks: The First Women Detectives, Operatives, and Spies with the Pinkerton National Detective Agency. Guilford, CT: TwoDot, an Imprint of Globe Pequot, 2017.

Mortimer, Gavin. Double Death: The True Story of Pryce Lewis, the Civil Wars Most Daring Spy. New York, NY: Walker & Company, 2010.

Nolan, Jeannette Covert. Yankee Spy: Elizabeth Van Lew. New York: Messner, 1970.

Recko, Corey. A Spy for the Union: The Life and Execution of Timothy Webster. Jefferson, NC: McFarland & Company, Publishers, 2013.

Pinkerton, Allan. The Spy of the Rebellion: True History of the Spy System of the United States Army during the Civil War. New York, NY: GW Dillingham, 1900.

Scarborough, Ruth. Belle Boyd: Siren of the South. Macon, GA: Mercer Univ. Pr., 1983.

Velazquez, Loreta Janeta, and C.J Worthington. The Woman in Battle: A Narrative of the Exploits, Adventures, and Travels of Madame Loreta Janeta Velasquez, Otherwise Known as Lieutenant Harry T. Buford, Confederate States Army. Hartford, CT: T. Belknap, 1876.

L'AGENT DOUBLE PREVIEW

Stay tuned for the next in the Women Spy Series- *L'Agent Double: Spies and Martyrs in the Great War*
Join my mailing list at kitsergeant.com to find out how to get a FREE copy before its release!

CHAPTER 1: M'GREET

JUNE 1914

"Have you heard the latest?" M'greet's maid, Anna, asked as she secured a custom-made headpiece onto her mistress's head.

"What now?" M'greet readjusted the gold headdress to better reflect her olive skin tone.

"They are saying that the Mr. K from the newspaper article is none other than the Crown Prince himself."

M'greet smiled at herself in the mirror. "Is that so? I think they're referring to Lieutenant Kiepert. Just the other day he and I ran into the editor of the *Berliner Tageblatt* during our walk in the Tiergarten." Her smile faded. "But let them wonder." For the last few weeks, the papers had been filled with speculation about why the famed Mata Hari had returned to Germany, sometimes bordering on derision about her running out of money.

She leaned forward and ran her fingers over the dark circles under her eyes. "Astruc says that he might be able to negotiate a longer engagement in the fall if tonight's performance goes well."

"It will," Anna assured her as she fastened M'greet's heavy gold necklace around her neck.

The metal felt cold against M'greet's sweaty skin. She hadn't performed in months, and guessed the perspiration derived from her nervousness. Tonight was to be the largest performance she'd booked in years: the Metropol could seat 1108 people, and the tickets had sold out days ago. The building was less than a decade old, and even the dressing room's geometric wallpaper and curved furniture reflected the Art Nouveau style the theater was famous for.

"I had to have this costume refitted." M'greet pulled at the sheer yellow fabric covering her midsection. When she had first began dancing, she had worn jeweled bralettes and long, sheer skirts that sat low on the hips. But her body had become much more matronly in middle age and even M'greet knew that she could no longer get away with the scandalous outfits of her youth. She added a cumbersome earring to each ear and an arm band before someone knocked on the door.

"Fraulein Mata Hari, are you ready?" a man's voice called urgently in German.

Anna shot her mistress an encouraging smile. "Your devoted admirers await."

M'greet stretched out her arms and rotated her wrists, glancing with appreciation in the mirror. She still had it. She grabbed an armful of translucent scarves and draped them over her arms and head before opening the door. "All set," she said to the awaiting attendant.

M'greet waited behind a filmy curtain while the music began: low, mournful drumming accompanied by a woman's shrill tone singing in a foreign language. As the curtain rose, she hoisted her arms above her head and stuck her hips out in the manner she had seen the women do when she lived in Java. She had no formal dance training, but it didn't matter. People came to see Mata Hari for the spectacle, not because she was an exceptionally wonderful dancer. M'greet pulled the scarf off her head and undulated her hips in time with the music. She pinched her fingers together and moved her arms as if she were a graceful bird about to take flight. The drums heightened in intensity and her gyrations become even more exaggerated. As the music came to a dramatic stop, she released the scarves covering her body to reveal her yellow dress in full.

She was accustomed to hearing astonished murmurs from the audience following her final act—she'd once proclaimed that her success rose with every veil she threw off. Tonight, however, the Berlin audience seemed to be buzzing with protest.

As the curtain fell and M'greet began to pick up the pieces of her discarded costume, she assured herself that the Berliners' vocalizations were in response to being disappointed at seeing her more covered. Or maybe she was just being paranoid and had imagined all the ruckus.

"Fabulous!" her agent, Gabriel Astruc, exclaimed when he burst into her dressing room a few minutes later.

M'greet held a powder puff to her cheek. "Did you finalize a contract for the fall?"

"I did," Astruc sat in the only other chair, which seemed too tiny to support his large frame. "They are giving us 48,000 marks."

M'greet nodded approvingly.

"That should tide you over for a while, no?" Astruc asked.

She placed the puff in the gold-lined powder case. "For now. But the creditors are relentless. Thankfully Lieutenant Kieper has gifted me a few francs."

"As a loan?" Astruc winked. "It is said you have become mistress to the *Kronprinz*."

She rolled her eyes. "You of all people must know to never mind such rumors. I may be well familiar with men in high position, but have not yet made the acquaintance of the Kaiser's son."

Astruc rose. "Someday you two will meet, and even the heir of the German Empire will be unable to resist the charms of the exotic Mata Hari."

M'greet unsnapped the cap of her lipstick. "We shall see, won't we?"

Now that the fall performances had been secured, M'greet decided to upgrade her hotel to the lavish Hotel Adlon. As she entered the lobby, with its sparkling chandeliers dangling from intricately carved ceilings and exotic potted palms scattered among velvet-cushioned chairs, she nodded to herself. *This was the type of hotel a world-renown dancer should be found in.* She booked an apartment complete with a private bathroom featuring running water and electric Tiffany lamps.

The Adlon was known not only for its famous patrons, but for the privacy it provided for them. She was therefore startled the next morning when someone banged on the door to her suite.

"Yes?" Anna asked as she opened it.

"Are you Mata Hari?" a gruff voice inquired.

M'greet threw on silky robe over her nightgown before she went to the door. "You must be looking for me."

The man in the doorway looked to be about 40, with a receding hairline and a bushy mustache that curled upward from both sides of his mouth. "I am Herr Griebel of the Berlin police."

M'greet ignored Anna's stricken look as she motioned for her to move aside. "Please come in." She gestured toward a chair at the little serving table. "Shall I order up some tea?"

"That won't be necessary," Griebel replied as he sat. "I am here to inform you that a spectator of your performance last night has lodged a complaint."

"A complaint? Against me?" M'greet repeated as she took a seat in the chair across from him. She mouthed, "tea," at Anna, who was still standing near the door. Anna nodded and then left the room.

"Indeed," Griebel touched his mustache. "A complaint of indecency."

"Ah," M'greet nodded. "You are part of the *Sittenpolizei.*" They were a department charged with enforcing the Kaiser's so-called laws of morality. M'greet had been visited a few times in the past by such men, but nothing had ever come of it. She flashed Griebel a seductive smile. "Surely your department has no issue with sacred dances?"

"Ah," Griebel fidgeted with the collar of his uniform, clearly uncomfortable.

Mirroring his movements, M'greet fingered the neckline of her low-cut gown. "After all, there are more important issues going on in the world than my little dance."

"Such as?" Griebel asked.

The door opened and Anna discreetly placed a tea set on the crisp white tablecloth. She gave her mistress a worried look but M'greet waved her off before pouring Griebel a cup of tea. "Well, I'm sure you heard about that poor man that was shot in the Balkans in June."

"Of course—it's been in all of the papers. The 'poor man,' as you call him, was Archduke Franz Ferdinand. Austria should not stand down when the heir to their thrown was shot by militant Serbs."

M'greet took a sip of tea. "Are you saying they should go to war?"

"They should. And Germany, as Austria's ally, ought to accompany them."

"Over one man? You cannot be serious."

"Those Serbs need to be taught a lesson, once and for all." Upon seeing the pout on M'greet's face, Griebel waved his hand. "But you shouldn't worry your pretty little head over talk of politics."

M'greet pursed her lips. "You're right. It's not something that a woman like me should be discussing."

"No." Griebel set down his tea cup and pulled something out of his pocket. "As I was saying when I first came in about the complaint—"

"As *I* was saying..." M'greet faked a yawn, stretching her arms out while sticking out her bosom. The stocky, balding Griebel was not nearly as handsome as some of the men she'd met over the years, but M'greet knew that she needed to become better acquainted with him in order to get the charges dropped. Besides, she'd always had a weakness for men in uniform. "My dances are adopted from Hindu religious dances and should not be miscon-strued as immoral." She placed a hand over Griebel's thick fingers, causing the paper to fall to the floor. "I think, if the two of us put our heads together, we can definitely find a mutual agreement."

Griebel pulled his hand away to wipe his forehead with a hand-kerchief. "I don't know if that's possible."

M'greet got up from her chair to spread herself on the bed, displaying her body to its advantage as a chef would his best dish.

"Perhaps we could work out an arrangement that would benefit us both," Griebel agreed as he walked over to her.

Griebel's mustache tickled M'greet's face, but she forced herself to think about other things as he kissed her. Her thoughts at such moments often traveled to her daughter, Non, but today she focused on the other night's performance. M'greet always did what it took to survive, and right now she needed the money that her contract with the Berlin Metropol would provide, and nothing could get in the way of that.

M'greet was glad to count Herr Griebel as her new lover as the tension between the advocates of the Kaiser—who wanted to "finish with the Serbs quickly"— and the pacifists determined to keep Germany out of war heightened throughout Berlin at the end of July. Although Griebel was on the side of the war-mongers, M'greet felt secure traveling on his arm every night on their way to Berlin's most popular venues.

It was in the back room at one such establishment, the Borchardt, that she met some of Griebel's cronies. They had gath-ered to talk about the recent developments—Austria-Hungary had officially declared war on Serbia. M'greet knew her place was to look pretty and say nothing, but at the same time she couldn't help but listen to what they were discussing.

"I've heard that Russia has mobilized her troops," a heavyset, balding man stated. M'greet recalled that his name was Müller.

"Ah," Griebel sat back in the plush leather booth. "That's the rub, now isn't it?"

Herr Vogel, who seemed to be Griebel's closest compatriot, shook his head. "I'd hoped Russia would stay out of it." He flicked ash from his cigar into a nearby tray. "After all, the Kaiser and the Tsar are cousins."

"No," Müller replied. "Those Serbs went crying to Mother Russia, and she responded." He nodded to himself. "Now it's only a matter of time before we jump in to protect Austria."

As if on cue, the sound of breaking glass was heard.

M'greet ended her silence. "What was that?"

Griebel put a protective hand on her arm. "I'm not sure." He used his other arm to flag down a passing waiter. "What is going on?"

The young man looked panic-stricken. "There is a demonstration on the streets. Someone threw a brick through the front window and our owner is asking all of the patrons to leave."

"Has war broken out?" M'greet inquired of Griebel as she pulled her arm away. His grip had left white marks.

"I'm not sure." He picked up M'greet's fur shawl and headed toward the main room of the restaurant. Pandemonium reigned as Berlin's elite rushed toward the doors. Discarded feathers from fashionable ladies' hats and boas floated through the air and littered the ground before stamping feet stirred them up again. M'greet wished she hadn't shaken off Griebel's arm as now she was being shoved this way and that. Someone trampled over her dress and she heard the sound of ripping lace.

She nearly tripped before a strong hand landed on her elbow. "This way," the young waiter told her. He led her through the kitchen and out the back door, where Griebel's Benz was waiting. Griebel appeared a few minutes later and the driver told him that there was a massive protest outside the Kaiser's palace.

"Let's go there," Griebel instructed.

"No." M'greet wrapped the fur shawl around her shoulders. "Take me home first."

"Don't you want to find out what's happening?" Griebel demanded, waving his hand as a people thronged the streets. "This could be the beginnings of a war like no one has ever seen."

"No" M'greet repeated. It seemed to her that the Great Powers of Europe: Germany, Russia, France, and possibly England, were entering into a scrap that they had no business getting involved with.

"I don't care about any war and I've had enough tonight. I want to go home."

Griebel gave her a strange look but motioned for the driver to do as she said.

They were forced to drive slowly through the streets, as they had become jammed with motor cars, horse carts, and people rushing about on foot. M'greet caught what the crowd was chanting as they marched past. She repeated the words aloud: "*Deutschland über alles.*"

"Germany over all," Griebel supplied.

The war came quickly. Germany first officially declared war on Russia to the east and two days later did the same to France in the west. In Berlin, so-called bank riots occurred as people rushed to the banks and emptied their savings accounts, trading paper money for gold and silver coins. Prices for food and other necessities soared as people stocked up on goods while they could still afford them.

Worried about her own fate, M'greet placed several calls to her agent, Astruc, wanting to know if the war meant her fall performances would be cancelled. After leaving many messages, she finally got word that Astruc had left town, presumably with the money the Metropol had paid her in advance.

She decided to brave the confusion at the bank in order to withdraw what little funds she had left.

"I'm sorry," the teller informed her when she finally made it to the counter. "It looks as though your account has been blocked."

"How can you say that?" M'greet demanded. "There should be plenty of money in my account." The plenty part might not have been true, but there was no way it was empty.

"The address you gave when you opened the account was in Paris. We cannot give funds to any foreigner at this time."

M'greet put both fists on the counter. "I wish to speak with your manager."

The teller gestured behind her. M'greet glanced back to see a long line of people, their exhausted, bewildered faces beginning to glower. "I'm sorry Fraulein, I can do nothing more."

She opened her mouth, about to let him have the worst of her fury, but a man in a police uniform appeared beside her. "A foreigner you say?" He pulled M'greet out of the bank line, and roughly turned her to face him. "What are you, a Russian?"

M'greet knew her dark hair and coloring was not typical of someone with Dutch heritage, but this was a new accusation. "I am no such thing."

"Russian, for sure," a man standing in line agreed.

"Her address was in France," the teller called before accepting a bank card from the next person.

"Well, Miss Russian Francophile, you are coming with me." For the second time in a week, a strange man put his hand on M'greet's elbow and led her away.

M'greet fumed all the way to the police station. She'd had enough of Berlin: due to this infernal war, she was now void of funds and it looked as though her engagements were to be cancelled. She figured her best course of action would be to return to Paris and use her connections to try to get some work there.

When they arrived at the police station, M'greet immediately asked for Herr Griebel. He appeared a few minutes later, seemingly amused to see her. "You've been arrested under suspicion of being a troublesome alien."

M'greet waved off that comment with a brush of her hand. "We both know that's ridiculous. Can you secure my release as soon as possible? I must get back to Paris before my possessions there are seized."

Griebel's amused smile faded as his lip curled into a sneer. "You cannot travel to an enemy country in the middle of a war."

"Why not?"

The sneer deepened. "Because..." His narrowed eyes suddenly softened. "Come with me. There is someone I want you to meet." He led her to an office that occupied the end of a narrow hallway and knocked on the closed door labeled, *Traugott von Jagow, Berliner Polizei.*

"Come in," a voice growled.

Griebel entered and immediately saluted.

The man behind the desk had a thin face and heavy mustache which dropped downward. "What is it, Herr Griebel? You must know I am extremely busy." He dipped a pen in ink and began writing.

"Indeed, sir, but I wanted you to meet the acclaimed Mata Hari."

Von Jagow stopped scribbling and looked up. His eyes traveled downward from the feather atop M'greet's hat, stopping at her chest. "Wasn't there a morality complaint filed against you?"

M'greet stepped forward, but before she could protest, Griebel cleared his throat. "We are here because she wants to return to Paris."

Von Jagow gave a loud "harrumph," and then continued his writing. "You are not the first person to ask such a question, but we can't let anyone cross the border into enemy territory at this time. People would think you were a spy." He abruptly stopped writing and set his pen down. "A courtesan with known powers to seduce powerful men..." he shot a meaningful at Griebel, who stared at the floor. "And a long-term resident of Paris with admittedly low morals." He finally met M'greet's eyes. "We could use a woman like you. I'm forming a network of agents who can provide us information about the goings-on in France."

M'greet tried to keep the horror from showing on her face. *Was this man asking her to be a spy for Germany?* "No, sir," she replied. "As I told Herr Griebel, I have no interest in the war. I just want to get back to Paris."

Von Jagow crossed his arms and sat back. "And I can help you with that, provided that you agree to work for me."

She shook her head and spoke in a soft voice. "Thank you, sir, but it seems I'll have to find my way back on my own."

"Very well, then." Von Jagow picked up his pen again. "Good luck." His voice implied that he wished her just the opposite.

Enjoyed the sample? Join my mailing list at www.kitsergeant.com and find out how you can get a FREE copy of L'Agent Double before it's release!

Don't forget to check out my Amazon Author Page for more great Women's Fiction books!

ACKNOWLEDGMENTS

Thank you to my critique partners: Ute Carbone, Theresa Munroe, and Karen Cino, for their comments and suggestions. I am eternally thankful to the gracious Kathy Lance for her superb editing skills. And as always, a special thank-you goes to my wonderful family, especially Tommy, Belle, and Thompson, for their unconditional love and support.

Made in the USA
San Bernardino, CA
16 June 2019